# *WORTH WAITING FOR*

## *A NOVEL*

## *By*

## *K. L. McKee*

*Cameo Mountain Press*
Palisade, CO 81526

Copyright ©2018 by Karen Lea McKee
All Rights Reserved.
Cover Photo—Castle Peak—Photographer K. L. McKee
Threesome Photo—Photographer Kurt M. Kontour

First Edition
Book #1 in the North Fork Series

# Dedication

To my Dad, a World War II veteran, and to all the brave but forgotten Vietnam veterans. Those of us who value our freedom appreciate the sacrifices these brave men and their families made for our country.

# Notes and Acknowledgments

None of the characters in *Worth Waiting For* exist except in my imagination and bear no resemblance to people living or dead or any relation to persons of the same name, with the exception of Barbara Walters. Ms. Walters is so well known for her in-depth celebrity interviews, particularly those done in conjunction with the Oscars each year, that it seemed inappropriate to use any other name. I have tried to capture, as best I could, Ms. Walters' expertise in interviewing celebrities. My apologies if I've erred in any way.

In order to keep the 1985 Oscar nominees for best actor at five, I was forced to eliminate one of the original nominees. My apology to Tom Hulce, who was so aptly nominated for *Amadeus* in 1985.

Some geographic locations in the book are real. Although the North Fork Valley is an actual location in Western Colorado, the town of North Fork does not exist. It is here that I took liberties with geography, creating the fictional town of North Fork, set against the West Elk Mountain Range and the Castle Range.

The mountains defining the North Fork Valley that are mentioned in *Worth Waiting For* are real. Mountains bordering the valley range in elevation from 9,719' to 12,641'. Black Mesa is real, but Hansen Creek and Crawford Mesa are imaginary.

As with all fiction books, many hours of research went into keeping the historical facts accurate. Any mistakes are purely my own.

Because I did not attend the dedication of the Vietnam Veterans Memorial, I relied heavily on the book *To Heal a Nation: the Vietnam Veterans Memorial* by Jan C. Scruggs and Joel L. Swerdlow for descriptions and incidents to give me a feel for the events of the dedication. To add authenticity to my story, I took the liberty of using one of the actual events that took place during the Candlelight Vigil of Names, adapting it to my story.

As with all books, numerous individuals contributed to the writing of this book. Many thanks to Vietnam veterans Jim Rupe and Bill Hutchins for their stories and experiences. The author takes full responsibility for any mistakes or misunderstandings. Thanks also to Randy Edwards and Wayne Cox, and to numerous online acquaintances for their input. A special thanks to Claudette Tuxhorn for her Christmas tree story which I adapted to this novel.

Every writer needs a support group. Jane Heitman Healy and Virginia LaCrone became my friends, my best critics, and my cheering section, along with Lucinda Stein, Pamela Larson, Brenda Evers, Patti Hill, and Joyce Anderson. And last, my family blessed me with their support and understanding during my many hours "chained" to my computer in order to put my story into words.

Most of all, I thank the Vietnam veterans that lived through an unwanted war, were treated horribly when they returned, and who still struggle with nightmares from the conflict and feelings of abandonment from the citizens of their country. My heart and respect goes out to all of them and the families whose loved ones did not return. Our nation owes all of you a great debt.

## Introduction

*T*he Vietnam War, the United States' most controversial war, began when President Truman sent military personnel to Vietnam to aid French forces in June of 1950. In 1954, the Geneva Accords divided Vietnam into North and South Vietnam, and President Eisenhower committed U.S. aid to the South Vietnamese government. By 1959, the United States was providing military advisors to the South Vietnamese infantry, artillery, and naval forces.

President Kennedy announced on May 5, 1961 that sending U.S. troops to Vietnam might be necessary. Although the U.S. commitment of troops was small at first, President Johnson gradually escalated the number of troops in Vietnam, and by December of 1964, U.S. ground forces had more than tripled. By June of 1969, the U.S. fighting force numbered 541,000.

The election of President Nixon brought with it a new resolve to end the fighting in Vietnam and bring U.S. troops home. Henry Kissinger, President Nixon's peace negotiator, and Le Duc Tho of North Vietnam reached a cease-fire agreement, which was finally signed in Paris on January 27, 1973.

Although a cease-fire had been signed, North Vietnam launched a final and successful offensive in the spring of 1975. With the evacuation of the remaining troops and the fall of Saigon on April 30, 1975, came the official end of U.S. involvement in Vietnam.

No other war in U.S. history caused more dissension or deeper resentment than the war in Vietnam. At a cost of more than 50,000 lives and a war that lasted more than twenty years, Vietnam made a lasting impact on Americans' view toward government and the question of war.

Hundreds of thousands of people demonstrated against the war, more than at any other time in our history. Many young men were caught between a deep-seated loyalty to their country and the prospect of fighting what was, to many of them, a senseless and hopeless war perpetuated by politicians and the threat of communism. College enrollment reached a record high; draft card burning and defection to Canada became ways to protest and avoid military service.

For the first time, nightly television news brought the horror of war into American living rooms. Dissension over the war became so intense that soldiers returning home were spit on and verbally assaulted by those who opposed the war. Americans became intolerant of war and its effect, and the soldiers who fought the war became the villains. Perhaps worst of all, the silent majority failed to thank the young men who came home wounded—physically and emotionally.

For soldiers fighting in the rice paddies and jungles of Vietnam, the frustrations were unending. They fought an often unknown enemy. Small children were sometimes rigged with grenades, and older children carried rifles and launched hit and run attacks. Women, too, became the enemy. To add to the frustration, some Vietnamese that fought with U.S. troops one day, fought against the U.S. soldiers the next. Instead of a war of acquiring or winning land

and then advancing, it was a war of attrition—the number of enemy casualties was directly proportional to the success of a battle.

Hardest of all for the soldiers to deal with was the rising resentment at home. Instead of feeling they had the support of the American people, soldiers were constantly reminded they were wrong and not worthy of support. And by the end of the war, many Americans blamed the soldiers for "losing" the war.

Healing over the bitterness and dissension caused by the Vietnam War was a slow process. In March of 1979, Jan Scruggs, a former rifleman of the U.S. Army 199th Light Infantry Brigade vowed to build a monument to all Vietnam Veterans, listing the names of all who gave their lives during that conflict. After several years of hard and sometimes frustrating work, and using only donated money, the Vietnam Veterans Memorial was dedicated on November 13, 1982 in Washington, D.C.

This stark but beautiful black granite wall, designed by Maya Ying Lin and listing the names of all who were killed or missing in Vietnam, began a healing process that continues today. No one who visits the wall goes away feeling ambivalent. Not a day goes by that something is not left at the wall in memory of someone whose name is etched in its stone. Flowers, poems, pictures, and medals are only a few of the mementos that are scattered along the walkway. Most cannot resist tracing with a finger the name of someone they knew. Few walk away dry-eyed.

If history teaches us anything, it teaches us that war, any war, leaves scars, and the worst scars of all are the emotional scars, for they cannot easily be healed.

*Worth Waiting For* begins with a defining year in our country's history—May 1968 through June of 1969:

**June 5, 1968**--Robert Kennedy is fatally shot after winning the California primary.

**August 26, 1968**--Riots occur at the Democratic National Convention in Chicago.

**September 30, 1968**--U.S. Strength in Vietnam is 537,000.

**November 5, 1968**--Richard Nixon is elected president and promises to stage a U.S. troop withdrawal in Southeast Asia, and to bring about the Vietnamization of the war.

**April 3, 1969**--The U.S. death toll in Vietnam reaches 33,641.

**June 8, 1969**--President Nixon orders the first troops out of Vietnam.

In *Worth Waiting For,* Stacey "Sam" Murcheson, Brian "Butch" Murcheson, and JD "Mac" MacCord are forever affected by the Vietnam War, its aftermath, and the healing that spans nearly two decades.

# WORTH WAITING FOR

## A NOVEL

# Prologue

## North Fork, Colorado—August 1985

Stacey Murcheson sat at her vanity and picked up her brush. With angry, deliberate strokes, she brushed her long blond hair and swept it up into a soft twist. Her hands shook as she struggled with a few stray strands. Her attempt to capture them failed. Setting her jaw, she grabbed her brush again, determined to succeed on the next try.

Her image in the mirror stopped her short, and she paused in mid-stroke. Green eyes, tired, reddened, and rimmed with heavy dark circles, stared at her. She hadn't slept well all week.

"Great look for a bride on her wedding day." She thought of her fiancé Ken and smiled. He had dealt with the past few months better than most men, exhibiting far more patience and understanding than JD. If JD had only stayed away…

Stacey slammed the brush on the vanity, knocking the airline ticket to the floor. She glared at it, picked it up, and flung it across the room.

"*Damn* you, JD MacCord!" Hot tears stung her eyes. "Why did you have to pick now to show up?"

She spent years trying to forget JD and the feelings and passion he stirred in her. Then, without warning, he barged back into her life and into her heart, causing her desires to resurface along with the guilt.

"*Damn* the feelings and *damn* the guilt. And *damn you*, Mac, for making me want you again."

She stalked to the window. The stillness and beauty of the early morning belied the disquieting events that transpired minutes earlier. Bare spots in the gravel drive marked where JD had peeled out. She closed her eyes and tried to remember his smile. Instead, she saw anger and pain. Pain that would last far longer than the anger JD unleashed.

She swiped at a tear trickling down her cheek. "I've made my decision, Mac," she said to the empty room. "I intend to honor my commitment to Ken. I won't betray another man over you again. I *won't*."

The morning sun cast golden rays as it inched above the West Elk Mountains, promising a beautiful day. A perfect day for a wedding.

Stacey sighed and forced a smile. She could be happy with Ken. There were so many things about him she loved. His sense of humor. His compassion. He provided stability and logic to her life; two things she needed. *Does Ken stir hunger and passion in you?* She shoved JD's words aside.

She turned from the window. "Marrying Ken is the right decision." Lingering tears glistened in her eyes. "Now all I have to do is put a smile on my face, a song in my heart, and say 'I do' to a wonderful man who loves me."

But her declaration failed to evoke any kind of smile. She sat at the vanity and gazed at her image. Why didn't she feel the same excitement and joy she felt the first time she married? Were only the young allowed the anticipation and wonder? If only she could turn back the clock. If only Brian was waiting for her.

## Part I

"...Of this I am certain: never before in American history have as many loyal and brave young men been as shabbily treated by the government that sent them to war; never before have so many of them questioned as much, as these veterans have, the essential rightness of what they were forced to do."

Murray Polner

*No Victory Parades: the Return of the Vietnam Veteran*

# Chapter 1

*A*utomatic gunfire ripped the air. Bombs exploded around him. Smoke blurred his vision. He couldn't shut out the screams of pain. Was that him or someone else? Then everything went black.

Brian Murcheson bolted upright, sweat pouring down his face, his heart pounding in his chest. The same nightmare, coming more frequently the last few weeks.

He wiped the moisture from his face with the edge of the sheet, fell back against his pillow, and closed his eyes. But sleep played tag with the cold reality of the nightmare, so he pulled on his jeans and a T-shirt and slipped quietly downstairs and out the front door.

He sat on the porch steps of the ranch house he'd come to know as home, leaned against the support post, and inhaled deep gulps of fresh mountain air. The stars winked at him, so close he swore he could reach out and touch them. One of the perks of living in rural Colorado, he thought. Closer to God.

He'd been luckier than most, although he had often wondered if he'd outlive the stigma of illegitimacy. When he was fourteen, his mother committed suicide. He felt the disdain of the local residents toward him. On several occasions, he heard people comment that he'd never amount to anything. He smiled at the thought that he had proved them wrong, and would continue to prove them wrong.

His best friend Jess and his family had believed in him and offered him a home, a family, and a nickname—Butch—that had stuck. They even helped him get a college education. Jess became more like a brother than a best friend, and when Jess's little sister Stacey, six years his junior, had matured into a beautiful young woman, Brian had fallen in love.

The previous week Stacey had graduated from high school. Brian wondered if he was pushing things a little. Although more mature than most girls her age, she had never lived away from home. Brian, however, couldn't wait any longer. In the morning, Stacey would become his wife. He should be content with that, but the constant need to prove himself had prompted him to volunteer for another tour in Vietnam.

A board creaked behind him. He jumped and turned in one movement.

"Hell, Mac, you nearly took two years off my life. What're you doing up?" He swallowed and tried to banish the nightmare and raw nerves that followed.

"I might ask you the same thing." JD "Mac" MacCord sat beside Brian and leaned forward, his arms resting on his thighs. "You having second thoughts about getting married tomorrow?"

"Naw. A little nervous, maybe, but not second thoughts. Stacey's the best thing that ever happened to me. Hell, her family's the best thing that ever happened to me. I'm definitely not having second thoughts. Just wish the wedding was over, that's all. Sorry I woke you."

"You didn't. I was having trouble sleeping myself."

"What have you got to be nervous about? You're not the one getting married." Brian tried to laugh, but it came out like a grunt. He couldn't shake the fear the nightmare left behind. A combat veteran, yet he couldn't handle a simple nightmare.

"I may not be getting married, but I have to make sure you do. Big responsibility, buddy."

"Yeah, well don't worry about me. I'll get through it. If I can get through a tour of Nam, I can get through a wedding."

JD rose. "Then I suggest you get some sleep so you can enjoy it." He stopped at the door and turned toward Brian. "You sure you're all right?"

"I'm sure." Brian rose and took a deep breath. He wanted to tell JD about the nightmare, but he didn't know how. Fear was something Brian couldn't understand. How could he expect someone else to understand? He clamped his hand on JD's shoulder and forced what he hoped looked like his usual grin on his face. "Come on, Mac, let's get some sleep. Tomorrow's a big day."

# Chapter 2

### *June 7, 1968--Oceanside, California*

*J*D MacCord unlocked the door to apartment 4B and stepped inside. Hard work and late hours had readied the apartment for the newlyweds. JD had painted and cleaned, unpacked all the boxes that Brian and Stacey sent ahead, and stocked the refrigerator and cupboards with a few groceries, all in a week's time. He hadn't bought his friends a wedding gift yet, so JD bought two sets of towels, one yellow and one blue.

After he hung the yellow towels in the bathroom, JD collapsed on the couch with a well-deserved beer. Flipping on a small television set, he tried watching a special on Robert Kennedy's life and the events of his tragic death, but JD's mind soon wandered. Since the wedding, he had struggled with some unexpected feelings. Feelings that left his nights sleepless; feelings he couldn't talk to Brian about; feelings he couldn't resolve; feelings of envy.

"Maybe I'm just envious of Brian living off base. Or because he's happily married."

JD downed several swallows of beer. Unable to conjure any more excuses, he finally admitted to himself what he had tried so hard to ignore. He envied Brian, not because Brian had an off-base apartment, or because he was happily married. He envied Brian because of the girl he married.

JD met Brian his freshman year of college. Both attended Fort Lewis College on football scholarships and were assigned the same dorm room. They also played baseball and rodeoed together. JD had spent an occasional weekend in North Fork with Brian, when his dad could spare him from the family ranch in Aztec, New Mexico. Brian had reciprocated with JD's family.

Stacey's parents had welcomed Brian into their family after Brian's mother committed suicide. Brian, fourteen at the time, didn't know who his father was, and his only relative was an aging grandmother. Since Brian was Stacey's brother's best friend, it seemed only natural to make him a part of their family.

JD's memories of Stacey during his visits to the Atkins' ranch were of a girl not unlike his two younger sisters. But when JD arrived in North Fork a week before the wedding, a couple of years had passed since he had seen Stacey, and he was astounded at the difference. She was no longer the cute young daughter of Brian's surrogate parents. She had grown up.

Although she had graduated from high school a week earlier, she seemed far more mature than her eighteen years. His sudden desire for Stacey blindsided him. The need to become better acquainted with such a beautiful, intelligent, and vivacious young woman had been overshadowed by the terrible truth that in a few days she would marry his best friend.

JD sauntered into the kitchen, deposited his empty beer bottle in the trash, and leaned back against the counter. "Face it, JD," he said to the empty kitchen, "you've really done it this time. You're more than just attracted to your best friend's wife. You could fall in love with her like that." He snapped his fingers. "Not a great idea, stupid."

He ran his hands over his Marine haircut and tried to push aside the memory of the many outings and talks he had with Brian and Stacey during the week before the wedding. Grabbing his third beer from the refrigerator, he pried off the cap and tossed it into the trash.

"Ah, hell," he said as he returned to the living room, "maybe I'm feeling lonely because my best friend got married. Or maybe I should have kept Stacey when I kidnapped her."

He smiled at the memory of Stacey's fury over him carting her off right before she and Brian were to leave for their honeymoon. She had sworn she'd get even with him, no matter how long it took. JD had delivered her safe and sound to the ranch and Brian, but only after Brian had collected enough money to "ransom" her. Brian's angry red face matched the dark red of his hair when JD returned with Stacey. He still wasn't sure Brian or Stacey had forgiven him, although giving them the collected "ransom" for their honeymoon helped a little.

Plopping onto the couch and resting his boots on the coffee table, JD took a gulp from the fresh bottle of beer. He leaned his head back and closed his eyes, but all he could see was Stacey—her long, thick, golden blond hair framing the soft features of her face, her shimmering green eyes, and a warm smile that could melt a Titanic-sinking iceberg in a few seconds flat. He rubbed his eyes, trying to chase away her vision, but her vivid green eyes lingered.

Raising his beer into the air, he declared, "Here's to you, Butch, you lucky son-of-a-bitch."

~

JD groaned and shifted his body, trying to find a comfortable position on the couch. In spite of a pounding headache, the kink in his back shouted at him to move. He eased open one eye. Sunlight

13

streamed through the window, and his eye slammed shut against the glare. Draping his arm over his face, he tried to swallow the "wad of cotton" that had taken up residence in his mouth.

"That's the last time I kill off a six-pack with whiskey as a chaser," he muttered.

Wincing at the throbbing in his head, he stumbled to the bathroom, his eyes open only enough to keep him from slamming into the walls. After splashing cold water on his face, he forced his eyelids open and glanced in the mirror.

"Death warmed over. Definitely a new look for you."

After a hot and cold shower, he shaved and dressed in a blue plaid short-sleeved western shirt, Levi's and boots. Two cups of coffee failed to cure his headache, so he drove to a shopping center, bought a bottle of aspirin, a dozen powdered-sugar doughnuts, and on a whim, a six-inch potted ivy. He had slept until almost 11:00 a.m., and he expected Brian and Stacey by early afternoon.

JD barely finished straightening the apartment when he heard the familiar rumble of Ol' Bess, Brian's beloved 1964 blue Chevy pickup. Taking a deep breath, he stepped outside and sprinted down the stairs to greet the newlyweds.

~

Brian set Stacey in the middle of the small living room. "Welcome to your new home, Babe. Hope you like it."

Stacey surveyed the small apartment. Gold carpeting covered the floors from the living room through the hallway and into the bedroom, showing signs of wear from numerous former occupants. The smell of fresh paint permeated the room. From where she stood, Stacey could see a Coppertone stove and gold countertop through the kitchen doorway.

"Mac and I found it a few weeks ago. Mac offered to paint and do some cleaning. I tried to talk him out of it. Told him we'd do it, but he insisted."

Brian turned toward JD, who was leaning against the front door. "Hey, buddy, the place looks great."

"Thanks. The landlord paid for the paint, but I sloshed it on. He had a professional outfit do the carpets." JD pushed away from the door. "You want to unload now, or wait till later?"

"Now," Stacey answered. "If we wait it might not get done before tomorrow morning." She smiled at JD. "You haven't seen all the boxes of stuff we brought with us."

"Hey, where's all the stuff we shipped ahead?" Brian asked.

"I unpacked everything and put it away. I hope it's where you want it. If not, it won't take much to change it." JD stuffed his hands in his hip pockets. "I took the liberty of stocking the cupboards and refrigerator with a few groceries. There are two sets of new towels, too. I hung one set in the bathroom."

Stacey pointed to the ivy on the coffee table. "And the plant?"

JD shrugged. "And the plant," he said.

Stacey smiled. "Thanks." She put her arms around JD's neck and gave him a big hug. "That was really thoughtful, JD," she said and kissed him on the cheek.

"I'm forgiven for the kidnapping?"

"Not if you keep hugging my wife like that," Brian complained.

"You're forgiven," Stacey said, "but I reserve the right to get even."

"I'll have to be on guard, then. And *she* hugged me, Butch, so back off."

"Matter of opinion." Brian scowled at JD. "Seriously, Mac," Brian said as he clamped a hand on JD's shoulder and grinned, "thanks for everything. Now, let's go relieve Ol' Bess of her load before her back breaks."

15

Working together, the three of them unloaded Brian's pickup in record time. By that night, they had unpacked and put away everything the newlyweds brought with them. With the last item in its proper place, Stacey collapsed on the couch.

"Whew! I'm glad that's done. We make quite a team, don't we?" Stacey smiled at Brian and JD, who lay sprawled on the rug along with a couple of empty pizza cartons.

Brian groaned. "I think that's worse than boot camp. I didn't know we had so much stuff. Or such a mean drill sergeant." He winked at Stacey. She scowled back.

"I didn't know you were bringing most of North Fork with you. If I had, I would've been gone when you showed up." JD lifted his head and grinned at Stacey. "How'd you talk Butch into bringing all this stuff, anyway?"

"Aside from being a 'mean drill sergeant,' I have great powers of persuasion. Don't I, Butch?"

Brian sat up, wiggled his eyebrows, and grinned. "You sure do Babe. You owe me."

"I think that's my cue." JD stood and headed to the door.

"You're comin' to the beach with us tomorrow, aren't you buddy?" Brian asked.

"I don't think you want a third wheel around."

"Sure we do, Mac."

"You're more than welcome, JD," Stacey said.

"Then I'll see you tomorrow."

~

JD and Stacey occupied their usual spot on San Onofre Beach, while Brian surfed. San Onofre and Del Mar beaches had become the usual weekend destination for Stacey, Brian, and JD. Both beaches provided a welcome environment free from the harassment military personnel and their families experienced on the more public beaches.

"Want something to drink, JD?" Stacey asked as she grabbed a Coke from the cooler.

"No thanks. I'm fine for now."

JD tried not to take notice as Stacey stretched her bare legs along the blanket and rested her heels in the warm sand. As she swallowed a drink of Coke, a distant "Yee-haw!" floated on the breeze toward the beach. Stacey and JD both waved toward Brian cresting a distant wave.

Brian was hooked on surfing, comparing it to riding an ornery bull. He tried to teach Stacey to surf, but after several tries, she insisted Brian could take all the chances.

"Do you think Butch has some kind of death wish, JD?"

JD turned from watching Brian and looked at Stacey. "Are you serious?"

"Yes, I'm serious. Look at him. He has no fear. If it's dangerous and provides a challenge he tries it. Doesn't think twice. Isn't that what you'd call a death wish?"

"For some, maybe, but not Butch. He just thinks he's invincible."

"Well, I hope he is, since he's doing his best to test it."

"He'll be all right, Stacey. Quit worrying. He's pretty levelheaded even when he's taking chances."

"That's a contradiction."

"That's Butch." JD studied Stacey as she chewed on her bottom lip and watched Brian. She had changed in the short time since she arrived in Oceanside. Marriage to Brian appeared to agree with her and landing a job at a local bank had boosted her self-confidence.

JD could still feel the warmth of her arms around him and the softness of her lips when she thanked him for his work on the apartment. As he watched her, he realized she had grown more

17

beautiful, something he probably shouldn't take note of, since she was married to his best friend.

He cleared his throat and stood. "I'm going for a swim. Want to join me?"

"Naw, I'll guard the cooler."

~

Stacey watched JD as he jogged toward the water, weaving in and out, avoiding other sun worshippers scattered on the beach. His dark brown hair showed signs of natural curl, even with a Marine cut. About six feet tall—a couple of inches shorter than Brian—JD had broad shoulders, a thick chest, muscular arms and legs, and walked slightly pigeon-toed, a condition Stacey equated with football players. JD had been quarterback to Brian's tight end on their college football team.

JD, more comfortable riding a horse than a wave, hadn't taken to surfing like Brian. Instead, he spent time with Stacey swimming and digging clams, or just talking. Stacey appreciated having someone to talk to while Brian rode wave after wave.

JD stepped into the water a moment before Brian landed on the beach. Brian picked up his surfboard, said something to JD, then turned and waved at Stacey. Stacey smiled and waved. In the next instant, Brian jumped on his board and headed back out to catch another wave. JD swam part of the way with him before turning back to the shore. He joined Stacey a couple of minutes later.

"I'll take that Coke now," he said.

Stacey reached into the cooler and pulled out a bottle. "You know, I've been thinking..."

"Dangerous pastime."

Stacey threw a handful of sand at JD's chest. "Next time you get it in the face."

"So you've been thinking. About what?"

"You."

"Me?" JD's brow curled into a frown.

"Butch calls you Mac most of the time. Never JD. What does JD stand for? I don't remember ever hearing your full name."

"John Douglas. My dad's name is John, too, so the family got to calling me JD to save confusion."

"Are you a junior?"

"Nope. Dad's middle name is Everett. But even if I was, there'd be no way anybody'd call me junior. Not even Butch."

"Junior doesn't fit you anyway. Does your family call you Mac?"

JD smiled. "Nope. That's Butch's doing."

"Mind if I call you Mac? It fits you."

"It's okay with me. You're welcome to call me most anything, as long as you call me."

Stacey giggled. "Be serious. I prefer Butch and Mac to Butch and JD. Has a better ring to it."

"Butch, Mac, and Stacey." He shook his head. "Spoils the rhythm." JD watched Stacey out of the corner of his eye. "Looks like Butch and I will have to ditch you." He paused. "Or give you a nickname."

"I have one. Stace. Or Babe. Butch calls me both."

"I don't think I'd better call you Babe. Butch would knock my block off. Stace isn't a real nickname, just a shorter version of your name. Let's see..." JD scratched his head and swallowed a drink of Coke. "What's your middle name?"

"Anne, with an 'e.'"

"Stacey Anne Murcheson. S...A...M... That's it! Sam. Butch, Mac, and Sam."

# Chapter 3

*J*D watched Stacey, waiting for her reaction to the nickname. A golden French braid hung down her back. Her one-piece bathing suit enhanced her slim, tanned, and well-proportioned figure. Years of ranch work had given her muscular arms and legs, but rather than detracting from her femininity, they added sensuality to her tomboyish nature.

"Sam?" Stacey frowned at him

"Yeah. Your initials spell Sam."

"Sam. Hmmmmm. I like it," she said. "When I was little, I was jealous of my brother, Jess, because he'd been born a boy. I guess the name Sam is the closest I'm gonna get."

"You'd make a lousy boy."

Stacey blushed. "You mean that?"

"I do. Believe me."

"You do what?" Brian asked as he jammed his surfboard in the sand beside the blanket.

"Believe Sam would make a lousy boy," JD answered.

"Sam?" Brian raised an eyebrow. "Who's Sam?"

"Me," Stacey answered. "JD thinks my nickname should be Sam, since that's what my initials spell." She laughed as Brian curled one side of his upper lip and frowned.

"I don't know...I'm gonna feel pretty funny going to bed with a Sam. I think I'll stick with Babe."

"Well, I kind of like Sam," JD countered. "You don't mind if I call your wife Sam, do you?"

"Not one bit, buddy. Have at it." Brian winked at Stacey. "Hand me a beer, Babe, I think I'm soberin' up."

"You know beer's not allowed on the beach, and you are sober, Butch," Stacey said. "Here's a coke. Don't choke on it." Brian grinned and winked again at Stacey.

"Hell, at least it'll wash down all that saltwater I've been swallowin'. But you better not wait too long to get me to a beer. I'm slowly wastin' away. I need *nourishment*." He grabbed Stacey around the waist and planted a kiss on her. "Mouth to mouth resuscitation will do till we get to Jarheads'."

"Honestly, Butch," Stacey managed between kisses, "you'd think beer was the most important thing in your life."

"It is," he declared, "right after the Corps and you."

~

JD stepped inside Jarheads' Pub and glanced toward Brian's favorite corner booth. Stacey waved. He smiled and worked his way around tables toward his friends, avoiding collisions with Sailors and Marines and their dates. The din of laughter, conversation, and jukebox music filled the smoke-hazed room.

The newlyweds and JD spent most of their Friday and Saturday nights at Jarheads'. The proprietor was a retired WWII Marine everyone called Pappy. The pub provided a jukebox, a small dance floor, and an atmosphere free of harassment by the locals.

JD slid onto the bench across from Brian and Stacey. "How do you always manage to get this booth, Butch?"

"It's my personal charm, Mac. Besides, everybody knows this booth's off limits when I'm here. They just get up and let me have it." Brian poured JD a beer from the pitcher on the table.

"Don't let him kid you," Stacey said. "He had to bribe the two Marines sitting here with a pitcher of beer to encourage them to move."

"What's the matter, Butch? The old 'my wife and I met here, and I proposed to her in this very booth' story not working anymore?"

"Hell, the new guys have no sentimentality in their bones."

"More like they know a snow job when they hear one."

Brian grinned. "Ain't no snow in California, Mac. Just pure BS, and I'm full of it."

JD raised his glass toward Brian. "No truer words were ever spoken. Here's to being full of it."

Brian drained his glass and poured himself more beer, emptying the pitcher. "Hey Pappy," he yelled toward the bar, "the well's gone dry!" Grabbing the pitcher, Brian strode to the bar to get a refill.

Stacey shook her head as she watched Brian waiting for Pappy to refill the pitcher. "I don't remember him being quite this crazy before I married him. Not that I'm complaining, mind you." She smiled at JD.

He returned the smile. "He's just cramming a lot of cutting loose into life before he becomes a father and has to set an example."

Stacey frowned. "Do you really think he's going to settle down even when faced with fatherhood?"

JD chuckled. "Quit worrying, Sam. There's nothing like responsibility to mellow a person."

She grinned and looked down at her hands curled around a glass of Coke. "To be honest, I hope he doesn't mellow too much."

"He won't, Sam. Just enough to make believers out of his kids when they do something wrong. You should see him with his

Marines. He's all business during training, and they know it. Yet they also see him cut loose when he's off duty. They know the difference between the two, and they never make the mistake of mixing them up."

"He's really that good of an officer? I've never seen that side of him."

"He's one lieutenant that commands a high level of respect from his men. Too many rely heavily on their non-coms for discipline and command. Not Butch. He takes charge and demands perfection, and the men respect him enough to do everything they can to please him. He doesn't ask anything of them he wouldn't do himself."

"Butch says you go along on some of the training exercises. I thought you'd be happy not to have to do that anymore."

JD shrugged. "It helps me keep in shape and keeps my mind sharp. It also gives me a chance to see what kind of Marines we're getting and how well they're doing. And that helps me do my PR job better."

"Well, I'm proud of both of you. I don't care what people say about the military. If they knew you two guys, they'd be less critical and more impressed."

"Why, thank you ma'am. You're right complimentary." JD raised his glass in a toast. Stacey giggled.

Brian set a pitcher of beer on the table. "Just what kind of things are you tellin' my wife, mister, that's makin' her twitter like a young school girl?" Brian sat down, grabbed his glass, and chugged half the contents.

"*Twitter?*" Where in hell did that word come from?" JD asked.

"From my mouth, buddy. And don't forget it."

Stacey had to cover her mouth to keep from spurting Coke all over the table. JD leaned his head back and laughed till his sides hurt, and Brian nearly choked on his beer, laughing and coughing at the same time.

Stacey spoke first. "I'm not sure it's safe to be out with you two guys. A girl could get a bad reputation."

Brian raised an eyebrow. "A bad reputation, you say? Why ma'am, we're the pillars of the community and are sworn to protect your reputation with our very lives. Isn't that right, Mac?"

"Absobloominlutely, my friend. Our very lives." JD poured himself another beer. "Just don't ask us after we've had a few beers, ma'am, or you could be in grave danger."

Stacey laughed. "Now that I believe."

The jukebox came to life with the strains of *When a Man Loves a Woman.* Brian grabbed Stacey's hand. "Come on, Babe, they're playin' our song," he said and pulled her toward the dance floor.

"That's not our song, Butch."

"It is if you can slow dance to it."

JD watched them, Brian holding Stacey tightly in his arms, Stacey's eyes shut, her head nestled under Brian's chin, her hand caressing Brian's neck, and no matter how hard he tried not to, JD envied Brian.

~

June slipped unnoticed into July. Beach outings on Saturdays and Sundays became a habit. JD, Brian, and Stacey singing to the accompaniment of JD's guitar signaled a perfect end to their weekends as the sun sank into the ocean on Sunday evening. On one occasion they had headed inland to try a change of pace, but Brian complained so loudly about not being able to surf that Stacey and JD gave up trying to get Brian to agree to anything but the beach.

"He can be so infuriating sometimes, Mac," Stacey said one afternoon. "He doesn't take into consideration that you or I might enjoy doing something different every now and then. He assumes everybody's going to enjoy doing what he wants to do."

"Don't be too hard on him, Sam," JD said. "He meets life head-on. Doesn't think twice about it. Besides, once you get back to North Fork, he won't have an ocean to play in."

Stacey sighed. "No, but he'll find some other crazy thing to do. You can bet on it."

JD chuckled. "I don't doubt that one bit. Sometimes I envy his ability to cut loose like he does."

Stacey smiled at JD. "You have every bit as much fun as Butch, but you know better than to take stupid chances. And you don't try to tell everyone else what they'll enjoy doing. You're flexible."

"I just enjoy being with the two of you. Doesn't matter where or what."

"At least I have someone to talk to while Butch is ignoring me. You, at least, are willing to have a serious discussion every now and then. Butch can't be bothered about anything serious."

"Butch has a lot on his mind right now. Believe it or not, volunteering for a second tour in Nam wasn't easy for him. He's painfully aware of what it's like there. When he's training the new grunts, he's also aware there'll be some who won't come home. The weekend is his time to cut loose, relax, and have fun. Don't begrudge him that."

"You're a good friend, Mac. Not everyone would defend him like you do."

"Not everyone has a friend like Butch."

Stacey understood what JD meant, but every so often, she yearned for Brian to discuss something important with her. Since JD never invited a date to their weekend get-togethers, she and JD had plenty of time to talk about anything and everything, while Brian played. Brian spent all his free time squeezing fun out of the time he had before he deployed. He didn't want to waste time discussing serious issues with Stacey.

Brian's lack of care about the world and its troubles frustrated Stacey. When demonstrations against the military and U.S. involvement in Vietnam increased, Stacey and JD discussed the growing unrest at length. Brian commented that those who demonstrated against the government and military in particular were unpatriotic traitors. He couldn't be bothered with what brought about the demonstrations in the first place.

With growing division throughout the country over the government's role in Vietnam, Stacey found her loyalties divided. She loved Brian, but she believed his gung-ho attitude and his belief that "we're doing the right thing" were misdirected.

Through their conversations, Stacey learned that JD, although a loyal Marine, believed the United States government had no business continuing their involvement in Vietnam. Recent policies implemented made the military vulnerable and ineffective. Stacey knew JD didn't share his feelings with Brian.

Stacey didn't let Brian know how she felt. She had expressed her feelings only once since they had moved to Oceanside. Brian exploded when she suggested the government was wrong.

"You just don't understand," Brian said. "Women *never* understand." He threw his hands up in despair.

"You're right, Brian, I don't understand. You're hell-bent on self-destruction over a war that's senseless and that no one will ever win. Why can't you see that?"

"And you have no faith in the superior American fighting forces, the Marines, or me!"

"Brian, you're not listening. I—"

"I've heard all I want to hear," Brian snapped. The windows rattled as he stormed out the door, slamming it behind him.

Stacey stood in the middle of the living room, tears streaming down her face. Unwilling to pursue Brian and perpetuate the argument, she crumpled onto the couch and sobbed out her misery and frustration.

~

Brian strode down the sidewalk, his anger pushing him to put as much distance between them as he could. *Why can't Stace understand how I feel?* With no destination in mind, his thoughts urged him on. *She knew when she married me how I feel about Vietnam and the Marines. I've explained to her a thousand times the importance of the American presence in Vietnam.*

He believed the South Vietnamese didn't want Communist rule. And if the Communists weren't stopped in Vietnam, it would be harder to stop them the next time they tried to overrun a country. Americans and democracy had to make a stand. Brian's first tour taught him that. Rather than walk his anger away, it built stronger with each step. "I need a beer," he muttered.

Scanning the street, he spied a bar on the opposite side and crossed over. Still wearing his Marine fatigues, Brian stepped inside, ignoring the cold stares from the locals. Taking a seat at the bar, he tossed out a twenty and ordered a boilermaker.

"Keep 'em coming until I tell you to stop," Brian said. The bartender set the mug of beer and the shot glass of whiskey in front of him.

Brian threw back his head and gulped the whiskey, then chugged half the beer. Carrying the mug with him to a pay phone in the corner, Brian dialed JD's number.

"I need to talk." He gave JD the location of the bar.

Brian returned to his barstool and settled in for some serious drinking.

"Mighty strong drink, but it won't drown out what you've done."

Brian frowned and glanced to his left. Still fuming over his argument with Stacey, the last thing he needed was hassling from some stranger. A burley, longhaired man, about thirty-five, sat four stools away. The man swallowed a drink of beer, never glancing in Brian's direction.

Brian eyed the man a moment, then focused on finishing the last of the beer in his mug. Ordering another boilermaker, he gulped the whiskey, chased it with half the beer, and began to feel some of the tension in his neck and shoulders drain away.

"You know, George," the man said, directing his remarks to the bartender, "I thought there was a law against murderers walkin' the streets."

"Don't be making trouble, Roy," George warned. "Keep your opinions to yourself."

"It's a free country. Anyway, it don't matter if I speak my mind or not, George. Guy's deaf anyway."

Brian made a point of looking at Roy. "I heard you. Didn't figure you were referring to me."

Roy stared straight ahead. "You see anybody else sittin' here?"

Brian ignored the question and finished his second beer. He ordered a third boilermaker.

"I'm talkin' about you, *Jarhead*," the man bellowed. The hum of conversation in the bar halted. Roy turned on his stool and glared at Brian. "We don't want no murderin' Marines in here drinkin' more'n they can handle, then pukin' all over the place. So I suggest you go back out the way you came in, little girl. We don't want your kind in here."

"Leave him alone, Roy," warned George. "Just ignore him, buddy," he said to Brian. "He gets a few beers under his belt, and he starts looking for a fight."

Brian's half smile lacked any humor. "If he doesn't shut up, he

29

just might find one." He grabbed his mug of beer. "Where's my whiskey?"

"You sure you want another one?"

"Right here." Brian tapped the bar in front of him.

George shrugged his shoulders and set another shot glass on the bar. Brian downed the whiskey and took a long swallow of beer.

"So tell me, *Jarhead*," Roy said, "how many innocent people you murdered in the name of the righteous United States and the Marines?"

Brian's already hot temper flared hotter. He slammed the nearly empty mug onto the bar, knocking over the empty shot glass as the mug hit the polished counter. His jaw tightened, and he glared at Roy. Brian eased his six-foot-two-inch marine-toned frame off the barstool and planted himself next to Roy.

"Unless you've served in Vietnam or any war," Brian said in a controlled but deadly voice, "I suggest you apologize for your cowardly and treasonous remark."

Roy cleared his throat, spit, and smiled as the spittle ran down Brian's face. "That's as close to an apology as you're gonna get you murderin' son-of-a-bitch."

Brian cleaned the spit off his face with the palm of his left hand, then carefully wiped it on Roy's shirtsleeve. Roy grinned and started to clear his throat again. Brian doubled his right fist and swung it toward Roy's face, but before he could land the blow, George grabbed his arm.

"You start something in here and I call the cops. Go home, Marine. He's not worth it."

Brian jerked his arm away from the bartender, never taking his eyes off Roy. "I'll see you outside for that apology," he said and stalked from the bar.

Brian didn't have to wait long. Roy charged out of the bar with the dozen or so locals that had witnessed the exchange.

"My disagreement's with Roy," Brian said to the small crowd. "No one else."

"We're just here to watch," someone said.

Roy stepped toward Brian and swung his fist. Brian ducked and landed a blow to Roy's midsection. Roy doubled over, staggered back, regained his balance, and charged Brian. Brian sidestepped the charge, clutched his hands together, interlocking his fingers, and struck Roy in the back.

"Oomph!" Roy crumpled to the ground. Brian shrugged his shoulders and walked away.

The blow to Brian's back caught him by surprise. He staggered and turned in time to see Roy's doubled fist homed in on his jaw. The blow jarred Brian's teeth and his head snapped back. Before he could recover, Roy's other fist connected with Brian's eye. Brian staggered again and heard Roy snicker.

"Damn Marines have glass jaws. No wonder they're gettin' their asses kicked in Nam."

Brian's rage spoke through his fists. Roy's face caught blow after blow until his nose and mouth spewed blood. As Brian pulled back to throw another punch, someone caught his arm, preventing his assault. He spun around, ready to take on his new opponent, and came face to face with JD. Brian tried to focus on JD but the combination of adrenaline, beer, and whiskey clouded his judgment and his eyesight.

"That's enough, Butch!"

"Mac, you're just in time for the fun." He grinned.

"Fun's over, Butch. Let's go home."

JD steered Brian away from the fight and toward his pickup.

"Hey!" Roy called. He heaved himself off the sidewalk and wiped his bloody face on his shirtsleeve.

JD turned toward Roy. "Fight's over, buddy."

"The hell it is!" Roy lunged toward JD and Brian.

JD let go of Brian long enough to stop Roy's charge with his fist. Roy fell backwards onto the sidewalk.

"Some people never learn," Brian said.

JD shook his hand. "Damn that hurt. Guy's jaw must be made of granite."

"Naw, glass," Brian said.

Roy raised himself up on his elbow and shook his head to clear it, spitting out a tooth as he did. "You broke my tooth! Who's gonna pay for it?"

JD pulled out his billfold and dropped forty dollars on the sidewalk next to Roy. "Let's get out of here, Butch, before the cops or the Shore Patrol show up."

# Chapter 4

Stacey opened the door and blinked. Brian's arm was draped over JD's shoulder and a lopsided grin spread across his face. His eyelids hung half open.

"What happened?" Tears of anger and worry stabbed at Stacey's already red and swollen eyes. "I've been worried sick."

"I had an unfor... mis... encoun..." Brian slurred, "with an unpatriotic bas... " He passed out in JD's arms.

Stacey slipped her arm under Brian's free one and around his back. She and JD half-carried and half-dragged Brian to the bedroom. With JD's help, Stacey undressed Brian and put him to bed.

Back in the living room JD explained Brian's remark. "Butch called from a bar and said he needed to talk." JD sat on the couch and Stacey joined him. "By the time I'd gotten to the bar, he was outside, beating the crap out of some long-haired creep."

Stacey sucked in her breath.

"Seems the unfortunate civilian, taking note of Brian's fatigues, made a derogatory comment about the Marines in general and Brian specifically."

"Oh no."

"Yep. Well, you know Butch," a frown creased JD's forehead,

"he'd already had a few drinks. He insisted the gentleman, and I use the term loosely, apologize. Rather than apologize, the man spit on Butch and said that was the closest a 'murdering son-of-a-bitch' would get to an apology."

Stacey threw up her hands in disgust. "So Brian proceeded to beat him up."

"He did have the presence of mind to invite the 'gentleman' outside to discuss the apology." JD shook his head and a smile tugged at the corners of his mouth. "The guy got in a couple of lucky shots, but that was it. When I arrived, Butch was more than holding his own. I managed to back Butch off, but the guy insisted somebody should pay for his broken tooth. I threw some money at him, and we left before the cops or the Shore Patrol showed up."

"We owe you, then. Big time."

"You don't owe me anything. Butch would have done the same for me."

Stacey frowned. "You would have walked away from the fight, Mac."

"I'm not so sure. Besides, I got in a lick of my own."

"*Mac.*"

"The guy charged us when we were leaving. I stopped him with my fist." JD grimaced and flexed his aching hand. "I was tempted to finish the job Butch started, but one look at the guy told me he wasn't worth it."

"That just shows you're more mature than Butch."

"Don't judge Butch too harshly. The guy had it coming. He had no right to insult Butch or the Marines the way he did. I don't understand people these days. They used to respect soldiers, but since Vietnam..." He shook his head.

"Nevertheless, he should have had the presence of mind to ignore the guy." She tucked one leg up under her. "So, if Brian only had a few drinks, how come he's so drunk?"

"Even though he was well on his way to drunk, Butch insisted we go to Jarheads'. Said something about an argument and he wasn't ready to face you just yet. After several beers, Pappy and I convinced him he belonged at home."

"Why didn't he go to Jarheads' in the first place? Pappy would have listened and maybe talked some sense into him. He knows he has a good chance of being hassled at other bars."

"According to Butch, he hadn't intended to go to a bar. Just wanted to walk off his anger and clear his head after your fight. But the longer he walked, the angrier he got, so he walked into the first bar he came to. He probably would have walked away from the fight if he hadn't had so much pent up anger still gnawing at him."

"So you're saying I'm to blame?"

"Nope. I'm saying that Butch doesn't let go of his anger easily. The guy at the bar just added to what Butch already had eating at him."

"Well, he needs to learn to control it." Stacey closed her eyes and shook her head. "He's so touchy about things lately. When's he going to grow up, Mac?"

"I don't know. It's part of his charm." JD grinned. "Go easy on him, Sam. Whether he'll admit it or not, he's scared."

"Butch scared? Of what?"

"Of being a husband. Of going back to Nam. Maybe a little of growing up. But he will grow up, Sam. We all do. Eventually. Just be patient."

"My patience is wearing thin." She shook her head and a grin inched across her face. "You're right though, Mac, it is part of his charm. Want some coffee?"

"Yeah, and some aspirin, if you have some. And a bag of ice for my hand."

"Coming right up."

~

"Never again, Brian," Stacey warned the following day.

"You have my word on it, Babe," Brian promised. "I'll avoid trouble like the plague. I'll learn to grit my teeth and walk away." He grinned and grabbed Stacey around the waist, pulling her against him. "Scout's honor."

Stacey dodged Brian's attempt to kiss her. "You were never a Boy Scout."

"Damn, you remembered." Brian cradled Stacey's face in his hands. "The s.o.b. deserved it, you know," he said and kissed her.

Brian promised Stacey he would never again walk out on an argument with her and spent the next few days trying to make amends for his behavior. By the weekend, he had won Stacey over with his usual carefree charm, and the incident was never discussed again.

Stacey, determined to repay the debt she felt she and Brian owed JD over the incident, took it upon herself to find JD a girl. She decided he would be much happier having a date along on the weekends, instead of always being alone with them. She worried about him and wanted him to be as happy as she and Brian.

The following weekend at the beach, Stacey cautiously brought up the subject of JD dating. He was lying on his back, his sunglasses covering his eyes, making it impossible for Stacey to tell if he was asleep. She chewed on her bottom lip, trying to decide how to tell him she and Brian had invited someone to meet him the next weekend.

"Mac," she said.

"Yeah?"

"Butch and I...would you mind if we invited someone to join us next week?"

"Who?"

"A girl I work with."

JD lifted his head and moved his sunglasses down his nose enough to peer over the rim at Stacey. Before he could say anything, Stacey plunged ahead.

"She's really nice, and Brian and I think you'd really like her."

JD turned on his side and propped himself up on his arm, facing Stacey. He removed his sunglasses. "This Brian's idea?" he asked without looking up.

"No, it was mine. But Brian and I talked about it, and he agreed with me that it'd be nice if you had someone to do things with—besides us."

"If I wanted to do things with someone besides you two, I would." JD looked at Stacey. "Do I look lonely or something?"

"Yes."

He raised his eyebrows at her answer.

"It's most noticeable on Sunday night after we've done a little singing and it's getting dark," she said. "You know how Brian sometimes gets a little frisky." She grinned and gazed toward the ocean, away from JD's sky-blue eyes. "Anyway, you always very politely take a long walk. You look so lonely when that happens."

He looked down at his sunglasses again. "Hell, what else can I do? I don't think you want an audience."

"No, but wouldn't you like to get a little frisky with someone?" The minute the words spilled from her, Stacey blushed

~

JD smiled and watched the crimson patch spread from Stacey's neck up to her cheeks. He tried to imagine Stacey's reaction if she knew she was the one he wanted to get frisky with. Would she be

37

embarrassed, flattered, or slap him? She would never know how he felt, however, for he would never betray his friendship with Brian, nor jeopardize his friendship with Stacey. They were the two most important people in his life. And, he decided, she'd slap him.

"She's nice, huh?" JD asked.

"Mac, I think you'd really like her. She's got a great sense of humor, and she's smart."

"And homely."

"I suppose so, if you consider long, black hair, blue eyes, and a face that resembles Elizabeth Taylor homely."

"Liz Taylor, huh?" JD sat up and hooked his sunglasses over his ears.

Stacey stood and stepped off the blanket, waiting for an answer.

"Oh, hell, why not? What have I got to lose?" He gazed out over the ocean, his arms resting on his bent knees.

"You won't be sorry, Mac, I promise," Stacey called over her shoulder as she trotted toward the water.

But he was already sorry. He watched as Stacey met Brian at the water's edge and wondered how life could be so cruel. No matter how hard he tried, he had not avoided falling in love with Stacey.

"You're an idiot, Mac. Sam won't ever belong to you." He picked up a handful of sand and let it sift through his fingers. "Maybe Sam's friend is exactly what I need. I'm sure as hell miserable the way things are." He watched as Brain drew Stacey close and kissed her.

JD knew, however, he was not entirely miserable. His happiest times were the hours he spent with Stacey and Brian. He watched the newlyweds, burying the jealously rising in him, and promised himself he'd make every effort to get on with his life and find someone like Stacey to share it.

~

38

JD sipped his Coke and observed Jacqueline as she and Stacey walked along the beach, the waves rushing across their feet then receding in perfect rhythm. Jacqueline made their group a foursome, spoiling the exclusive friendship he shared with Brian and Stacey. He tried not to resent the intrusion, focusing, instead, on Jacqueline's finer qualities. Stacey was right, JD thought. Jacqueline resembled Elizabeth Taylor a lot, except for Liz's violet eyes. He liked blue better.

Although definitely beautiful, Jacqueline did seem a little stuck-up. She sure didn't like him calling her Jackie. *Hell, it was an honest mistake.*

He had apologized, but wondered how many other things she might object to, like having fun. She didn't seem the type to get crazy like the three of them often did. After several minutes of awkward silence, Stacey had invited Jacqueline for a walk. When Brian landed on the beach, Jacqueline rejoined JD, leaving Stacey at the water's edge with Brian.

"So, you enjoy the walk?" He asked as Jacqueline settled on the blanket near him.

"Very nice. It's a beautiful day."

JD deposited his empty Coke bottle in a trash sack and watched the waves cresting and rushing toward the shore.

"Stacey tells me you work in public relations at the base," Jacqueline said.

"Uh huh."

"Do you like it?"

"It's a job."

"What do you do?"

"Write press releases, go over comments before they're released to the public, try to make it look like we're winning the war. Public relations kinds of things."

"Oh."

Silence stretched thin. JD berated himself for his ill temper and short answers. If she was Stacey's friend, she must have some redeeming qualities. He was about to apologize for his gruffness when Jacqueline spoke.

"Look JD, I'm sorry about earlier. I'm afraid I got us off to a rocky start when I said I didn't like to be called Jackie."

"It's okay. I shouldn't have assumed."

"No, it's not okay. I'm afraid I'm a little touchy about my name, and I shouldn't be. It's just that when my father named me, he insisted I would never be called Jackie. He thought it sounded too masculine. Since I've always insisted on being called Jacqueline, some people think I'm stuck-up."

"Are you?"

"My father died when I was ten. I've always tried to respect his wishes."

"I'm sorry." JD grabbed another Coke from the cooler. He felt like a heel and was thankful Brian and Stacey joined them at that moment, rescuing him from further embarrassment.

"Hey Mac, toss me a Coke."

"Sure, Butch. Heads up." JD launched a bottle in Brian's direction. "You want something, Sam?"

"A Coke, please."

"Jacqueline?"

"If there's still a 7-Up I'll take it."

"One 7-Up coming up."

"You two *finally* getting acquainted?" Stacey asked.

"Well," JD answered, "I keep opening my mouth to change feet, and Jacqueline keeps handing me a towel to wipe them off." JD grinned and glanced at Jacqueline.

She smiled and shook her head. "That towel's not nearly as wet as

JD thinks it is. But his feet are staying *very* clean."

A laugh burst from Stacey, then all four of them howled with laughter. When he stopped laughing, JD grabbed the football he'd brought for the day hoping to distract Brian from surfing for a change.

"Hey Butch, head out for a pass."

Brian handed Stacey his Coke and raced down the beach. JD threw a perfect spiral in Brian's direction. Brian trapped the ball against his chest and ran a zigzag pattern back to the blanket.

"Just like old times, Mac. Perfect throw, perfect catch. No wonder Fort Lewis College was conference champs three years in a row." Brian tossed the football at JD and loped away from him.

JD launched a bullet pass at Brian, hitting him in the chest. Brian dropped the ball, feigned injury, and sprawled spread-eagle on the sand.

"Now *that's* like old times!" JD yelled. "You dropped half the passes I put right in your hands."

Brian grabbed the football and threw it at JD. Stacey jumped up and intercepted Brian's pass. Tucking the ball under her arm, she ran down the beach toward Brian. When he grabbed for her, she swerved and bolted past him. He caught her on the run and they both hit the sand, a tangle of arms and legs, Stacey still clutching the ball. As they fought over the football, their laughter drifted back to JD and Jacqueline.

"Do you guys always play this rough?"

"Don't know," JD answered. "This is the first time we've had a football at the beach. Butch's antics I expected, but Sam's move," he shook his head, "totally unexpected."

Stacey managed to extricate herself from Brian's grasp and headed back toward JD and Jacqueline at a dead run, Brian in hot pursuit. Stacey collapsed on the blanket, gasping for breath between laughs. She tossed the ball at Jacqueline, who ducked.

"Grab it, Jacqueline!" Stacey shouted as Brian lunged for the football.

JD snatched the football away from Brian. Stacey recovered enough to stand and receive a lobbed pass from JD. Brian moved toward Stacey, but as she arched the ball back to JD, Brian jumped and intercepted it.

"Yee-haw!" Brian yelled, but before he could escape, Stacey and JD sandwiched Brian between them and dragged him down, knocking Jacqueline over as they did.

Laughter mingled with grunts and groans and feeble attempts at corralling the football. It was JD who realized Jacqueline was in solitary possession of the football, standing over them grinning and watching the three of them grapple for something that was no longer there.

"Hold it!" JD yelled. Brian and Stacey froze. "We've been out-maneuvered." He hoisted himself off the sand and grinned at Jacqueline as she handed him the football. "In answer to your question, yes. How 'bout a little touch football? You and me against them."

Jacqueline laughed. "I think your touch football is going to get a little too physical for me. I'd settle for some volleyball, though."

The volleyball game attracted a few others on the beach. Brian, Stacey, JD, and Jacqueline pitted their skills against all other takers. While Jacqueline did her best, she didn't have the athletic skills or killer instinct the rest of them had when it came to sports.

Jacqueline apologized later for not pulling her weight during the volleyball matches.

"It's okay," JD assured her. "It's only a game."

"I get the feeling that with you three it's more than just a game. I'm afraid I was a bit of a handicap. I don't have the skill or the win or die attitude you guys have."

"We were all born competitive. We won most of the matches, anyway. But it doesn't hurt to remember it doesn't always matter who wins. Don't fret about it. Just have fun, okay?"

"Okay."

"Hey Mac," Brian said, "play us a tune or two, or did you bring your guitar just for show?"

"I'll play, Butch, if you'll hand it to me along with another Coke. Can't sing when I'm thirsty."

Brian handed JD his guitar and reached into the cooler. "Hey, the Coke's all gone. What gives?"

"It can't be all gone." Stacey said. "We had the usual amount."

They all looked at JD.

"Hey, I was thirstier than usual today, okay?"

"Hell, you drank all my Coke," Brian complained.

"So have a 7-Up, Butch. There's plenty of that. Geez, you'd think I drank all your beer."

"Hey, you two," Stacey said, "it's not worth arguing over. Next time we'll bring more. And 7-Up won't hurt you, Butch."

"You're right, Babe, but Mac's buying the beer on Friday." He grinned. "Come on, Mac, let's do some singing."

Well into the evening, they sang songs made popular by Ian and Sylvia, Bob Dylan, the Brothers Four, the New Christy Minstrels, Peter, Paul and Mary, the Kingston Trio, Joan Baez, and Judy Collins. Jacqueline listened, Brian sang out of tune, and Stacey harmonized with JD's smooth baritone.

"Enough," JD protested when Brian suggested they repeat *Sloop John B*. "My voice is shot."

"Then there's nothing left to do but attack my wife," Brian declared. He grabbed Stacey, pushed her down on the blanket, and kissed her, leaving her no chance to protest.

"That's our cue to go for a walk." JD helped Jacqueline to her feet, and they strolled down the beach, hand in hand.

## Chapter 5

*J*D picked up Jacqueline the following Friday night, and they met Brian and Stacey at Jarheads'. As usual, Brian and Stacey occupied their favorite corner booth.

"That your first or second pitcher, Butch?" JD asked as he waited for Jacqueline to slide across the bench.

"Second, Buddy. You guys are late."

"Sorry, I got delayed at the base." He picked up an empty glass. "Beer, Jacqueline?"

"No thanks. I'll share Stacey's pitcher of Coke, if she doesn't mind."

"There's plenty." Stacey poured a glass for Jacqueline. JD filled his glass with beer and downed half of it. *I Got You Babe* drifted from the jukebox.

Butch grabbed Stacey's hand. "Come on, Babe. They're playin' another one of our songs."

JD offered Jacqueline his hand. "Now's as good a time as any to find out if I can dance or not." He escorted Jacqueline to the dance floor and guided her smoothly across the well-worn wooden planks. JD proved he could not only slow dance with ease, but could jitterbug with the best of them and polka till he had Jacqueline's head spinning. The only time he balked at dancing was when she suggested the Watusi or Twist.

"You'll have to get a few more beers into me before I attempt the Twist, and two is my limit." JD swallowed a drink of Coke.

"Hell, Mac," Butch said, "I'm beginning to think you're turning into a sissy. Two beers doesn't even get the heart beating."

"I can drink you under the table any time, buddy. I just don't like the results the next day."

"Okay, then, I'm swiping your girl, 'cause they're playing *Good Vibrations*, and we can Twist to that."

JD chuckled at Brian's wild attempt to dance to the Beach Boys. "I never thought I'd see Butch doing the Twist, but anymore I believe he'd try anything. He called it a sissy dance when it first came out."

"I guess that's my fault." Stacey grinned. "I made him try it at my junior prom. He was hooked after that."

JD smiled at her. "That's another thing about Butch. He'd do about anything you asked him to do." And so would I, he thought, and noticed her expression change from happy to somber.

"Except stay home instead of doing a second tour in Nam."

"You can't ask him to do something that goes against everything he believes, Sam. You know that."

Stacey's eyes glistened as she drained her glass of Coke. "I think I need a beer," she said and groped for the half-empty pitcher.

JD reached out and took her hand. "I think you need to dance," he said and helped her out of the booth.

As they reached the dance floor, the record changed to *Cherish*. JD nodded toward Brian, and Brian gathered Jacqueline close to him. JD slipped his arm around Stacey and guided her away from Brian and Jacqueline. He noticed Butch leading Jacqueline smoothly through the slower dance.

"You can't let Butch see you upset like this," JD said.

"I know." Stacey leaned her forehead against JD's cheek.

JD closed his eyes and drank in Stacey's soft, sensual perfume. He seldom had an opportunity to hold her like this, and he savored every fleeting moment, wishing the world would go away and leave them alone.

~

Brian lay awake, thinking back over the evening at Jarheads'. The image of JD and Stacey dancing filled his thoughts. He had seen the look on JD's face as he held Stacey. He also noticed Stacey appeared upset about something.

As soon as they set foot inside their apartment, Brian had confronted Stacey. "You and Mac had a lot to talk about tonight."

Stacey shrugged her shoulders. "We always have a lot to talk about. You're too busy doing other things to notice."

"What's that supposed to mean?"

"Nothing. That's just you. You like to be busy, that's all. So while you're busy, Mac and I talk." Stacey headed toward the bedroom. "It's late and I'm tired. Let's go to bed."

Brian followed. "It was different tonight. What'd he say that upset you?"

Stacey stopped and turned toward Brian. "He didn't say anything to upset me."

Brian grabbed Stacey by the shoulders. "Something upset you. What was it?"

Stacey shook her head and tried to turn away, but Brian held her fast. "What? Was it because I danced with Jacqueline?"

Tears filled Stacey's eyes. "No."

"What then? Tell me."

"All right. It's because you're set on doing another tour. Okay? Are you satisfied?"

Brian pulled Stacey against him, and held her as she cried. "We've been over this before, Babe. You know why I'm going back."

"J-just because I know," she sobbed, "doesn't make it easier for me."

"I know, Babe. I'm sorry." He rubbed her back and kissed the top of her head. "So what did Mac say?"

"H-he said I should support your decision."

"He's right, you know."

"I guess so," she whispered.

Once Stacey calmed down, they made love, more intense than usual. Afterwards, Stacey fell asleep in Brian's arms. But Brian lay awake. He couldn't forget the look on JD's face as he danced with Stacey.

~

JD had agreed to meet Jacqueline for Stacey's sake. He continued seeing Jacqueline because she kept his loneliness at bay, and their threesome became a regular foursome. He especially liked having company on his Sunday evening walks along the beach. Sunday evenings still ended the same—Brian "attacked" Stacey, so JD and Jacqueline took long walks together.

After several weeks, JD didn't need to say anything. He would hold out his hand for Jacqueline and they would slip away. Their walks always ended with a kiss or two, nothing more.

On the most recent of such evenings, JD and Jacqueline walked toward the parking lot, instead of along the beach as they usually did. They stopped under the railroad bridge to watch the sunset. JD leaned his back against a bridge support and pulled Jacqueline close to him. With one arm around her waist, he slid his other hand along her cheek and to the back of her neck. He lowered his mouth to hers and kissed her. But like all the other times, his heart yearned for Stacey.

JD ended the kiss more quickly than he intended. When he tried to pull Jacqueline against him and hold her, she shoved away from him.

"I've had enough, JD," she said and turned her back to him.

"What are you talking about?"

She whirled and faced him. "This! Us! Quit pretending you care. It isn't working." Tears stung her eyes.

"Jacquelyn," JD reached for her, but she batted his hand away.

"Face it, JD, you'll never get serious about anyone until you've gotten Stacey out of your system. I'm tired of her being a third party whenever we're alone. I can't do this anymore. There'll never be a future for us. I know your secret."

JD's jaw tightened. "I don't know what the hell you're talking about. I'm just not ready to get serious. It has nothing to do with Stacey. She's a good friend."

"Who's married to your best friend. You can't have her, but you can't stop loving her, either. Quit trying to deny it."

"I'm not denying *anything*. Maybe *we* need to call it quits."

"That's *fine* with me."

JD walked away from Jacqueline toward the ocean, not caring whether she followed him or not. He picked his way around the scrub brush and stopped when he reached the open sand. His thoughts in turmoil, he barely noticed the waves rushing onto the beach. Unsure of how long he'd been alone, he flinched when Jacqueline's hand touched his arm.

"JD, we need to talk, a little more calmly," Jacqueline said. "I think if we don't talk about this, it's going to eat you up inside. And

I'm going to continue to be a miserable outcast."

The quiet whoosh of the waves rushing endlessly onto the beach and an occasional muffled voice were the only sounds permeating the quiet of the mostly deserted beach. JD tried to ignore Jacqueline's offer. He didn't want to talk about his feelings for Stacey, least of all with Jacqueline. The muscles in his arms contracted with the clenching of his fists. He heard Jacqueline sniff. He hated it when women cried, particularly when he was the obvious cause.

"It's already eating me up inside," JD said, surprised at his willingness to admit Jacqueline was right. "I didn't mean to hurt you. I like you, Jacqueline. You're a great gal."

"But it won't go beyond friendship, will it?" When JD didn't answer, Jacqueline continued. "For what it's worth, I know you didn't mean to hurt me, but you did. I had high hopes for us. I guess we just weren't meant to be together."

JD took a deep breath and asked the question he knew he needed an answer to. "Are my feelings for Sam that obvious? I've tried so hard to hide them." He cleared his throat. "The last thing I need is for Butch or Sam to know. I value their friendship above everything. I don't *ever* want to jeopardize that."

With the admission, his shoulders slumped, and his hands relaxed at his side. He turned to look at Jacqueline. "I didn't intend...I'm sorry. I honestly hoped that you would be the one to help me forget." He shrugged his shoulders. "Please don't tell Sam."

"Let's sit down," Jacqueline said. When they were settled on the sand, she continued. "First of all, your secret's safe with me. I couldn't do that to any of you, let alone Stacey. She's too good a friend."

He closed his eyes. "Thanks."

"No thanks necessary." After a few minutes' silence, she said,

"Tell me about it. Maybe it will help."

"Maybe not." JD rubbed his hand over his face and rested his arms on his bent knees, letting his hands dangle in front of him. "Hell, I didn't mean to fall in love with her," he said, more to himself than to Jacqueline. "It just happened." He watched the waves cresting and rushing onto the sand. "How did you know? I thought I hid it."

"Little things. Things Stacey or Brian would never pick up on. But an outsider like me—well, it didn't take long." JD glanced at her, and she smiled. "The first thing I noticed was the way you look at her, especially when she or Brian isn't aware you're watching. There's an unmistakable longing in your eyes. You've never looked at me that way."

JD stiffened and clenched his fists again.

"It's also obvious," Jacqueline pressed on, "to me, anyway, in the way you interact with her—your teasing, conversations, everything. Even when you disagree." Jacqueline grew silent.

JD noticed her hesitation to continue. His uneasiness over what she said grew with each revelation, but he knew he had to hear everything. "Go on," he said. "You've gone this far. You might as well finish."

"Okay. It's most obvious when Brian kisses Stacey or touches her. The first night we took a walk together you were so quiet. I could feel the turmoil inside you."

"I've been a real jerk, haven't I?"

"Yes, but I'll get over it, in time. You've never said you love me, so I can't say you've deceived me, but I kept hoping. I've finally had to admit you're a lost cause. Every time you kiss me, she's there between us as big as life. After that kiss a few minutes ago, I decided it was time I brought it out in the open. I can't go on like this, JD. I was starting to care too much, and you aren't available."

"So what do we do now?"

"First, I'll give you a little advice, then we go back and act like we normally do. After a weekend or two I'll begin making excuses for not coming. You can act hurt and pretend you don't know why I've lost interest. Before long, it'll be the three of you again, and I'll be history."

"What about your friendship with Sam? She'll be hurt. She needs a friend like you."

"I'm not giving up my friendship with Stacey, but it will be just be the two of us. I'll tell her things didn't click with you. That I like my men a little more sophisticated. You know, suits and ties and executive positions. Not the macho military type. There's a new loan officer that started at the bank last week. He's single and 4-F. I think I'll give him a try."

"Macho military type?" JD raised his eyebrows.

"Well, you aren't nearly as bad as Brian, but there's a little of it in you. I think the Marines inject you with something when you join." She smiled.

He grinned. "I'll have to check that out."

After a few minutes, JD took Jacqueline's hand and placed it between his two. "You're much too understanding about this, you know," he said.

"Oh, I know when I'm licked. I think the sooner we part company, the better it will be for both of us."

"You said something about advice. I could use some good advice about now."

"Get on with your life."

"That's it?"

"In a nutshell. If you continue to spend every weekend with her you're going to be more and more miserable. Do something on your own for a change. Quit spending all your time with them. Pretty soon it'll get easier to do. And you might even establish a relationship with someone."

"And what do I tell them?"

"Tell them you're tired of being a fifth wheel. Tell them you think they ought to have some time together by themselves. Isn't Brian shipping out to Vietnam soon? Give them a chance to be married."

"If I do that, will you give me a second chance? Just the two of us on a date sometime?"

"No."

"No?"

"It would never work. I know your secret, and it would always be between us. But if you ever need a friend to talk to, give me a call. And I mean that."

"Some guy's going to be real lucky to get you." JD put his arm around Jacqueline and kissed her on the cheek, pulling her close as he did. They watched the persistent waves wash over the sand, while the stars, one by one, ushered in the night.

~

Stacey and Brian sat together on the blanket, watching the twilight fade into night. Brian put his arm around Stacey's shoulders, and she snuggled against him.

"You're awfully quiet, Babe. Everything okay?"

"Uh huh."

"You sure?"

"I'm sure. Quit asking." Stacey leaned forward and hugged her legs against her, resting her chin on her knees. "You think there's something serious going on between Mac and Jacqueline?"

"How should I know? Why don't you ask them?"

"That's just like you Brian. Why don't you ask them?" she mimicked.

"What's bugging you Babe? You're a little touchier than usual."

"Nothing. Just tired I guess."

"What made you wonder about Mac and Jacqueline, anyway?"

"Oh, I don't know. I'm not sure she's right for him. I worry about him getting mixed up with the wrong person."

"Several weeks ago you thought she was perfect for him. Now you're not sure?"

"Haven't you noticed? For one thing, she's not athletic. She's nice, but I don't think she'd fit Mac's lifestyle."

Brian moved forward on the blanket so he could turn and face Stacey. He hooked her hair behind her ear and let his hand rest on her shoulder.

"If I didn't know better, I'd swear you were jealous. Don't worry about Mac. He knows his own mind. Come on, I'll race you to the water." Brian jumped up and took several steps toward the ocean.

"It's time to go home, Butch," Stacey said. "The beach is closed." She turned her back to Brian and gathered up the blanket. Tears filled her eyes, and she wiped them away. *This is stupid. Jealous. How can Butch even say such a thing? Ridiculous. I'm just concerned about Mac.*

Brian grabbed Stacey around the waist, pulled her against him, and kissed the back of her neck. "I love you, Babe," he whispered as he nibbled at her soft skin.

"Please, Brian," Stacey said and pulled away from him. "Let's go home."

"Sure, Babe, whatever you say."

On the walk to the parking lot, Stacey wondered if Brian was right. Whenever JD paid special attention to Jacqueline, it bothered her. And when JD and Jacqueline took off on their nighttime walk along the beach, Stacey couldn't help but wonder what happened when they were out of sight.

She kicked at a piece of scrub brush, hoping to rid herself of the turmoil she felt. She was a happily married woman, and nothing or no one could ever change that.

## Chapter 6

*S*tacey answered the phone on the second ring.

"Sam? Mac."

"Hi, Mac." Stacey took a deep breath and tried to sound normal, but anticipation over talking to him and then hearing his voice left her nerves jumbled. She thought it odd that talking to JD could make her nervous. Weeks had passed since he had spent any time with them at the beach or Jarheads'. She wondered if he resented her for introducing him to Jacqueline.

"I had a message to call you. What's up?"

"Brian and I wanted to invite you to spend the weekend with us. He's shipping out on Wednesday, you know." She held her breath, hoping he wouldn't refuse.

"Yeah, I know. I'd love to. Where're we spending it?"

A sigh of relief slipped past her lips. "The beach. Where else?"

"Don't you guys know it's October? Won't the water be cold?"

"Not here. You're thinking October in New Mexico. The weather's been perfect lately. The water and the beach are just right."

"Where do you want to meet?"

"Why don't you come here Saturday morning, and we'll drive to the beach together."

"Sure. What should I bring?"

"The usual. Coke and some chips. We'll furnish the rest."

"Okay. See you Saturday. Sam?"

"Yes."

"Thanks for inviting me."

Stacey replaced the receiver and wandered into the kitchen. She didn't realize how much she had missed JD until she heard his voice. Stacey still did not understand what had happened between JD and Jacqueline. She was not sure she believed what either of them said, and Jacqueline refused to give details. They both insisted their breakup was mutual.

Stacey had only seen JD a couple of times since he quit spending his free time with her and Brian. Both times were at Jarheads'. She watched him flirt with one of the regular barmaids. The first time, he stopped by their booth long enough to say "hi" and visit a few minutes, then left alone. The second time, the barmaid left with him.

"Rats. I forgot to tell Mac to bring someone if he wanted."

Stacey returned to the living room and dialed the base.

"Lieutenant MacCord. May I help you?"

"Mac. It's Sam again. I'm sorry to bother you."

"No bother."

"I forgot to tell you to bring someone if you wanted."

"If you don't mind, I think it ought to be just the three of us this weekend. Like old times."

"That's fine. But if there's someone special, I wanted you to feel free to bring her."

"No one special, Sam. See you Saturday morning."

Stacey could not explain the relief she felt as she replaced the receiver. JD did not have anyone special. The three of them would spend the weekend together, the way it should be. She looked forward to Saturday. She missed him.

~

JD arrived at his friends' apartment early Saturday morning, anxious to spend as much time as possible with them. Stacy opened the door before he could ring the doorbell. JD deposited the cooler he carried inside the door.

"You guys ready?" JD asked.

"Shhh. Butch is still asleep. Come in."

"I figured he'd be raring to go."

"He hasn't slept well the last few nights, so I decided to let him sleep in." Stacey glanced toward the bedroom, then back at JD. "Wednesday's going to get here too soon. I'm not ready for him to leave, Mac. I'm not sure he is either."

"I understand. He's determined to go, but I know he has reservations about leaving you."

Stacey smiled. "How 'bout a hug," Stacey said. "It's been a while. I've missed you."

JD gathered her in his arms. Holding her felt natural. He had stayed away, believing Jacqueline's advice would work, but the longer he stayed away, the more he missed Stacey.

"I've missed you, too," he said as he released her.

"Want some coffee?"

"Sure."

They sat at the kitchen table, sipping coffee and nibbling donuts.

"So, Mac, did Butch or I do something to make you mad?"

JD nearly choked on his bite of donut. "Why do you ask that?" He washed the donut down with coffee.

"You seem to be avoiding us."

"I'm here today, aren't I? Besides, I see Butch at the base nearly every day."

"Then you're mad at me." She frowned.

He smiled at her. "No, Sam, I'm not mad at you." He averted his eyes and stared at his coffee. "I've just had other things going. I hadn't meant to avoid you."

"Truth, Mac. I know when you're lying."

JD shook his head and looked at her. "Truth is, Sam, I decided I was getting in the way."

Stacey started to object, but JD held up his hand. "With Butch's second tour getting so close, I thought maybe you needed to spend a little more time together alone. Besides, when things didn't work out between Jacqueline and me, I kind of started feeling like a fifth wheel. You know, 'two's company, three's a crowd.'"

"Oh, Mac, you know Butch and I don't feel that way." Stacey placed her hand over his and his heart skipped a beat. "You're part of the family. You should know that by now."

He covered Stacey's hand with his free one and squeezed it. "Even family can get in the way when a couple is just starting out. You two needed some time by yourselves. I managed to find things to do. Even dated a couple of different girls. Nothing serious. Just had fun." He took his cup to the sink.

"I'm sorry things didn't work out between you and Jacqueline."

"She's a nice girl. We were just too different to get serious. How's she doing?"

"She and Jack, the new loan officer at the bank, seem to be hitting it off pretty good."

"Jack, huh? That's great." JD rinsed his cup and set it in the dish drainer. A grin spread across his face at the mention of the loan officer.

"Hey, you two goin' with me to the beach?"

Stacey jumped at the sound of Brian's voice. "Don't scare me like that, Butch! Since when did you start sneaking up on people?"

"Just practicin' for all those night patrols in Nam." Brian grinned.

"That's not funny, *Brian*." Stacey took her cup to the sink. "How long've you been up?"

"About five minutes. Why? You two up to somethin'?"

JD moved out of Stacey's way and playfully hit Brian's arm with his fist. "What're you thinkin,' Butch? She's your wife, not mine."

"Just remember that, buddy." Brian laughed. "Otherwise I'd have to beat the crap outa ya."

"You and who else?"

JD and Brian boxed at each other, moving into the living room and knocking over a lamp.

"Will you two grow up?" Stacey set the unbroken lamp back on the end table. "You want some coffee before we go, Butch?"

"Hell, no. Let's get goin.' We're wastin' daylight."

~

At the beach the three settled in their usual spot. The weeks JD spent without Brian and Stacey faded, and it felt like old times. Brian donned a wetsuit and braved the cold water with his surfboard.

"Do you think he'll ever grow up, Mac?" Stacey asked.

"You've asked me that before, remember?" JD watched as Brian caught a wave.

Stacey shook her head. "I must not have liked the answer."

"I believe I suggested patience. Unfortunately, besides patience, the answer's still pretty much the same."

"And that is?"

"Eventually." JD smiled, shrugging his shoulder and winking at her. "Truth is, though, probably not. At least not completely. Your kids will probably be more mature than their old man."

"Then I guess we'd better have only one, since I never wanted to raise more than two kids." Stacey chuckled, then sobered. "Want to take a walk, Mac?"

"No thanks. I'll stay and guard the food." JD wanted more than anything to take a walk with Stacey, but he didn't think it proper or trust himself. He watched her as she strolled along the beach, her thick blond hair trailing behind her, the sun-bleached strands shimmering as the breeze lifted and separated them. Her slender frame packed energy and softness.

A picture of Stacey practicing her barrel racing at the ranch filled JDs thoughts. She sat a horse like a seasoned cowboy, was not offended by the smell of a barnyard, knew the ins and outs of ranching, and could mend a barbed wire fence alongside the best. Yet she was all woman—soft, feminine, and destined to drive men to distraction. Especially him.

JD shook his head to clear it. *Unfortunately, they don't make too many girls like Sam.* The thought depressed him. He set it aside as Brian approached the blanket.

"Where'd Stace go?" Brian asked as he plopped next to JD.

"For a walk."

"She's been kind of different lately, Mac. I'm not sure what to make of it."

"What do you mean different?"

"I don't know...she seems quieter, more inside herself. And every time I mention something about my second tour coming up, she gets even quieter. Won't talk about it."

"You know why, don't you? Every time she tries to talk about it, you get mad or change the subject. Besides, she's scared. She wants you safe and sound and you're hell-bent on heading to a war zone."

"Hell, I'll be all right. Doesn't she know that?"

"No, she doesn't." JD clenched his teeth to keep from saying more. *You can be really insensitive sometimes, Butch.*

"Well, she shouldn't worry about me. I know the ropes."

"It's different this time, Butch. Haven't you heard the talk around the base from the guys just returning?"

"Yeah, but they whine too much. It won't last long. There's an election comin' up and Johnson ain't runnin'." Brian opened a bottle of Coke and took a swig. "Got a favor to ask, Mac."

"Sure. What?"

"Keep an eye on Stace for me, okay?"

"Some reason you don't trust her?"

"Trust hasn't got anything to do with it. She's only eighteen and a little naïve about some things. I don't want something bad happening. She'll be living alone in the apartment, and well, I just worry, that's all. You're my best friend. I trust you. Just check on her every few days or so. Make sure she's all right."

"I'm not sure she'll appreciate me keeping tabs on her."

"Tough. At least I'll know she's safe."

JD took a long swallow of his Coke. If Brian knew how he really felt, he wouldn't ask him to keep an eye on Stacey. On the other hand, he knew he would never do anything behind Brian's back. Friends did not betray friends. Ever.

"You haven't answered me Mac."

"You know I'll do it for you. You and Sam are like family."

"Thanks, buddy. I'll sleep better knowing you're there for both of us." Brian saw Stacey walking toward them. "Don't say anything to her, okay, Mac? I don't want her to get the idea I don't trust her or something. She'd never understand about the safety bit. She thinks she can take care of herself just fine."

"Whatever you say."

Brian smiled in Stacey's direction, watching her as she moved toward them. "I'm one lucky son-of-a-bitch, huh, Mac?"

"That you are," JD agreed. "Real lucky."

The weekend passed quickly for JD, and all too soon he was back in his weekday routine. He savored the time he had spent with Brian and Stacey, realizing with every passing moment that in a few days their lives would change forever.

Once Brian returned from his second tour in Vietnam, he and Stacey would leave for Colorado, leaving JD and their friendship to drift apart. It was a truth he wished he had not realized while sitting on the beach, enjoying a last weekend with his friends. No one ever planned to drift apart from friends, but it happened, and he knew it.

Brian and Stacey would never exclude him from their lives, nor would he intentionally exclude himself, but miles and time would separate them enough that even occasional visits would never completely recapture the old times.

On the day Brian shipped out for Vietnam, JD couldn't exorcise the feeling that he was in mourning. At Brian's request, JD took the day off to drive Stacey and Brian to the base.

"Stacey'll get all bleary-eyed when I take off, and I don't want her driving home by herself," Brian explained.

At the base, JD shook Brian's hand and resisted the urge to give him a brotherly hug. He knew the gesture would embarrass Brian in front of the other Marines.

"Be careful, Butch, and take care of yourself," he said. "I like having you around." The courage to say "I love you like a brother," deserted him. The words stuck in his throat, unspoken and lost.

JD turned his back while Stacey and Brian said their good-byes. Brian climbed aboard what the Marines called a "cattle car" with the rest of his platoon. JD watched Stacey fight back tears when Brian disappeared inside the truck.

"It's all right to cry, Sam."

"No, not till the truck is out of sight. Then I'll have a good cry."

The eighteen-wheeler rumbled through the gate, its destination El

Toro Marine Corps Air Station. JD watched helplessly as tears streamed down Stacey's cheeks. The rain-threatening sky did little to alleviate the gloom that hung over them as the truck with its human cargo crammed together on makeshift seats disappeared from sight. JD could not shake the image of beef cattle on their way to slaughter.

## Chapter 7

Stacey climbed inside JD's pickup, and he drove away from the base. Tears streamed down her cheeks, and she leaned her head against the side window, occasionally wiping away the wetness with her fingers. As they neared her apartment, she sat up straight and sucked in a shuddering breath.

"I can't go home yet. Could we just drive around a while?"

"Sure."

JD turned left at the next intersection, instead of the usual right, and drove aimlessly through the streets of Oceanside for the next thirty minutes. Stacey barely moved, staring out the passenger window. The wipers swished a monotonous rhythm, while Stacey's tears matched the steady drizzle that trickled down the windshield.

"He's not coming home, is he?" Stacey mumbled, still staring out the window.

Her comment took JD by surprise, and a noticeable silence elapsed before he spoke. "That's crazy, Sam. Butch will be home before you know it, and you'll laugh at yourself for even thinking such a thing."

"I hope you're right, Mac, but I have this awful empty feeling."

"That's the same empty feeling every wife has when she ships her husband off to Nam."

"But I didn't feel this way the first time. I was scared for him, but this empty feeling wasn't there."

"You weren't married to him the first time, either. It's a perfectly normal feeling for a wife and doesn't mean a thing, except that you love Butch, and you're going to miss him like hell."

"Really?"

"Really."

Stacey turned toward JD and managed a small grin. "That's a relief."

He smiled and shook his head. "Speaking of relief, I had one too many cups of coffee this morning and nothing to eat. How 'bout we make a pit stop, and I buy you breakfast?"

"I'm not hungry, but I'll have some tea while you eat."

Once they found a restaurant, JD convinced Stacey she would feel better if she ate something. He ordered a stack of pancakes with eggs, bacon, and hash browns for both of them. JD ate and Stacey picked at her food. With a little effort, he managed to get a smile or two out of her. By the time he dropped her off at her apartment, her mood had improved.

He returned to his quarters with his emotions in turmoil. In spite of all the reassurances he had given Stacey, he failed to convince himself everything would be all right. He heard too many horror stories from returning Marines to feel good about Brian's second tour in Vietnam.

Career officers confided they dealt with too much ambiguity in policy. They also disclosed that even though the Marines were well trained and prepared, the enlisted men in the Army units they served with had too little discipline and know-how. Added to all that, since the Tet Offensive in January, the general policy was "don't shoot unless shot at." Things weren't the same, the officers lamented off the record, and this was no way to run a war. To add to his worries, the casualty numbers escalated steadily, along with the war.

For the first time in many years, JD prayed—for Brian's safe return and for an early end to the war. But it had been too long since the last time he'd talked to God, and he wasn't sure God was listening.

~

The first few weeks without Brian were empty and endless for Stacey. She rattled around the apartment, looking for things to do, keeping the television on more for company than entertainment. At night she tossed and turned, unable to adjust to sleeping alone. JD called once a week to see how she was doing and if she needed anything. Trips to the beach and Jarheads' stopped. She had no reason to go without Brian.

Stacey wrote to Brian every night, finished each weeklong letter on Sunday, and mailed it every Monday. Mail coming from Brian was slow. His first letter arrived two weeks after he shipped out. The letter barely covered two pages. His platoon was preparing to move "in country," as he called it, to a remote base. He didn't say where. Every night Stacey asked God to watch over Brian.

The last Saturday in October dawned gray and wet. Stacey awoke to drizzle, and it took all her will power to climb out of bed. She had promised herself she would clean cupboards. They were the only things in the apartment she hadn't cleaned since Brian left. She had the cupboards half empty, with dishes and food piled everywhere in the kitchen, when the doorbell rang.

"Crap," she grumbled as she climbed off the stepladder and headed for the door. "Probably some stupid salesman." She peered through the peephole, ready to tell the unlucky bell ringer she was not interested. Instead, she saw a familiar face.

Stacey flung the door open. "*Mac.*" A smile spread across her face. "What a great surprise. Come in."

~

As soon as JD stepped inside, Stacey gave him a big hug, unaware his leather jacket, face, and hair were damp from the weather. When she stepped away, moisture glistened on her cheek.

"Whoops," he said and wiped away the wetness with his hand. "I'm afraid I got you a little wet. I'm sorry."

"It's okay. I don't think I'll melt, though you never know. Let me take your jacket. What in the world brings you out in this awful weather?" Stacey asked as she led the way to the kitchen. She grabbed a towel and wiped the rain from JD's jacket.

"Had some errands to run not too far from here, and decided since I was in the neighborhood, I'd stop by and see how you were doing." It wasn't a complete lie he reminded himself. Checking on Stacey was the errand in the neighborhood, but she didn't need to know that.

"Well, I think I'm glad for errands, then. How about some coffee? I think there's still a cup or two in the pot."

"Sure."

Stacey draped his jacket over the back of a chair and poured him some coffee. "Black, right?"

"Right." He smiled and really looked at Stacey for the first time since he walked in the door. She wore patched jeans, an old shirt of Brian's, ragged sneakers, and no makeup. A red bandanna scarf, secured at the back of her neck, kept her hair pulled back and out of her eyes. She was beautiful.

Stacey blushed at JD's scrutiny. "I must look a sight. I promised myself I'd clean my cupboards today, so the kitchen and I are a mess."

"You look fine. The kitchen's a mess, though. Want some help?"

"Do I? I hate doing jobs like this by myself." She frowned. "You sure you want to get involved in this?"

Absolutely. I've got nothing planned for the rest of the week. I think we should finish by then." He winked and a grin spread across his face.

"It's not that bad." She eyed the mess spread over the table and countertops. "At least I don't think so."

JD set his cup in a small open spot on the table. "Just point me in whatever direction you want me to go and tell me what to do when I get there."

Stacey pointed toward the bathroom. "Go dry your hair and face. You're still wet."

"Yes, ma'am." JD saluted.

Stacey laughed. "There are fresh towels in the hall closet. Help yourself," she called after him.

With JD's help, the cupboards were cleaned in half the time it would have taken Stacey by herself. He did the high cupboards and Stacey the lower ones. With the last dish in its proper place, Stacey sighed and slouched onto a chair, stretching her legs out in front of her and crossing her ankles.

"Thank goodness that's done. I don't know how I get myself into these projects."

JD sat in a chair opposite her and rested his right foot on his left knee. He leaned back and watched Stacey as she closed her eyes and rubbed her neck. He couldn't remember when he had spent a more enjoyable day. Just being in the same room with Stacey left him content.

"Maybe you're just a glutton for punishment," he said.

She opened her eyes and smiled at him. "No, I'm just bored. I don't know what to do with myself since Butch left."

"That's understandable. He wasn't the kind to sit around on a weekend. You guys were always on the go."

"I worry about him, Mac. I've only gotten a couple of letters." She stopped rubbing her neck.

"Don't let the lack of letters worry you. He's busy. And if he's in country, he probably has little time for writing. The main thing is to keep writing to him. And don't *ever* let him know you're worried or depressed. Keep your spirits up and tell him you love him."

"Oh, I do, don't worry." Stacey rubbed her eyes and yawned. "I need a Coke. Want one?"

"Sure."

Stacey sat forward and groaned. "Oooh, I think I pulled a muscle or something."

"Sit still." JD stepped behind Stacey's chair. "Sit up straight." She obeyed. "Now where does it hurt?"

"Right here." Stacey pointed between her shoulder blades.

He gently moved her long hair aside and began massaging the tightness out of Stacey's shoulders and neck. Her head slumped forward, and he felt her relax.

"Mmmmmm that feels wonderful, Mac."

As JD worked, he fought the desire to take Stacey in his arms and make love to her. His mouth went dry, and he had difficulty swallowing. *What the hell do I think I'm doing?* He gave Stacey's shoulders a last squeeze, draped her hair down her back, and stepped away.

"There, that should help. I'll grab us a couple of Cokes." His hands shook as he opened the refrigerator and reached for the drinks.

"Don't stop. I was just beginning to feel better." Stacey turned to look at him as he closed the refrigerator with his elbow. Their eyes met, and a moment of awkwardness passed between them.

He cleared his throat and handed Stacey one of the cans. He pulled the tab and pitched it into the waste basket. "Sorry. I'm worn out. You worked me too hard." He forced a smile and settled onto the chair he had vacated.

"Just can't take woman's work, huh?"

"You got it." He smiled and raised his Coke in tribute. "Here's to women and their work. God love ya."

Stacey laughed and nearly choked on the swig of Coke she had taken. "You're nuts, Mac."

"You got that." The smile faded from his face.

Stacey rose from her chair and stretched. "Well, after all that hard work, you deserve a little pay. Let's see what I can find to fix for..." she glanced at the clock, "whatever. It's a few minutes after four. Too late for lunch, too early for supper. Any ideas?"

"Yeah. Pizza. I'll treat."

"No way. I owe you."

JD stood and put his hands on Stacey's shoulders. "I've been paid, Sam. You brightened up an otherwise dreary day for me. Save your money for when Butch has his six-month R & R, so you can meet him in Hawaii. I'll spring for the pizza."

"Okay," she said, "but you brightened up my day, too. Go ahead and order the pizza. I'm going to take a quick shower."

As Stacey disappeared into her bedroom, JD ordered pizza. When he replaced the receiver, he noticed the rain had stopped, and the late afternoon sun threatened to peek through the clouds. He stepped out on the deck, took in a deep breath of rain-fresh air, and leaned against the railing. A rainbow stretched across the sky, its colors bright and shimmering.

JD inhaled another deep breath and released it slowly in an effort to expel his turbulent emotions. He gripped the railing with both hands and gritted his teeth, then shoved away from the railing and ran a hand over his short hair.

"I've got no business being here. Damn it, Sam, why did it have to be you I fell for?" He shoved his hands in his jeans' pockets and watched new clouds drift toward him from the west. "God help me."

In spite of his reservations, JD stayed until after midnight. They devoured the pizza, then spent the remainder of the evening playing gin rummy. When JD left, he was in debt to Stacey for over a hundred toothpicks.

~

Strong hands massaged away Stacey's loneliness, their smooth deep strokes penetrating her whole body, warming her throughout. She turned and slipped her arms around JD's neck and pulled his face toward hers. His lips parted, and she felt them brush hers.

Stacey awoke with a start and reached for the light. She closed her eyes against the glare and rubbed the sleep from her eyes. When her eyes adjusted to the brightness, she glanced around the bedroom, making sure she was alone. Satisfied no one was there, she switched off the light and stared into the darkness. The vivid dream left her shaken.

"It was Mac I wanted, not Butch," she whispered. "I kissed Mac." Stacey put her fingers to her lips and wept. "Oh, Butch, I'm so sorry. It's you I love. Not Mac. Please forgive me."

## Chapter 8

*B*y convincing himself that it was his way of keeping his promise to Brian, JD arrived at Stacey's every Saturday night with pizza and a determination to win back his toothpicks. He left each time deeper in debt and deeper in love.

"Unlucky in cards, lucky in love," Stacey teased whenever he lamented the fact he could not beat her often enough to get even, let alone ahead.

JD laughed. "I hope you're right, Sam," he said, knowing he was doomed with bad luck in both.

JD didn't write Brian about spending every Saturday losing toothpicks to Stacey. He reported some of the truth. "Stacey's okay. Misses you like hell, but doing good otherwise."

Every week JD reminded himself he was treading on dangerous ground, yet he couldn't stop. His need to be near Stacey outweighed his better judgment.

~

In spite of the unsettling dream about JD, Stacey looked forward to Saturday nights with him. The morning after the dream, she reasoned that because of Brian's absence and her loneliness, she merely focused on the last person she had seen. She convinced herself it meant nothing to have dreamt about JD. Dreams, after all, could be deceiving.

Stacey didn't write Brian about the weekly rummy game. She wasn't trying to hide anything, since there was nothing to hide; she just didn't think it proper to write about JD, other than an occasional comment that they had talked.

The third week of November, Stacey called JD at the base. "I need a really sturdy rectangular cardboard box, about two and a half to three feet in width, and about five and a half to six feet tall," she said. "Do you think you can scrounge up a box like that at the base?"

"I don't know," he answered. "What do you need it for?"

"I need it to ship something, and you need to come Friday night instead of Saturday. Can you do that?"

"I suppose so. What if I can't find a box?"

"Oh, you will, Mac. See you Friday night."

On Friday evening, JD arrived at Stacey's door, a rectangular cardboard box obscuring him from sight. He maneuvered his way inside and set the box in the middle of the living room and grinned.

"Just like you ordered, Ma'am. The United States Marine Corps always comes through." He saluted and in the next instant found a delighted Stacey hugging him.

"I can't believe it!" she squealed and planted a kiss on his cheek, and then turned her attention toward the box. She walked around it, her arms folded across her chest, sizing it up and shaking her head.

JD watched in wonder and amusement, unable to recall ever seeing her this excited. His heart pounded in his chest, and he found himself caught up in her excitement without knowing why.

"Well, you going to keep me guessing, or am I going to have to subject you to standard Marine questioning to find out what's going on?"

Without saying a word, Stacey took JD's hand and led him to the bathroom. She pulled him through the door and pointed toward the bathtub. He blinked a couple of times to clarify the bluish-green and brown mass soaking in a tub full of water. The pungent odor of pine pricked at his nostrils.

"Is that what I think it is?"

"Yep." Stacey beamed. "It's a Christmas tree. A Colorado blue spruce."

JD stepped to the tub and stuck his hand in cold water. A heap of twine and wire lay in a corner of the bathroom floor. He sat on the edge of the tub and looked, first at Stacey, then at the tree, and back at Stacey.

"It's for Brian." Tears clouded Stacey's eyes. She sank Indian-style onto the floor and smiled up at JD.

"Brian's coming home for Christmas?"

"No, silly, we're going to send him the tree."

"Send him the tr—how are you going to do that?"

"In the box you brought."

JD rubbed his hand across his face, then removed his jacket, laying it carefully across his lap. He rested his arms on his legs and noticed the expectant look on Stacey's face. "You want to start at the beginning?"

Stacey brought her knees up under her chin and wrapped her arms around her legs. "I've been racking my brain, trying to figure out what I could send Brian for Christmas, and nothing seemed appropriate. And then one night I got a brilliant idea." She grinned. "Why not send something he couldn't get in Vietnam? And the answer was..." She gestured toward the bathtub.

"A Christmas tree."

"A Christmas tree. Not an artificial one. A real one."

"So what's it doing in the tub?"

"Soaking."

JD cocked his head. "I can see that."

She shrugged. "I went to the library to find out how to ship an evergreen. I discovered that if you soak a pine tree, or in this case a spruce tree, in cold water for several days, it makes it pliable and helps preserve it for shipping. So, this tree has been soaking for a little over three days."

She hooked a stray strand of hair behind her ear. "It's made showering a little difficult, but it's worth it."

"Ah, that's what I smell." He wrinkled his nose and fought back a smile.

Stacey's eyes widened. "Is it that bad? I've been taking spit baths and washing my hair in the kitchen sink." She sniffed at herself.

JD laughed. "I'm teasing, Sam. You smell fine."

"Whew, that's a relief."

"So tell me how we're going to do this." He tried to wipe the grin from his face.

"We're going to wrap the twine and wire around the tree to compact the limbs against the trunk, add it and the decorations to the box tonight, and first thing in the morning, I'm going to ship it to Brian."

"You've got decorations, too?"

"Lights and everything."

JD shook his head at her. "Where'd you get the tree?"

"I found it at a Christmas tree lot across town."

"I didn't know anyone was selling trees yet."

"Well one lot is. I happened to drive by it the other day, and that's what gave me the idea."

"So, did you have to pay an arm and a leg for it?"

"Butch is worth it." Stacey's grin faded, and she bit her lip. "You think he'll like it?"

JD reached out and wiped away a tear slithering down Stacey's cheek. "The last weekend the three of us spent at the beach, you went for a walk. As Brian and I watched you return from your walk, he said to me, 'I'm one lucky son-of-a-bitch, Mac.'" JD smiled. "Do I think he'll like the tree? He'll love it, because it came from you. From your heart. And that's all that really matters, Sam."

"Thanks, Mac." Her grin returned. "Well, don't just sit there, we have a tree and decorations to pack."

~

Stacey paced the living room floor and checked her watch for the umpteenth time in the last fifteen minutes. Brian said in his letter that he would call at 9:00 p.m. California time, but "don't worry if the call is late. It sometimes takes a while to patch the calls through from in country."

The minute hand on her watch inched to 9:12. When the telephone rang two minutes later, Stacey jumped like she had touched a live wire and reached the receiver in the middle of the second ring.

"Hello?"

"Stace?"

"Brian?" Tears flowed freely at the sound of his voice.

"Hi, Babe. It's good to hear your voice."

"Yours, too, Butch." Stacey sniffed. "I've missed you so much. Are you all right?"

"I'm great." He paused. "I love you, Babe. God, I've missed you."

"I love you too, Brian." Stacey sniffed again and wiped her eyes.

"Hey, you're not crying are you? Never mind. Don't answer that. I know you too well. Just dry your eyes. I'm okay."

"You're sure? Your letter said you were going to call, but you didn't explain why."

"Sorry. I don't get much time to write these days. Things have been pretty busy. But I had to be sure you'd be home. We seldom get to call home from in country. After mail call last week, the old man gave me special permission." Brian cleared his throat. "He thought your package warranted a special call."

"I don't understand."

"It's because of the Christmas tree. Geez, Stace, what a surprise when I pulled that tree out of the box. And lights and decorations, too. It's incredible."

"Everything made it okay? I was afraid it—"

"The tree looks and smells like we just went out and cut it." Brian's voice wavered. "You sure know how to get a bunch of Marines blubbering like babies." He paused. "Well, blubber maybe isn't a good word, but things sure got quiet around here, and I don't think there was a dry eye in the place, though nobody would admit it. You've really made our Christmas. I've put the tree where everyone can enjoy it. Thanks, Babe." His voice cracked. "It's really incredible."

"You're welcome. I'm glad it made it okay."

"It's better than any box of goodies, although we don't turn those down either. The whole company wants to thank you, so listen up."

After a moment's silence a chorus of male voices yelled, "Thank you, Stacey, and Merry Christmas!"

"Did you hear that?"

Stacey giggled. "Yes, loud and clear. You can tell them they're welcome, and Merry Christmas."

"She says you're welcome and Merry Christmas," Brian yelled. Stacey heard cheering in the background.

"We were going to sing you a Christmas song, but the way we sing, you would've thought we hated the tree. We also figured we wouldn't have enough time, so the guys said since I was married to you, they thought it'd be okay if I used the time."

"I'm glad they felt that way."

"Me, too." He paused. "It's so great to hear your voice. It makes the world seem sane again, even for just a minute."

"Are you sure everything's all right?"

"Everything's as right as it gets in a war zone." Brian cleared his throat. "The world's gone crazy, Stace. The things I've seen this time...Well, you just wouldn't believe... it's so different. Tell Mac he was right."

"Right about what, Brian?"

"Shit. They're already signaling time's up. I love you, Babe, and I miss you."

"I love you, too, Brian. I—"

The line went dead before Stacey could say anything more. Tears streamed down her face. "—miss you, too," she whispered as she placed the receiver on its cradle. The entire call had taken less than five minutes.

Stacey collapsed on the couch and sobbed. She treasured their few minutes of conversation, but hearing Brian's voice made the distance between them more unbearable. She ached to touch him, kiss him, and see the sparkle in his eyes that told her everything was all right.

Only the thought of going home to Colorado for Christmas comforted her. She silently cursed the war and prayed for an early end to the conflict, and Brian's safe return. Loneliness wrapped around her, and she turned on the television for company. Unwilling to sleep alone in her own bed, she fell asleep on the couch, watching *Casablanca.*

## Chapter 9

*J*D inhaled the crisp New Mexico air, the scent of cedar, sagebrush, and cattle welcoming him home. With Stacey in Colorado, JD hoped that going home for Christmas—returning to his roots—would put things in perspective and help him deal with his feelings for her.

On Saturday nights during their rummy games, JD and Stacey talked about their hopes and dreams. When she expressed the dreams she and Brian had for their future, JD found himself wanting the same things—marriage, kids, and a ranch where he could raise his family on hard work and love.

Like Brian and Stacey, JD grew up on a ranch near a small town. He knew the stability and quality of life a ranch and small-town atmosphere could provide. He had learned to appreciate his roots during college. Most of the people he met yearned for the excitement and opportunities of a metropolis. He missed the simplicity and solitude of ranch life.

None of the women he dated understood his need for space and fewer people. Only Stacey knew what it meant to him. And because she understood, he loved her more. But Stacey belonged to Brian and his dreams, not JD and his. That Stacey didn't belong to him and never would was a reality he struggled with every day.

While at home, JD escorted his sister's friend to dinner and a movie, but all she talked about was escaping New Mexico and going to California or New York. She expressed no desire for the things he yearned to have. It was their first and last date.

He spent his time at home working alongside his father, hoping the hard work would help him forget about Stacey and his ever-increasing need for her. But the joy of spending time with his family only added to his desire to share it all with Stacey.

On a crisp, clear morning while JD helped his father fix fence, he decided to seek his advice about Stacey. John MacCord had always been easy to talk to, and JD trusted his father's wisdom. As they worked, each knowing the other's moves and needs, JD steeled himself to broach the subject. His father beat him to it.

"You don't seem yourself since you've been home, son. Something bothering you?"

JD's resolve left him. "Nothing specific, I guess."

He regretted the lie the moment it passed his lips, but he still had reservations about admitting his feelings for Stacey to his father, fearing his father's reaction.

"Sick and tired of the war and seeing our country torn apart because of it. And I'm worried about Butch." *At least that isn't a lie.* "The two letters I've gotten from him indicate he's in the thick of things." JD shook his head. "I'll just be glad when he's home safe. For his sake and Stacey's."

"Must be hard on her, Brian doing a second tour."

"She didn't want him to go, but he wouldn't listen. She's handling it the best she can. She puts on a brave front, but I can tell she's scared to death."

"That's only natural. I'm sure she appreciates having a good friend like you to depend on."

JD hammered a fence staple into place and leaned against the cedar post. Staring at the hammer in his hand, he confessed. "Truth is, Dad, I'm a lousy friend." When his father didn't comment, he blundered on. "I'm in love with Sa—Stacey, and I don't know what to do about it."

John MacCord regarded his son for a moment. "You done anything you shouldn't have?"

JD met his father's steely gaze. "Hell no. You raised me better than that."

"I hope so." John moved to the next cedar fence post.

"You're a grown man, JD, not some little boy wishing he had another boy's favorite toy. It's not easy to quit loving someone. It'll take time. But there's no future in it, so that's what you have to do. You don't covet another man's wife. Find a way to distance yourself."

"How? I promised Butch I'd watch out for her. I can't just act like she's no longer a friend."

"I didn't say quit being a friend. But you damn well better find a way to distance yourself emotionally." He hooked the top fence wire with the claw of his hammer and twisted.

"Look, I understand what you're going through. When the right woman comes along, the natural thing is to make her yours, no matter the adversity. Your grandfather thought I was a good-for-nothing young buck that would never be able to provide a decent home for his only daughter. But I proved him wrong. She was worth going after. But then she wasn't married to someone else. Engaged, but not married. I figured that still made her fair game." A grin pricked the corner of his mouth.

"Dad, I've never tried to go after Stacey. Even if Brian wasn't my best friend, it would still be wrong. They don't know how I feel, and they never will. Problem is, I don't know how to stop loving her. I've tried to find her faults, and I've tried dating other women.

Nothing works. I need help." He drove a staple deep into the post, leaving a gouge in the wood.

John chuckled. "Well, that oughta hold."

A look of chagrin spread across JD's face. He shook his head. They worked in silence until they reached the corner post. With the last staple hammered into place, John spoke.

"Son, I can't tell you how to forget Stacey. Chances are, if you love her as much as you say you do, you won't forget her. The best thing is time and distance. The sooner you can do that, the better." He lifted his hat and readjusted it on his head, then clasped JD on the shoulder. "Let's go get some supper."

Sharing his guilt with his father lifted some of the burden JD carried. The advice his father gave him was no different than what he had told himself for months, but it helped to hear it from someone he respected. He returned to California with a new resolve to put his life in order.

~

Stacey returned to California the Saturday after Christmas. JD met her at the airport and drove her home. At her apartment, Stacey offered him a cup of coffee and set out a box of surplus Christmas cookies her mother sent with her. She'd missed him and wanted him to stay for a while.

"These are good. Just what I need." JD rolled his eyes as he munched a cookie.

"You're welcome to take some home with you if you want," Stacey said.

"Thanks, but Mom sent a bunch of food back with me, including more than my share of cookies. She thinks I starve when I'm away from home." He chuckled. "I think that's all I did while I was home for Christmas. 'Eat this. Try this.' I hope I can still fit in my uniforms."

Stacey smiled. "My mom did the same thing to me. Oh, that reminds me." Stacey jumped up and disappeared for a minute, returning with a small package. "This is for you. Sorry, but it's more food. Mom and I spent a day making several batches, and I thought you'd like some."

JD took the package and opened it. "Toffee. Now I really will need bigger uniforms. Thanks." He grinned and popped a piece in his mouth.

"You're welcome."

"Mmmmmm, this is great," he said between crunches. "By the way, I have a little something for you and Butch in the pickup. I'll be right back."

A minute later, he handed Stacey a flat package. "I would have given it to you before Christmas," he said, "but part of it had to be finished while I was home and could use Dad's workshop."

Stacey ripped open the package, uncovering an 8 X 10 photograph of the three of them taken at the beach—Stacey in the middle with her arms behind Brian's and JD's backs, and each of them with an arm across Stacey's shoulders. Burned into the frame of twisted juniper were the words "The Three of Us" at the top, and at the bottom all three names, Mac, Sam, and Butch. The varnished frame was made to sit on a table or hang on a wall. Stacey's eyes filled with tears as she held the picture.

"I wanted to make the frame myself," JD said, "and I wanted to use New Mexico juniper. That's why I had to wait till I went home for Christmas to finish it."

"It's wonderful, Mac. I'll treasure it always." She blinked away the tears, remembering the day they'd taken the picture.

"I thought we ought to have some kind of record of the three of us and our weekend excursions."

Stacey set the frame on the table and wiped at the tears trickling down her cheeks. She grabbed a Kleenex from the top of the refrigerator, buried her face in her hands, and sobbed. Without thinking, JD gathered Stacey into his arms and rubbed her back while she cried on his shoulder.

"I didn't mean to make you cry, Sam. I just thought the picture of the three of us would be something you and Butch would enjoy."

Stacey stepped away from him and blew her nose with a fresh Kleenex that he handed her. "We will enjoy it, Mac. It's a wonderful gift." She wiped her eyes and inhaled, shuddering as she did. "I don't know what's wrong with me lately. I can't seem to control my emotions." Stacey crossed her arms, rubbing her hands along them as if to warm them. She bit her lip and tried to smile.

JD rubbed his face and the back of his neck with his hand. With Stacey less than an hour, he had already broken his resolve to distance himself. Shoving his hands in his hip pockets, he cleared his throat.

"Don't be embarrassed about showing your feelings, Sam."

"Butch would think I was being silly." She tore at the Kleenex she held.

JD exhaled through his half-open mouth. "Butch would joke about it because he thinks it makes *him* look weak to show his feelings. And because he can't, he thinks it's silly when someone else does. It makes him uncomfortable.

"Our friendship is very special, Sam. The picture is my way of letting you two know how special it is." He placed his hands on Stacey's shoulders. "For once I'm glad Butch isn't here to spoil the moment. It doesn't bother me that you get emotional over things. I'm flattered the picture means so much to you."

"Sometimes I think you understand me better than Butch does." She put her arms around his neck and kissed him on the cheek.

"Some girl is going to be very lucky to get you, you know."

"Thanks, but you're probably a little prejudiced. Friends usually are."

"Maybe." She dropped her arms from around his neck and stepped back. "It's still early. How about a game of rummy?"

JD shook his head. "I think I'd better get back to the base. Early day tomorrow." He picked up his coat and grabbed the toffee from the kitchen table. "I'll call you later in the week. Thanks again for the toffee."

~

Stacey watched JD's pickup disappear, then locked the door. She had not expected such an unsettling homecoming. She had enjoyed her Christmas in Colorado, but the ranch and her family were a constant reminder of how much she missed the two most important men in her life. That realization left her questioning her loyalty to Brian and her friendship with JD. But missing, she reasoned, was not the same as loving.

JD's friendship kept the loneliness of Brian's absence from overwhelming her. She missed Brian because she loved him; she missed JD because he was a friend she and Brian had shared so much of their life with.

Stacey unpacked her bags and crawled into bed, but she couldn't stop thinking about the picture. In the living room, she sat on the couch, held the picture, and studied the images, looking first at Brian and then at JD, wondering if it was possible, or even right, to love two men at the same time.

~

JD settled uneasily into his job. Two weeks' vacation away from the constant reminders of the war had helped him forget how much he dreaded the daily reports from Vietnam. Americans fighting in Vietnam numbered over 500,000 and the death toll rose alarmingly with the escalation of the war. The distressing numbers compounded his worry over Brian, but did little to distract him from his tortured thoughts of Stacey.

JD had missed her far more than he expected, and his plan to put his life back on track was in danger of derailing. Her image filled his mind, and he couldn't forget the way she felt in his arms as she cried on his shoulder.

"Can I talk to you a minute, JD?" His co-worker's request jolted him back to the present.

"Sure, Bob."

"Let's go outside where it's a little more private."

JD followed him outside and waited while Bob lit a cigarette. "What's the problem?" JD asked.

"To put it bluntly, I've heard some talk around the base about you and Brian Murcheson's wife."

"What? What kind of talk?" JD's gut told him what it was before Bob spoke.

Bob took a drag on his cigarette, then exhaled, the smoke dissipating slowly in the still morning air. "Some of the guys think you're, well, making a move while Brian's in Vietnam. Personally, I don't think so, but one of the guys says you're at her place every Saturday night."

The end of his cigarette glowed as Bob inhaled, then exhaled the smoke through his nose. "Look, I know the three of you are close friends, but it doesn't look too good, you being there every Saturday night," he said and flicked cigarette ashes onto the concrete.

JD rubbed his face. "You're, right, it doesn't look good, does it? I assure you nothing's going on. I promised Brian I'd keep an eye on things—make sure Stacey's all right while he's away."

"Couldn't you do it by telephone?"

"Sounds like I'd better start, huh?"

"Yeah, I think so." Bob ground his cigarette out with his shoe and turned to go back inside. "Wouldn't hurt if you dated a little, either. Might look better to everyone."

"I'm not movin' in on Stacey. I wouldn't do that to a friend, and you can take that to the bank." JD opened the door and stepped inside. "Thanks for letting me in on the gossip."

"Just thought you ought to know."

Unable to get the conversation out of his mind, JD called Stacey that night and canceled the Saturday night rummy game. Unwilling to lie to Stacey, he repeated his conversation with Bob. They agreed JD would keep in touch by calling once a week instead of the weekly visits.

Careful checking through base files revealed that one of the junior officers in JD's unit had recently moved into the same apartment building as Stacey. He cursed himself for his carelessness. The last thing he wanted was to damage Stacey's reputation.

## Chapter 10

*O*nce JD's visits stopped, the weeks became longer and lonelier for Stacey. She spent as much time as she could with Jacqueline, but even Jacqueline had limited time since she'd begun dating Jack, the new loan officer. Stacey realized her two closest friends in California were no longer as accessible as they had been. She longed for the days before Brian shipped out; days when it was proper for JD to be a friend. Stacey took on extra projects at the bank in order to avoid the loneliness of her apartment.

With the additional projects came extra pay, and she saved diligently, anticipating the day she would meet Brian in Hawaii. In his letters he had told her to make tentative plans to meet him in March. Hawaii was the only destination the Marine Corps allowed wives to meet their husbands on R & R. Since she had worked at the bank less than a year, Stacey hadn't accrued enough vacation time for the entire week, but the bank agreed to let her have extra days off without pay, as they had at Christmas.

The days between January and March moved at a snail's pace. With Richard Nixon's election to the presidency, Stacey had hoped for an early end to U.S. involvement in Vietnam. But politics and politicians moved slowly. Stacey clung to President Nixon's promise to withdraw U.S. troops from Southeast Asia and bring about the

Vietnamization of the war. But as the months slipped by and no change came, Stacey's hope faded that Brian might come home early.

Stacey avoided watching the nightly news on television. Vivid firsthand images of the gruesome realities of war sickened her and reminded her that Brian was part of the horror. As upsetting as the reports from Vietnam, however, were the reports from home.

Unrest over the war grew steadily, with clash after clash between those opposing the war, and those supporting the government and its policies. The soldiers fighting for their lives in the swamps of Southeast Asia were blamed for not winning the war. And those who supported the soldiers, but not the war, kept silent. Demonstrations against the military and the war increased number and intensity with draft card burning becoming a popular occurrence on college campuses.

More than once, Stacey witnessed ugly encounters between civilians and soldiers from the base. The verbal abuse of military personnel and their families increased, angering Stacey. She couldn't understand why people blamed the soldiers for policy decisions the government bureaucrats made. Troop morale in Vietnam plunged in direct response to the rise of anti-war demonstrations stateside.

Stacey tried her best to keep her letters to Brian upbeat, and avoided writing him about the turmoil at home. She emphasized how proud she was of him and what he was trying to do. In her heart, she resented the government and its policy in Vietnam, but she kept her resentment to herself. Brian was putting his life on the line for his country and the freedom of the South Vietnamese people. The problems of the war lay with the leaders in Washington, not the men fighting bloody battles on foreign soil.

Since Brian's departure, Stacey struggled with sleepless nights and a waning appetite. She had difficulty concentrating on the simplest tasks. JD's weekly call was one of the few things that bolstered her spirits. His optimism was infectious. Stacey's nightly prayers for Brian's safety always included a prayer of thanks for JD's friendship.

At long last, March arrived, and along with it, Stacey's trip to Hawaii. She spent the night before her departure packing and repacking her suitcases, checking and rechecking her lists. The moment JD arrived to take her to the airport, she met him at the door and handed him a suitcase before he could utter "Hi."

"We have plenty of time before your plane leaves, Sam," he said, taking the suitcase and setting it down on the deck outside her apartment.

"I don't want to take any chances. What if there's a traffic jam or something? I'd die if I missed the plane."

JD took hold of Stacey's arms. "Sam, there's not going to be any traffic jam. It's early Sunday. There's very little traffic. We have plenty of time, and you're not, I repeat, *not* going to miss your plane. I promise. Relax. Okay?"

"I'm sorry, Mac. I'm just so anxious to get there. I didn't sleep much last night, and I've been pacing the floor waiting for you." She smiled sheepishly. "Want some coffee?"

"No. We'll get some at the airport. That way you won't worry about getting there on time. Is this your only suitcase?"

"There's another one inside plus my overnight bag. I'll get them."

"I'll get the other suitcase. You worry about your overnight bag and your purse." JD stepped inside the apartment and picked up the second suitcase. "Make sure everything's turned off, the windows are all closed, and the door's locked."

Stacey double-checked everything and joined JD at his pickup. On the way to the airport, Stacey gave JD her keys to the apartment and Ol' Bess, assuring him he could use either while she was away. After confirming her ticket and checking her bags, Stacey and JD went in search of coffee and a place to pass the time until her flight was announced.

~

Stacey fidgeted with her coffee cup. JD smiled to himself and wished he were lucky enough to have someone as anxious to see him.

"Don't expect Butch to be the same as when he left. And don't push him to tell you about the war. He's on R & R to forget the war for a while."

"What do you mean he won't be the same? Do you know something I don't know? Has he told you something?"

"No, Sam. Calm down. Butch hasn't said anything to me. But I know what war can do. And things have steadily gotten worse over there. You know that. I have a feeling he's not going to be as free-wheeling as we're used to."

JD glanced away from Stacey for a moment. When he looked at her again, she had tears in her eyes. "All I meant is that you'll need to be extra patient and understanding. He's straight out of a war zone, and he's going to be jumpy as hell."

"You're right, Mac. I've been so excited about this trip that I haven't stopped to think about how different Butch may be. His letters have sounded more serious, more, I don't know, depressing lately. I can't exactly put my finger on it, but he has seemed different. I promise I'll do my best to be sensitive to his needs.

"That's my girl," JD said and patted Stacey's hand. "Another thing, remember how Butch talked incessantly about surfing at Ewa Beach and especially Makaha?"

Stacey nodded.

"Well now he's going to have the chance, and knowing Butch,

he'll do it."

Stacey smiled. "I can already see me spending endless hours on the beach watching him catch wave after wave. At least I'll get back some of my tan."

"Don't be afraid to remind him there are things you want to do and see."

"I won't."

Stacey's flight was announced and JD walked her to the gate. She hugged him and promised to give Brian his best. JD watched as the plane lifted its bulk from the runway and spirited its precious cargo away from him. He spent only a short time with Stacey, but he treasured any amount of time with her. He looked forward to picking her up in a week—a long week for him, and a short one for Stacey.

The day following Stacey's departure, an unexplained dread invaded JD's mundane workday. He tried ignoring his uneasiness, but no matter what he did, the feeling haunted him all day. There was no rational reason for his edginess. His nerves were so frayed by the time he returned to his quarters Monday evening that he chugged a beer before he went through his mail.

With a second beer in hand, he dropped onto a chair, propped his right foot on his left knee, and picked up the stack of mail from the table. He tossed aside two magazines, laid a letter from his mother on his lap, and pitched several pieces of junk mail into a wastebasket. That left a letter bearing a Hawaii postmark and JD's address scrawled in Brian's handwriting.

He trembled as he held Brian's letter, the unexplainable dread returning. The Hawaii postmark itself said Brian didn't want the contents censored. He set his beer on the table, opened the envelope, and made a mental note that there were far more handwritten sheets than usual for a letter from Brian.

JD settled back and unfolded the pages. His mouth went dry, and his hands shook as he read the first two sentences. He reread the unsettling words, hoping he'd misread them. Praying he'd misread them.

*Friday, February 28, 1969*

*Dear Mac,*

*This will probably be the last letter you ever get from me, so please read it carefully and with an open mind. I'm not going to make it home this time. Don't ask me how I know, I just do. Believe me when I tell you I'm not suicidal. I don't have a death wish, and I'm not going to intentionally do anything stupid. It's a feeling I just can't shake.*

*I wish I didn't have to tell you this, but you're the best friend I've got, and the only one I feel I can confide in. I hope I can make you understand everything I want to say. It's important you understand everything. You're the only one I can trust with my feelings. My deepest feelings.*

*You're probably thinking to yourself right now that this doesn't sound like me. Well, you're probably right, but it is me. It's the me I don't usually let people see. But this so-called war has changed everything.*

*You were right about it being different this time than when you and I were here before. I've never seen anything like it. We're stationed in the same spot as an army unit, and I've never seen such an undisciplined bunch of guys. Drugs are abused flagrantly and regularly. Some guys have no respect for authority, but you can hardly blame them. I'm as confused as they are.*

*We aren't allowed to launch any kind of maneuver that might be construed as being offensive. Heaven forbid if we do or we'll be dubbed as the aggressor. We can't move forward and take any land or use that as a measure of success. All the brass wants is the number of Vietcong we've killed. That's how we measure success. Somehow, I don't feel very successful.*

*Our recon missions are filled with danger, and the information we gather seems to fall on deaf ears. Our CO is clearly frustrated, although he tries to hide it. He must follow orders, but the messages we get from Washington are confusing. It seems as though Congress, the Pentagon, and the President are constantly at odds. And the American people call us murderers. I tell you this only because I think, no, believe that all these mixed messages from home give the Vietcong all the ammunition it needs to continue this war indefinitely, killing more and more of us. And I see no escape.*

*You've been the best friend a guy could ever ask for. You've been like a brother to me. Even more so than Stacey's brother, Jess. You and I always seem to know what the other is thinking or feeling without saying anything. With that said, you have to know I've suspected for a while that you're in love with Stace.*

"Shit!" JD sprang from the chair, knocking it over and bumping the table. Magazines and beer spilled onto the floor. Clutching the letter in his right hand, he rubbed his left hand across the top of his head. He had caught the edge of the table with his arm, but he barely noticed the pain. Righting his chair, he sank onto it and rubbed his hand across his face.

"I'm sorry, Butch," he whispered, shaking his head slowly. "So sorry you had to know. I didn't mean for you to know." He propped his left elbow on the table and rested his head against his hand. His stomach ached like an ornery mule had kicked him. He took a deep breath and continued reading.

*...have to know that I've suspected for a while that you're in love with Stace. Please, Mac, believe me when I say I understand. I know without a doubt that you've never done anything, or would ever do anything that would destroy our friendship. If I thought different, I'd pound the shit out of you. But I know you too well. You've kept your feelings to yourself and from Stace. And, I'm sure, you thought from me. You're going to think I'm crazy, but I think you've got great taste—and have great restraint.*

JD closed his eyes and gritted his teeth. "Geez, Butch, you *should* want to pound the shit out of me." He shook his head, then returned to the letter, as though drawn to it by a magnet.

*...have great restraint.*

*All this said, I need to ask a favor. Stace is going to need you when I'm gone. She's going to need your strength and friendship. Without me, the two of you belong together. Of course, if I thought I was going to make it home, I wouldn't say this, but things have changed. I must think of Stacey's future.*

*I want Stace to be happy—to have the family and life she wants, and you can do that for her. The three of us, well, we make a great team. We fit together. Belong together. I'll always be there in spirit, you know that. We can't break up a good team. And Stace, in her own way, loves you. Stace and I could have been happy together forever, but it's not going to happen. I blew it. I wouldn't listen. I had to be a man and come back to Nam.*

*I know how you're going to react to this letter, Mac. You're going to feel guilty and frustrated, maybe even get mad, and then you're going to do something really stupid and write to me and tell me I'm full of bullshit, and how could I ever think such a thing, and that I am going to make it home, and that I should have my head examined, and hell, you know. Do me a favor, Mac. If you really love me as a friend (yes, I'm using the 'l' word, because that's how I feel about you buddy), you'll do the following things:*

*First, you will not respond to this letter. You can write me, but not about this letter. I don't want to have you tell me I'm full of crap. I trust that you understand and will do what I've asked.*

*Second, don't be afraid to tell Stace you love her. She'll need to know. Give her a little time. You'll know when it's right. Be patient. She's worth waiting for. As I've said before, you two belong together, if Stace and I can't be.*

*Third, promise me you'll never tell Stace about this letter. I don't think she'd understand. She thinks I'm a free-wheelin,' devil-may-care kind of guy. I don't want to spoil what she loves about me.*

*And last, but not least, name your first kid after me. You'll have to be creative if it's a girl.*

*I guess that's about all. I'll say it again. I love you, Mac, like a brother, and I know you feel the same about me. You've been a stabilizer in my life, and I wish I'd listened to you more often—if I had, I wouldn't be here or writing this letter. I intend to enjoy every minute of my last week with Stacey. It will be hard to leave her, but I don't have a choice. I don't have any control over my life any more. My fate is sealed, as they say. Take good care of our girl, Mac. She deserves the best.*

*Your buddy,*

*Butch*

*P.S. If I make it home, burn this letter. Hell, burn it anyway.*

Still clutching the letter, JD kicked the fallen beer can across the room, then cursed himself and the war. As his anger subsided, he rested his arms on his legs, the letter dangling in his hand. The pages drifted, one by one, to the floor. Tears stung his eyes, and he buried his face in his hands and wept.

# Chapter 11

Stacey spotted Brian the minute she stepped on the tarmac at the Honolulu airport. "Brian!" She raced toward him and into his arms.

Brian scooped her off her feet and kissed her. "God, I've missed you, Babe," he said when he came up for air. He set her on her feet, gathered her carry-on luggage, and guided her to the baggage claim. The two of them wasted little time getting reacquainted once they arrived at the hotel. They ordered room service the first twenty-four hours.

Stacey noticed a change in Brian the instant she saw him at the airport. Although his infectious smile spread over his face as he scooped her into his arms, his demeanor lacked his usual carefree, teasing style. At first Stacey thought she had imagined the change, but as their time together rushed headlong toward the day they'd part, the difference in Brian became increasingly obvious.

The change was subtle, but noticeable to Stacey. He had aged— the lines in his face deeper, his eyes strained and hard, unlike the Brian she had known most of her life. He still laughed and joked and called her Babe, but she noticed an underlying intensity in everything he did and said. Most of all, Stacey noticed Brian watching her the way he might study a model he intended to paint. He scrutinized her as though trying to etch each part of her into his memory.

The Tuesday after Stacey's arrival, they rented a car and drove to Pearl Harbor, visited the USS Arizona Memorial, then spent the remainder of the day at Ewa Beach. Brian surprised Stacey when he showed no interest in renting a surfboard and catching a few waves.

"I've missed you too much to waste any time surfing, Babe," he explained.

"But you love surfing, Butch. It's all right. I understand."

"I can surf any old day, but I only have a few precious days with you." Brian smiled at her.

"I'm really glad you want to spend the time with me," Stacey said, "but it's just not like you." She stroked his cheek and searched his gold-brown eyes.

"You're lookin' at the new me." He shrugged his shoulders. "Hell, maybe I'm growin' up," he said and winked.

Stacey grinned and playfully poked him in the ribs. "Fat chance!"

"Hey, you callin' me fat or a liar?"

Brian grabbed Stacey, wrestled her onto the sand, and tickled her. Stacey fought and kicked, but her giggling made her efforts at self-defense futile.

"Butch," she gasped, "I give up. Stop!"

"Say you believe me. Tell me I'm not a liar." Brian straddled Stacey and captured her hands above her head. "*Say it.*" Hard as he tried, he couldn't stifle the grin spreading across his face.

"Let's...just say...I'm skeptical," Stacey said between giggles. She tried to frown, but the look on Brian's face made her effort impossible.

"Why you..." Brian attacked Stacey with renewed fervor. He playfully bit her neck, but his assault quickly turned from fun-loving to passionate and needful.

"Brian, it's the middle of the day, and we're on a public beach."

"Come on, Babe. I need you. I haven't gotten enough of you yet."

"I know, but let's save this for later."

"Okay, but look out for later." He smiled and stood, offering his hand. "Let's walk."

They walked along the beach, their arms around each other's waist, oblivious to everything around them.

~

On Friday, Brian sat in a chair next to the bed and watched Stacey sleep. Moonlight streamed into the room, highlighting her face and hair. He hadn't been able to sleep after making love to her. It was their last night together, and Brian dreaded returning to Vietnam.

Leaving Stacey behind was tearing him apart. After his mother died, Brian hated the world and everything in it. But Stacey and her family changed his hatred into hope and love, and he was throwing it all away. He was throwing it away for duty and country, and he couldn't stop himself.

He had hoped leaving the battlefields of Vietnam behind would erase the unsettling feeling he couldn't shake. The feeling he would never see Stacey or home again; the feeling he would never have the house he'd built over and over in his mind, or the kids to fill the empty bedrooms.

He knew he would climb aboard the plane in the morning and never look back. He couldn't...wouldn't run away from the commitment he had made to the Marines. He regretted his choice anyway. That choice left him with sleepless nights and haunting visions of Stacey in black.

Stacey stirred and sat up. "Is something wrong, Butch?" she mumbled. She hugged her knees around the sheet that covered her.

"No, Babe. Go back to sleep. Just a little insomnia is all."

"Are you sure?"

"Positive." Brian smoothed Stacey's hair away from her face and tucked it behind one ear. "You're sure pretty when you sleep, Babe." He leaned over and kissed her on the forehead.

Stacey slipped her arms around Brian's neck. "Come to bed, Butch. Maybe I can wear you out enough so you can sleep."

Instead of his usual flippant retort, Brian slipped into bed next to Stacey and propped himself up on one elbow in order to look into her face. "I'm a very lucky guy, Stace. You've made my life everything I could've ever wanted it to be. Thank you."

"You can spend the rest of your life thanking me, Butch."

"Believe me, Babe, I'm trying to do just that."

Brian left for Vietnam the following day. Stacey discovered it was far harder to let him leave this time than when he shipped out in October. Oddly enough, Brian said little to reassure Stacey he would be all right.

"Pray for me," was all he said. Stacey couldn't shake the fear that seeped into her heart as she watched his plane disappear into a gray, overcast sky.

~

On Sunday, JD picked Stacey up at the airport. She said little during the trip to her apartment. After he deposited her luggage in her bedroom, Stacey offered him a cup of coffee. He accepted.

He sat at the kitchen table and caught himself watching Stacey as she picked up her cup and took a sip.

"You've been awfully quiet since I picked you up," he said.

"I'm sorry. Jet lag, I guess."

"Nope. I think it's more than that. Want to talk about it?"

Stacey leaned her arms on the table and stared into her cup. "You were right, Mac. Butch was different this week. There were times when I wasn't sure I knew him at all. He wasn't his usual carefree self. He wasn't this way the first time he came home from Nam. Why is this time so different?" Her calm voice contradicted the uncertainty and fear in her eyes.

JD had slept little since receiving Brian's letter, a letter he couldn't and wouldn't share with Stacey. She raised her soft green eyes to his, demanding an answer. JD looked away and searched for words of comfort and reassurance, but found none.

"It's different this time," he said, "because the war is different. Everything's different." His answer was, in part, the truth.

"I suppose so." She sighed. "He's gotten old, Mac. I can't explain it. His eyes were especially telling. They lacked their usual liveliness. He joked and teased me, but the orneriness just didn't spark from his eyes like it usually does." Tears brimmed in her eyes. "Why the *hell* can't grown men see how stupid war is?" She buried her face in her hands.

JD squirmed in his chair, wanting to hold her, needing to hold her, knowing he couldn't. He leaned his arms on his legs and contemplated the floor. Stacey rose and grabbed a Kleenex from the top of the refrigerator. She blew her nose and wiped her eyes, then knelt in front of JD and took his hands in hers.

"Tell me Brian's going to be all right, Mac," she said. "Promise me he'll be home before I know it."

He gazed into Stacey's eyes and gritted his teeth. "As much as I want to promise that, Sam, I can't. I'm not God. You'll just have to think positive and keep praying for him." He forced a smile, but it quickly faded. He wished he had never received Brian's letter.

Stacey slumped the rest of the way to the floor and rested her head against JD's knee and sobbed. He rubbed her back and let her cry. He had nothing else to say, no words of comfort or hope. The one time she needed reassurance, JD was painfully aware of letting her down.

After only a few minutes of what felt like an eternity, he cleared his throat. "Sam," he said, "it's late. You need some rest, and I should get back to the base."

He stood and pulled Stacey to her feet. Forcing normalcy into his voice, he added, "You're tired from the trip and missing Butch. You'll feel better once you get a shower and a good night's sleep. Tonight you can dream about all the fun you had with him this week, and how great it'll be when he comes home."

"You're right, Mac. Thanks for understanding." Stacey managed a faint smile. "Butch said to tell you he's sorry he didn't get to see you. He would have liked to."

"I'll see him when he gets home next fall." He hoped he sounded more convincing than he felt. He pulled on his jacket and stopped at the door on the way out. "Get some rest, Sam. You'll feel better tomorrow." He smiled, hoping to receive one in return. He wasn't disappointed.

When he arrived at his quarters, he showered and turned in early, but sleep hovered out of reach. Desolation surrounded him like a silent enemy. He prayed Brian was wrong. Once he fell asleep, Brian crowded his dreams, saying over and over again, "I'm not coming home, Mac. Take care of Stacey."

JD awoke with a start, drenched in sweat. He knew before he was fully awake he had heard Brian scream. "Please, God, not Butch," he prayed. "*Please.*"

~

Brian climbed aboard the Huey and settled in, his flak jacket beneath him for protection. He knew from experience he was in more danger from enemy fire penetrating the bottom of the helicopter than from bullets piercing the sides of the aircraft. As the Huey lifted, Brian glanced at his companions. He noticed two of them followed his example with their flak jackets.

Besides himself, the pilot, copilot, and a single gunner, there were six new grunts transporting to Brian's base in-country. A second gunner was conspicuously missing, but Brian didn't ask why.

As discretely as possible, Brian observed each one of the grunts. He guessed they were eighteen or nineteen, although one didn't look a day over sixteen. They joked about killing Vietcong, but underneath the joking, Brian felt their fear.

*They're just kids. Dammit! What's wrong with a country that sends such young, naïve kids into war?* He gritted his teeth. *Well, they won't be kids anymore when they go home. They'll be old men. If they're lucky enough to go home.*

He felt a prickling sensation at the back of his neck and shivered, in spite of the warm and humid day. *Obviously a week away from the war zone didn't help much. I'm still jumpy as hell.* Brian closed his eyes, leaned against the side of the Huey, and forced himself to think of something more pleasant. Stacey's soft smile and vibrant green eyes filled his thoughts. He lost himself in visions of her and their last night together.

The explosion jolted Brian awake followed by the pilot's declaration, "Mayday! Mayday! Mayday! We've been hit!" Smoke trailed behind them. The gunner opened fire with his machine gun, and Brian grabbed his M-14. He heard the pilot giving their position over the radio. Taking a spot near the gunner, Brian returned the fire coming from the jungle below them.

"Marines! Return fire!" he ordered.

Only one of the grunts reacted, returning fire along with Brian and the gunner. Brian turned away from the bay door long enough to spur the others to action. As he did, searing pain bit into his thigh and his leg buckled under him. A dark red stain spread over his fatigues. Brian removed his belt and fashioned a makeshift tourniquet around his leg. The initial pain numbed and he continued barking orders. The Huey lost altitude as the pilot fought to control it.

A groan escaped the gunner, and he slumped over his M60, blood flowing from his head. Brian pushed him aside and took over the machine gun, firing rapidly into the trees as the Huey continued its descent.

"Brace yourselves!" the pilot yelled. "We're gonna hit!"

## Chapter 12

*U*nder heavy enemy fire, the Huey slammed to the ground in a small clearing. As soon as he recovered from the jolt of the landing, Brian surveyed the surrounding landscape.

"*You*," Brian pointed at the nearest Marine, "set up a firing line over there," he indicated a stand of trees about a hundred yards away. "I'll keep firing from here until you're in position. Move it, move it!"

The young Marines scrambled from the Huey. At the edge of the trees, they set up a firing line as ordered, forcing the enemy to concentrate on their position instead of Brian's.

Brian checked the gunner for life signs. Finding none, he lifted the heavy machine gun from its tripod, balanced it on his shoulder, grabbed an extra belt of ammunition, and turned toward the opposite bay door. When he did, he realized the pilot and copilot hadn't evacuated the Huey. Hefting the gun from his shoulder, Brian moved toward them.

"Get outa here," the pilot croaked. Danny's dead," he said, nodding toward the copilot, "and I'm done for. Get outa here *now*."

"No way, buddy." Brian could see blood dripping from the pilot's limp left arm.

"My arm and my leg are shot to hell. I'll never make it to the trees. Just leave me and take care of your men."

Brian grinned as he unbuckled the pilot. "Looks to be about the length of a football field to the trees. Nice easy return for a touchdown on the kickoff. Done it once or twice." Sweat streamed down Brian's face as he eased the pilot out of his seat and dragged him to the bay door, ignoring the other man's grunts and groans of pain.

"Don't do this man," the pilot begged. He noticed the bloodstain on Brian's leg. "You're hurt. No sense both of us dying."

"*Can it,*" Brian ordered. He jumped onto the ground, grabbed the pilot's good arm, and eased the injured man over his shoulder into a fireman's carry.

Brian grimaced as new pain exploded in his injured leg under the weight of the pilot. He took a deep breath and gritted his teeth. "You're the football and I'm about to make the biggest touchdown of my life, so hang on buddy and pray I don't fumble."

About ten yards away from cover, two of the Marines rushed out to help Brian while the others continued firing. When they reached the cover of the trees, Brian collapsed on the ground, fighting for breath. Sweat poured down his face, and he wiped it away from his eyes with his arm. Enemy fire became sporadic, but enough to keep them pinned down.

The uneasiness Brian felt earlier pricked again at the back of his neck as he assessed their situation. Their position left them vulnerable. The enemy could easily flank them, and they had little firepower. Upon questioning, the pilot could not reassure Brian the Mayday had gotten through, or how soon they could expect a rescue attempt. Brian tended the pilot's wounds as best he could, then crawled to where the grunts had set up their line of defense.

"I'm going back for the M60 and ammo, and send the Mayday again just to be sure," Brian said. "Cover me. And watch your backs."

Brian sprinted across the clearing in a zigzag pattern, ignoring the pain from his injured leg. Bullets exploded around him. He flinched as something stung his hand.

Inside the Huey, he set the machine gun and ammo near the bay door and collected the dog tags from the gunner and the copilot. He grabbed the pilot's discarded headgear and broadcast another Mayday. Throwing aside the headset, he moved to the bay door and reached for the M60 in time to see a wave of Vietcong rush the helicopter. Shouldering the M60, sweat pouring off his face, he positioned himself in the bay door nearest the oncoming enemy and fired, ignoring the pain in his shoulder from the repercussion of the big gun.

Adrenaline coursed through his veins. "Take that you bastards!" he yelled and emptied the gun at the onslaught. He grabbed another belt of ammunition, and when he looked up, he realized more than half the enemy had fallen, the rest in retreat.

"Yee-haw!" Brian yelled at their backs and lowered the M60. He cringed as a sharp pain exploded in his shoulder and fresh blood ran down his arm. Ignoring the pain, he slipped the remaining ammunition belts over his head and across his uninjured shoulder, hefted the M-60, and turned toward the bay door behind him. As he prepared to jump, an explosion rocked the helicopter.

~

JD jolted awake, drenched in sweat. Another nightmare had interrupted his sleep. He remembered gunfire, and then the unmistakable sound of Brian screaming, although JD couldn't be sure he hadn't screamed himself. Unable to sleep, he showered—

cold first, then hot. He returned to bed, only to spend the few hours till dawn afraid to fall asleep and have the nightmare return.

He dragged himself to work on Tuesday and buried himself in reports to keep his mind off Brian and the nightmares. After two hours of concentrating on his job, he stretched and gave in to the need for fresh coffee. But before he could pour himself a cup, he was summoned to Captain Nolan's office.

"At ease, Lieutenant. Please sit." Captain Nolan directed. "It's my understanding you're a good friend of Lt. Brian Murcheson."

JD fought the sudden fear rising in him. "Yes sir. He—Lt. Murcheson and I have been friends since college. We enlisted together."

"We just received word that Lt. Murcheson was killed in action. I'm sorry, Lieutenant."

JD's mind numbed. He could see the captain's mouth moving, but he could no longer hear any words. He only heard Brian's screams.

"Lt. MacCord. Did you hear what I said?"

Captain Nolan's raised voice jolted JD back to reality. He swallowed the bile rising in his throat. Sluggish, raspy words stumbled from his mouth.

"Sir, you informed me that my friend is dead."

"I'm sorry, Lieutenant. I know this is a shock."

"Yes sir."

"The base chaplain and CAO will contact his wife."

JD gritted his teeth and clenched his fists, summoning all his resources in order to control an overwhelming need to lash out at someone or something. "Sir, if it's all the same to you I'd prefer to be the one to tell her. If I might have the rest of the day off...I sure as hell don't want her hearing it from strangers, or getting the news from a goddam telegram, which is probably already on its way."

"Permission granted, Lieutenant. Does she have family here?"

"No sir. I'm it, so to speak."

"If you have any leave coming, you might want to take it. She'll probably need help making arrangements."

"Yes sir. Thank you, sir." JD felt his emotions unraveling. He fought to keep control. "Sir, may I ask how it happened?"

Captain Nolan related the events that led to Brian's death. When he finished, he paused and leaned forward, resting his arms on his desk. "The Vietcong made a direct hit on the chopper's fuel tanks with a B40. The chopper exploded and burned. I'm afraid there weren't enough remains left to send home.

"Two Cobras responded to the Mayday, taking out the remaining enemy, but not before Lt. Murcheson bought it. The rescue chopper reached the survivors within a few hours. They retrieved the extra dog tag that Lt. Murcheson kept in his boot. It had blown clear. There's already talk of nominating him for the Medal of Honor. He not only gave his life unselfishly to save others, but he took out a significant number of enemy in the process. It's a proud day for the Marines."

"Yes sir." JD shuddered. Pride was not what he felt at the moment.

"Dismissed, Lieutenant."

JD rose, uncertain his legs would hold him. "Sir." He saluted, then turned on his heel and walked stiffly from the room. He ignored the stares that followed him as he hurried through the office. He headed straight to the bathroom and vomited into the sink.

When the vomiting subsided he doused his head with cold water, but when he tried to leave, his legs buckled. Staggering against the wall, he slid to the floor, bent his knees, and rested his head against the wall.

"*Dammit*, Butch, why did you have to be right?" JD closed his eyes. *How in hell am I going to tell Sam?* He fought back tears of pain and loss.

When he summoned enough strength to stand, he left the restroom and went directly to his quarters. If anyone asked where he was going, he didn't hear. He was numb with the knowledge Brian's prediction had come true.

~

JD paced the floor of his quarters and prayed for the words to tell Stacey her husband wasn't coming home. He had seen his share of battle during his tour of Vietnam. He remembered the adrenalin that accompanied every firefight. Adrenalin that made ordinary men do extraordinary things. And he tasted the fear. Fear he had faced more than once. The fear he knew Brian must have felt.

Through sheer will power he pushed his own emotions aside, knowing he had to be in control for Stacey's sake. In desperation, he called Jacqueline at the bank.

"JD, this is a surprise. What can I do for you?" she asked.

He cleared his throat and closed his eyes, trying to picture Jacqueline's smile. "I need a favor."

"If I can."

"I need you to bring Stacey to Guajome Park for lunch. Would that be possible?"

"I don't know. I'm not sure what her plans are. Why don't you ask her?"

"Whatever they are, I want you to make her change them. It's very important."

"JD, what's wrong?"

He took a deep breath and braced himself.

"JD?"

"Butch isn't coming home. He's..." JD's voice trailed off. He couldn't say aloud that Brian was dead.

"Oh, God, no," Jacqueline whispered. "When? How?"

JD swallowed the lump in his throat. "Sunday. I'll explain at the park. I need you to be there for Stacey, but I don't want you to let on that something's wrong. Just tell her you had an urge to have a picnic in the park and didn't want to eat alone. Do you think you can do that?"

"Of course." Jacqueline bit her lip. "Should I tell her you're meeting us?"

"No. She'll suspect something."

"We'll need to pick up something to eat first, or she *will* suspect something."

"Do whatever is necessary. Just get her to the park."

"May I ask why the park instead of here or at home?"

"I sure as hell don't want to tell her at the bank with so many people around." JD silently berated himself for his burst of temper. "I'm sorry, Jacqueline, I shouldn't have snapped at you like that."

"It's okay. Go on."

"It will be better to tell her on neutral ground. Lunch at the park is less suspicious than suggesting you go home with her. And not hearing the news at home, well, it will be someplace she'll want to go instead of avoid. And I don't want her picking up a damn telegram if it's already arrived."

After a short silence Jacqueline spoke. "Are you going to be all right?"

"No. But for Sam's sake I have to be. I don't know how I'm going to tell her, but I'll find a way. I'll see you in a little while."

"We'll be there."

~

JD leaned against his pickup and watched as Stacey and Jacqueline settled on a bench and opened their McDonald's sacks. A brisk breeze picked up a carelessly discarded Milky Way wrapper, sending it scooting across the ground ahead of him as he forced his feet to move toward them. He heard Stacey laugh as he neared and committed the sound to memory, knowing it would be a while before he heard it again.

Stacey glanced up from her hamburger and saw JD. "Mac! What a surprise. What are you doing here?"

He stopped short of the bench. Jacqueline glanced toward him, and he nodded at her. "Thanks for coming."

"What's going on?" Stacey asked. She looked at Jacqueline and then at JD. Stacey set her partially eaten hamburger down. "This isn't a coincidence, is it?"

"No." JD glanced away from Stacey's inquiring stare.

"Brian," Stacey whispered as tears stung her eyes. She put her hand to her mouth. JD fought for some way to tell Stacey what she didn't want to hear. Jacqueline put her hand on Stacey's arm.

"Tell me he's injured, and they're flying him to a hospital somewhere."

JD grimaced as he watched fear turn to hope in Stacey's eyes.

"*Tell* me, Mac," she demanded, jerking her arm away from Jacqueline. "Butch is just wounded, right?" She rose and stepped toward JD, searching his eyes as she did. "He *has* to be," she whispered.

JD searched Stacey's stricken face and fought back his own tears. "I can't Stacey. I wish to God I could, but I can't. Butch—"

Stacey clamped her hands over her ears. "Noooooo," she wailed. "I don't want to hear this!"

Before JD and Jacqueline could react, Stacey bolted blindly away from them.

"Sam!" JD sprinted after Stacey. She was halfway across the park when he caught her. "Sam, stop!" He grabbed her arm and swung

118

her around.

Anger flashed in her green eyes. "Let me go!"

"I can't, Sam." He pulled her tightly against him. "It won't change anything. What's done is done."

"Oh, Mac," she moaned. Sobs wracked her body and her tears soaked his shirt.

JD's own tears ran down his face into Stacey's hair. "I'm sorry," he whispered. As inadequate as the words sounded, he could think of nothing else to say. "I'm so sorry."

## Chapter 13

Clouds drifted in lazy patterns across the sky, and shadows under the trees lengthened inch by inch. Time had little meaning for Stacey and JD as they held each other. After a time, her tears subsided, and she sucked in a deep breath. Her body trembled, and JD held her tighter, rubbing her back to calm her.

When he thought she was ready, JD guided Stacey back to the bench and coaxed her to sit next to Jacqueline. He sat on the other side of Stacey and offered her his handkerchief. As she blew her nose, he smoothed her hair away from her face. Jacqueline put her arms around Stacey, easing Stacey's head down on her shoulder, rubbing Stacey's arm in comfort as she gently rocked from side to side.

Knowing he had to face questions Stacey would inevitably ask, JD stood and walked a few feet away, summoning the words to answer those questions. He smoothed his hand across the top of his head and down the back of his neck while praying for guidance. He returned to the bench, knelt on one knee in front of Stacey, and took her hands in his.

"I wish I could change things, Sam." He paused, searching for words of comfort, voicing, instead, his own troubled thoughts. "I wish I could turn back the clock and make everything right. It's all so senseless."

"I wish you could, too, Mac." Stacey shuddered. "How can this be? I was just with him. He was alive and laughing." She lifted her head from Jacqueline's shoulder, her eyes searching JD's face. "There's got to be a mistake. They're wrong. They have to be. It's somebody else. Brian can't be...I would have felt something."

JD closed his eyes and shook his head. "I'm sorry, Sam. He didn't die alone. There's no doubt."

Stacey grasped JD's hands. "Then tell me what happened," she said. "I have to know."

"Maybe now isn't a good time."

"*Now*, Mac. I have to know now."

Unable to ignore the determination etched on her face, JD cleared his throat and with difficulty repeated the information he'd heard earlier from Captain Nolan. As he told Stacey how Brian died, her grip on his hands tightened and tears streamed down her face. By the time he finished, his hands were numb from Stacey's grip.

She remained silent for a few minutes, her face taut, brows furrowed. Slowly loosening her grip, Stacey peered into his eyes, bewilderment written on her face.

"How can I say good-bye if there's nothing to say good-bye to?" she asked.

JD closed his eyes, unable to face the haunted look in Stacey's. "I don't know, Sam." He opened his eyes and looked away from her. "But somehow we'll find a way. I promise."

JD and Jacqueline eventually convinced Stacey to go home. At the apartment, Jacqueline fixed Stacey hot tea and soup, but she refused them both. JD coaxed Stacey into lying down for a while. He covered her with a blanket and left her bedroom door ajar. When he returned to the living room, Jacqueline was placing the telephone receiver on its cradle.

"I promised my boss I'd let him know how things went," she explained. "He thought it best to wait to tell everyone else until after I called." Jacqueline laid her head on the back of the couch and rubbed her eyes. "What now, JD?"

"I don't know." He sat at the opposite end of the couch and rested his arms on his knees, his head bowed. "I'm afraid I didn't handle things too well."

Jacqueline leaned toward him and put her hand on his arm. "You did just fine. There's no easy way to tell someone that kind of news." She squeezed his arm and stood. "Want some coffee?"

"Sure."

When the coffee finished brewing, JD joined Jacqueline at the kitchen table. His lifeless eyes focused at the cup in front of him.

"JD, what can I do for you?"

"What do you mean?"

"You're not handling this any better than Stacey. Brian was your best friend. You've got dark circles under your eyes, and you look like you're about to fall apart. Is there something, anything, I can do to help ease the pain you're going through?"

"No. Nothing." He sipped his coffee. "Only time will help. Thanks anyway." He set the cup down. "I haven't slept very well the last few nights." He closed his eyes and rubbed them. "I'd give anything to have Butch back, Jacqueline. *Anything.*"

JD leaned his arms on the table and cupped his hands around his coffee. "Would you think I was crazy if I told you I heard Butch scream in my sleep the last two nights?"

"Oh, JD, I'm so sorry."

JD wanted to tell Jacqueline about Brian's letter, but knew he couldn't. The letter was meant for him and him only. "Brian was like a brother to me. We were always on the same wavelength. I usually knew what he was thinking. God, I'm going to miss him." He rubbed his hand over his face. "I would have gladly taken his place. That way Stacey would still have her dreams…and her husband."

"Stacey's young. She'll survive this."

"I hope so." JD took his cup to the sink. "Do you think you could stay with her tonight? She shouldn't be alone, and it wouldn't be proper for me to be here."

"I'd be happy to, if you'll stay long enough for me to go home and get a few things."

"No problem."

Jacqueline had been gone only a few minutes when Stacey emerged from the bedroom. JD explained that Jacqueline had agreed to spend the night. He could see the relief on Stacey's face, knowing she wouldn't spend the night alone.

"Will you stay while I call my parents?" she asked.

"Sure."

Stacey dialed the number, but when her mother answered, she froze and handed the phone to JD. For the second time that day, he found himself relaying the tragic news about Brian. After returning the phone to Stacey, he moved to the window and watched the semi-busy parking lot.

"Oh, Mom, he's gone." Stacey sobbed. "Brian's gone."

JD gritted his teeth and turned to watch Stacey. His heart ached for her. She reminded him of a lost little girl.

She wilted onto the couch and drew her knees up against her chest. "Mom, I need you. Can you and Daddy come out?" She listened for a minute and nodded. "Thanks," she whispered. As she placed the receiver on its cradle, new sobs racked her body. JD put his arms around her, and held her as she wept.

After a while, her sobbing quieted into hiccups and sighs. JD suggested Stacey splash cold water on her face. He had a hot cup of tea and a piece of toast waiting for her in the kitchen when she returned. She tried to refuse the nourishment, but he insisted.

"Are your parents coming?" He watched Stacey nibble on her toast.

"Mom said she'd come, even if Dad couldn't get away. He's in the middle of calving, so he may not be able to come. Mom said she'd call once she had her plane reservations."

"It's good she's coming out. You need your family right now."

Stacey reached across the table and placed her hand over JD's. "You're the best friend I have, Mac. I don't know what I'd do without you." She took a deep breath and shuddered. "You're family." A smile tugged at the corner of her mouth. "You're hurting, too."

He covered both their hands with his free one. "I'll always be here for you, Sam." He squeezed her hand and smiled. "I promise."

~

The days following the news of Brian's death blurred one into another. Stacey slept little, pacing the floor when she couldn't sleep, crying when she thought she had no more tears to shed, and finding herself, on more than one occasion, furious at Brian for dying.

"Damn you, Brian!" she raged one night when she couldn't fall asleep. "How could you do this to us? We had plans," she sobbed. "You were going to build us a house. A beautiful house. And now there won't be one. There'll be no place to raise our kids, no place to grow old together in, no place...." Stacey hugged her pillow and soaked it with her tears. "How could you be so selfish?" Her fist pounded the bed. "How could you leave me alone like this?"

Through her rage and her grieving, JD and Jacqueline provided Stacey with support and comfort. Jacqueline stayed with Stacey until

Kate and Phil arrived. The Atkins' neighbors had offered to take over the calving, making it possible for Phil to get away. Having her parents with her, helping her cope and giving her strength during the days that followed was a godsend to Stacey.

She was disappointed her brother, Jess, couldn't abandon his law school midterms to make the trip. He called and talked to Stacey for over an hour, giving Stacey added comfort and encouragement.

On Thursday, the base chaplain and a Casualty Assistance Officer arrived to express their sympathy and offer their services. Her coworkers, and other Marines and their families stopped by, bringing food and offering help.

Saturday morning, friends and family gathered at the base chapel to bid Brian farewell. At Stacey's request, JD gave the eulogy. His stories about Brian evoked both tears and chuckles from those in attendance. He faltered at times while speaking about his friend, but when he finished, he had given a complete picture of Brian— Marine, son, friend, and husband.

Captain Nolan presented Brian's dog tag to Stacey, along with a United States flag "from a grateful nation," and the Purple Heart. He stated with pride that Brian's commanding officer in Vietnam had nominated Brian for the Medal of Honor, "for conspicuous gallantry and intrepidity at the risk of his life above and beyond the call of duty."

When the *Navy Hymn* was sung, Stacey tried to sing along, but her voice failed her. She stood quietly as tears flowed down her cheeks, and took comfort from JD's voice as it blended with the others in the chapel.

At the conclusion of the service, the mourners stood outside the chapel for a final military salute. Rigid and stone-faced, the honor guard focused unseeing at the field before them, awaiting their orders. Stacey steeled herself and stood erect and proud in honor of

Brian and his dedication to the Corps. As the volley of gunfire exploded in the morning air, she flinched and her knees threatened to buckle. JD sensed her distress and slipped his arm around her waist, providing support until the final note of *Taps* faded.

Friends were invited to Stacey's apartment after the services for "a wake of sorts," as she put it. The apartment overflowed, and Stacey heard countless stories about Brian and his escapades. She laughed as much as she cried, each tear and smile slowly chipping away at her pain.

Pappy attended the services and stopped by the apartment afterward. "I'm going to put a bronze plaque in your favorite booth at Jarheads' and call it *Brian's Place*," he told Stacey.

"What a wonderful thing to do Pappy. Brian would be proud."

"Brian used to confide in me before you two were married," Pappy said. "Told me about growing up without a father, and what your parents had done for him." Tears glistened in his eyes and his voice cracked. "His real father missed out on knowing such a great kid. I would have been proud to have been his father."

Stacey hugged him. "Oh, Pappy, he thought the world of you and would have been proud to have you as a father."

After all the guests had departed, Jacqueline stayed to straighten up the apartment, while JD and Stacey drove Kate and Phil to the airport.

"I hate leaving you so soon after the services, honey," Kate said. "I could stay a little longer, if you want."

"I'll be all right, Mom. I've got Mac and Jacqueline for moral support, and besides, Dad needs you." She winked at her father. "He's terrible at bachin' it.

Phil grinned at his daughter. "Honey, if you want your mother to stay, I don't think I'll starve to death,"

"Thanks, but you're only a phone call away if I need something. I need some time to sort things out and decide what to do. I'll be in touch and let you know what's happening."

Stacey said little on the return trip to her apartment. Jacqueline had gone by the time Stacey and JD returned. Stacey collapsed on the couch. JD shed the jacket of his dress uniform and sat beside her.

"Do you think Mom was upset that I didn't want her to stay longer?"

"No. I think she's worried about you, but I think she understands."

"I hope so. Mom and Dad and I talked a lot about what I should do now." Stacey sighed. "It's just that I feel I need to make decisions about my future without my parents' advice. Is that wrong?"

JD took Stacey's hand and squeezed it. "No. It's very independent and mature."

"Thanks." She smiled at him. "I needed that."

"Are you going to be okay by yourself tonight?"

Stacey grimaced. "I don't know, Mac. I feel lost. Unsettled. I still don't feel like I've said good-bye to Brian." Tears glistened in her eyes. "It sounds awful, but if there'd been a body, or a casket. Something." She bit her lip and sniffed.

JD brushed a strand of hair away from her face and up onto her head, tucking it into the knot it had strayed from. "I understand, Sam. I'm having the same problem."

He stood and sauntered to the window. Stacey joined him, put her arm around him, and lightly rubbed his back. The late afternoon sun cast long shadows across the parking lot of the apartment building. She closed her eyes and thanked God for JD. She valued his friendship above all others—a friendship far stronger than she had with anyone else, including Jacqueline.

"Thanks for doing the eulogy," she said. "I know how hard it was for you, but it wouldn't have been right coming from anyone else."

"I was honored you asked me, Sam." They stood together in silence a few minutes longer. "That's it!"

Stacey flinched at JD's sudden outburst.

He grabbed Stacey's shoulders and turned her to face him. "I know how we can say goodbye to Butch. What did he like doing the most?"

Stacey shook her head and frowned. "Lots of things. He was always doing something."

"Here, I mean. Every weekend."

"Surfing."

"I'm going to my quarters and change into my jeans. You do the same, and I'll be back in a few minutes. We're going to give Butch a proper send-off."

Before Stacey could react, JD hurried out the door, leaving her wondering what he had in mind.

~

JD and Stacey stood on a deserted San Onofre Beach, Brian's surfboard propped between them. They had shed their sneakers and rolled up their jeans.

"Well, what do you think, Sam? Will this do?"

Stacey grinned. "It will do, Mac. I just hope we don't get caught."

"Have a little faith. Anyway, if we do, I think we can make even the toughest Shore Patrolman or cop understand what we're doing and why."

Together they duct-taped a full bottle of Brian's favorite beer onto the surfboard, waded out into the cold water, and gave the surfboard as hefty a shove as they could manage. They watched the board drift out to sea as the water ebbed and swirled around their legs. After a few minutes, they returned to the beach and sat down.

JD opened a bottle of beer and Stacey a Coke.

"To you, Butch," JD toasted. They clinked their bottles together. "Happy surfing."

Tears stung Stacey's eyes as she took a sip. "Do you think he's watching us?" she asked.

JD turned to her and grinned. "He's probably already chugged the beer and is ready for another one." He put his hand on Stacey's cheek and wiped away a tear with his thumb. "He's in God's hands now Sam. I truly believe that. He's looking down on us right now, and I can almost hear that high pitched '*yee-haw*' he'd always cut loose with when he caught a good wave."

Stacey smiled and put her arm around JD, resting her head on his shoulder. "You always know the right thing to say and do, Mac." She raised her coke toward the ocean. "Surf your heart out, Butch. I love you."

## Chapter 14

*T*he days following the memorial service, JD either called Stacey or stopped by the apartment after work to check on her. On Saturday, she invited JD to supper and challenged him to a game of rummy, "for old times' sake."

"I've made a decision, Mac," she announced while shuffling the cards.

"Oh?"

"I can't stay here." She didn't look at him and forged ahead before he could react. "Somehow it's just not right to stay. I returned to work sooner than I needed to because there were too many reminders of Brian in the apartment—his civvies, his favorite mug, his denim jacket and cowboy boots. I thought working would help, but I still come home to them every night."

"It would probably help if you gave some of those things away. I know it will be hard, but it would be a start."

"It's more than that. I need a change of scenery. I've decided to go home and maybe start college next fall." She looked at JD and could see the disappointment in his eyes. "Western State College isn't too far away, and I've always wanted to teach. It's a good teacher's college." Stacey set the cards on the table for JD to cut.

"I can't fault your reasoning, Sam. You know I'll support you no matter what you decide," he said, "but you might want to consider that this is where you asserted your independence. Getting your degree is definitely a good idea, but there are good colleges here, too."

"I know, but without Brian here, there's no one—"

"I'm here."

"Oh, JD, I'm sorry. I didn't mean..." She touched her chest. "You'll always be here, in my heart. And I know I can call you anytime I need to talk, but I have to go home." Tears stung her eyes. "I need to be near my family. I hope you understand."

"You're sure it's what you want to do?"

"It is. Without Brian, this isn't really home, just a stopping off place. I miss Colorado and the mountains. That's where Brian wanted to settle. He wanted to be close to his mountains." Her eyes pleaded with JD. "Please understand, Mac."

"Of course I do, Sam. But I want you to know I'm here if you ever need anything." He smiled and tapped the deck she set in front of him. "I'm going to miss you."

"I'll miss you, too, but Colorado's my home, and Brian's, and I feel the need to be there. You'll have to promise to come visit me whenever you can. I don't want to lose touch with you."

"You can count on that," he promised.

Stacey dealt. "I'll have to find someone to take over the lease on the apartment, but that shouldn't be too hard. There's usually a waiting list."

JD picked up his cards one at a time. "I think I know someone who would be willing to take over your lease."

"Really? Who?"

"Me."

"You?"

132

"Yep. I'm due to muster out in about six months, and I'm sick of living on base. This would be perfect for me."

"You've got a deal." Stacey set the deck down and picked up her cards. "So, what are you going to do once you're out of the Marines?"

"I was thinking I might take some graduate courses at UCLA or USC. I've always wanted to teach at a college, and I need at least a Master's Degree to do that."

"Sounds like a good plan." Stacey arranged and rearranged the cards in her hand. "Well, now that that's settled, gin." She laid her cards on the table.

JD shook his head. "I should've cut the cards," he mumbled and counted up his points.

~

Stacey resigned her job at the bank, effective the following Friday. She began the tedious job of packing, deciding which items of Brian's she wanted to keep, and which items she would give to charity. Some choices were difficult to make. She gave JD the bull riding championship belt buckle Brian won while in college.

JD helped Stacey with the packing as much as he could. Some things they boxed and shipped ahead. He insisted he drive Ol' Bess and Stacey home, then fly back to California. "It's the least I can do for you and for Brian. That way I can delay saying good-bye for a few days longer, and I'll know you got home safe and sound."

For a moment, Stacey thought she detected a longing in his voice that went beyond friendship, but she decided it was only her own reluctance to say good-bye to him that had her imagining more than what he said.

The day before Stacey and JD were to leave for Colorado, they finished last-minute packing and loaded Ol' Bess. By the end of the day, exhaustion had set in and Ol' Bess bulged at the seams. Stacey and JD leaned against the tailgate and forced it closed. When it was secured, Stacey stood back and surveyed the pickup. A laugh started somewhere deep inside her and burst out without warning. She crumpled to the pavement in hysterics.

JD knelt in front of her. "Sam, are you all right?"

"It looks like something out of the *Grapes of Wrath*," she said. "All my worldly goods are crammed into Ol' Bess."

"Sheez, Sam." JD crumpled to the ground, his laughter nearly drowning out hers.

But tears of laughter gradually turned to tears of heartbreak for Stacey. "Why can't I take him home with me, Mac?"

His eyes softened, and then he smiled. "You are, Sam, in your heart. Where it counts."

The two of them sat in silence for a few minutes, then they hauled boxes out of JD's pickup and carried them into the apartment. Stacey offered to help him unpack, but he assured her his things would wait until he returned from Colorado.

Jacqueline stopped in to say good-bye about the same time their pizza arrived. At their urging, she joined them for supper. After Jacqueline left, JD showered, then Stacey took her turn.

Stacey emerged from the shower and found JD standing barefoot on the deck, dressed in Levi's and a T-shirt and gazing out toward the ocean. He was so handsome and strong. Her rock. The one person she could always depend on.

*If he could hold me I'd feel safe and cared for.* It seemed so natural to want his arms around her. He was a part of her life she didn't want to lose. An anchor to hold on to. More than a friend. Someone she loved. The thought startled her.

She tightened the tie on her terrycloth robe and joined him. "Penny for your thoughts," she said.

"Wondering how far out the surfboard got."

"I hope far enough to catch a big one." Stacey swallowed the lump in her throat. "I feel so alone, Mac, so lost. When did life get so serious?" She sighed and leaned against the deck rail. "I'm not even nineteen, and I'm already a widow." A frown creased her forehead. "Where's the justice in that?"

~

JD said nothing. He had no answers to mend her broken heart. His own heart ached—for Stacey, for Brian, and the injustice of it all. The tears forming in her vivid green eyes glistened. She turned abruptly, stepped into the apartment, and hurried into the kitchen. JD followed.

He stood in the doorway to the kitchen and watched Stacey pull a bottle of Chardonnay from the refrigerator. Brian's words invaded his thoughts. *"I know you're in love with Stace, Mac. Take good care of her. You two belong together since Stace and I can't be. I'll be there in spirit."* JD closed his eyes. *Now is not the time.*

"There's a little bit of wine left. Want some?" Stacey offered.

"You go ahead, it'll probably help you sleep."

JD leaned against the doorjamb and tucked his thumbs in his front pockets. Stacey had never looked more beautiful to him than she did at that moment. Her thick blond hair was twisted into a knot secured loosely on top of her head. Long tendrils escaped both sides. Her white terrycloth robe enhanced her tan and hugged her trim figure. He fought the urge to gather her into his arms.

*Patience.*

Stacey poured the last of the Chardonnay into a small paper cup and sat at the kitchen table. She closed her eyes and sipped the soothing liquid. Setting the cup down, she rested her elbows on the table and massaged her neck with both hands.

"How 'bout one of your famous neck rubs, Mac?"

"Sure." JD wasn't sure he could trust himself if he touched her. But he couldn't say no, either. He thought about the afternoon he had helped her clean the kitchen cupboards. The massage had been an innocent gesture as it must be now.

Stacey loosened her robe to allow it to slip an inch or two down her back. JD took a deep breath, thankful that Stacey couldn't see his trembling hands. He gently massaged her neck, then her back between her shoulder blades.

"Mmmmmm. That feels so good. You have great hands, Mac. You should get into the massage business."

"You think so?" He tried to keep his voice light.

"Mmm hmmm."

He sensed Stacey relaxing as he kneaded her neck and shoulders. He tensed at the softness of her skin under his hands and willed himself to stop while he still could. Slipping her robe up against the back of her neck, he retreated to the kitchen doorway.

"If we're going to leave at the crack of dawn," he said, "we'd better get some sleep."

"You're probably right." Stacey downed the last of the wine. She crumpled the paper cup and tossed it in the trash. "Do you want some help making up the couch?"

"No. I can get it."

Stacey stopped in front of JD and put her hand on his cheek. "Thank you for everything you've done, Mac. I don't know what I would have done without you." She kissed him on the opposite cheek and hugged him.

He returned her hug. "I'm glad I could be here for you."

As her arms dropped from around him, JD's self-control crumbled. His imaginings became reality as his lips brushed her cheek, then found their way to her lips, softly caressing them before claiming them.

If he surprised her, he didn't notice. His only reality was the softness of her lips and her body pressed against his. Stacey slipped her arms around his neck and kissed him with an urgency and hunger that equaled his.

Barely lifting his lips from hers, he said, "I love you, Sam. God forgive me, I can't help myself."

"Oh, Mac, I love you, too," she whispered and guided his lips back to hers.

His desire for Stacey overcame any misgivings he might have had about his timing. Patience abandoned him. "You're all I've ever wanted, Sam," he said between kisses. "I can't wait any longer." He lowered his head and nuzzled her neck, nibbled her earlobe, and kissed her cheek. Taking her face between his hands, he searched her eyes. "I need you, Sam."

Stacey smiled and touched his lips with her fingers. "I know," she said. "I need you, too."

JD lifted Stacey in his arms and carried her to the bedroom. Setting her down next to the bed, he loosened her hair from its knot, letting it tumble down her back. He slipped his fingers through the golden strands and kissed her forehead. As his lips found hers again, he loosened the tie on her robe and slipped it from her shoulders.

~

Stacey awoke with a start, her heart throbbing in her chest. She could still see Brian's face and hear his voice. "You couldn't even wait until I was cold," he accused. "And with my best friend. I thought you loved *me,* Stacey."

Tears trickled down Stacey's cheeks and onto her pillow. She could hear JD's heavy breathing in the bed next to her. The clock on the nightstand showed 2:11 a.m. She slipped out of bed and groped for her robe, finding it on the floor where it had fallen.

Closing the bedroom door quietly behind her, she crept into the living room. Light from the parking lot flooded past the open curtains into the room. Stacey crumpled onto the floor and hugged herself, rocking back and forth, unable to stem the flood of tears.

She had no excuse for what happened. Her reaction earlier that evening to the sight of JD standing on the deck had startled her. She wanted him to take her in his arms and hold her. She couldn't get the image out of her head. When he kissed her, she had abandoned all misgivings. The warmth of his mouth and the strength of his arms sparked life into Stacey's grieving heart. She put all thoughts aside except JD and the passion building between them. She hadn't thought of Brian once, until the nightmare awakened her.

"Oh, Brian, I'm so sorry," she sobbed. "What have I done?"

~

Sunlight streaming in the bedroom window coaxed JD awake. Feeling rested for the first time in weeks, he closed his eyes for a moment longer, then bolted upright.

"Shit!" He looked at the clock. "Sam, we're two hours late getting started," he said and swung his legs over the edge of the bed.

He glanced behind him at the empty mattress. As he tugged on his jeans, he wondered why Stacey hadn't roused him. The aroma of fresh coffee greeted him in the hallway.

"Sam, why didn't you wake me?" he called as he rushed barefoot down the hall. When he entered the kitchen, Stacey was nowhere in sight. A folded sheet of paper with his name on it rested against an overturned cup on the table. Panic washed over him. He sprinted to the front door, struggled with the lock, and flung it open.

JD gripped the deck railing and stared at the empty spot where they had parked Ol' Bess the night before. He scanned the parking lot, hoping Stacey had only moved the pickup, but Ol' Bess was gone. He raced to the bedroom, grabbed a shirt and fumbled with his socks and boots, forcing them on, then grabbed his keys and ran to his pickup.

The engine sprang to life. But instead of releasing the clutch, JD turned the key off. He slammed his palm onto the steering wheel, then gripped it with both hands. His head slumped onto his hands as he realized he had nowhere to go.

Inside the apartment, he sank onto a kitchen chair and reached for the note. Taking a deep breath, he unfolded the paper. The ink was smudged in several places. As he read the note, he absently played with the empty cup it had rested against.

*Dearest Mac,*

*I'm so sorry things must end this way. What has happened between us should never have happened. ~~We~~ I've betrayed Brian's trust and hurt you because of it. I believe the best thing for both of us is to go our separate ways. Any relationship we might've had would always have Brian between us. I must start to put my life back together—alone. And so should you.*

*Please don't come after me. It will only make things worse. If you care about me, you will respect my wishes. We can't see each other again. I can't forgive what happened. Maybe time can heal the guilt and maybe we can be friends again someday.*

*I'm so sorry it has to be this way, Mac. I wish you the very best life has to offer. You certainly deserve it. You were a good friend to Brian and me, and I'm grateful to you for that. Take care, Mac, and God bless you.*

*Sam*

JD's fingers tightened around the empty cup as he crumpled the note in his other hand. "You *stupid* son of a bitch!" he hissed through clenched teeth. The cup crashed against the wall, scattering colored shards across the kitchen floor.

## Chapter 15

Stacey tightened her grip on the steering wheel of Ol' Bess as traffic raced past, a blur through the tears she fought. Each passing mile she struggled to hold herself together. Each passing mile reminded her of her pain, her guilt, and her cowardice. She bit her lip, gulped back a sob, and tried to focus on the gray asphalt ahead.

All her worldly goods, crammed high in the bed of Ol' Bess, blocked her view through the rearview mirror. She always thought of Ol' Bess as Brian's, not hers. Brian. She slammed her open hand against the steering wheel as the tears spilled onto her cheeks.

"How could you, Brian? How could you do this to us?"

The blast of a car horn jerked her back to reality and her own lane. She signaled, eased the pickup to the side of the road and stopped, letting her head fall back against the seat. The sobs burst from her like a sudden summer thunderstorm. She ached with the pain of loss. "Why can't I turn the clock back, Lord?" she sobbed. "Why can't I have Brian back?"

She wouldn't be returning to North Fork alone if Brian hadn't died. And what about JD? She had done the unthinkable, not to mention taking the coward's way out. She had lost Brian, JD, and her self-respect. She had lost everything—everything but her few possessions jammed in the back of a pickup.

Thirty minutes passed before she exhausted all her tears and pulled onto the highway again. She promised herself a stop in Las Vegas to eat and refresh before going on, but as she neared the desert city, her stomach began to churn and roll. She swallowed the bile rising in her throat and remembered she hadn't eaten anything since leaving Oceanside. She had long since discarded the stale cup of coffee she bought in Barstow. She needed to rest a while.

Stacey found a mid-priced motel near the airport and paid for a room, deciding to sleep first before eating. She crumpled onto the bed and let exhaustion take over. As she closed her eyes, the guilt and pain pricked and poked at her like demons starved for attention.

"Lord," she sobbed, "how did this happen? What have I done to deserve this? Please, I don't want to feel like this anymore. I want my life back. I want things to be the way they were."

~

Stacey splashed cold water on her face and groped for the towel. She wiped her face with a long, slow stroke, then threw the towel carelessly onto the rack. After rinsing her mouth out with warm water, she made her way to the bed, nausea threatening again with each step.

She groaned as she eased herself onto the hard mattress and rolled onto her back. This last bout of vomiting had been little more than dry heaves. Resting one arm across her forehead and the other across her stomach, she closed her eyes and waited for the queasiness to subside. She hadn't been able to keep anything down since early morning. Even the water she drank didn't stay with her long, and the Coke she had sipped to settle her stomach hadn't helped at all.

She wondered why her brother, Jess, hadn't returned her call and fought the panic rising inside. She left the name and number of the Las Vegas motel with Jess's roommate several hours earlier.

Tears stung her eyes as her thoughts once again drifted over the events of the last few days. Her quiet but hurried departure from Oceanside and JD was cowardly, but her guilt over giving herself to him so soon after Brian's death haunted her. As much as she knew she should have stayed and talked things out with JD, she couldn't face him. She couldn't face herself.

Her eyes flew open at the telephone's intrusive ring. She fumbled for the receiver, and barely whispered, "Hello?"

"Stacey?"

"Jess."

"Sis, what's up? What're you doing in Vegas?"

Stacey fought back tears and raised herself up on one elbow. "Oh, Jess, I need your help. Can you come and get me?"

"What's wrong? Where's JD? Isn't he with you?"

Stacey heard the worry in Jess's voice. "His leave got canceled at the last minute, and he couldn't come with me," she lied. "So against his advice, I started out anyway." Another lie, but she didn't want her family blaming JD for her impulsive decision, and the truth required too much explanation. "When I got to Las Vegas, I stopped because I wasn't feeling very well. I've been here since yesterday afternoon."

Stacey coughed and blew her nose. "I started throwing up early this morning. I think I have the flu." She paused a moment and swallowed the bile rising in her throat. "I need you to come drive me and the pickup home. I'll pay for your plane ticket to Vegas. *Please.*"

"What about the folks? They'll be worried."

"I called them and said we'd been delayed. Can you come?"

"Give me a little while to make arrangements, and I'll call you back. I was planning to go home for spring break, anyway, so I guess getting there by way of Vegas will work."

"Thanks. You're a life saver." Tears of relief trickled down her cheeks. "Jess, promise me you won't tell Mom and Dad, okay? I don't want them to worry." She paused and waited, Jess's silence sending a clear message that he wasn't at all sure he should agree with her request. "Please, Jess."

"They should know, Stace."

"I'll tell them when we get home. I'll take full blame if they get mad." She held her breath.

"Okay. I'll call you back in a little while. Just get to feeling better."

Stacey could hear the resignation and worry in his voice. "Thanks, Jess. I owe you. Big time."

"No sweat," he said and hung up.

~

In spite of Jess's attempts at conversation during the trip home to North Fork, Stacey refused to say much. She used her illness as an excuse. They left Las Vegas late in the afternoon the day Jess arrived, spent the night in Richfield, Utah, and arrived home by afternoon the next day. When Jess pulled to a stop in front of the house, their mother, Kate, rushed out the door to meet them.

"Where in the world have you two been?" Kate demanded, tinges of anger and worry in her voice. But one look at Stacey's pale face and lifeless eyes brought her up short.

She guided Stacey toward the house. "We've been worried sick. JD called yesterday morning to see if you arrived safely. That's when we found out you started home alone. Your father has the State Patrol out looking for you.

"And *you*," she accused, turning her attention to Jess. "I called you to see when you were coming home, only to have your roommate tell me you'd flown to Las Vegas two days ago. You two have a *lot* of explaining to do."

"I'm sorry we worried you, Mom." A wave of nausea flooded over Stacey just as she entered the house. She clamped a hand to her mouth. "I'll explain in a minute," she mumbled and ran for the bathroom.

Stacey heard her Mom open the bathroom door. Kate pressed a cold washcloth against Stacey's forehead as she hovered over the toilet.

"I'm sorry, honey. I didn't know you were sick. When JD called, expecting you to be here, we got worried."

Stacey slumped to the floor and leaned against the wall, managing a wan smile. It felt good to be home.

"Oh, Mom, I'm really sorry. I didn't expect Mac to call. I should have, though." Stacey closed her eyes and waited for the room to stop spinning. It's so like Mac to worry about me arriving safely, she thought. He may hate me for running out on him, but he'd still check on me for Brian's sake.

"He was quite concerned you hadn't arrived yet," Kate said. "I must say I'm a bit confused. When you called to say you were delayed, I expected JD to come with you. Honey, what's going on? Why did he let you start out alone? And why is Jess with you instead?"

Stacey opened her eyes. "Mom, none of this is Mac's fault. Or Jess's. I take full responsibility. And I'll explain everything, but right now I just want to lie down."

"Oh, honey, I don't mean to be mad at you or Jess, but we've been worried sick." Kate helped Stacey to her feet and held her.

"I know. Will you call Mac for me and let him know I'm home? I'm not up to it right now. Please?" Stacey knew she wasn't up to hearing his voice or explaining her actions to him. And she knew him well enough that if she talked to him, he would want answers. Or worse, insist on seeing her. She wasn't ready for that, either.

"Of course I'll call, but let's get you to bed first."

~

Once Kate had Stacey settled in her old room, she returned to the kitchen where Phil and Jess sat at the kitchen table, drinking coffee.

"Stacey okay?" Phil asked, a frown creasing his forehead.

"She's resting. She's had a rough few weeks, and it's finally caught up with her." Kate sat down and glared at Jess. "Okay, I'm waiting for an explanation. But make it quick. I need to call JD."

Jess looked away from his mother's glare and fiddled with the coffee cup resting on the table in front of him. He turned the cup nervously between his hands as he explained.

"Stace called me three days ago from Vegas and said she was sick with the flu and would I fly out and drive the pickup for her. When I asked about JD, she said his leave had gotten canceled, and she had set out on her own against his advice. She told me she called to tell you they'd been delayed, so you wouldn't worry. Then the flu hit her and that's when she called me."

"You should have called us," Kate said.

"She didn't want you to worry, and she knew Dad couldn't get away. I'm sorry we worried you."

"If JD hadn't called, we wouldn't have known the difference." Kate put her hand on Jess's arm. "I'm just glad you're both all right." She rose. "I'd better call the State Patrol and let them know you've arrived safely."

"I already have," Phil said.

"Then I'd better call JD. He was ready to set out looking for Stacey. I talked him into waiting until he heard from us."

146

~

After several days of rest, Stacey still lacked energy and nausea continued to plague her. Her fourth morning home, Stacey sat at the kitchen table, sipping a cup of tea. Most of her breakfast of bacon, eggs, and toast remained on her plate, untouched and cold.

Kate cleared the table and sat opposite Stacey. "Honey, are you still taking your birth control pills?" she asked.

Stacey's eyes met her mother's. "I stopped taking them after Butch shipped out to Vietnam. They were making me gain weight, and I was moodier than usual. With him gone, I didn't see any need to take them."

"I see. Did you start taking them again before you went to Hawaii?"

"No." Stacey caught her breath as her mother's implication registered in her mind. "Butch and I...we used other means."

Kate stepped to the wall phone. "Nevertheless, I think we'd better make an appointment with Dr. Miller and get you a pregnancy test. 'Other means' aren't always reliable."

A wave of panic rushed over Stacey. She and JD hadn't taken precautions. She buried her face in her hands, barely hearing her mother make the appointment.

Late the following morning, Dr. Miller confirmed what Kate suspected. Stacey was pregnant. He prescribed vitamins the size of horse pills and gave Stacey a strict lecture on eating right, along with a suggestion that a soda cracker or two before getting out of bed in the morning might help alleviate her morning sickness.

The shock of Dr. Miller's diagnosis hadn't worn off by the time Stacey and her mother arrived home. After lunch, Stacey went to her room to lie down, but whenever she closed her eyes, the memory of her night with JD loomed before her. The walls of her room crowded

147

in on her, pushing at her until she wanted to scream.

With nothing better to do for the remainder of the afternoon, Stacey grabbed some juice, a few cookies, and bridled her horse. Dr. Miller had given her permission to ride as long as she was careful. Promising to be home in time for supper, Stacey set out for the piece of land she and Brian dreamed of building their home on.

∼

Perched on a rock next to Hansen Creek, Stacey watched the water swirling past her. Snow had disappeared from the valley, and the March winds had dried out the ground, but the surrounding mountains were still blanketed in white.

She took a deep breath of fresh air and shivered. Although the temperature had reached the mid-sixties, the cool breeze reminded her that, in Colorado, snow still threatened, and even in April, spring was only a promise.

Stacey crossed her arms over her bent knees and rested her forehead on her arms. The tears trickling down her cheeks changed to rivulets. She sobbed until her lungs hurt, and she had no more tears. Wiping her face with her palms, she fished a Kleenex out of her pocket to blow her nose.

"What am I supposed to do now, God?" she asked. Tears stung her eyes again. "How in the world did I manage to completely screw up my life in so short a time?"

She picked up a small stone and rubbed it between her fingers before flinging it into the water. "In three short weeks I managed to lose a husband, make love to his best friend, and get pregnant. And I haven't got a clue as to which one is the father. What's *wrong* with me?" She sniffed and sucked in a shuddering breath. "I can't confide in Mom. She'd never understand. I don't understand this whole mess myself."

Stacey swiveled on the rock and slipped to the ground. She wandered toward the tree she and Brian dreamed under a few days after their wedding. Fresh tears gathered in her eyes as she remembered that day.

The afternoon before leaving for California, they had ridden out to their ten acres of land, a wedding gift from her parents. After tethering their horses, they sat on the edge of Hansen Creek. Stacey could remember the day as if it had happened only yesterday.

"You've been awful quiet since we got here," Brian had said between bites of cookie,

"I can be quiet if I want." She couldn't stop thinking about Brian's second tour, but every time she brought it up, he changed the subject.

"Not like you, Babe. You're usually chattering away at close to ninety miles an hour. Most days I can't get a word in edgewise."

"Maybe I just want to sit here and enjoy some peace and quiet." Stacey frowned at him.

"Whew, something's definitely bothering you. I can't even get a rise outa you when I insult you." He grinned and glanced sideways at her, but she ignored him.

The spring runoff rushed along the banks of the creek. As the rapids churned and foamed before her, Stacey's fears about Brian's second tour boiled to the surface.

"All right," Stacey said, still staring at the rushing water. "I'll tell you what's wrong. Vietnam. *That's* what's wrong. You *don't* have to go back."

Brian shifted and glared at Stacey. "I thought we settled this. No, I *don't* have to go back. I've *chosen* to."

"I *know* that, but it's more like you're obsessed with it."

"I'm not obsessed with it, Babe. I just think it's the right thing to do. Since I've been there, I can show the new grunts how to survive.

149

They're green and headed to a war zone. It's my responsibility to show them the ropes."

"Do it stateside, then. Just don't go back."

"What good is it to train them here and then send them off on their own? If I'm there with them, they'll have a better chance of surviving."

"That's just it. You've already survived once." Tears welled in Stacey's eyes. "What if they survive, but you don't?"

"Nothing'll happen, Stace. I'm a survivor and—"

"*Stop it.* You can't just nonchalantly push this aside. You're gambling your life, our future, on the fact you're a survivor. What if you've used up all your luck? Geez, Brian, don't tempt fate." Stacey shuddered and crossed her arms, resting them on her bent knees.

"When I joined the Corps I took an oath—"

"*Oath.* A few days ago you took another oath. What about that one?"

"You never have understood loyalty and duty, the very essence of the Marine Corps. I'm aware of my responsibility to you, but as long as I'm a Marine, the Corps comes first. God, Corps, country, and then everything else. That's what it means to be a Marine and a man. It's time you understood that."

"I'll never understand putting the Marines before *us.* All I understand is that I love you, and I want you alive and out of danger." Tears streamed down Stacey's face.

Brian slipped his arm around her shoulder and pulled her against him. She tried to squirm away, but he held tight. "You know I love you more than anything in the world, Babe. If you love me as much, you'll support my decision."

He kissed Stacey on the cheek and helped her up. Turning her back to him, he pulled her against him and wrapped his arms around her. Brian rested his head against hers.

"Look at the West Elk Mountains and Castle Peak, Babe. A wall of protection and comfort—tall, rugged, and invincible, just like me. They've endured everything Mother Nature has thrown at them. Those mountains are part of me. I'll be all right as long as I have my mountains to come home to. And this land, well, it's a perfect spot to build a house."

Brian stepped away from Stacey and began scraping lines in the dirt with his boot heel. Stacey wiped the tears from her face and watched.

"What are you doing, Butch?"

"Aha!"

"What?"

"You're not mad at me anymore." He grinned, dimples creasing the sides of his mouth. "You can't be mad at me and call me Butch."

"Who says," she challenged.

"I say. Now be quiet while I finish."

Brian continued scraping lines in the dirt, stepping off measurements and scraping more lines inside the others. Stacey's curiosity peaked.

"You want to tell me what you're really doing so intently?'

"Buildin' that house. Just sit tight. I'll be through in a minute." Brian pushed his cap back and scratched his forehead. He looked at Stacey and grinned again, set his cap forward, and gouged one last line in the dirt. He surveyed his work, then beckoned Stacey to join him.

When she reached him, he swung her up in his arms and pretended to open a door and carry her inside. Once "inside," he set her down and bowed, sweeping his hand before him.

"Your new home, Mrs. Murcheson. Allow me to give you the grand tour. As he guided her through the "house," he described each room in detail. Stacey giggled at his overzealous descriptions. Near the end of the tour, he swept his hand to the side and declared, "The first two bedrooms are for the kids." Brian raised his eyebrows several times in succession. "You were planning to have a couple of kids, weren't you?"

Before she could answer, he steered her into the last room. "And this is the master bedroom with a big bed right here." He pointed to the ground in front of them. "We can listen to Hansen Creek while we're making love." He turned to face Stacey. "So, what do you think, Babe? You like it?"

"I love it, Butch. But only two kids?"

"Once we build this house, we'll only be able to afford two kids." He took Stacey's face between his hands and kissed her. Lifting his head, he peered into her eyes. "You know where we're standing, don't you?"

Stacey nodded. "The bedroom."

"Mmmmm, yes, but we're actually standing in the middle of the bed." Brian began unbuttoning Stacey's blouse. "You know what beds are for, don't you?"

"It's broad daylight. Someone might see us."

"And who would that be?" We're on private land. The closest house is Hansen's, which isn't even visible from here. We've got a nice grassy, shady spot, and no one to bug us. I think we ought to 'break ground' on this house the right way."

Brian kissed her again, demanding more. "I love you, Babe. I just can't seem to get enough of you. Don't turn me down." He succeeded in removing her blouse and dropped it on the ground. "Don't be so uptight, Babe. We're married, remember?" As he eased her onto the grassy carpet, he whispered, "Yee-haw."

Stacey and Brian had left Colorado the next morning for California, but she had never forgotten the afternoon and the dreaming they'd done about their future.

She wiped the tears streaming down her face and searched desperately for even a small scratch that would indicate Brian's outline of their house, but the winter snow and wind had obliterated his hard work. Falling to her knees, she grabbed a handful of dirt and let it sift through her fingers.

*Ashes to ashes; dust to dust.* The words assaulted her. Settling against the heels of her boots, she scraped at the ground around her. Thin tufts of new grass battled for survival under the shadow of the towering cottonwood.

"Ashes," she whispered. "That's all I have left, Brian. No dreams. Nothing to build on. Only ashes."

She swiped at the tears again and rubbed her hand across her abdomen. "I'm not ready to be a mother. And obviously I wasn't ready to be a wife. Oh, Brian, how could I do that to you? *Why* did I do it?"

Stacey rolled onto her back, oblivious of the cold seeping through her denim jacket. Small, marshmallow clouds floated across the deep blue Colorado sky. She closed her eyes, trying to remember Brian the way she had last seen him. He had smiled and winked at her before disappearing into the plane. His smile always had a hint of orneriness to it, as though he was about to pull some prank. A smile crept across Stacey's face. Brian's orneriness was one of the things she loved about him.

New tears seeped from the corners of her eyes. Then without warning, Brian's face faded, a new one taking its place, with sky-blue eyes, dark hair, and a warm smile. Stacey's eyes flicked open, and she sat up.

"*No,*" she cried. "I can't think of you. Why do I always come back to you, Mac? What *is* it about you?"

## Chapter 16

Stacey drew her legs up, wrapped her arms around them, and rested her chin on her knees. For the first time since she had fled California, she faced what happened.

JD's friendship had been important to her. As important to her as it was to Brian. JD served as a buffer between Brian's impulsiveness and her practicality. When she wanted craziness, she turned to Brian. When she needed reassurance, she turned to JD. Brian's sense of adventure made life exciting, but sometimes she needed calm and logic. JD provided that. He was solid. Settled. Brian lived life on the edge.

A tentative smile tugged at the corner of her mouth. Even their lovemaking reflected their differences. Brian made love with impatience and abandon; JD gentle and unhurried. When JD had taken Stacey in his arms, she wanted to be there, and she hadn't thought of Brian once.

Stacey closed her eyes. Countless times she tried to have a serious conversation with Brian about their future, but he would manage to avoid it, saying they could worry about it later. JD talked to Stacey often about the future and his plans. Brian needed her understanding;

JD understood her. They both loved her, and she loved both of them.

She shook her head, realizing she could no longer deny, proper or not, that she loved them both. She plucked at a tuft of grass poking up through the rich brown earth. But even if she did love JD, her actions so soon after Brian's death were wrong.

*How could I? Had I so easily accepted Brian's death that I could give myself over to JD without even thinking?* Was it loneliness that drove her into JD's arms? Or a need to feel alive in the face of death? Her unanswered questions troubled her. *How could I do that to you Brian? How could I abandon you so easily? Was I that desperate to feel alive and loved again?*

Stacey rocked gently for a few minutes. "I did love you, Brian, with all my heart," she whispered. Tears streamed down her face. "I still do."

She rose, and her gaze wandered toward the West Elk Mountains. Brian called them his mountains. He used to say that as long as the mountains were there to come home to, all was right with the world. The sight of their snow-covered peaks made Stacey shudder. Brian hadn't come home to his mountains, and all was not right with the world.

She rubbed a hand across her stomach again. "Have I betrayed you so completely, Brian, that I'm carrying another man's baby?" She grimaced. "Damn you! This would never have happened if you hadn't died. I prayed for you every night," she cried. "Why did you have to die?" Tears rushed down her cheeks, and she lashed out at the only One who was listening.

"Damn you, God! It's all Your fault. If You had answered my prayers, Butch would still be alive, and I wouldn't be in this predicament. How could You *do* this to me? To us?" She lifted a large rock and heaved it at the cottonwood. The rock found its mark, slicing away a chunk of bark as it hit. Stacey crumpled to the ground and sobbed, pouring out her hurt and anger.

~

The days following Stacey's sudden departure were hell for JD. More than once he decided to set out for North Fork, but each time the memory of Stacey's note was a reminder she wanted nothing to do with him. The day after she left, he had gotten as far as packing his duffel before he stopped himself. After he called Kate and discovered Stacey hadn't arrived home, he cursed himself for not going after her the first day. When Kate called, instead of Stacey, to report she was home and safe, he got the distinct feeling he wasn't wanted or needed.

Kate explained that the flu had delayed Stacey, and that Jess met her in Las Vegas and drove her home. The fact that Stacey called Jess instead of him made JD realize she meant what she said in the note. He had clung to the hope he could talk to her and straighten things out, but it was clear that would never happen.

He questioned over and over again his reckless behavior, when he had never done anything reckless in his life. Brian was the reckless one. Not him. JD always thought through the consequences before he acted. Until the night he made love to Stacey. His impulsive actions had lost her forever.

With both Brian and Stacey gone from his life, loneliness surrounded JD. His perfect world had crumbled, and he didn't know how to pick up the pieces. He needed someone to talk to, but without Brian and Stacey, he had no one.

He missed Brian more than he could have imagined. When he first met Brian at college, JD's impression was of someone completely out of control. He soon learned Brian's antics were part of his basic nature, consequences be damned. Brian provided a vicarious dimension to JD's ordered life.

JD discovered in Brian and Stacey a friendship he could not only depend on, but two people he could talk to about anything and everything. And now when he needed a friend most, he had no one to turn to.

"Dammit, Butch, who am I supposed to talk to about this? You warned me to be patient, but I didn't listen. Now what?" JD snickered at the irony of his dilemma.

He knew he could never confide in his father about making love to Stacey. John MacCord hadn't been sympathetic about JD's feelings for Stacey in the first place. He definitely wouldn't understand JD's impulsive act; an act that had driven Stacey away.

In order to forget, JD buried himself in his work. But each night the memories haunted him. Over and over he replayed in his mind the last night with Stacey, knowing what he should, or could, have done differently. But he had ignored his own inner warnings, and all he had left was the bittersweet memory of holding her in his arms and making love to her.

After nearly two months of self-recrimination, he realized he was wallowing in self-pity. "It's time I did something to forget," he declared. He tried dating, but his heart refused to take any pleasure in seeking other women. None of his dates interested him enough to ask them out a second time.

One evening, unable to stand the apartment and its memories any longer, JD drove to Jarheads' Saloon. Sitting in the booth designated *Brian's Place*, JD nursed a beer and wished he could turn back the clock. The three of them spent countless hours in this very booth laughing at life, unaware of the cruel joke it had in store for them.

"You look like you could use a friend, son." Pappy scooted across the bench opposite JD and lit a cigarette. "Guess you miss Brian, just like the rest of us," Pappy remarked and took a long drag on his cigarette. He slowly released the smoke and reached for the cup of coffee he had set on the table in front of him. "That kid sure could liven up the place." He chuckled.

JD smiled. "That he could, Pappy. It's just not the same without him."

Pappy tasted his coffee and took another drag on his cigarette. The smoke seeped from his nostrils and mouth. JD twisted his beer mug in his hands.

"What happened to that pretty little wife of his? She still around?"

JD looked past Pappy. "She went home to Colorado," he answered and noticed a couple dancing to "Cherish." He pushed away the memory of dancing with Stacey to the same song.

"You want to talk about it?"

"What? Talk about what?" JD tried to sound perplexed.

"Whatever it is that's got you lower than a snake's belly. I'm a good listener," Pappy offered.

JD looked down at his half empty mug. He did need a friend to talk to, but not just anyone. He needed to talk to someone who really understood how he felt about both Brian and Stacey. Pappy would never understand. Only one other person knew how JD felt, but he hadn't wanted to impose.

JD made a quick decision. "You're right Pappy, I do need a friend. Excuse me. I have to make a phone call."

"Glad I could help," Pappy said to JD's back.

JD deposited a dime in the pay phone and dialed the number, praying she was home. He closed his eyes in relief when a familiar voice answered on the second ring.

"Jacqueline. It's JD. "

"JD, it's good to hear from you. What's up?"

"I was just wondering if you've heard from Sam." He tried to keep his voice neutral, hoping Jacqueline wouldn't suspect anything.

"Actually, I haven't. I wrote to her a week after she left, but she

159

didn't answer. I've tried a couple of times since, but I still haven't heard from her."

JD took a deep breath and rubbed his eyes. "Oh," was all he could think of to say.

After a moment of silence, Jacqueline asked, "JD, what's wrong?"

"I need to talk to you. I need a friend."

"Where are you?"

"Jarheads'."

"I'll be right there."

JD hung up and leaned his head against the wall next to the pay phone. Relief flooded through him. He had done the right thing to call Jacqueline. For the first time in many weeks, he had finally done the right thing.

~

A memorial service was held for Brian three weeks after Stacey arrived home. Jess gave the eulogy. Numerous classmates of both Brian and Stacey attended, as well as teachers and other townspeople who knew them both. The outpouring of concern and sympathy for Stacey was both comforting and difficult. Stacey placed a headstone in memory of Brian in the local cemetery, engraved with the Marine Corps emblem and a riderless horse.

Over the next few months, Stacey wrestled with bouts of depression. The news from Vietnam of increased U.S. air activity, and President Nixon's promise of withdrawing troops from Vietnam, only added to Stacey's difficulty in dealing with Brian's death. She struggled with the contradiction of his senseless death and her pride in the way he had conducted himself as a soldier.

As demonstrations against the war increased, Stacey's anger and bitterness also increased. She hated the war, she hated the insensitivity of the anti-war protesters and their maligning of the soldiers fighting in Vietnam, and she hated the refusal of the silent majority to speak out in support of the soldiers doing their best for their country.

In June, President Nixon announced the first troop withdrawal from Vietnam in accordance with his plan for Vietnamization. Stacey grieved for Brian and his untimely death. And she prayed for a quick end to the war that divided a nation.

In the weeks following President Nixon's announcement, Stacey, at her mother's urging, did a lot of soul searching. Her bitterness and depression was affecting her health and mental well-being, and she had a baby to think about. Still struggling with Brian's death, she sought advice from her minister.

With Reverend Sparks' counsel, she made peace with God, realizing she unfairly blamed Him for Brian's death and for a war no one but the bureaucrats wanted. That young men still fought and died so far from home in an unwanted war made no sense to Stacey, or to millions of Americans. Yet the war raged on, and America's young men continued to die.

Doing her best to put the war aside, Stacey focused on her baby. The due date Dr. Miller gave her did nothing to relieve her anxiety about who had fathered her child. She hoped and prayed the baby was Brian's, partly because it would make things right, but mostly because she desperately wanted to have a part of Brian live on. He had looked forward to having children. But Stacey knew she had to prepare for the fact that the baby could also be JD's. And if it were, would she tell him? She had no answer, no matter how many times she pondered the possibility.

Stacey made no effort to get in touch with JD. Her mother's call to let him know she arrived safely had been the last contact with him. He hadn't called after that, and Stacey had felt the need to leave things as they were.

She had chosen the coward's way out. JD wouldn't forgive easily, and she had done the unforgivable. Like a frightened animal, Stacey fled rather than face the consequences. She believed JD's concern that she had arrived home safely was for Brian's sake. All things considered, Stacey knew she would never see JD again. She had hurt him, and in the process, lost his friendship.

What happened between them that fateful night happened too fast. Perhaps, she reasoned, if she'd taken time to let things take their proper course...but she hadn't. She'd given in to her impulses, and no matter how hard she tried, she couldn't rid herself of her guilt over betraying Brian.

She blamed only herself and made a conscious effort to bury any feelings she had for JD. She had more than she could handle with her pregnancy and Brian's death. And her baby came first.

Out of necessity to move on, Stacey convinced herself she carried Brian's baby. As her guilt and fears turned to happiness and anticipation, the old Stacey emerged.

In an effort to preserve Brian's memory, she had his Purple Heart framed, leaving a space for his Medal of Honor that still awaited final approval. Both medals would share a place of honor on the top of the piano, next to their wedding picture, and among other family pictures.

As a final gesture of making a new start, she boxed and stored the picture JD gave her of the three of them. She wanted reminders of Brian, not of her indiscretion with JD.

In order to make a complete break with the past, Stacey didn't answer Jacqueline's letters. Afraid Jacqueline would attempt to mend her rift with JD, Stacey thought it best to break all ties that connected her to him. She thought it was safer, too, if Jacqueline didn't know about her pregnancy. In her self-created isolation, she grieved for Brian and for lost friends.

The nightly news kept Stacey informed of the events in Vietnam. Every major network had film crews covering the war, and graphic pictures fueled the American public's outrage over the events in Southeast Asia. Stacey's compulsion to watch the news came out of a loyalty to Brian.

When President Nixon announced in November 1969 what had happened at My Lai over a year earlier, Stacey realized she'd had her fill of war news. Although a single isolated incident, opponents of the war used My Lai as an excuse to further malign the men still fighting in Vietnam. Sick of the hate leveled against all soldiers, she avoided detailed reports and discussions about the war.

~

In early December, when Stacey's due date arrived without any labor pains, her fears about who had fathered her baby returned. When she questioned Dr. Miller about the due date, he assured her that first babies often arrived late.

Three weeks later, Dr. Miller discussed inducing labor, or if necessary, a Cesarean section if Stacey went one more day without delivering. As if on cue, the next day, December 30th, 1969, Stacey gave birth to an eight pound, two ounce baby boy.

Propped in her hospital bed, Stacey gently rubbed the soft blond down of her son's head and smiled at his contented face. "Whose little boy are you?" she wondered. "The whole world thinks you belong to Brian, but do you?"

Tears stung her eyes. She would have to at least pretend he belonged to Brian. Anything else required an awkward and embarrassing explanation.

"But if you are JD's son," she whispered, "he deserves some kind

163

of recognition." She decided to name her son, Brian John Murcheson. Brian for the father Stacey hoped he had, and John, JD's first name, for the father he possibly had.

As her son grew, Stacey and the rest of her family began calling him BJ. About the only physical features that Stacey could lay claim to were his blond hair and green eyes. The rest was all BJ, a bundle of high-octane energy.

With BJ making demands on most of her time, Stacey slowly healed emotionally. She seldom thought of JD, except for those rare moments when some small unexpected incident or antic from BJ triggered a memory.

She concentrated on her memories of Brian and wrote down as much as she could remember about him for BJ's sake. She also concentrated on putting the horror of the war out of her mind. In February 1970, peace talks between Henry Kissinger and Le Duc Tho made headlines worldwide. Stacey offered a prayer of thanks at the announcement.

With peace talks making slow, but hopeful progress, Stacey, too, began making peace with herself and the world around her. Needing to move forward with her life for her sake and BJ's, she began thinking about her future.

In November of 1970, the state highway department finished paving the Black Mesa road between North Fork and Gunnison, keeping this shorter route open all winter and making the trip between the two towns just under an hour. By living at the ranch, Stacey could commute to Gunnison, reducing her living expenses and making college more affordable. She promised herself she would rely on her parents only until she finished school.

With a new resolve, a little fear, and a touch of excitement, Stacey enrolled the fall of 1972 as a freshman at Western State College in Gunnison. Two and a half-year-old BJ, a bundle of kinetic energy, no longer needed Stacey's constant attention.

With careful course scheduling, Stacey could leave BJ with her mother while she attended school. She finally put aside the dreams she and Brian had made and replaced them with dreams of her own.

## *Part II*

"When you, the visitor, pass before the granite slabs and read the names, you suddenly see beyond the names the faces of living Americans, moving, looking, touching, whispering—and in their midst your own face reflected in the shining mirror. It seems to say, Vietnam was not theirs alone, it is all of ours; if you wish peace, love them."

Howard K. Smith
"Introduction" from *To Heal a Nation:*
*the Vietnam Veterans Memorial*

## Chapter 17

Stacey glared at her registration form and fought back the tears trying to force their way out. For the fifth time that day, she scratched out her schedule and started over.

"I don't know about you, but I'm ready to dump the whole mess into a garbage can and split."

Stacey looked up to see a mirror image of her own frustration on another student's face. They stared at each other for a moment, then burst into laughter.

"Rachel." The dark-haired, brown-eyed young woman offered her hand in introduction, a few giggles still lingering in her throat.

"Stacey."

"If I'd known just registering would be this hard," Rachel complained, "I would have told my parents I was joining a convent instead. And I'm not even Catholic."

Stacey grinned. "Classes will be a breeze compared to this. *If* we stick it out. Right now that convent is sounding pretty good."

"Tell you what," Rachel offered. "If you'll do my schedule, I'll do yours. Maybe that will work."

"I'm willing to try *anything*," Stacey admitted and handed Rachel her schedule. Two hours later, they'd each come up with a schedule and a newfound friend.

Although Rachel, a drama major, had few common interests academically with Stacey, a science and physical education major, their personalities complemented each other. Stacey found Rachel's candid nature refreshing, and Rachel depended on Stacey's stability to keep her focused. Their schedules often had them at opposite ends of the campus, but they managed to see each other every day.

Addicted to soap operas, Rachel scheduled her classes around her favorite soaps. Stacey seldom had to look farther than the freshman dorm lounge and the television to find Rachel.

One day in mid-October and suffering from one pop quiz after another, Stacey trudged to the dorm in search of Rachel. She found her friend curled up in front of the television, a book open on her lap, her eyes focused on the screen.

"What in the world do you see in these awful soap operas?" Stacey asked as she plopped onto the floor beside Rachel.

"Are you kidding?" Rachel said, a look of excitement on her face. "They're the best thing to study the art of acting, other than movies, which I can't afford right now. They have a wide range of characters and emotions. Even when the acting is bad, I learn something. Sometimes the script leaves something to be desired, and the problems are endless. And nobody ever stays married for very long, but they sure know how to cry, and fight, and be really evil and bitchy."

Stacey laughed. "You're nuts. You know that, don't you?"

Rachel giggled. "Yep. But it's better than being crazy. Besides, right now on *Another Day,* there's the best looking hunk you ever saw. He's got dark curly hair, dreamy eyes, a great smile, terrific bod, and he's even a decent actor."

Stacey's heart skipped a beat. She hadn't thought about JD in a long time, but Rachel's description conjured up his image. "So you're telling me you have a thing for a guy on a soap opera?"

"Hey, there's worse things, ya know. Seriously, you ought to see this guy. He's got really rugged features. He's not what some people might call extremely handsome, like Sean Connery. He's more like Clint Eastwood, but I like 'em rugged like that. And this guy's got this charisma that nearly swallows you up when you're watching him. He plays a drifter, a cowboy-type that plays guitar and sings, and has all the women interested in him, and he's only been in town a short time. He's new on the soap, showed up a couple of weeks ago, so I don't know his real name yet. It takes the network a while to decide if the character is important enough to list the actor's name at the beginning. Otherwise, the names scroll by so fast at the end you can't read them."

Stacey smiled and shook her head. With Rachel it was sometimes hard to tell when she referred to the fictional world and when she referred to the real world, but Stacey was used to sorting out Rachel's gibberish.

Rachel closed her book. "Stick around for a few minutes and you'll see what I mean. It's time for *Another Day,* and you just *gotta* see this guy."

The last thing Stacey wanted to do was watch a soap opera, but she had a couple of hours before her next class and nothing better to do. She decided to humor Rachel and satisfy her own curiosity to see if this actor resembled JD at all.

Several other girls filtered into the lounge and parked themselves on the couch behind them. Stacey set her books on the floor next to her and took a deep breath.

"Okay," she said, "let's see what all the excitement's about."

The opening scene of the soap took Stacey's breath away. She barely heard the "oohs" and "ahs" of the girls around her. It can't be, she thought. But the actor *was* JD with long hair. Long, anyway, compared to his Marine cut. His hair fell just below his ears, thick and wavy and sexy. The shock of seeing him with longer hair was minor, however, to the shock of seeing him. A stab of regret pierced her heart. *If only...*

"See, what'd I tell ya? That's him." Rachel whispered over the sighs and comments of the other girls. "Isn't he something?"

Stacey barely nodded her head, mesmerized by JD's presence on the small screen. Rachel was right. JD projected ten-fold on the television screen what Stacey always found physically attractive about him. She couldn't take her eyes off him, and found herself disappointed whenever the story line switched to another character.

When the soap ended, Rachel lamented that she still didn't know "Dirk's" name.

"JD," Stacey whispered, more to herself than to Rachel.

"What?"

"His name is JD MacCord," Stacey said a little louder.

"Where'd you see that? I didn't see his name." Rachel frowned at Stacey.

"Unless he's changed it."

"Are you telling me you know this guy?"

Stacey swallowed the lump in her throat. "He was my husband's best friend and best man at our wedding. I haven't seen him since Brian died."

"So you're saying you used to know him."

"Y-yes." Stacey bit her lip and glanced at Rachel. She forced normalcy into her voice. "He's a very nice guy. Totally opposite the manipulating kind of guy he's playing."

"Tell me more."

Stacey looked back at the television and shrugged her shoulders. "He's quiet, reserved, but he can be a lot of fun, too." Stacey missed JD and the good times they had enjoyed together, and she was unprepared to be pumped by Rachel about him. "Look, I have to go to the library. I just remembered some research I need to do before I go home tonight." Stacey gathered her books before Rachel could say another word. "I'll see you later, Rach," she called as she hurried away.

From that day on, Stacey found herself unable to resist watching *Another Day* as often as she could. She emphasized to Rachel that JD was more Brian's friend than hers, a necessary deception in Stacey's mind.

As the months flew by, Stacey toyed with the idea of getting in touch with JD. For several years she had managed to put him out of her mind, but seeing him again dredged up feelings she thought she had buried. Equally upsetting was the renewed guilt she felt over their one night together.

No matter how hard she tried to put the incident out of her mind, she had betrayed Brian. Over time she had learned to deal with it, but not forgive herself.

Stacey eventually realized that getting in touch with JD served no purpose. She reasoned that if JD thought of her at all he probably hated her for running out on him. There was no future in renewing an old, and most likely dead, friendship.

When JD's character was murdered in the soap's story line, Stacey was depressed for days. She missed watching him, although she didn't miss the character he played. If she hadn't known the real JD, she would have believed he was a "sleaze," as Rachel had put it, "but fascinating."

Stacey couldn't hide her disappointment, however, when JD didn't reappear on another soap, as Rachel explained often happened, and she wondered if he had given up acting for something else. Reasoning it was better that she couldn't see him nearly every day, Stacey did her best to put thoughts of JD aside.

With renewed effort, Stacey concentrated on her classes. She found college stimulating and exciting, and had forgotten how much she enjoyed learning. But the college atmosphere was also an active reminder of the country's plight in Vietnam.

In spite of the progress of the peace talks over the last year, students held demonstrations and debates on college campuses across the country. Western State College was no exception. Constant bickering over America's involvement in the war left the nation divided. Stacey's divided heart ached over her loyalty to the soldiers fighting the war and her anger at the government for perpetuating the war.

The spring quarter of Stacey's freshman year, she enrolled in American Social Problems. Professor Axtel spent time each week during class discussing the Vietnam War and its effects on American society, creating heated debates among the students. Stacey never engaged in any of the discussions about Vietnam, for fear her emotions would overwhelm her before she made her point. She bit her lip and remained silent, except on one occasion.

When the last American troops left Vietnam in March of 1973, one of the students remarked during class discussion, "I'm glad we're out of Vietnam, but now what're we going to do with all those murderers that will be coming home?"

The comment appalled Stacey, and she interpreted it as a personal attack on Brian. "Pardon me?" she snapped, breaking the silence that had descended on the classroom at the young man's remark.

He turned to look at her. "I said, 'What're we going to do with all those murderers that will be coming home?' Everyone knows our government has trained the soldiers in Vietnam to kill women, babies, and old men. Not to mention the bombing of North Vietnam that killed innocent people. Jane Fonda proved that."

Stacey's anger exploded full force. "Anyone who thinks the same way you do is not only a fool but should be kicked out of this country for thinking that way! And Jane Fonda didn't prove anything, except that she is terribly naïve. She let the government of North Vietnam deceive and use her. And our soldiers consider her a traitor."

"What about My Lai? Do you deny that happened?"

"My Lai," she answered, "was a terrible tragedy and an isolated incident. Don't you *dare* judge our soldiers on one tragic incident. They fought and died in an unwanted war because they felt an obligation to their country. My husband fought in Vietnam because he loved his country and its freedoms. He died defending your right to sit here in this classroom and safely voice your opinion, however wrong it is."

Stacey's voice cracked and tears streamed down her face. Still she continued, fighting to speak through her tears, unwilling to let senseless remarks go unanswered.

"Brian fought in Vietnam for his country and the freedom it stands for. He knew that the South Vietnamese people wanted desperately *not* to live under Communist rule. He went back to Vietnam for a second tour because he loved his country and felt his experience would help the young Marines going into a war zone for the first time. He died saving the lives of several Marines and received a Medal of Honor for his selfless act.

"He *never* murdered babies, women, or helpless old people, although he often wrote that it was hard to tell who the enemy was. He once saw a woman carrying a baby wired to grenades, and it left him feeling sick and helpless.

"Daily he faced an unknown enemy, often the same Vietnamese men that fought beside him the day or week before. When he entered a village, he never knew if his Marines would be welcomed or ambushed."

Stacey glared at him. "Don't you *dare* condemn the men who've fought in Vietnam or any war. Unless you've been there, you have no idea what it's like. War is senseless, tragic, and brutal. Not just Vietnam, but any war. Someday I hope leaders of all nations will realize what a waste war is. Until then, our best resource, young men, will die."

She took a deep breath. "But no one, *no one,* has the right to condemn the soldiers for doing their job. We should welcome them home with gratitude, not spit on them and call them murderers. I, for one, am thankful they're coming home.

"And if you have any sense of decency, you will welcome them home with open arms, not condemnation. God help us if we can't put this behind us and stop blaming the men who were there because their country asked—no demanded—they serve."

When Stacey finished, silence crowded the room. The student who had spoken out looked down at his books and said nothing more. Stacey, unable to bear the surprised stares of the other students, grabbed her books and fled from the room. Later she heard about the clapping that started with a single student and grew to involve almost everyone in the room.

She was still shaking when she found a corner table in the student center. Her tears had stopped but her anger hadn't. She breathed deeply to settle herself down. As calm descended on her, she put her arms on the table and rested her forehead on them. *Oh, Brian, I miss you so.*

"Stacey, are you all right?"

Stacey raised her head to see Professor Axtel standing across the table from her, concern written on his face. The fact that her professor took time to seek her out surprised her. Although only two or three years older than Stacey, he had never spoken to her outside of class. One of the younger professors at the college, Professor Axtel taught sociology while working on his doctorate.

"I'll be fine. I'm sorry I disrupted class, but I'd had all I could take of Gary's uninformed opinion."

"I'd say that was a kind description of his comments." Professor Axtel smiled. "May I buy you a cup of coffee?"

"That would be nice."

When Professor Axtel returned with the coffee, he told Stacey about the support she'd received from the class. They spent the rest of the afternoon talking first about the war in Vietnam, then Brian, and finally about Stacey.

When her sociology class met again, many of the students greeted Stacey and talked to her about her impromptu speech two days earlier. Gary avoided her and Professor Axtel treated her the same as he always had during class. When class ended, Professor Axtel asked her to remain.

"This is going to sound rather odd, I'm sure," he said, "but I thoroughly enjoyed our talk the other day, and I want to see you again. Outside the classroom, that is."

Words failed Stacey. A good portion of the coeds at Western State would envy her. The blond, brown-eyed professor's classes were in demand, partly because he was handsome and eligible. Rumors abounded on campus about Professor Axtel and some of his female students, but Stacey always considered the stories just that— rumors with no basis in fact.

Before Stacey could respond, he spoke again. "I realize dating one of your professors is awkward, but I find myself infatuated with you."

Stacey blushed at his comment. "I think it would be best if we continued our relationship as student and teacher. There's no other choice. I need the class, and it's too late to drop it. But I am flattered at your interest." She smiled and turned to go, clutching her books to her in order to calm her shaking hands.

177

"Once the quarter is over, would you consider going out with me?"

Stacey turned toward him. "I don't know. Perhaps you will have lost interest by then."

"I doubt I will lose interest anytime soon."

Stacey surprised herself by answering, "Then if you're sure it won't be considered improper by the college, yes." She left the classroom with a new outlook. Having a handsome and mature man interested in her put a smile on her face and a lilt in her step.

~

The following June, Stacey received a call from Professor John Axtel. "I'm in North Fork," he said, "and I'm not familiar with the restaurants here. Would you care to make a recommendation and join me for dinner?"

Stacey hesitated only a moment. "I would love to."

At dinner that night, Stacey listened intently as John talked about his work. She laughed at his anecdotes about teaching, sure he embellished the stories a bit for her benefit, but she enjoyed them nonetheless. Her initial nervousness at meeting him for dinner melted away, and she found herself enjoying his company. Over dessert, John unexpectedly brought up his popularity with young women.

"Stacey, I'm sure you're aware of the numerous stories about me circulating around campus, and I want to set the record straight." He smiled at Stacey's frown and continued. "I discovered a long time ago that, for whatever reason, I have a certain appeal to women. And I'm certain you've heard the stories that link me to any number of coeds. One of the rumors is that I've been known to give A's in return for sexual favors."

Stacey, uneasy over John's openness, scraped at the residue of lemon meringue pie with her fork. "John, you don't have to—"

John reached across the table and took Stacey's hand. "Stacey, look at me. I'm not trying to embarrass you or make you uncomfortable, but we need to address this from the start."

Stacey searched his face and saw sincerity. "All right," she conceded, "what about the rumors?"

"That's just what they are. Rumors. I would never jeopardize my teaching position or my reputation by doing something that stupid. Oh, I've had girls offer themselves to me if I'd give them an A. I tell them they can get an A the old-fashioned way—by studying hard. I believe that a couple of the girls I've turned down started the rumors to salve their wounded pride."

John squeezed Stacey's hand and pulled it closer to him. "Those girls don't interest me in the least. They're immature and for the most part brain dead. You, on the other hand, have interested me since the day you signed up for my class."

Stacey blushed. John smiled. With the index finger of his free hand, he traced the path of the blush from Stacey's cheekbone to her neck.

"The moment I saw you," he said, "I knew I wanted to get to know you better. And after that impassioned speech you gave in class, I knew I couldn't wait until the quarter was over. That's why I sought you out in the student center. It's been hard for me to wait, as you prudently suggested. Thank goodness one of us was thinking straight. But you're no longer one of my students, and I want to spend the summer getting to know you better."

Unable to resist his warm brown eyes and personable smile, Stacey replied, "I think that would be very nice, John."

Their dinner together that evening was the first of many that summer for Stacey and John. Although her parents expressed concern that she was rushing into the relationship, Stacey didn't share their misgivings. Overwhelmed by John's attention and devotion, she found herself falling in love again.

The best part for Stacey, however, was John's interest in BJ. Her young son had become his grandfather's shadow, but Stacey thought it unfair for her father to have to raise his grandson, instead of simply sitting back and enjoying him. John spent almost as much time with BJ as he did with Stacey. And BJ talked incessantly about John.

In August, John proposed, catching Stacey completely off guard. The day began like many of the days Stacey and BJ spent with John that summer. He had suggested a day of fishing at North Fork Reservoir. They settled in their favorite spot under a large cottonwood tree near the water. John assembled his fly rod while Stacey helped BJ with his pole.

After lunch, John resumed his fly fishing, and BJ curled up on the blanket for a nap. Stacey enjoyed watching John as he deftly cast his fly out over the water, then slowly pulled the line toward him until he pulled in enough line to cast again. After several casts to play out the line, the slow process of pulling the fly across the water began again.

John made several casts without getting a strike. Stacey teased him about not holding his mouth right in order to catch fish. After a few minutes of her teasing, he surprised her with a challenge that left her speechless.

"Marry me, Stacey," he said without turning around. When she didn't answer, he turned and smiled at her. She stopped stroking BJ's head and rested her hand on his blond curls.

"How about it?" John asked.

He reeled in the line he'd patiently flicked out onto the lake and hooked the fly on his rod handle. He walked to the blanket and laid down his fly pole. Kneeling in front of Stacey, he cupped her chin in his hand and kissed her.

"Your lips are still warm; I don't detect any bluing; I can feel your breath on my face, so I'll assume you're still alive." His grin made her smile. "I know it's not very romantic. No candlelight or champagne, but being with you and BJ today has seemed so right. I feel like we're a family, and—"

"Yes," she whispered.

He tipped his head. "What did you say?"

"I said yes."

John pulled her against him and kissed her. "You've made me very happy, Stacey. I know you won't regret this."

Believing she was doing the right thing, Stacey expended a great deal of energy convincing her parents that marrying John was right for her and BJ. Her parents worried about her impulsive decision and suggested she take more time, but Stacey refused. In spite of her parents' concern, Stacey began her sophomore year at Western State College as Stacey Murcheson Axtel.

## Chapter 18

By September, Stacey, BJ, and John had settled into their new home. Stacey registered for her fall classes, taking a full load at John's urging. He didn't want her to delay her education because of their marriage, and he promised to help with BJ so she could study. With John's help, Stacey juggled mothering, school, and housework along with adjusting to her new marriage. She was truly happy for the first time since Brian's death.

A new police drama, *The Streets of L.A.*, debuted on television that September, with JD MacCord as one of its stars. Although Stacey had little time for television with her busy schedule, she always found time to watch JD's show. She saw his new series as a sign of a new chapter in his life. With her marriage to John, she had moved forward and begun a new chapter, as well.

"What is it you see in that show?" John asked her one night while the credits rolled across the screen. "It's just another cop show." Stacey ignored the slight irritation in John's voice.

"An old friend is one of the stars, and I enjoy watching it for that reason," she said. "The guy that plays Lt. Anderson was our best man when I married Brian."

"You seem a little obsessed with watching it."

"Are you jealous?" Stacey teased.

"No." John frowned. "Should I be?"

"Of course not. I haven't seen or been in touch with JD since Brian died. He was Brian's friend. Actually, acting is the last thing I expected him to do, but he's very good at it. I'm happy for him."

"Just as long as you're happy with me."

"I am, John."

Stacey kissed him on the cheek and sat down to study, but she had trouble concentrating. She was happy for JD, but every time she saw him she felt a tug on her heart and a longing to see him, talk to him, and set things straight. Under the circumstances, she knew that would never happen. JD most likely despised her, if he thought of her at all, which she doubted. She needed to let the past go, and her marriage to John was a step in the right direction.

Stacey worked hard at making her new home a pleasant and loving place for both BJ and John. As fall slipped into winter, however, John spent less and less time at home. Blaming herself and her busy schedule, Stacey cut her class hours by half for winter quarter in an effort to give more attention to John, but it didn't seem to help.

As weeks turned into months, Stacey noticed John's increasing lack of interest in BJ. At first he had been a wonderful stepfather, playing with BJ and taking him places. But then John began to find fault with everything BJ did and complained that he was an undisciplined and spoiled child. John yelled at BJ for no reason and accused Stacey of being too lenient with him.

Stacey tried her best to keep peace and smooth things over with John and BJ, but her efforts failed miserably. One evening in early April, Stacey's frustration over John's inability to deal with BJ came to a boiling point. John was working at his desk, and BJ was sprawled on the floor drawing pictures. Stacey had curled up in a chair to read a chapter in her kinesiology textbook.

BJ scrambled up and grabbed his drawing, leaving his crayons in the middle of the floor. Planting himself next to John's chair, he tapped John on the arm. Beaming, he shoved the drawing in front of John.

"Look, John."

John shoved BJ's hand with the drawing away. BJ's lower lip protruded into a pout.

"BJ," Stacey said, "leave John alone. He's working."

BJ turned back to John and shoved the drawing at him again. "John, look."

John snatched the drawing from BJ's hand, wadded it into a ball, and threw it across the room. "I don't want to see your stupid scribbling, BJ. And pick up your crayons before someone steps on them," he snapped.

BJ wailed and ran after his drawing.

"Shit!" John slammed his pen onto the desk and turned toward Stacey, who had gotten up and gone after BJ. "Can't you keep the little brat out of my hair while I'm working?"

Stacey's temper flared, but she squelched it in order to comfort her crying son. She picked him up as he tried to unfold the crumpled drawing.

"It's okay, BJ. John didn't mean to snap at you. He's very busy right now. You can show him your picture later."

BJ laid his head against Stacey's shoulder and sobbed. Stacey rubbed his back.

"John," she said with an effort to keep her voice calm, "it will take less than a minute to look at his picture. Surely you can manage that."

John stood, tipping his chair over with a crash. Gathering his papers together and shoving them in his briefcase, he snarled, "Thanks to your inability to make your son behave, I have to find someplace else to work. I'm going to my office."

"His name is BJ, and you need to treat him with more understanding."

"Children should be seen and not heard," John said as he shoved into his coat. "When you both figure that out, things will be a lot better around here. Don't wait up for me."

After John left, Stacey sat down with BJ and helped him smooth out his drawing. Between the shudders and hiccups left over from crying, he explained his art work to Stacey. When he finished, Stacey attached it to the refrigerator with a magnet, then gave BJ a bath and put him to bed.

The confrontation left Stacey more than unsettled. Unable to find a logical reason for John's change in attitude toward BJ and needing to confide in someone, she called Rachel.

~

"Whew!" Rachel closed her umbrella as she hurried through the open door. "It's raining poodles out there!"

Stacey smiled as she took Rachel's coat and hung it in the hall closet. "They'll most likely be frozen poodles by morning," Stacey said.

They laughed and hugged each other. Rachel was the breath of fresh air Stacey had needed for many months. She regretted not spending more time with Rachel since her marriage to John.

Rachel followed Stacey into the kitchen and plopped on a chair next to the kitchen table. Stacey set a steaming mug of coffee in front of Rachel, poured one for herself, and sat opposite her friend.

"So what's up? You sounded stressed when you called." Rachel set her mug down. "It's the professor, isn't it?"

Tears trickled down Stacey's cheeks. She wiped them away with her fingers, then gripped her mug with both hands.

"It's me. John's just not happy. BJ and I can't seem to do anything right." Stacey sniffed and fought back the tears.

"I *knew* it. It's not your fault any more than it's mine."

"What?"

"I should have said something the minute you told me you were getting married to the jerk. But *no,* I had to keep my mouth shut for the first time in my *uninhibited* life."

"Rach, what are you babbling about?"

"I'm saying I should have warned you about good old Professor John Axtel, *that's* what I'm saying."

"If you're referring to his rumored reputation with some of the female students, I already knew about that. But they're just rumors. John and I discussed it before we even started dating. There's no truth to any of the stories."

"You don't really believe that, do you?"

Stacey glared at Rachel. "Yes, I do. Trust between John and me is not the problem."

"Then what is the problem?"

"The three of us aren't adjusting well. Adjusting to marriage is difficult enough, but adding a live wire like BJ makes it twice as hard. Practically everything BJ does gets on John's nerves, and then BJ gets cranky, and I get blamed for not being a better disciplinarian.

"John's been spending more and more time away from home, working late at his office and coming home after I'm asleep. I can't say as I blame him." Stacey took a deep breath. "Oh, Rach, I don't know what to do, but something has to change."

Anguish and frustration surfaced in sobs Stacey could no longer contain. Rachel remained quiet until Stacey's tears were spent. Stacey wiped her nose and eyes, and absently swirled the coffee in her mug.

"So, what are you going to do?" Rachel asked. "Put BJ up for adoption?"

Stacey's head shot up, but when she noticed the grin on Rachel's face an unexpected laugh escaped. She shook her head. "You always make me laugh, Rach, even in the worst circumstances." She sighed. "Of course I'm not going to put BJ up for adoption. That's obviously not an option."

"Then I guess you'll have to confront the professor."

"I've tried, but he finds ways to change the subject and avoid talking about our problems. Or he manages to make me feel guilty and apologize, like everything's my fault."

"Where is he now?"

"At his office."

"Can't think of a better place. No interruptions from little Mr. Trouble, and he'll be a captive audience, particularly if you lock the door and throw away the key. Insist he listen for a change and don't take 'no' for an answer."

"I don't have a car. John took his, and mine's at the garage for repairs."

"Take my car." Rachel handed Stacey her keys.

"What about BJ?"

"I'll watch the little troublemaker. Now go and straighten things out."

"Thanks, Rach. I owe you. BJ's already in bed asleep."

"I'm here till whenever," Rachel said.

Stacey dreaded arguments with John. He twisted everything around until she apologized or accepted the blame in order to restore peace. On the way to John's office, she practiced what she was going to say to him and promised herself she wouldn't give in this time.

As she placed her hand on the doorknob to John's office, she heard a woman's voice. Realizing he might be with a student, Stacey turned to leave, then changed her mind. Whoever was with John could reschedule. She took a deep breath, opened the door, and froze.

A young coed Stacey didn't know personally, sat astride John's lap, her blouse unbuttoned. Startled by Stacey's unexpected entrance, the young woman turned toward Stacey and gasped. John closed his eyes for a moment, then looked at Stacey. Calmly putting his hands on the girl's waist and helping her off his lap, he spoke, never taking his eyes from Stacey's.

"Beth, why don't you put yourself together and go back to the dorm. We'll discuss your test score tomorrow after class."

Beth buttoned her blouse and grabbed her coat. She sidled past Stacey, avoiding Stacey's glare, and exited quickly.

"I see grading papers has taken on a new twist," Stacey said. She clenched her hands and fought the urge to slap him. "You should have remembered to lock the door." She turned to go, but John grabbed her arm.

"*Let go of me.*" Tears stung Stacey's eyes.

John dropped her arm and moved to block the doorway.

"Let me out, John," Stacey said, fighting the hurt and anger rising in her.

"Not till we talk." He took hold of Stacey's arms and backed her onto a chair. "I'm sorry you had to see that," he said and sat opposite her on the corner of his desk, one foot resting on the floor.

"I'll *bet* you are. Apparently, the propriety of a professor being involved with a student no longer has meaning for you."

"I never pretended it did. You insisted on that."

"I should have listened closer to the gossip before I married you. But you assured me the rumors weren't true, and I was gullible enough to believe you. Obviously, you lied. Our whole marriage is a lie."

"Unfortunately, the marriage isn't working out. I thought I could make it work. I never meant to hurt you."

"If you hadn't meant to hurt me you wouldn't have gotten involved with a student. Or is it students?"

Her question was met with silence. She bit her lip and waited a beat. "We haven't even been married a year and already you've turned to other women. Why? What haven't I given you?"

His eyes darted away for a moment, then he quietly said, "Your love, Stacey. You say you love me, but you keep talking about Brian. And then there's the guy on TV—JC something or other."

"*JD.*"

"Whatever. I've seen the way you look at him, so don't accuse me of seeking other women. You're no better."

Stacey glared at him. "That's *absurd.* He's an old friend I haven't seen in years, so don't turn this around. I'm sick of you always making everything my fault." She shuddered and took a deep breath. "You're the adulterer, John. Not me."

He shrugged his shoulders. "The truth is, I'm not cut out to be a father."

"Or a husband, for that matter." Stacey took another deep breath and wiped the tears from her face. "So, when did you decide all of this?"

"I'm not sure. When I asked you to marry me, I thought we could make things work. You and BJ were perfect for me. You're beautiful and smart, and we make a good-looking couple. And with you and BJ, my income taxes really went down. Instant family, instant deduction. But having BJ around was too much. I should never have tried being an instant father."

Stacey shook her head in disbelief. "That's *all* we meant to you? How I looked with you and deductions on your income tax?"

"What can I say? I was going to have to pay a bunch in taxes this year because of some well-timed investments, so the whole situation was perfect. A beautiful wife, a new son, and less to pay Uncle Sam. Besides, you wouldn't sleep with me before we were married, so how else could I find out how you were in bed?"

"And how am I?" Stacey asked without thinking.

"I've had better."

His words stung. "So have I," she said. Moments of silence stretched between them.

He shrugged. "You haven't lived up to my expectations, so I've turned elsewhere. It happens. I guess I just haven't been happy."

"*You* haven't been happy. I cut down on my classes because things weren't going well. And BJ is no longer the happy-go-lucky little boy he used to be. We've both been walking on eggshells around you. Well no more, John. I may have been gullible, but I learn quickly." Stacey rose to go. "You'll hear from my lawyer."

John slipped off the desk and stood in front of her. "Don't be too hasty, Stacey. Maybe if we came to an understanding. This isn't going to look good with administration. If they learn about this..."

John's comment drove the stabbing pain a little deeper into her heart. "An understanding, John? No. Not ever. Don't worry, though, I'm not vindictive enough to ruin you. I just want out. I do expect you to pay for the expense of the divorce. Maybe you can deduct *that* from your taxes.

"Just to save you further worry," she continued, "I don't want any money from you. I'll leave with what I brought to the marriage. But I do expect to be able to stay in the house *alone* until this quarter is over. After that, I don't care if I *never* have anything to do with you."

Stacey pushed past him to the door. "I hope you and your cute little coed can work things out." Stacey opened the door and with her back to John delivered one last dig. "I'm curious. Did she earn her A? After all, she's worked for it the old-fashioned way."

Stacey slammed the door behind her and leaned against it, unable to move any further. Her stomach churned and tears burned her eyes. After a few moments, she forced herself to walk to the car and drive home.

John didn't come home that night, and the following day Stacey left a message with his secretary that he could pick up his clothes and any personal items he might need, and then he was no longer welcome in the house until she was gone. Stacey made sure she wasn't at home when John moved his things out.

That summer, Stacey and BJ moved back to her parents' home in North Fork. Instead of recriminations, Stacey's parents offered understanding and love. She spent hours trying to understand why she had been so easily deceived by John. Her only conclusion was that she wanted desperately for BJ to have a father and had been lonely and needed someone to love her. But needing to be loved, Stacey realized, was far from being loved, and she resolved never to trust so easily again.

Setting aside her own needs, Stacey concentrated all her love and energy on BJ. They went on picnics and spent time hiking, riding, and fishing. By summer's end, BJ was energetic and happy again, and his grandfather's shadow once more.

Returning to school the next fall was difficult for Stacey. She had prepared herself, as much as possible, for her first inevitable encounter with John. But Stacey discovered that John's reputation had caught up with him. He had quietly resigned before the fall quarter and sought employment elsewhere. Stacey was relieved she wouldn't have to face seeing him on campus. She began her junior year with renewed enthusiasm instead of dread.

## Chapter 19

*April 1977-- North Fork, Colorado*

*T*he sun inched its way above the West Elk Mountains, painting the scattered clouds pink and lavender, while bathing snowcapped peaks in the gold of early morning light. Stacey sat at the kitchen table sipping her morning coffee and drinking in the beauty of another spring day.

Like Mother Nature, Stacey felt she was waking up from a long winter, ready to begin again. The excitement of starting something new, of independence, burned inside her. As a way of celebrating that independence, she cut her waist-length hair into a feathered, shoulder-length cut.

The previous December, Stacey graduated with honors from Western State College. She had worked hard to finish her schooling and the payoff was a secure future for her and BJ.

Since graduation she had worked as a substitute teacher in the North Fork schools, and by March, the school district offered her a contract to replace a retiring teacher at the high school. In the fall, she would become a full-time teacher and realize her dream.

Stacey smiled as she watched the sun continue its early morning journey. She cherished the challenge of teaching and the new beginning it offered her and BJ. She had finally made her way in the world on her own terms.

"Care for some company?"

"Dad. I didn't hear you come downstairs. Want some breakfast?"

"In a little while." Phil Atkins stopped next to the table and glanced out the window. "Gonna be a beautiful day." He filled a mug with coffee. "BJ still asleep?"

"Yes, thank goodness. I think he wore himself out fishing yesterday." Stacey smiled at the memory of seven-year-old BJ, his mouth set with grim determination, concentrating on his fishing pole and hoping for the tiniest movement.

Phil chuckled. "He sure gets serious when it comes to fishing." He swallowed a gulp of coffee. "How about taking a ride with me after breakfast? We haven't had a good ride together in quite a while."

"I'd like that." Stacey suspected more than the ride her father offered. He rarely took time away from ranch work just to take a horseback ride with his daughter.

The late morning ride took Stacey and her father to Hansen Creek and the piece of land Stacey's parents had given her and Brian for a wedding present. Because the land had meant so much to Brian, Stacey always felt his presence there. She often spent an hour or two reading under the big cottonwood tree, or pitching stones into Hansen Creek with BJ. Without Brian, Stacey balked at following through with the dreams they had envisioned together.

Stacey knew better than to ask her father why he had ridden to this particular piece of land. She waited patiently. They sat together on the creek bank, shared a few cookies, and talked about the weather and when the alfalfa would be ready for cutting. Finally,

Stacey's father steered the conversation in a new direction.

"Honey, your mother and I are real proud of you. In spite of everything that's happened, you've managed to get your college degree and raise a great boy at the same time, sometimes under very difficult circumstances." He took hold of Stacey's hand, squeezed it, and then stood and turned around.

Stacey joined him. "Thanks, Dad. I had a lot of love and support from home. I couldn't have done it otherwise."

"Your mother and I will always be here for you, you know that." He cleared his throat. "But I think it's time you became a little more independent. You can't live with your old folks forever. We'll get to be a drag one of these days."

"Never."

"Now don't be so quick to deny it. In spite of what you may think now, one of these days the right man will come along, and you'll need some space."

"I'm through with men for a long time, Dad, believe me."

"Maybe. Maybe not."

"I do understand what you're saying, though. It's time I became independent of you and Mom. I'll start looking for a place in town. With any luck I'll find something and be settled before school starts in the fall."

"Not so fast." He cleared his throat again. "I was thinking that it might be nice to build you a house right here. This is your land. We don't want you and BJ too far away, you know. Besides, it's good for a boy to grow up on a ranch. Teaches him responsibility. For only being seven, he's already a big help. Does a lot of chores by himself, and as he gets older, he'll do more and more. If he's living in town, he'll be too far away to help much."

Tears tugged at Stacey's eyes. "I know you mean well, Dad, but—

"Now don't you fret any about the cost. With your job you should qualify for a loan, and I can do a good bit of the work, so that should cut down on expenses. I think that together we can swing it. Won't be fancy, but it'll be yours."

Stacey put her hand on her Dad's shoulder. "Dad, I've thought a lot about this land lately, even looked into building a house on it, but I just can't." She swallowed the lump in her throat. "Brian and I had so many plans for this place. I can't do it without him. It doesn't feel right. I've decided that this land should be BJ's. He can build the house on it. I can't."

She stuffed her hands in her hip pockets. "I know you probably don't understand, Dad, but I won't change my mind." She bit her lower lip and waited.

"Honey, I think I do understand. Can't say as I blame you." He put his arm around her shoulders and hugged her. Stacey rested her head against her Dad's shoulder. "Your mother was pretty sure you'd refuse, so we came up with an alternate plan."

Stacey raised her head to look at her father, and as she did, he winked and smiled at her.

"An alternate plan?"

"Yep. How 'bout we turn the garage into a small house for you and BJ? That way you two can have your privacy and still live on the ranch. I don't really think you want to leave your horses, and I can't imagine you living in town."

"You'd really do that?"

"Absolutely. Your mother and I discussed it at length the other night. We can build another garage over by the shop, next to the tack room. What do you think?"

"The cost and the payments will be my responsibility," Stacey said, a determined look on her face. "Otherwise, I won't agree to it. I'll move to town, instead. Deal?"

"Deal." They hugged to seal the bargain.

~

By September, Stacey and BJ had new quarters attached to her parents' house. The garage became a cottage with a living room and kitchen/dinette combination. Adding a second story provided two bedrooms and a bath. The remodeled garage was joined to the main house by a laundry room and storage area that served as a buffer between the two households.

Stacey and BJ had the best of all circumstances. They had their privacy, but still enjoyed the simple but busy pleasure of living on a ranch. Stacey began her new career content with her life.

From the moment she walked into the classroom on her first day of teaching, Stacey demonstrated a natural ability to capture her students' interest and bring out the best in them. In addition to teaching two biology classes, a general science class, and two physical education classes, Stacey also coached the girls' volleyball team in the fall, the girls' junior varsity basketball team during the winter, and the coed tennis team in the spring.

Much to the delight of her principal, Stacey's coaching techniques paralleled her teaching abilities. The fall of 1978 and her second year of coaching, Stacey's volleyball team won their conference and placed second in state competition. Although her basketball team only placed second in the conference, her tennis team surprised everyone. Stacey took players who demonstrated average talent for tennis and transformed them into top competitors. Throughout the state, the North Fork Eagles' tennis team became the team to beat.

Although Stacey's professional career was on an upward track, her personal life continued its ups and downs. BJ was a source of unending joy and sometimes frustration for Stacey. As he grew, she began to see little things—things that others would miss—that reminded her of his father, making Stacey wish she could turn back the clock. But wishing for what might have been only caused her more pain. Nothing practical could be gained by wishing for something she knew would never be.

In February of 1979, Stacey's safe and comfortable world was jolted when her father suffered a mild heart attack. Though the doctor's prognosis was good, Stacey still worried about her father. Stacey's brother, Jess, resigned from his position as a junior partner in a prestigious Denver law firm and moved back to North Fork to help with the ranch, relieving some of Stacey's and Kate's worries.

Also in the spring of 1979, Jan Scruggs, a former army infantryman in Vietnam, began a drive to establish a memorial for Americans killed in the Vietnam War. Stacey had rejoiced with most of the nation when America's involvement in Vietnam came to an end during the Nixon administration. The sight of American prisoners of war setting foot on American soil after years of isolation, torture, and abandonment brought tears of joy that they were home, and tears of regret that they and their families had suffered for so long.

Although the conflict in Vietnam had ended, the conflict at home had not, putting Vietnam veterans on the defensive regarding their involvement in the war. Many Americans blamed Vietnam veterans for losing a war and refused to afford them the same status as World War II veterans. In spite of their sacrifices, Vietnam veterans felt they had never been properly acknowledged for putting their lives in danger and their futures on hold for other Americans and their freedom. Bitterness waged its own war in America.

Stacey saw Jan Scrugg's dream of a Vietnam memorial as an honorable means to pay tribute to those who had died or were still missing in action. She also saw the memorial as a means to bring healing to the nation. She sent a generous donation to the fund, and waited anxiously for news of its completion.

Stacey's life settled into a busy routine. Content with her life as it was, she had little time to miss having a man around. Her priorities became BJ and her career.

In spite of her busy schedule, however, Stacey managed to keep track of JD's career, silently celebrating his steady run of successes. She was disappointed when he left the television series *The Streets of L.A.* after only a year. When he won a supporting role in a major movie, she understood his reason for leaving the series. In fact, JD's first movie role was so successful that he starred in his next movie. From then on, his career skyrocketed, and Stacey made sure she saw all of his movies. In only a few years, JD became the number one box office attraction, and the heartthrob of American women.

It was with mixed emotions that Stacey read the announcement of JD's marriage to Sabrina Branson. The movie industry's newest and prettiest starlet had managed to win the heart of America's most sought after bachelor.

Although Stacey knew she had no future with JD, she experienced unwelcome jealousy over his marriage and regret over the loss of his friendship. But life, Stacey reminded herself, moved forward, and she had a son she loved above all else, and a rewarding career. She set aside her regrets and concentrated on her future.

## Chapter 20

*March 1980--San Onofre Beach, California*

On a balmy Saturday afternoon in March, JD MacCord sat on San Onofre Beach lulled by the ocean's relentless pursuit of the shore. He contemplated the odd direction his life had taken since mustering out of the Marines. He hadn't pursued fame. He'd taken up acting on a whim and discovered he enjoyed it. Success at something he loved was a bonus.

He formed his own production company after several consecutive hits, allowing him to exercise more choice in the roles he played and giving him creative control over the finished product. With his latest movie, he added directing to his list of accomplishments.

He watched a gull soar over the water, and wondered what happened to Brian's surfboard after he and Stacey sent it out to sea eleven years ago. Did someone find it? Had it sunk to the ocean floor? Or after all these years, was it still floating somewhere in the vast Pacific Ocean?

In all the weekends he'd spent on this very beach with Brian and Stacey, he never once imagined he'd no longer have them as friends. Brian's death and Stacey's sudden departure from his life left him devastated, and for a while, angry at both of them. Angry at Brian for dying and even angrier at Stacey for not facing what happened between them. Unable to sort out his feelings on his own, he had turned to the only friend who understood. The night in Jarheads' he had sought Jacqueline's advice became a turning point in his life. She voiced what he already knew. He had two options.

"Stop feeling sorry for yourself," Jacqueline admonished, "and quit being angry at Stacey. You share half the blame. Either go to North Fork and confront her, or put the past where it belongs and get on with your life."

He chose the latter, afraid that confronting Stacey would only alienate her more. In her note she asked him to stay out of her life, and he made the decision to honor her request.

When he mustered out of the Marines, he planned to look into graduate school at USC or UCLA, but without Stacey to share his dream, his enthusiasm for continuing his education waned.

JD returned to Aztec, New Mexico to help his dad with the ranch and to take some time to decide on his future. He contemplated teaching in Aztec or Farmington and did some substituting in the local schools, but no immediate full-time teaching positions opened. When a movie company chose Albuquerque and the area around it to film a rodeo flick, JD signed on as an extra, more out of curiosity and boredom than anything. He never guessed that impulsive act would launch a new career for him.

Life has a funny way of throwing you a curve, JD thought as he watched the waves caress the beach. "God, Butch, I miss you and Sam."

His heart ached at the thought of them. So many memories and too much time in between. *I have two regrets—Butch's death and alienating Sam.* He had only himself to blame for the latter, and he couldn't turn back the clock.

"I let you down, Butch," he murmured. "You asked me to take care of Sam, and I blew it. I failed you, I failed Sam, and I failed myself. I'm sorry, buddy. Truly sorry."

He let his gaze wander along the beach, lost in the past and half expecting Brian to crest a wave and yell "Yee-haw!" JD's heart skipped a beat as his gaze settled on a shapely, long-haired blond sauntering in his direction, and for a fleeting moment Stacey walked through the sand toward him.

Removing his sunglasses, he rubbed his eyes and looked again. He'd never consciously noticed the resemblance before, although there had been something familiar about Sabrina the first time he saw her on the studio lot. Now he knew why. He slipped his sunglasses on, hoping to hide his unsettled thoughts as the object of his attention stopped in front of him.

"You look like you're miles away from here, JD." She eased down beside him on the sand. "Want to tell me about it?"

JD forced himself to sound normal. "Sorry, Sabrina. This beach holds a lot of memories for me." His eyes drifted over her, and the resemblance to Stacey faded.

"Is this where the picture that sits on your desk was taken?" When he didn't answer, she pressed the point. "You know, the one of you and Sam and Butch."

"Yes," he answered, remembering the last weekend he'd spent with his friends at the beach. A passerby had snapped the picture.

"You've never talked about that picture, but it must have some meaning. Who are the other two? Every time I ask, you say it doesn't matter, but it does. It matters to you, so it matters to me, too. I'm your wife. Don't shut me out."

"I'm not shutting you out," he said, a little more sharply than he intended. "Look, Sabrina, they're a part of my past. Let's just leave it there."

"No, they're not."

"What?"

"A part of your past. If they were, you wouldn't still have that picture on your desk, or be miles away right now."

"We probably shouldn't have come here." JD stood. With Sabrina intruding on his thoughts, his walk down memory lane lost its appeal. "Let's go home."

"Not till you tell me what's going on," she said, pursing her lips into a pout.

JD despised Sabrina when she whined or pouted to get her way. Why hadn't he seen that side of her before he married her? He realized then that he might have married her because subconsciously she reminded him of Stacey—physically, anyway. The resemblance stopped there. Sabrina's youthfulness had appealed to JD when they starred together in her first film. He soon discovered she was spoiled and immature, although she had hidden it well before they married.

Today was the eleventh anniversary of the night JD and Stacey taped the bottle of beer to Brian's surfboard and sent it out to sea. The trip to San Onofre was intended as a private pilgrimage for JD, but Sabrina discovered his plans and whined and cajoled until he relented and allowed her to accompany him. But her presence intruded on his need to reflect, and he had no desire to share Brian and Stacey, or his memories, with Sabrina.

JD offered Sabrina his hand. "Come on, let's go."

Sabrina took his hand and pulled herself up. Wrapping her arms around his neck, she kissed him on the cheek, then the lips. JD slipped his arms around her and tried to lose himself in her soft caresses, but his mind and body refused to respond. Regret stabbed at his heart. He yearned to hold Stacey in his arms, not Sabrina. But wish as he might, Sabrina wasn't Stacey, and he would never hold Stacey again.

He pushed away from Sabrina, then felt guilty for feeling the way he did. He took her hand and pulled her toward the waves rushing onto the shore. As they walked along the beach, his guilt nagged at him. It wasn't fair to shut Sabrina out like he did.

*Maybe if I told her a little bit about Sam and Butch, I could put the memories aside and get on with my marriage.* He'd been in love with Sabrina when he married her ten months ago. At least he thought he loved her. And if he loved her, he should be willing to share all aspects of his life with her.

"Butch and Sam were my best friends," he said. "Sam was Butch's wife. Butch and I were both stationed here at Pendleton during the Vietnam War. The three of us spent a lot of time together at this beach before Butch shipped out to Nam. He was killed there eleven years ago this month."

JD stopped and turned toward Sabrina. "Today I felt the need to come here and remember him, that's all."

Tears brimmed in Sabrina's eyes. She touched his cheek with her hand. "I'm so sorry, JD. Why didn't you tell me this before I insisted on barging in on your trip?"

JD's guilt ate at him. He'd been too harsh in his assessment of Sabrina earlier, failing to give her enough credit where his feelings were concerned. He gathered her into his arms and held her tight.

"I'm sorry, Sabrina. You haven't deserved my mood today. Forgive me?"

"If you promise you won't shut me out anymore."

"I promise." JD crushed his lips to hers, hoping to drown out the memories San Onofre Beach had conjured. He didn't need to dwell on the past. His future was with Sabrina.

~

Over the next six months, JD's efforts to concentrate on Sabrina

205

and their marriage proved less than effective. Sabrina's self-centeredness only worsened. No matter what he tried, JD seemed unable to make Sabrina, or himself, truly happy. Despite the trip to Europe Sabrina begged for on their first anniversary, she wasn't content. She complained that JD never did anything for her, never took her anywhere. No matter what he gave her, she always wanted more.

Sabrina's constant demands rankled him. The simple things in life—home, friends, family—made him happy. But Sabrina balked at his suggestion they start a family. She insisted she wasn't ready, and JD feared she'd never want children.

Sabrina's tentative contentment came with things—clothes, jewelry, and cars. If it was expensive, she wanted it. Yet no matter how many things she acquired, she always wanted more. Most of all, she was dissatisfied with her career. She made a second movie, but the part was a small supporting role given to her as a favor to JD. Sabrina wanted star billing, and that wasn't happening fast enough for her. She badgered JD to find her a script with a starring role.

That fall a screenwriter JD had worked with early in his career sent him a screenplay hoping he might produce it. On a dreary, wet October afternoon, JD sat behind his desk reading the screenplay, enjoying the peace of the rain drumming against the windows. Flames danced and crackled in the fireplace, warding off the fall chill.

JD had nearly finished reading the screenplay when Sabrina entered his office. She glided over to his desk, planted her hip on the corner, and leaned toward him, propping herself up on one arm. Her silk blouse fell open enough to expose the top of her breasts.

"New screenplay?" she asked.

"Yep," he answered.

As he read the script, he contemplated casting Sabrina as the female lead just to keep her happy. Then he reminded himself he hadn't gotten where he was by making foolish decisions. Other more seasoned actresses were much better suited for the role. He wouldn't compromise his high standards to further his wife's career just to keep her happy.

"Any female leads?" She glided her tongue slowly across her upper lip.

Sabrina's attempt to seduce him into giving her a part irritated him. JD dropped the few remaining pages onto the desk and leaned back in his chair.

"None for you."

Momentary surprise registered on her face at his abrupt answer. As she raised up, she knocked the picture of JD, Stacey, and Brian off the desk.

"Be careful." He rose from his chair to retrieve the picture, but Sabrina beat him to it.

"There's never a part in any of your movies for me," she said and cradled the picture against her.

"That's because I haven't found a part that fits you. This one definitely doesn't."

"You could have it rewritten so it would."

"No. The script works the way it is." JD could see the anger building in her, but he refused to give in to her immature manipulation.

"You're not being fair. You owe me this part."

"I don't owe you anything, Sabrina. You're more than welcome to seek parts elsewhere." He held out his hand. "Now hand me the picture and leave me alone so I can work."

Sabrina spun on her heels and headed for the fireplace. Her hand had barely grasped the handle of the protective glass doors when JD caught her. He spun her around and grabbed the picture. Defiance danced across her face.

"Don't even think about it." Rage burned in his eyes.

"What's the matter, *Mac?* Afraid you'll forget them if you haven't got a picture to remind you?"

JD's hand tightened on Sabrina's arm. "Don't *ever* call me that."

"Why? Because *she* called you that? What makes *her* so special? Did you love her? Your best friend's wife?"

JD fought the urge to slap her. He'd never hit a woman in his life, but Sabrina was dangerously close to becoming the first. He dropped her arm like he'd been burned and returned to the desk.

"What makes you say that?" he asked, his back to her.

"I've seen the way you look at that picture when you think no one's watching. And more than once I've seen you reach out and touch her face with your fingers."

He winced at her revelation and realized she had just admitted to spying on him.

"I think you better leave," he said.

"*No.* Not till you tell me what was so special about her."

JD turned, forcing himself to remain calm. "Don't push it, Sabrina."

Tears surfaced and spilled onto her cheeks. "Please help me understand, JD. *I'm* your wife. I don't know how to compete with a ghost."

JD sighed and leaned against the side of the desk. "It isn't a competition. Just try being who you are. The woman I married...or thought I did."

She gestured toward the picture. "Then stop trying to make me into *her*." She stormed from the room.

JD took a deep breath and rubbed his hand through his hair. Regaining his composure, he sat in his chair, placed the picture in a bottom drawer of his desk, and locked it. No sense taking any chances, he thought. When angered, he knew Sabrina was capable of anything.

He leaned back in the chair and closed his eyes. Sabrina's parting shot hit a nerve. Whether she realized it or not, she had effectively turned the tables on him and used his guilty conscience against him. He would never stop loving Stacey, but in the process, he was hurting Sabrina. When he married her, he made a commitment. It was up to him to make their marriage work.

Sabrina's idea of making a marriage work meant gifts, and JD obliged her. Appeasing her cost him a large and expensive diamond and sapphire pendant and a fresh bouquet of exotic flowers each day for a week. Sabrina's jealously waned in direct proportion to the gifts she received from him. Three months after the picture incident, Sabrina landed a major role in a TV movie produced by someone other than JD.

With Sabrina temporarily content with her career, JD settled into a more peaceful existence. Stacey was never mentioned again, and Sabrina behaved as though she'd never accused him of loving Stacey. He began to believe that Sabrina had finally matured and viewed their relationship as something worth saving, until a comment from Jack, his business manager, shattered any hope JD had of making his marriage work. He usually paid no attention to the constant rumors running rampant throughout the industry, but JD wasted little time confronting Sabrina with the latest rumor from several reliable sources.

Arriving home after his meeting with Jack, JD found Sabrina on the patio next to the pool, soaking up the warm April sun. His shadow fell across her face and Sabrina opened her eyes.

"Hi, sweetie," she said. "How was your lunch?"

"Very informative."

"You look upset." She swung her legs off the chaise longue and sat up. "Has something happened to your new project? Sit down and tell me about it." She patted the cushion beside her.

JD shoved his hands into the hip pockets of his Levi's and turned his back. "There's a rumor going around that you slept with the producer of your last project in order to get the part, and continued sleeping with him until it was done. Is it true?"

Her silence was the only answer he needed. He turned to find her staring at him, an indifferent expression on her face.

"That's what I thought," he said. In spite of their rocky relationship, her betrayal hurt.

She shrugged her shoulders and rose. "I did what I had to do to get the part."

JD gripped her shoulders and searched her face for any sign of guilt or regret, but found none. "You didn't have to do that," he said. "Nothing is worth that kind of betrayal. *Nothing.*"

"It is to me." She twisted away from him and stepped back. "Besides, you've betrayed me for another woman. Why isn't it okay for me to do the same?"

"I haven't been sleeping with another woman, Sabrina."

"Maybe not in reality, but she's always there between us."

Her accusation stunned him, but he refused to let her twist things around to her advantage. "Only because you assume she is. I've done my *damnedest* to make you happy. I thought you were."

Her smile lacked softness and sincerity. "Which just goes to show you how good an actress I am. The truth is, you haven't made me happy because you haven't provided me with the career I thought our marriage would bring. This wouldn't have happened if you'd given me a part in your latest project, but you screwed up. Sorry, JD."

"No," he said through clenched teeth. "You screwed the wrong guy." He stalked into the house and slammed the patio door behind him, cracking the glass.

By mid-April, front-page headlines in the tabloids announced the separation of JD MacCord and Sabrina Branson. The details of the breakup and the settlement Sabrina received in the divorce were greatly exaggerated, but JD didn't care. For the first time since he married Sabrina, JD was thankful Jack and his attorneys had insisted on a prenuptial agreement. And for the first time since he'd locked it away for safe keeping, JD set the picture of him, Stacey, and Brian on his desk in its proper place.

## Chapter 21

Stacey stood in the grocery checkout lane and read the headline about JD's divorce. Unexpected feelings of jealously had surfaced when JD married Sabrina Branson. The night she heard the news, she cried herself to sleep. The following morning, ashamed of the way she reacted and trying to explain her feelings away, she had convinced herself she cried only because of her own losses, and because she had no one to love and no one to love her. Staring at the headline, she finally admitted to herself how much she still missed Brian and JD. Stacey ached with emptiness.

Two years had passed, yet the new headlines evoked unsettling emotions toward JD again. The news of his separation and divorce triggered sympathy for JD, while at the same time, Stacey experienced unexpected relief. She had prayed for his happiness, so her relief at the news of his divorce made no sense.

One of the tabloids suggested another woman was involved, but Stacey knew JD too well to believe he cheated on Sabrina. The remainder of the tabloids, however, reported that Sabrina had an affair and used JD for her own career gain. Compassion and sympathy for JD and his failed marriage filled Stacey's heart. Because of the hurt she experienced over John's infidelity, she understood what JD must be feeling. Renewed guilt pierced her heart over running out on him years ago, an act she was sure had embittered him toward her.

On her drive home from the store, Stacey contemplated how different things might have been if Brian had lived, or if she and JD had allowed more time for their relationship to grow. She set aside the latter thought immediately. Guilt over betraying Brian colored every thought she had of JD and any future they might have had. As for his friendship, she had destroyed that the night she made love to him, then stole away like a coward.

Tears slid down her cheeks as she turned down the lane to her house. She realized that she'd never have the chance to make amends for the past, and she finally accepted that her friend was lost to her forever.

~

After his divorce, JD took some much-needed time for himself and visited his parents in Aztec. Getting back to his roots rejuvenated him. Both his sisters had married and settled in Aztec to raise their families. JD took his nieces and nephews fishing, enjoyed long talks with his family, and took solitary rides to ponder his future. By the time he returned to Los Angeles, he had rediscovered himself.

Sick of the cramped living conditions, smog, and traffic congestion of Los Angeles, he sold his home and bought a hundred acres in the Carmel Valley. He and a former stunt man formed a partnership to raise Quarter Horses and rented their stock to rodeos and the film industry.

Working alongside the builder he hired, JD used his carpentry skills to build a two-story country-style house, a guesthouse, and stables. Once settled into his new home, his career became his focus, and his newest project, *Wind River Wars,* became an obsession. As producer, director, and star, he worked tirelessly on every aspect of the movie, determined to make it his best work yet.

In his spare time, he built furniture, cabinets, and bookshelves for his new home. Given too much free time, he tended to dwell on the regrets of his life—the loss of Brian and Stacey, his marriage to and divorce from Sabrina, and his final regret that he had fathered no children.

JD wanted a family, but that possibility seemed more and more unlikely. Concentrating, instead, on loving his nieces and nephews without interfering too much, he resigned himself to a future without children of his own. To compensate for his loss, a good portion of his charitable contributions went to groups devoted to helping children.

He settled into a busy and satisfying existence. He seldom dated and avoided most social functions, keeping a small group of trusted friends. The paparazzi soon tired of trying to photograph him in compromising situations or dig up gossip about him.

Rather than hurt his career, JD's self-imposed seclusion gave him an air of mystery. His popularity soared, particularly with his female audience. His most recent movies attained the top spot for box office gross the first weekend they opened and remained on top for many weeks. Success professionally eased the loneliness JD experienced personally.

~

By the spring of 1982, Stacey had established an outstanding coaching record at North Fork High School with winning seasons in all three of the sports she coached. She was named coach of the year for Colorado high schools with state championships in volleyball and tennis, and a perfect season for her junior varsity basketball team. Twelve-year-old BJ became active in Little Britches Rodeo, and Stacey began dating again.

After moving to North Fork, Stacey's brother established a law practice while continuing to help his dad on the ranch. With the success and demands of his law practice taking up more of his time, he added a partner, an old friend from law school, Ken Larsen. Unable to continually resist Jess's relentless efforts at matchmaking, Stacey agreed to a date with Ken.

The first date led to more until they were seeing each other regularly. With Ken a permanent presence in her life, Stacey tried shoving any past feelings about JD out of her mind. Avoiding his movies was out of the question, since Ken was a fan and insisted on seeing them all. Stacey did her best to view JD only as the character he played, burying, as best she could, the feelings of jealousy she experienced during the inevitable love scenes.

Content with the direction of her life, Stacey concentrated on her future and her relationship with Ken. It was BJ who dredged up past feelings Stacey thought she had successfully buried. Stacey had gone shopping and asked BJ to help his grandmother clean the attic.

Juggling sacks of groceries, Stacey struggled to open the front door. BJ sat in the middle of the living room floor with several boxes and their contents scattered around him. Stacey pushed the door closed with her hip.

"I could use some help, BJ."

"Oh, hi Mom." He greeted her without looking up.

"What in the world is this mess?" Stacey asked, lowering a sack of groceries onto the arm of an easy chair. "You were supposed to be helping Grandma this morning."

"I did. We cleaned out the attic, and this stuff is yours. She had me bring it over here for you to sort through."

"What's it doing all over the living room?"

"I wanted to see what was in the boxes." He shrugged his

shoulders and spread his hands and arms open. "I guess I got a little carried away, huh?" He looked at Stacey and rested his arms on the box he was about to open.

"Just a little." She shook her head. "Did it occur to you that what was in the boxes might be private?"

"Gee, Mom, I'm sorry. It's just pictures and stuff."

Stacey sighed. "No harm done. I'll need to go through the boxes before I store them away. Now's as good a time as any."

"Can we go through them together? I found some pictures and some letters and stuff. Grandma says one of the boxes has all your wedding pictures, but I haven't found that one yet. All I've ever seen is the big one of you and Dad you keep in your bedroom. How 'bout it Mom, wanna take a history trip with me?" He winked, a big grin on his face.

Stacey couldn't stop the grin spreading across her face. "Okay, but first we have to put the groceries away."

Stacey and BJ spent the remainder of the day wading through stacks of pictures, letters, and trinkets—reminders of the special times she spent with Brian. Stacey even found the journal she'd used to write down her memories of Brian in the months following his death. She had packed the journal away and forgotten about it. She handed it to BJ, explained what it was, and suggested he read it in private.

For BJ, the boxes revealed treasure after treasure. Tired of his constant requests to keep something, Stacey finally told him, "Keep whatever you want. Just stop asking." By the time they got to the last box, BJ had a small stack of pictures and items he wanted, including Brian's dog tag, which he hung around his neck.

While Stacey finished reboxing what they'd gone through, BJ opened the box he had been about to open when she arrived home. She finished labeling the last box and turned toward BJ. He had his back to her, and she couldn't see what he held.

"You're awfully quiet. What are you studying so intently?"

"Who're Mac and Sam?"

Caught off guard, Stacey choked on the answer. BJ turned around, holding an 8 X 10 picture framed in polished juniper.

"I know it sounds stupid, but this Mac guy looks a lot like JD MacCord. You know, the movie star, except younger. Butch is Dad, and I'm sure that's you in the picture, but I've never heard you called Sam." He handed the picture to Stacey.

Stacey took the picture, willing her hands not to shake. Three happy faces stared back, without a clue as to what the future held. She bit her lip and fought back the tears. Her fingers caressed the frame as she tried to find a way to explain JD to her son.

"Mom?"

"Sorry, honey, it's just that this picture brings back a lot of memories." Stacey swallowed the lump in her throat and rested the picture on her lap. "Mac looks like JD MacCord because he is JD MacCord." She waited a moment for BJ's reaction.

He grinned. "You're kiddin', right?"

"Wrong."

"You're telling me you're in a picture with my favorite movie star in the whole world?"

"Yes."

His eyes widened. "You know him?"

"Knew."

"No way."

"Wanna bet?" Stacey smiled.

"So how come you've never told me you knew him?"

"It's a long story." She couldn't tell him that she insisted, long before BJ was born, that she didn't want JD mentioned by anyone. Mentioning him brought back too many painful memories of happier times. Her parents and Jess had reluctantly complied.

"So, I got all night."

"How about a shortened version? Mac and your dad were college roommates, rodeo buddies, and best friends. When we got married, Mac was your dad's best man, so when you were born, I named you after both your dad and Mac."

"That's where my middle name came from?" BJ's eyes widened at Stacey's revelation.

She nodded. "JD's first name is John."

"Cool."

"I'm sure that box has our wedding pictures in it, and Mac will be in those, too."

BJ sorted through the pictures in the box. "*Wow.*" He pulled out a white album and began thumbing through it. "You're right, Mom. What's this?" He held up the album and pointed to a picture. "Looks like somebody's getting carted off."

Stacey chuckled at the picture of her "kidnapping" the day of the wedding.

"Mac and one of the other groomsmen kidnapped me and held me for ransom. Your dad had to pass the hat and collect money from the wedding guests to get me back, and your Uncle Jess nearly got a black eye over it. Once your dad collected enough money, Mac brought me back safe and sound. Jess gave us the sack of money for our honeymoon."

"How much was it?"

"Oh, I don't remember. Close to $300, I think."

"Cool." BJ grinned. "So then what happened?"

"Well, we spent a few days at Mountain Valley Resort, then we moved to Oceanside near Camp Pendleton, where your dad was stationed. Mac was stationed at Pendleton, too, and the three of us spent a lot of time together. Mostly at the beach, where this picture was taken." Stacey hugged the picture to her. "Mac gave us this picture the Christmas before your dad died."

Swallowing the lump in her throat, Stacey realized she'd never completely get over the loss of JD's friendship any more than she'd get over Brian's death. JD had been someone she could talk to about anything. She missed him. She missed Brian. And she missed the carefree days the three of them shared.

"I'm sorry, Mom."

"It's okay, hon."

"It's okay if you don't want to talk about it."

"No, it's all right." Stacey took a deep breath. "The reason I've never mentioned Mac is because I haven't seen him since your dad died. We sort of lost touch. Too many memories, I guess. It was just easier for me to start over by leaving some things—people—behind."

She put her hand on her son's shoulder. "I'm sorry, BJ. Maybe I should have said something. Told you a little more about your dad's friends."

"Well," he smiled, "you're telling me now." He took the picture from Stacey. "Dad really looks happy in this picture."

"We were all happy then," Stacey answered. "And your dad was doing what he loved best, with the two people he loved the most."

"Surfing and you and Mac, right?"

"Right."

"So where did the name Sam come from?"

"That was Mac's nickname for me. Sam is a result of my initials. You know, Stacey Anne Murcheson. Mac decided since he and your dad both had nicknames, I needed one, too."

"Did Dad call you that?"

"No. Just Mac. Your dad called me Stace and Babe." Stacey rose and tousled BJ's hair. "Let's get some supper and finish this box later, okay?" She turned and wiped away the tears spilling onto her cheeks.

"Mom, I think we should put this picture out where we can see it. You and Dad look really happy in it. We can put it over on the piano with Grandma's and Grampa's, mine, and Uncle Jess and Aunt Lisa's pictures."

"Oh, I don't know..."

"Please, Mom. It's a great picture. And not because JD MacCord's in it. Because you and Dad look so neat in it."

Stacey looked at BJ, then at the picture. I wonder, she thought, if BJ will notice the resemblance between him and his father like I do. They look so much alike in that picture. Same smile and sparkle in their eyes. She nodded her head. He had a right to have his father's picture on display in the house. "Okay, if you can make room on the piano for it, go ahead."

"Thanks, Mom."

BJ rearranged the other pictures on the piano and placed the new picture in the middle. He stepped back and admired it for a minute.

"Mom, tell me about the things you guys used to do."

"There isn't much to tell, hon. What do you want to know?"

"I don't know. The funny things that used to happen. Maybe how Dad used to crash and burn when he was surfing. You know."

"Your dad seldom 'crashed and burned' as you so eloquently put it. By the time we got married, and I had a chance to watch him surf, he'd gotten quite adept at it. He said it was a lot like riding an ornery bull." Stacey smiled, remembering Brian's surfing technique.

"That's what I mean. Every time you talk about Dad, you tell me how proud he'd be of me, or how he'd expect me to act, or that he was brave, that he liked to surf and loved rodeos, but you never really talk about him—what he was *really* like." BJ sat in the middle of the floor and looked up at Stacey. "I want to know my dad."

221

Stacey sank to the floor opposite BJ and wondered, after so many years, how much she could tell him. "I'm sorry. It's just so hard for me to talk about him. I loved him and miss him very much, but I've needed to get on with my life, so I've tried, I guess, to put the memories behind me. You'll find a lot in the journal I gave you."

She noticed tears in her son's eyes and realized she had deprived him of something very precious. Taking a deep breath and wiping the tears from her eyes, she began telling BJ about Brian, from the time she first remembered him coming to the ranch, to when he died in Vietnam. She took extra care talking about JD and the friendship between the three of them.

BJ became so involved in Stacey's stories, and Stacey so engrossed in telling them, supper was forgotten, and they snacked on fruit, cheese, and crackers. Between them, they emptied a box of Kleenex tissues, and by the time Stacey talked herself out, it was well past midnight.

## Chapter 22

*November 1982--North Fork, Colorado*

*K*en Larsen sat at the kitchen table, watching Stacey as she finished clearing the last of the supper dishes. "Are you sure you don't want me to go with you?" he asked. "I can easily rearrange my appointments, and I don't have any court cases pending. Anything urgent Jess can take care of."

"I appreciate your offer, Ken, but this is something BJ and I have to do alone. Together." Stacey shut the door to the dishwasher, turned it on, and joined Ken at the table.

"I understand that, but I worry about the two of you in D.C. with thousands of other people. Who knows what might happen? Besides D.C. having a high crime rate, this dedication has sparked a lot of emotions. There could be trouble." He paused. "I promise I'll stay out of your way."

"We'll be all right." Stacey put her hand on Ken's. "How can I make you understand that this is a very private thing for BJ and me? We're not trying to exclude you. It's just that..." Stacey groped for a way to make him understand. He hadn't served in Vietnam. How could he possibly understand? Squeezing Ken's hand, she continued.

"There's just not room for you on this trip, Ken. Emotionally, I mean. I'm sorry."

"I won't pretend I completely understand, or that it doesn't hurt to be excluded. Emotional support is the one thing I can provide for you."

"I don't mean to hurt you, but BJ and I will have each other. I'm afraid you'll feel left out." Tears stung her eyes. "Please understand, Ken."

Ken stood and pulled Stacey into his arms. "I'm trying," he said. "Really, I am."

~

Stacey had difficulty controlling the butterflies in her stomach as the plane made its final approach to Washington National Airport. She hadn't ventured so far out of her safe little valley for a long time. The school generously allowed her a week of personal leave to attend the dedication of the Vietnam Veterans Memorial. Although late season for her volleyball team, she had complete confidence that her assistant coach could handle things in her absence. One weekend without her wouldn't hurt the team.

Stacey peered past BJ out the plane's window and caught a glimpse of the Potomac River and the nation's capital city. The minute she did, however, the butterflies increased their frenzied flight in her stomach. Leaning her head back against her seat, she closed her eyes and wondered for the hundredth time if JD would come for the dedication, and what she would do if she ran into him.

"Sure are a lot of people showin' up in D.C. last few days," the taxi driver remarked as he loaded Stacey's and BJ's luggage in the trunk. "Hope you already have reservations. Ain't a room to be had in the city, so I hear."

Stacey and BJ slipped into the back seat of the taxi. She was thankful she had made both her plane and hotel reservations far in advance. Stacey sat silently in the taxi, her arm around BJ. They cleared the airport congestion and were well on their way to the hotel, when the driver broke the silence.

"You here for the dedication?" he asked.

"Yes," Stacey answered and watched the out the side window.

"Someone you know serve in Nam?"

"My husband. He was killed in 1969."

"I'm sure sorry, ma'am. I'm a vet myself. Served in '70 and '71. Worst time of my life. All these years and we still don't get no respect. Well, maybe this memorial will change things. I'm tired of gettin' blamed for losin' a war."

Stacey glanced up and smiled at the face in the rearview mirror. "You didn't lose the war. The politicians did that for you. If you did your job while you were there, you have nothing to be ashamed of."

"You got that right. Hell, maybe I'll see you at the dedication. I lost some buddies in Nam, so I told my boss I was takin' the day off, and if he didn't like it, he could take the job and shove it."

"He must not have minded, since you're still working."

"Found out my boss is a vet, too. He'd never said nothin' before now. Small world, huh?"

"Small world."

When they arrived at the hotel, the taxi driver refused Stacey's money. "This one's on me, ma'am. Have a good visit."

Stacey and BJ planned to rise early the following morning. They had a lot of sightseeing to get in before the week's events. A Candlelight Vigil of Names was scheduled at Washington's National Cathedral from 10:00 a.m. Wednesday morning until midnight on Friday. The priests of the cathedral had prepared a small chapel, and volunteers were scheduled to read the names of those killed or missing in Vietnam in half-hour shifts, day and night, until all

58,000 names were read. Stacey received notice that Brian's name would be read on Thursday afternoon.

"Mom," BJ said over breakfast Wednesday morning, "one of the hotel guys told me we could visit the wall any time before the dedication. How come we're waiting?"

Stacey set her toast down and smiled at her son. "I'm not sure I can explain. I suppose a small part of me is very reluctant to see your father's name chiseled on a wall of granite." Stacey swallowed back a lump growing in her throat. "When I planned this trip, I wasn't sure when we'd go see the wall for the first time. But when I got notification about the candlelight vigil, it seemed appropriate to wait to see the wall after your dad's name is read. But if you'd like to go sooner, we can."

"No, it's okay. I just wondered."

Early Thursday afternoon, Stacey and BJ were ushered into a small chapel in the National Cathedral. Large, slow-burning candles stood at either end of the chapel. Only twelve rows of seats filled the small room. Stacey drank in the sweet aroma of red roses placed in the chapel. In the comforting silence, every breath could be heard and each footfall echoed in the high-ceilinged room.

They chose a place near the back to sit. Stacey and BJ planned to leave as soon as Brian's name was read, making room for others wanting to hear the names of loved ones who gave their lives for their country.

Stacey held BJ's hand, thankful he didn't try to object. She knew the gesture might embarrass him, but on this occasion, her almost thirteen-year-old son seemed to understand Stacey's need to have his hand in hers.

They listened quietly as the readers, standing at either side of the altar, began reading names, clearly and with deep emotion. Stacey noticed one of the readers was in uniform, wearing proudly the

Medal of Honor around his neck. As he began reading, his voice was strong, but after a few names, it became difficult for him to speak, and he finally broke down. Tears of empathy trickled down Stacey's cheeks, and she bit her lip to keep from sobbing out loud. Then, as she watched in awe, the proud veteran knelt and read the rest of the names on his knees. The last name he read reached Stacey's ears loud and clear. "Brian Foster Murcheson." Unable to control her emotions any longer, Stacey sobbed.

BJ put his arm around Stacey and patted her shoulder. "It's okay, Mom." Someone behind Stacey and BJ put a hand on each of their shoulders and squeezed in a silent gesture of comfort.

At the end of fifteen minutes, the readers paused to allow a few minutes of prayer. Before they began reading again, Stacey and BJ slipped quietly from the chapel. A gray, overcast sky greeted them, and a cold breeze nipped at the wetness on her cheeks. Stacey took a deep breath, shuddered, and for the first time, noticed the tears on BJ's face. She gathered him into her arms and held him tight.

Stacey's first sight of the wall took her breath away. A v-shaped black, polished granite monument spread before her, over ten feet high at the point where the corners met, then descending both directions to less than a foot high at each end. The top of the memorial was level with the ground behind it, a "wound in the earth, eventually healed by the grass" as its designer, Maya Ying Lin, described it.

Stacey could see the Washington Monument, trees, people, sky, grass and a myriad of colors reflected in the polished black granite of the wall. All sorts of mementos—pictures, flowers, unopened cigarette packs, empty combat boots, medals, and notes—cluttered the walkway along the panels.

BJ snapped several pictures with the camera he bought for the trip. Stacey absorbed the wall and its stark beauty. She had read that when it rained, the names on the wall disappeared, as though the wall wept. When warmed and dried by the sun, the names reappeared. As she examined the black granite and the numerous names etched into its surface, emotions of pride, regret, sorrow, and loss overwhelmed her. She fought back tears as she and BJ approached the wall.

Together, they located the panel representing the year 1969 and scanned the black granite slab in search of Brian's name. BJ spotted it first.

"Look, Mom, there it is. About half way down." He pointed toward the wall.

Stacey's eyes rested on the capital letters that formed Brian's name. Oblivious to everyone around her and guided by an unseen force, Stacey stepped closer and placed her fingertips on Brian's name, her hand meeting its own reflection, giving life to the silent stone. Tears spilled onto her cheeks, and she bit her lip.

Her fingers lingered for a moment, then she moved aside to give BJ room. Stacey stood behind him, watching proudly his reflected image and gripping his shoulders as he touched Brian's name. He stepped back and snapped another picture.

"Are you related to Lieutenant Murcheson?"

The question startled Stacey. She turned toward the voice, not knowing what to expect. A man about Stacey's age nodded and smiled at her.

"You knew Brian?" she asked him.

His eyes clouded, and he looked away from Stacey toward the wall. "He saved my life," he said. After a moment he continued. "I was flying Lt. Murcheson and several new grunts in-country when we were hit by enemy fire." He cleared his throat and sucked in a deep breath. "Your husband carried me to safety. My left arm and leg were hit by shrapnel and I couldn't move."

Stacey noticed a scarred left hand. Looking back at the wall, she said, "Brian was my husband and this is our son, BJ. Brian died before he knew about his son." She gripped BJ's shoulders a little tighter.

"I'm sorry to hear that." The veteran extended his hand to Stacey. "Carl Wilson," he said. "I'm proud to meet you."

"Stacey Murcheson," she replied, but instead of shaking hands with him, Stacey put her arms around him and hugged him, tears streaming down her cheeks.

When they broke the embrace, Carl shook BJ's hand. "I'm pleased to meet you, too, BJ." He struggled through his next few words. "I've been coming to the wall every day this week, hoping to meet the relatives of the men I knew who were killed. I especially hoped to meet the family of the man who saved my life. My prayer has been answered." He paused, gaining control before speaking again. "My two crew members who died that day are on this panel, too."

He showed Stacey and BJ the names of the gunner and co-pilot. Silence followed as the three of them read the names, their own images reflecting back.

"Mom, where's the paper and crayon?"

Stacey retrieved the requested items from her purse. She and Carl held the edges of the paper, while BJ rubbed the crayon back and forth across Brian's name. When he was done, he carefully folded the paper and put it in his jacket pocket.

"I'd like a picture of you and Mom, Mr. Wilson, if you don't mind."

"Not at all. And call me Carl. Please."

After BJ snapped the picture, Stacey took one of Carl and BJ.

After visiting a few minutes longer, Carl turned to leave, hesitated, and turned toward Stacey and BJ.

"I had trouble, at first, getting my life on track after I got home from Nam," he said. "I spent a lot of time feeling sorry for myself. I couldn't deal with my injuries and the possibility of losing the use of my arm and hand. My leg alone took months of painful rehabilitation to make it useful again. There were many days when I wished your husband had left me to die with my crew."

His voice cracked, and he looked away for a moment. "But time, and God, have a way of healing. One day I realized that by feeling sorry for myself I was spitting in the face of the man who gave his life for mine. I realized if his sacrifice was to mean anything, I had to do something worthwhile with my life.

"After several surgeries, I began months of physical therapy on my hand and arm. Like my leg, I was determined to be able to use them again. A lot of guys couldn't."

He took a deep breath. "I eventually flew a helicopter again. My family thought I was crazy, but I knew I wasn't. It took a couple of trips just to get over my fear of being in a chopper again, but I overcame that." He smiled. "I fly an air life helicopter for a hospital in Denver. Have for several years now. It's good to know I'm doing my part in saving lives. I wanted you to know, Stacey, so that you know your husband's sacrifice meant something."

His gaze returned to the wall for several long moments. Stacey waited, her own emotions in turmoil. When he looked at Stacey and BJ again, he had regained his composure. A slight smile tugged at his mouth. "You two take care, now, and God bless." Before Stacey could respond, he walked away, a noticeable limp in his stride.

"God bless you, too," she said.

~

Stacey awoke at 5:00 a.m. on Saturday to the steady rhythm of rain beating against the window of their room. She tried to go back to sleep, but found it impossible. When she emerged from the shower a little after six, the rain had stopped, but the clouds remained.

Instead of trying to fight the crowds at the parade, Stacey and BJ made their way early to Constitution Gardens and the sight of the memorial. They took up their positions opposite Brian's panel and next to the ropes erected to keep the crowds away from the memorial during the dedication. Hundreds of people were already milling about.

By the time the dedication ceremonies began at 2:00 p.m., the grass and hillsides all around the memorial were a sea of humanity. Stacey clutched BJ's hand all through the numerous speeches of dedication, dropping it only long enough to wipe her eyes or blow her nose.

Stacey barely choked out the first few notes of "God Bless America" as the crowd began to sing at the end of the ceremonies, but to her surprise, her voice became stronger with each note. She ended the song with a strong voice, pride in her heart, and tears streaming down her face.

After a moment of silence, Jan Scruggs, the Vietnam infantryman whose dream had become reality, declared, "Ladies and gentlemen, the Vietnam Veterans Memorial is now dedicated."

Stacey and BJ stood again in front of Brian's name and touched it, this time also touching the names of the two crewmen who died with him. When three veterans walked up and touched Brian's name, Stacey asked, "Did you know my husband, Lt. Murcheson?"

They turned at her question and smiled. "We served proudly in his unit," one said. Another commented, "He was one hell of an officer." Each one, in turn, grabbed Stacey and hugged her, then

231

shook hands with BJ as he was introduced. Although Stacey thought she had exhausted all her tears, they flowed freely.

While the three veterans talked about Brian and told BJ what a fine man his father was, Carl Wilson joined them. Stacey introduced everyone, and BJ insisted on more pictures. In order to make room for others, the six of them left the wall together, finding a spot where they could sit in view of the wall and visit.

"Our unit had one of the lowest casualty rates," one of the vets, named Alex, related. "The Lieutenant had us well prepared for Nam. We were lucky to serve under him. He knew what he was doing and took an active role in our training. I remember a few times during those grueling months at Pendleton I wanted to clobber him he rode us so hard. But he taught us to survive. We were dumbfounded at the news that he'd died returning in-country."

Carl recounted the incident that took Brian's life. They chuckled a little when Carl told them about Brian referring to him as a football and that carrying him to safety was no different than making a touchdown on the kickoff. "I'm sure as hell glad he didn't fumble," Carl said, remembering Brian's words.

Each of the men, in turn, shared stories about Brian. Some were funny, others poignant, but all gave Stacey and BJ a new insight into Brian, the soldier and leader.

As the sun sank in the west, the three men who served with Brian invited Stacey, BJ, and Carl to have dinner with them. Stacey accepted and agreed to meet them later. Exhaustion from the day's events had set in, and she wanted to rest before going out that evening.

At dinner, the six new friends talked about their present lives and what they were doing. It was a relief to put the past behind them for a while, but before long the conversation found its way back to Vietnam. Each man expressed bitterness over the war, its length, and the lack of support they felt from the American people. In spite of their regrets over Vietnam, they still loved their country and believed in its future.

Stacey ignored BJ's normal curfew, realizing that what he learned about the Vietnam War, his father, and the men who knew him was too important for him to miss. History books, she knew, would never match the firsthand accounts he heard from the four Vietnam veterans.

At midnight, one of the men in Brian's unit stood and raised his glass. "To Lt. Brian Murcheson, a fine soldier, a good friend, a husband, and a father. We miss you." All at the table stood and drank a toast, then sat in silence for a few minutes, unwilling to admit to the tears glistening in their eyes.

"With the exception of today," Alex, one of the four said, breaking the uncomfortable silence, "the last time I saw you guys with such big tears in your eyes was the Christmas before we lost the Lieutenant."

He took a long swallow of beer before continuing. Staring into his beer and fighting the moisture in his own eyes, he recalled, for Carl and BJ's benefit, Christmas of 1968 and the Colorado blue spruce that arrived for Brian, decorations included.

"You can't imagine what that meant to all of us," he said to Stacey. "It made home so much closer. For the first time in my life, I wasn't ashamed of crying." A tear escaped, and he wiped it away with the back of his hand. "That tree touched my heart like no other gift I can remember, and it wasn't even for me. Even the Lieutenant had tears in his eyes." The veteran smiled. "He said it was just an allergy to pine trees, but we all knew better. We let him get away with it, though, because we knew he hated showing any kind of weakness."

Alex stood and declared, "Every time I've decorated a Christmas

233

tree since then, I think of that tree and what it meant to a bunch of guys so far from home. Here's to you, Mrs. M." Raising his glass of beer, he saluted Stacey, and the others at the table stood and joined him.

At one in the morning, Stacey and BJ said their good-byes, the address of each veteran tucked into her purse. Carl insisted on seeing Stacey and BJ safely to their hotel. Unable to fall asleep right away, Stacey packed for the return trip home, then sat by the window and wished for a clear, starry Colorado sky.

"Oh, Brian, I miss you," she whispered. "How wonderful to know you were so well respected and loved. I'm so proud of you. You made a difference in this world." She closed her eyes to hold back the tears and fell asleep in the chair.

# PART III

## Sam's Song

I stare at a photo,
Three friends from the heart.
Two are missing,
Why did we part?

Death stalks the young;
Love betrays trust;
Love overcomes guilt if God is just.

I stare at a photo,
Three friends took flight.
One gone forever;
One fled in the night.

Time separates lovers
Fate made us part.
Only a green-eyed lass can heal my heart.

JD McCord

## Chapter 23

*February 5, 1985—Carmel Valley, California*

*W*iping his sweaty palms on his Levi's, JD waited for the director to approve the lighting setups. He wished he hadn't agreed to the interview. He made a habit of avoiding personal interviews, and this would be his first allowing any questions other than those related to his work.

Jacqueline insisted that his Oscar nomination made it imperative that he let Barbara Walters "have a shot at him." For a moment, he questioned his decision seven years ago to hire Jacqueline as his personal assistant. He glanced at her watching from behind the camera. She gave him a thumbs up. He began plotting a way to get even.

Earlier in the day, JD had given Ms. Walters and her cameraman a tour of his hundred-acre ranch, ending with his home. For the tour, he was in control.

He watched as the makeup girl applied a last-minute touchup to Ms. Walters and reminded himself that when the interview began, Ms. Walters had the upper hand. She could be charming and unpredictable in her questions, and he would have to be sharp and ready for anything.

The thought produced beads of perspiration on his brow. He dabbed at the moisture with his hand and glanced at Ms. Walters. She smiled.

"Relax JD. This isn't as hard as making a movie."

"Worse." He grinned. "With movies, I'm prepared. This is unfamiliar territory. I can't say 'cut' whenever I want."

"We'll make it as pain-free as possible. The interview will air the night of the Oscars. I'll add an introduction, which will include the fact that here at the ranch you and a partner raise Quarter Horses for use in movies and rodeos. We'll edit in the tour of the ranch as a background to the introduction. Some parts of the interview may become narrative or be deleted completely to fit the allotted time. Right now we'll just start with questions and go from there."

"Whatever you say."

The closer they got, however, to the actual taping, the greater the urge to call it off. But he had agreed, and he wouldn't go back on his word.

The director gave the signal and the interview began. JD took a deep breath and leaned back in his chair, trying to relax as much as possible, his legs crossed, his forearms resting on the arms of the chair and his hands dangling loose over the ends.

Ms. Walters fired her first question. "You keep to yourself, and until now, you've refused to do any in-depth personal interviews. Why?"

"I think it's important to separate my private life from my professional life."

"But your fans are hungry for any information about you. Why not let them know who you are?"

JD smiled. "Because no interview will ever completely reveal the real me. I owe my fans my best work. I owe them quality performances. That's what they pay for. My private life should be just that. Private."

"To some you're a hero. Bigger than life."

"I find it odd that, based solely on my work, I can have such an impact on people." He shrugged. "I'm an ordinary guy who tells lies for a living. That hardly qualifies me as a hero."

"People believe in your characters and relate the real you to those characters. Are you those characters?"

"I suppose a tiny part of me is projected into each character, but every character I've played is far from who I really am."

"When you were growing up, did you have dreams of becoming an actor?"

"Far from it. My world was made up of working on my folks' ranch and going to school, with football, baseball, and rodeos thrown in to keep me out of trouble."

"You'll be forty in June."

He winced. "Don't remind me."

"Any regrets?"

He frowned. "Some."

"Such as..."

"Let's not go there."

Ms. Walters smiled. "We all have regrets. Tell me one."

JD returned her smile. "My regrets are personal and have nothing to do with my professional career."

"You're sure you won't tell me?"

"I'm sure."

"When you were eighteen, where did you expect to be at this point in your life?"

"Teaching...and ranching."

"Do you regret not doing that?"

"Sometimes." He looked past her, a faraway look in his eyes. "Life would certainly be simpler."

"Your first role was as a rodeo cowboy in the film *Bronco Busters*."

JD chuckled. "Where'd you dig that up?"

She smiled. "I have my sources. You're listed in the credits."

"It was filmed near my hometown in New Mexico, and they were looking for extras and stunt men to ride broncs." He shook his head. "I had one line in that film, so I was listed as one of the actors. I'm not even sure I remember the line."

"I believe the line was something like 'Go gettem' Rusty, you're due.'"

"You did your homework. The film didn't do well, but I was fascinated with the process. That's when the bug bit me."

"That break opened the door for a part on the soap opera *Another Day*."

"Not quite. You make it sound so easy. When I did *Bronco Busters,* I'd just mustered out of the Marines, and I found it difficult to settle back into ranching with my Dad. I was doing a little substitute teaching, but I was restless. So I signed up as an extra. When they were through filming, I headed for Los Angeles. No job, just a lot of high hopes."

JD cleared his throat and continued. "Growing up on a ranch you learn to be a carpenter, electrician, mechanic, and just about anything else you can't afford to pay someone else to do, so I sold those abilities to one of the studios. Then I signed up for some acting classes."

"Is that how you landed the job on *Another Day?*"

"My acting instructor recommended me to a friend of hers who was working as a writer for the show." JD lifted his hands in a half-shrug. "I auditioned and got the part."

"When you took the role as Dirk, did you know the character would be written out of the show?"

He smiled. "That's why I took the part."

"The producers offered to continue your character indefinitely. You turned them down."

"I didn't want to get stuck doing a soap opera. The part of Dirk was for experience only."

"You did the primetime show *Streets of L.A.* for only a year before leaving that series."

"You spend too much time in a role, you not only run the risk of being typecast, but it's very easy to stagnate. From the beginning I had my sights set on doing movies."

Ms. Walters smiled. "It's very unusual for actors to successfully make the switch from television to movies. Why do you think you were successful?"

"I made the jump before I became too well known as a television actor. I wasn't the only star of *Streets*. That made it easy for me to leave."

"Your big break came when you played a supporting role in the award winning film, *Back Alley*. Did you know when you were doing that film it would be so successful?"

JD leaned forward, putting more weight on his arms, uncrossing his legs. "When doing a part you can really sink your teeth into, you hope it will be recognized as quality work. I was lucky with *Back Alley*. It was a great story with a top-notch cast and director. I learned a great deal from everyone involved in that film."

She nodded. "And the rest, as they say, is history. You went on to do several leading roles for major studios, then formed your own production company—starring, directing, and producing most of your films since. You're considered America's number one box office attraction. Some very good actors work all their lives and never accomplish what you have, and in such a short time."

"Like I said, I've been lucky, and I've had very few distractions along the way." JD glanced at the floor, then back at Barbara. "I try not to take myself too seriously. The work, but not myself."

Leaning back, he continued. "I make films because I enjoy it. There's nothing more satisfying than to take a project from beginning to end, with total control over the finished product. When I stop enjoying the process, then I'll quit. Working hard and producing a quality film is the reward."

He licked his dry lips and waited for the next question. He was pleased the questions had centered on his work and hoped that continued.

"I'm sure the monetary reward is also quite satisfying. It's rumored you're one of the wealthiest people in the entertainment industry."

JD frowned. He didn't like talking about money, particularly his. "The money is secondary. It's the work that counts. I've never needed a lot of things, so money has never been my goal. Hard work and a quality product, that's what counts, and that's what growing up on a ranch taught me."

"You support numerous charities and educational projects and scholarships that help young people."

"Barbara, I was always taught to share with those less fortunate than myself. I do what I can. I can't cure all the world's ills, but I can share what I have."

She leaned forward in her chair. "Why do you guard your private life so carefully?" When he didn't respond, she added, "You're extremely selective with industry social events. Some say you don't like the Hollywood elite."

"I'm not particularly comfortable in crowds or hobnobbing with people. It's nothing personal." JD shifted in his chair.

Ms. Walters leaned back in her chair, and her voice softened. "You married for the first and only time in 1979 to Sabrina Branson. Two years later you were divorced. Since then, you've had no personal involvements. No one special, that we know of."

He squinted at her. *She changes her mind faster than a bucking bronc,* he thought. He ignored the comment.

"*Is* there someone special in your life?"

"No."

"There are many who say you were terribly hurt and disillusioned over your marriage to Sabrina."

"You believe everything you hear, Barbara?" JD tried to smile, but the result was more of a grimace.

"Not everything. But at the time of your divorce, rumors circulated that Sabrina married you only to advance her own career. When you found out, that was the end of the marriage."

"What happened between us is private."

"Was she that cold-hearted?"

"You're not going to let this rest, are you?"

"No. Sabrina said you were unfaithful. Now is your chance to defend yourself. Set the record straight."

JD had no intention of maligning Sabrina. "Sabrina was young and trusting, and I let her down."

"Are you saying you were unfaithful?"

"No." JD sighed and rubbed his hand through his hair. "I just tried to make her someone she wasn't."

"And who was that?"

"Try another question."

Ms. Walters raised her eyebrows. "You won't tell me? Come on, all America wants to know."

He frowned. *If she doesn't back off, I will cancel the interview right now, word or not.*

She tried another tack. "Do you think you'll ever find the right woman?"

JD's eyes clouded. "I've been successful at everything but romantic relationships. One too many ghosts in my past."

"We're not talking about Sabrina, are we?"

"No."

"This 'ghost' from your past...she hurt you."

"We hurt each other. It was a long time ago and best left in the past."

"Do you regret not having children?"

"Yes." JD looked away from her. "Some things are just not meant to be."

"That sounds so final."

"That's life. It doesn't always turn out the way we expect it to." JD shrugged. "I've learned to accept it."

He gave Barbara a cold stare, hoping to convey to her to try another line of questioning far removed from his painful personal life. She did. Or so he thought. He was unprepared for where her next few questions led.

"You helped build this beautiful home. Much of the finish work and furniture are your work—the dining room table and chairs and the oak desk in your office."

"Yes. Woodworking is therapeutic. Something I enjoy."

"It shows. Your work is exquisite. Tell me about the photograph sitting on that beautiful oak desk in your office. Three smiling young people at the beach. One of them is you. Who are the other two?"

JD shifted in his chair, turning slightly sideways and crossing one leg over the other. He hadn't expected the question about the picture with the juniper frame. If he ignored the question or refused to answer, she might get suspicious and push in a direction he didn't want to go.

"The picture is of me, my best friend, and his wife. He died in Vietnam in '69." He hoped his answer would satisfy her.

"You also served in Vietnam."

"Yes."

"Tell me about it."

At her simple request, JD realized how much he wanted to talk about Vietnam. It was time veterans like him spoke sincerely and honestly about the controversial war and the toll it exacted.

"My friend, Brian, and I joined the Marines right after we graduated from college. We felt it was our duty to serve our country." He paused. "Like all young men, we had an idealistic view of war and what it was about."

"How did you feel about our country's involvement?"

"After Korea, our leaders believed that Vietnam was our next best stand against Communism. But after Korea, we should have learned. Vietnam changed completely the way people perceive our government and its policies." He shifted to sit straight in his chair again.

"What was it like for you as a soldier?"

"Difficult at best. My tour ended just before the Tet Offensive." He raised his arms, allowing his elbows to rest on the arms of the chair, his hands meshed together in front of him.

"There's still a lot of bitterness over Vietnam," she prompted.

"In the end, it was very disillusioning." JD cleared his throat. "I still believe strongly in patriotism and serving my country, but the Vietnam War was wrong. We were committed so we went. It wasn't the dissension across the country that bothered me so much. That was necessary to make the politicians come to their senses.

"What hurt," he said and swallowed, "was the lack of support for the soldiers who were doing their best, and the lack of respect afforded them when they came home. My friend was spit on and called a murderer." His voice cracked, and he paused long enough to regain control of his voice. "During his second tour, he gave his life to save seven others."

Ms. Walters gave him a moment, then asked, "Do you think attitudes have changed in the last few years?"

"A little. The Vietnam Veterans Memorial did a great deal to heal many of the emotional wounds caused by the war. For veterans, particularly. That, and time, will eventually make a difference."

"Did you go to the dedication?"

"No. I was in the middle of filming, and we ran into some production problems. I couldn't leave, so I visited the following week. It worked out for the best. My visit was private."

"Your friend's name is on the wall."

"Yes." The memory of seeing and touching Brian's name was quite vivid, and dealing with his death was still difficult.

"Are you bitter over his death and the deaths of so many others?"

JD pondered the question a moment, then leaned forward in his chair. "The picture I was working on at the time of the dedication had a Vietnamese technician. He found out I was a Vietnam veteran and had visited the memorial. When I returned to resume work on the picture he approached me, and with tears in his eyes he thanked me for fighting for him and his freedom. He apologized for the agony and difficulties the war had caused the American soldiers and our country. Am I bitter? No. Do I have regrets? Many."

"I think we all do," she said, tears in her eyes. "Thank you for sharing that. I think it gives us all something to think about."

JD nodded in answer and hoped Ms. Walters would change the subject back to his career. He was grateful when she did.

"You've been nominated for an Oscar for your portrayal of a drifter caught in the middle of a range war in *Wind River Wars.* Your performance has been described as, and I quote, 'understated and brilliant.' Are you going to win?"

JD chuckled, relieved to have the conversation return to his work. "I doubt it." He let his hands drop to hang over the ends of the chair arms.

"Why not?"

"For starters, this is my first nomination. Few people win their first time out. And I've got some hefty competition. Jeff Bridges and Sam Waterston, not to mention Albert Finney. All three have been in this business longer than I have, and deserve it far more than I do. And F. Murray Abraham's performance in *Amadeus* was brilliant."

"Does that mean you think Mr. Abraham will win?"

"I never predict. I'm usually wrong, anyway."

"Where does JD MacCord go from here?"

"I continue to do what I do best and enjoy most—make movies."

"If all of this ended tomorrow and you were unable to make any more movies, unable to direct or act again, what would you do?"

JD smiled. He liked the question. "Barbara, I've had a good run. I won't deny that I've enjoyed every minute of it. But if it all ended tomorrow, I'd go back to ranching and maybe even teach a little. That's where your real heroes are found. I could be happy doing that the rest of my life."

## Chapter 24

*I*n his office, JD contemplated the framed photograph he held in his hands. Three carefree faces smiled back at him. He rubbed his thumbs along the polished juniper frame, remembering the day he gave one exactly like it to Stacey.

"Don't you think you've been spending entirely too much time staring at that picture lately?"

Unaware Jacqueline had entered his office, JD looked up to see her frowning at him. He set the picture back in its permanent spot on his desk and returned the frown.

Holding the thumb and first finger of his right hand about an inch apart, he said. "Do you know you came this close to getting fired over the Barbara Walters interview?"

She laid a stack of folders on his desk and sat opposite him. "You didn't answer my question," she said.

"You're changing the subject."

"You'd never fire me. I'm the only person you can really trust to handle your personal affairs. And I know all your secrets." She winked at him and smiled. "Besides, I thought the interview went quite well."

"You think so? I thought I said too much."

"Jack thought you did great."

"What does Jack know? He's just a banker." JD smiled.

"He's your friend and business manager, and my husband. He's always honest with both of us."

"It got too personal."

"It was supposed to. You knew going in Barbara would get personal. It's about time you let people know a little bit about you. It keeps them interested and sells tickets to your movies."

"I'm not in this business for the money. If I didn't enjoy doing what I do, I wouldn't do it."

"You still haven't answered my question, and no more avoiding the subject."

"What question?"

Jacqueline frowned at him and tapped her fingernails on the arm of her chair.

"It reminds me of happier times."

"It reminds you of what you lost." Jacqueline leaned forward in her chair. "The two people who mattered most to you. Isn't it about time you connected with Stacey again?"

"She told me to stay away. I have." He stood and stepped to the window behind his desk. Shoving his hands in the hip pockets of his Levi's, he stared across the expansive rose garden that began beneath the window and stretched a hundred feet toward a small pond.

"That was a long time ago, and she was understandably confused," Jacqueline said.

"I'm sure she's happily married with a dozen kids by now. I don't need to mess up her life again. Or mine."

"And she's probably fat and ugly and impossible to live with. For heaven's sake, JD, the only way you're going to know is to look her up and find out for yourself. You're never going to get on with your life until you exercise this ghost you're carrying around inside of you."

JD turned from the window and looked at Jacqueline for a moment. "You're not giving in on this, are you?"

She shook her head. "It's time, JD. You need to know one way or another. Not knowing is eating you up."

JD sat in his chair and leaned back. "Okay, Jacqueline, you win." He rubbed his hand through his hair. "But I'll do it on my terms. I want you to find a private investigator that will be discreet and do the investigation himself. I don't want anyone else involved."

Jacqueline took notes as JD talked. A small, almost imperceptible smile crossed her lips.

JD continued. "I want to know where she is, what she's doing, and if she's married. I want to know everything that's happened to her since she left Oceanside in '69. I don't want pictures or descriptions, only facts. Money's no object. I will pay for any reasonable expenses plus a bonus if the job's done right. He can start in North Fork, Colorado. I'm sure her parents still live there. Her maiden name was Atkins." He leaned forward and rested his arms on the desk. "Now, are you happy?"

"Ecstatic. No pictures?"

"I don't want to be influenced by the way she looks now."

"Okay. I'll get right on this. Jack has some pretty good contacts in the private investigators' field. The person we hire won't even have to know it's for you. I'll request a written report." She stood and turned to go. "Anything else, *boss?*"

"Yeah. How're the kids?"

"Making me crazy. I don't think I'll be ready when Jack Jr. starts driving in two years. He's already hounding us about the kind of car he wants. And Angelica has discovered boys. I don't think I'm ready for either one of these stages."

"You'll handle everything just fine. You always do, Jacqueline. You're the most competent person I know. Jack and Angelica are lucky to have you for a mother." He grinned.

"You have far more confidence in me than I do," Jacqueline said. She walked to the door, paused, and turned toward him. "You're doing the right thing, JD. It shouldn't take too long to get a report back. In the meantime, you have some papers and screenplays to go over. They're in the folders on your desk. Happy reading."

### *March 25, 1985--North Fork, Colorado*

In Colorado, the Barbara Walters Special aired after the Oscars and the local news. With a generous supply of Coke and popcorn, Stacey and Ken watched the Oscars and then the special together. BJ opted to spend the evening with his friends—Rick, Jake, and Cam—and planned to sleep over at Jake's.

Stacey tried to hide her disappointment when JD lost the Oscar to F. Murry Abraham, but a few tears managed to slither down her cheeks. She was relieved Ken pretended not to notice.

JD's interview was the last one to air. During the interview, Ken held Stacey's hand, and when JD talked about Brian and Vietnam, Stacey's tears flowed freely. Ken put his arm around her shoulders, offering silent comfort.

When the program ended, Stacey turned off the television and carried her empty glass to the kitchen. The interview left her in turmoil. JD's comment that "we hurt each other" kept replaying in her thoughts. Setting her glass in the sink, she gripped the edge of the counter and breathed deeply. Ken set the empty popcorn bowl on the counter and put his hand at the back of Stacey's neck underneath the clasp securing her long hair.

"Want to talk about it, honey?" he asked.

"No. I'll be all right in a minute."

Ken pulled her into his arms and held her. After a few minutes he gently pushed her away from him. "I think you do need to talk about it. You'll feel better and so will I." He smiled at her and guided her back to the living room.

Stacey sat on the couch and wondered how to start and what to say. Ken solved her problem.

"I know JD MacCord was an old friend of you and Brian. But I think there's more to it than that. Tell me about him."

Stacey bit her lip, trying to think of what to say. "He was," Stacey said, "more like a brother to Brian than a best friend. He was at our apartment or doing things with us as often as he could. The three of us had great times together. He and Brian were practically inseparable. At least until Brian's second tour.

"After Brian shipped out, JD checked on me weekly to be sure I was all right. I know Brian asked him to watch over me, though JD wouldn't admit it. When someone at the base suggested he might be making a play for me, he stopped coming around to the apartment. We both knew nothing was going on, but he didn't want idle gossip to ruin my reputation."

Stacey took a deep breath. "When Brian died, JD provided the strength I needed to get through everything. He was a rock, even though he was hurting, too." Stacey closed her eyes and leaned her head back. "The interview made me realize that he is still deeply affected by Brian's death."

Ken took hold of Stacey's hand. "It sounds like he was a very good friend. One you loved."

Stacey frowned at Ken, trying to hide the uneasiness she felt at his comment. "I don't know what you mean."

Ken looked at their hands. "Friends like that don't come along every day. I assume you miss him. You couldn't help but miss such a good friend. How did you lose touch?"

"It just happened," she said. "Once I moved back to Colorado, I got so busy trying to put my life back together that I just lost touch. I'm sure the same thing happened with JD."

"Did he know about BJ?"

Stacey pushed back the building panic that surfaced with each of Ken's questions. She hated lying, but she couldn't let Ken know the truth. It would serve no practical purpose, and she doubted he would understand. She still didn't completely understand herself. She only knew JD was a part of her past. Someone she'd never see again. She was even more convinced of that after hearing his comments during the interview.

"No. I never wrote him after I came home," she answered. "I figured he didn't need to be worrying about me and my life. He had a life of his own to get on with. Besides, he knew where I lived if he wanted to get in touch with me." She knew he hadn't wanted to.

"What you're saying doesn't make sense, Stacey. If he was such a good friend—"

"It was a long time ago, Ken, and we were very young."

"He talked so candidly about Brian in the interview. Maybe you ought to try to get in touch with him," Ken suggested. "I'm sure he'd like to meet BJ."

Stacey walked to the piano and picked up the picture of her, Brian, and JD. "I'm sure the picture Barbara Walters referred to in the interview was a lot like this. But this represents the friendship the three of us had. Brian was the common denominator, and he's gone. There's no reason to dredge up the past, for either of us." She returned the picture to its place on the piano.

Ken joined her and took her in his arms. "I think you still have feelings for JD."

Stacey slipped her arms around Ken's neck. "Of course I do. He'll always have a very special place in my heart, but only a tiny corner. What's left of it is completely yours—lock, stock, and barrel." Stacey rested her head against Ken's shoulder. "Thank you for understanding what I was going through tonight. That means so much to me."

Ken leaned back and placed his hands on either side of Stacey's head. "I love you very much, Stacey, and I want to share your life. Everything. The past, the hurts, the joys. All of it. Your past is what makes you who you are, and I love every tiny little bit of who you are. But I get the feeling you're leaving something out."

"Oh, Ken, I love you. Let's keep the past where it belongs. You're my future, and I want to concentrate on that."

Stacey realized even as she spoke the words of love to Ken, she still loved Brian and JD. Admitting her feelings for JD frightened her. She'd tried so hard over the years to purge her love for him, a love that lurked in the recesses of her heart, always waiting, and surfacing at the most unexpected times. But that love had betrayed Brian, leaving her with an unforgivable guilt.

The interview left her unsettled. JD hadn't mentioned her name, but she knew she was the "ghost" in his past—the woman who hurt him. Abandoning him instead of facing what happened was the coward's way out. Her guilt drove her away. But she couldn't reach into the past and fix what had gone wrong; the past was best forgotten.

Stacey lay awake that night, wondering what she would say to JD if she ever saw him again. No matter how many different ways she imagined saying, "I'm sorry," none of them seemed adequate. She fell asleep just before dawn convinced she'd never have the chance to apologize and thankful she wouldn't have to face the hatred and hurt in JD's eyes for what she had done.

~

### March 29, 1985--Carmel Valley, California

Jacqueline entered JD's office. After reminding him of his appointments for the following day, she handed him several notes concerning phone calls he needed to make, and then set a medium-sized manila envelope on the desk in front of him.

He looked up from the notes and frowned. "What's this?"

"The written report from the private investigator. He delivered it to Jack early this morning."

JD placed his hand on the envelope, afraid of what it might hold. Not quite two months had passed since he'd made the decision to find out about Stacey. He hadn't expected a report so soon.

"I'll make sure you're not disturbed." Jacqueline closed the door behind her.

JD picked up the envelope and leaned back in his chair, resting his right foot on his left knee. He stared at the envelope, afraid to open it. His hand shook as he removed the contents. He picked up the first page and set the remaining pages on his lap. His gaze lingered on the first line for a moment before he read on.

> *SUBJECT: Stacey Anne Atkins Murcheson*
> *ADDRESS: Rural Route 1, North Fork, Colorado 81414*
> *MARITAL STATUS: Married Brian Foster Murcheson, June 1968— Deceased March 1969;*
> *Married John Michael Axtel, August 1973—Divorced June 1974*
> *CHILDREN: One son, Brian John Murcheson (BJ); Born—December 30, 1969*

JD shot forward in his chair, spilling the envelope and its contents on the floor except for the sheet he held in his hand. He read the line listing *CHILDREN*, focusing in on the birth date. He counted the months between March and December on his free hand, then sank slowly against the chair back.

"It can't be," he whispered. "She would have told me. Wouldn't she?" He read the name again. Brian John. "Brian's middle name was Foster. I used to tease him about having two last names." JD leaned his head against the back of the chair and closed his eyes. "John is *my* first name. Could he be my son?"

## Chapter 25

*A*s he took a deep breath, JD pressed his fingers against his tear-stung eyes. The possibility that he had a son shook him as no other news could have. He gathered up the papers that had fallen on the floor and began to read. An hour later, he called Jacqueline into the office.

"Have you read this report?" he asked.

"No. It was for your eyes only. No one else has seen it. Why? Has something happened to Stacey?"

"Here," he said and thrust the papers toward Jacqueline. "Read for yourself."

JD paced the floor while Jacqueline read, stopping several times to stare out the window. Too many memories of Stacey crowded his thoughts. His head hurt. After reading the report, he knew a trip to North Fork was imperative. He mulled over scenario after scenario about how he would approach her; how he would handle seeing her again; what reason he might have for being in North Fork other than to see her.

When Jacqueline finished reading, she set the report on the desk. "A lot has happened in the last sixteen years."

JD sat down and leaned his arms on the desk. "It's possible BJ is my son, isn't it?"

Before Jacqueline could answer, JD said, "She was with Butch the first part of March. I was with her the last part. BJ wasn't born until December 30th. It's more than possible, right?"

"It's possible," Jacqueline answered. "But it's also possible he's Butch's son. Babies don't always come on time. Jack Jr. was a week past his due date."

"But this would be about three weeks if he's Butch's son." JD leaned back in his chair, the framed picture on his desk taunting him. "If you were recently widowed, had been with a man that wasn't your husband, and suddenly found yourself pregnant, what would you do?"

"That's not a fair question, JD. I'm not Stacey."

"Then what do you think Sam would do?"

"Considering the circumstances, I think she'd probably convince herself the baby was Brian's. And she certainly wouldn't have any other choice than to list him as the father on the birth certificate. Too much explaining any other way."

"But if she thought the baby was mine, would she have told me, even though she wanted me out of her life?"

"I think Stacey is the only one who can answer your questions."

"I know." JD stood and walked to the window. He watched the wind whispering through the trees, and thought of the night, so long ago, when he and Stacey had made love. It seemed as real as if it happened yesterday. She told him she loved him. But in a matter of hours she was gone. Her note said she had made a mistake and that she couldn't forgive him. Could she forgive him now?

He heard Jacqueline open the door and turned from the window. "Don't go just yet," he said.

"I thought you wanted to be alone."

"In a minute. There are some things I need you to do."

Jacqueline returned to her chair and opened her notebook.

"Jack's always after me to invest in more real estate. Contact a real estate agent in North Fork. I think it's time I bought myself a small ranch in Colorado. I've been thinking about getting back into cattle ranching. After all these years, I miss it. North Fork would be a good place. When he has some good prospects for me to look at, let me know. Let's keep this quiet. The world doesn't need to know I'm looking."

"Do you want to sell this place?"

"No. I'm not planning to get out of the Quarter Horse business. I'll leave that operation here. I also don't plan to abandon my film career, so I'll just have to maintain two homes. Besides, if things don't work out..." He took a deep breath.

"Have Jack contact the lawyers and set up a trust fund for BJ. Double the amount we've set for my nieces and nephews. Whether he's my son or not, I feel responsible for him." JD turned and gazed out the window, shoving his hands in the hip pockets of his Levi's. "Make sure Jack gives the private investigator a hefty bonus. He did a good job."

"Is that all?"

"What will I say when I see her again?"

"You'll think of something. You always do."

Still staring out the window, he said, "You have more faith in me than I do. I always seem to blow it where Sam is concerned."

"You only blew it once, JD," she said. "Big. But just once. You won't make the same mistake twice."

He turned his head and grinned at her. "Your confidence in me isn't particularly reassuring. I'll just be happy if she's willing to see me."

~

261

### *April 19, 1985--North Fork, Colorado*

JD took a deep breath and entered the North Fork High School office. He decided to surprise Stacey at school, reasoning that if she refused to see him, he could slip out of town without her family knowing. He would be unable to avoid visiting with them if they knew he was in town. That situation would be awkward for both him and Stacey if she wanted nothing to do with him.

He had deliberately waited until a few minutes after 4:00 p.m. when most of the kids had gone for the day. The young blonde behind the office counter looked up, tucked her long straight hair behind her left ear, and smiled.

"May I help you?" she asked.

JD removed his Stetson, laid it crown down on the counter, and smoothed his hair. "I'm told Stacey Murcheson teaches here. Is she still here, or has she gone home?"

The young woman stared at him for a moment. "Y-you're JD MacCord. I can't believe it!"

JD grinned. "I get that a lot."

A frown crept across the young girl's face. "Oh. You're not J—?"

"*Is* Ms. Murcheson still here," he glanced at her nametag, "Sarah?" he asked. He didn't want to be distracted now that he'd worked up his nerve to see Stacey.

"I think so. Would you like me to ring her room?"

"Actually, I'd like you to take this to her for me." He laid a single white rose surrounded by baby's breath and wrapped in green florist's paper on the counter. A small envelope dangled from a thin white ribbon tied in a bow around the middle of the paper. "I haven't seen her in a long time," he explained, "and I'd like to surprise her. I'll just follow along and wait to see how she reacts." He smiled again.

"Sure." Sarah shrugged her shoulders. "Follow me," she said as she moved from behind the counter and headed for the door with the rose in her hand. "Her room's down at the end of the hall," she said over her shoulder.

JD fell into step beside Sarah. As they neared the last room, he spoke again. "I would appreciate it if you'd hand her the rose and then leave, if you don't mind. I'll watch from the hall."

"Sure thing." Sarah glanced at him again. "Boy, you sure do look like JD MacCord. You could be his twin brother."

"So I've been told. I guess I should hire out as his stunt double, huh?"

"Yeah." Sarah hesitated a moment at the door. "Shall I tell her you're waiting?"

"No. Just give her the rose and leave." JD handed her a five-dollar bill. "A little something for your trouble."

"Nah, that's all right." Sarah grinned as she refused the money. "You keep it." She turned the doorknob and entered the room.

JD positioned himself so he could see through the glass window in the door. Stacey stood at the chalkboard, her back to him. Her long golden blond hair was pulled back into a loose wide braid, and the cranberry red scarf tied at the end matched her long-sleeved turtleneck. A denim vest, skirt, and burgundy dress boots completed the ensemble. She was still as slender as he remembered.

A twinge of panic hit him, and JD considered forgetting the whole thing. At the moment, not knowing how she'd react seemed better than outright rejection.

JD's apprehension made Sarah appear to move in slow motion. Then Stacey turned, and JD sucked in his breath. His memories of her face faded at the sight of her. Stacey was no longer a young girl, but a woman. A beautiful, desirable woman. All the old feelings washed over him, and he knew without a doubt he still loved her. The years of separation hadn't changed his feelings.

"Please," he whispered in prayer. "Please, God, let her forgive me."

JD held his breath as Stacey took the rose from Sarah and frowned. Stacey said something, but he couldn't make it out. He held his breath as Sarah pointed to the envelope and turned to leave.

Gripping the brim of his hat tighter in his left hand and clenching his right fist, he watched as Stacey removed the card and set the rose on her desk. Taking slow, deep breaths to calm his jumbled nerves, he waited as Stacey read the simple words he had written on the card.

*Sam*

*Have you finally forgiven me after all these years?*

*Mac*

Stacey looked toward the door as Sarah exited, and her gaze met JD's. He froze as the door closed between them. He knew he couldn't bear it if Stacey crumpled up the note and threw it and the rose away. Although she hesitated only a moment, to JD it seemed an eternity. Seconds took minutes to tick away as he watched her stare at him through the window in the door. Then she moved toward him, pushed open the door, and in the next instant threw her arms around his neck.

"Mac! I can't believe it's really you."

"Sam," JD whispered as his arms went around Stacey. He held her as tight as he could without squeezing the breath out of her, fighting the tears of relief forming in his eyes. Years of being without her, aching to feel her in his arms fell away, and he savored the moment as long as he could. Her familiar sensual scent, unchanged after so many years, filled his lungs.

For a time she seemed unwilling to let go of him, and for that he was not only grateful, but hopeful. Then he felt her lean her head back as her hands moved from around his neck and to his shoulders. He loosened his hold, and she took a step back. Soft green eyes searched his blue ones. He smiled at her, and with a strained voice said, "I stayed away as long as I could, Sam, but I need to be forgiven. I need you to forgive me."

Stacey's eyes glistened, and she shook her head slowly. "Forgive you?" she asked.

He frowned. "For sixteen years ago." Silence hung between them like an impenetrable wall, and JD held his breath.

"Oh Mac, I'm the one who walked out. I thought you probably hated me for not facing up to...can *you* forgive *me*?"

"What? Sam, the note you left said you couldn't forgive *me* for what happened."

"No." She shook her head. "No, I distinctly remember writing that I couldn't forgive myself for what happened. Not you."

JD searched her questioning eyes. "Does this mean I'm forgiven?"

"Oh, Mac, there's nothing to forgive. It was me. I was wrong."

JD noticed Stacey glance down the hall, and he heard several distant, youthful voices behind him.

"Let's go inside," she said. Taking his hand, she led him into her classroom and let the door shut behind them. Grabbing a Kleenex from the corner of her desk, she blew her nose and wiped her eyes, then sat down in her chair. JD sat in a chair next to her desk, rested his right foot on his left knee, and laid his hat near the still wrapped rose.

"I can't believe it's really you," said Stacey, staring at him and smiling. She glanced again at the card clutched in her hand. "But I'm still confused."

"So am I," he said. "The note you left said 'I can't forgive what has happened.' I read it enough times I committed it to memory. Those were your exact words." He leaned his elbow on the desk, smoothed his hair away from his forehead, and waited for her response.

Stacey closed her eyes and shook her head. "Mac, I'm so sorry. I must have left out a couple of words. I was so upset at the time. I didn't blame you. I've *never* blamed you." She bit her lip and wiped a tear from her cheek with the Kleenex. "I blamed myself. I betrayed Brian, and I couldn't face you. I couldn't forgive myself." New tears trickled down her cheeks. "That's why I asked you to stay away. I'm so sorry. You must really hate me."

JD leaned forward and took her hands in his. "No, Sam. I could never hate you. *Ever.*" He squeezed her hands and smiled.

Stacey's tears turned to sobs. JD stood and pulled her into his arms and held her while she cried into his shoulder. He heard someone open the door to the room and cough softly, but he didn't budge. Whoever it was could come back.

Stacey lifted her head and pushed herself gently away from JD. "It's okay, Sarah," Stacey said and sniffed.

JD reached for another Kleenex and handed it to Stacey.

"Is everything okay, Mrs. Murcheson?" Sarah asked.

"Everything is just fine, Sarah." Stacey took a deep breath and shuddered. "Did you need something?"

"BJ called and said he was going to study at Rick's and he'd have supper there. If he needs a ride home he'll call you."

"Thanks, Sarah."

"Are you sure everything's okay?"

"Absolutely. Mr. MacCord is an old friend of mine that I haven't seen in a long time."

Sarah gaped at JD as he turned toward her. He shrugged his shoulders and tipped his head to the side, raising his eyebrows as he did, a sheepish look on his face.

"You really *are* JD MacCord. You lied." she said, her eyes like saucers.

JD held up his hands in self-defense. "I didn't exactly lie. I just didn't admit that I'm JD MacCord."

"Geez. And I fell for it. I can't wait to tell everybody that JD MacCord is here."

"Uh, Sarah, how about an autograph and a promise to take you and some of your friends out for pizza if you'll not say anything for a couple of days?" JD reached for a piece of paper on Stacey's desk and a pen. "Deal?" he asked. He wanted a couple of days of privacy with Stacey before the world found out he was in town.

Sarah hesitated. "I-I guess so."

JD handed Sarah the paper on which he'd written, *Sarah, thanks for helping me out,* along with his signature. "Now the pizza deal's off if you tell anybody. Okay?"

Sarah took the paper and read it. She smiled at JD and nodded her head. "Okay. You've got a deal. Coupla days. See you then."

Sarah closed the door behind her and squealed as she tucked the note against her chest and skipped down the hall.

Stacey smiled. "She's madly in love with you now."

"She'll get over it." JD looked at Stacey. "Can she keep a secret?"

"Probably better than most girls her age. That's why she has a job in the office."

JD reached for Stacey's hand, cradling it in both of his. His face sobered, and he asked the question he knew he had to ask, afraid to look at Stacey when he asked it.

"Is BJ my son?"

He felt Stacey tense, and he held his breath. Now that he'd asked the question, he was a little afraid of the answer. Time stood still as he waited for her response.

267

"Is he, Sam?"

"How—when did you know about BJ?" she asked.

"Does it matter?"

"Yes."

"I promise I'll tell you later. Right now I need to know if he's my son or not."

Stacey took a deep breath. "No," she said.

Hope burst at her answer. He squeezed her hand, and she looked up at him. His gaze held hers. "Are you sure?"

"Positive." The fingers of her free hand touched his temple, and she smoothed his hair back. Renewed tears filled her eyes.

"I'm sorry, Mac, for you, but Butch is very much alive in his son, and I'm so thankful for that. When you meet BJ, you'll know for certain he's Butch's son. He has my blond hair and green eyes, but the rest of him is all Butch. Sometimes I think I'm seeing and hearing a ghost." She bit her lip.

A slow smile caught the corner of JD's mouth. "I have to admit I'm happy that Butch left a part of himself behind, but I can't help but be a little disappointed for myself. I hope you understand."

"Of course I do."

JD let go of Stacey's hand and took a deep breath. Shoving his hands in the hip pockets of his Levi's, he looked at her again. "Sam, if he had been my son, would you have told me? Contacted me?"

Stacey focused on the floor. "I don't know, Mac. I was very confused when I found out I was pregnant. I had no idea whose baby I was carrying." She turned her back to JD and crossed her arms. "I struggled with whether or not to write you, but in the long run, I decided it was best to believe I was carrying Butch's baby. I had to for my own sanity."

Stacey turned to face JD again. He tried to hide his pain. Tears trickled down her cheeks.

"Don't you see, Mac," she said, "I betrayed Brian. I was unfaithful to him. I had to cling to the hope I was carrying his child."

"You weren't unfaithful Sam. Butch was dead."

*"Barely."*

JD flinched.

"I was wrong, Mac. I should never have let it happen. Distancing myself from you was the best way to put it all behind me. I'm sorry. I did what I had to do."

She wiped the tears from her cheeks and blew her nose with the Kleenex she still clutched in her hand. "Realization that BJ really was Butch's son was gradual. The possibility that he was your son remained in the back of my mind for a long time, and I often wondered how you would react if you ever found out I kept it from you."

"Is that why his middle name is John?"

"Yes." A wan smile crossed Stacey's lips. "When he was born I still had no idea who he belonged to, so I gave him both names. I hope you don't mind."

JD grasped Stacey's shoulders. "I don't mind, Sam. I'm honored you cared enough to include me. It makes me feel as though he's a little bit mine." JD pulled Stacey into his arms and held her. She slipped her arms around his back and leaned her head against him.

"I promised Butch before he left for Nam I'd take care of you. I let him down." JD held Stacey a little tighter. "I let you both down, Sam. You should never have had to face that alone."

Stacey lifted her head and leaned back. "I had my family, Mac. They've been terrific. And Dad and Jess have been good father figures to BJ. He's turned out to be a fine young man. You'll see when you meet him."

"And when will that be?"

"Tonight, if you'd like."

"I'd like that." He smiled.

Stacey stepped from JD's arms and picked up the rose. "How about a pizza, some beer, and a little gin rummy until BJ gets home? For old times' sake?"

JD smiled and picked up his hat. "That sounds perfect."

## Chapter 26

Stacey set the vase holding the white rose on the kitchen table.
"You were lucky you caught me at school today." She sat
opposite JD "Ordinarily, my tennis team would have had a match,
but the team we were supposed to play forfeited."

"Let's hope my luck holds out," JD said.

Stacey wondered what he meant as she helped herself to a slice of
pizza. It was hard for her to believe he was here with her. She had
followed his career and watched him become more handsome over
the years. Age had added character to his face and depth to his sky-
blue eyes. And now he was sitting at her kitchen table, like he'd
done so many times in California. Old feelings crept into her heart.

"I can't believe you're here," she said. "Just like old times, huh?"

JD raised his bottle of beer. "Here's to old times, old friends, and
old memories. But most of all, here's to Butch."

"To Butch." Stacey raised her Coke and drank.

"Sometimes," JD said as he picked up another slice of pizza, "I
find it hard to believe he's gone. I half expect him to walk into my
office and ask what the hell I'm doing."

"I know the feeling," Stacey said. "It would be just like Butch to
suddenly show up. He was so unpredictable. I never knew what to
expect. On the other hand, I *always* knew what to expect from you,

Mac."

"Was I that predictable?"

"Until the night...you were very unpredictable that night." Stacey blushed. She hadn't meant to bring up the subject and wished she hadn't.

"I surprised myself that night, Sam." JD cleared his throat. "I never intended to hurt you." He looked at Stacey.

"I know." She stood and dropped her empty can in the kitchen trash. "Another beer? Or a Coke?" she asked.

"Another beer, please."

Stacey handed him a beer and pulled the metal tab on a fresh can of Coke. Air hissed out of the opening. "Do you know there were times when I felt like I was married to both of you?"

JD nearly choked on a swallow of beer. "What do you mean, married to both of us?"

"You spent so much time with us that it felt odd whenever you'd leave to go to your quarters on base."

"Are you saying I was a pest?"

Stacey smiled. "Absolutely not. You and Butch complemented each other so well. What he lacked in stability, you had. I think sometimes you were the glue that held us together."

"I don't understand. I thought you and Butch were happy."

"Oh, we were. But sometimes Butch could be so frustrating. He was so 'devil-may-care.' He never seemed to take anything too seriously, including me. At least until the week I spent with him in Hawaii." She fingered the fringe on the blue-striped place mat. "He was so different then, like he was trying to make every minute count. It probably sounds crazy, but thinking back on it, it was almost like he knew he wasn't coming home."

JD swigged some beer. "Maybe he did, Sam. I've heard some people just know."

"If he was feeling that way, why didn't he tell me?"

"He probably didn't want to upset you over some weird feeling he was having. No sense worrying you if he didn't have to."

"I suppose." Stacey settled back in her chair and sipped her Coke.

~

JD glanced into the living room and for the first time noticed the display of pictures on the piano. He rose and walked over to them, smiling as he saw the juniper-framed picture he had given to Stacey. His gaze wandered over the other pictures, then stopped abruptly at the sight of a blond Brian smiling back at him. He picked up the picture and turned toward Stacey.

"BJ?"

"Yes."

"I see what you mean. Definitely Butch's son." He studied the picture a moment before setting it back on the piano. He returned to the table and took another swallow of beer.

"Hey, you promised to tell me how you knew about BJ," Stacey said.

*Honesty is the best policy,* JD thought, but he wasn't sure how she was going to react to the truth.

"It's kind of a long story."

"I've got all night."

JD took a deep breath. "Jacqueline goaded me into it."

"Jacqueline? You're seeing Jacqueline? That's...great."

"No." JD realized Stacey wouldn't know about Jacqueline. "Jacqueline's my personal assistant."

Stacey frowned.

"Jacqueline's very happily married to Jack. You know, the loan officer she dated after we broke up."

"I liked Jack." Stacey smiled. "I'm happy for Jacqueline."

273

"Anyway, when I started producing and directing movies, I realized I needed a personal assistant. Someone I could trust. Someone who knew me before I was famous. Jacqueline fit the bill perfectly. Not long after I hired her, I hired Jack as my business manager. We make a good team."

"So you finding out about BJ is Jacqueline's fault?"

"A few months ago she got fed up with me sitting and staring at the picture of the three of us." He indicated the picture on the piano with the mouth of his beer bottle. "I have one just like it on my desk." He set the empty bottle on the table. "More than anything, she got tired of me blaming myself and feeling guilty over what happened. She blatantly told me it was time I looked you up and resolved the whole mess."

Stacey squirmed in her chair. "Jacqueline knows what happened between us?"

JD reached across the table and took hold of Stacey's hand. "You have to understand, Sam. I was devastated after you left. I loved you. In spite of the fact you were married to my best friend, I loved you. God knows I never intended anything to come of it. I tried very hard not to love you."

He closed his eyes for a moment before continuing. "If Butch had lived, you would have never known. I would never have betrayed my friendship with either of you. But Butch died. I should have had patience enough to give us both time to adjust to Butch's death, but I didn't think clearly. I acted impulsively for the first time in my life, and I lost you. I needed to confide in someone, and the only one I could think of was Jacqueline. She already knew how I felt about you. It's why we broke up."

Stacey bit her lip. "Jacqueline never said a word to me."

"What could she say? My feelings were private and not meant for anyone. I didn't tell her. She just figured it out. Not saying anything was best for everyone. Especially you."

He realized he was revealing more than he intended. "She's the only one who knows about that night, Sam. I promise you that."

JD slipped his hand free of Stacey's, sat back in his chair, and rubbed his hand through his hair. "Anyway, I was reluctant to look you up. Afraid you were married and had a dozen kids." He grinned, but failed to get a reaction from Stacey. "I didn't want to interfere in your life. And I was afraid you wouldn't want to see me."

JD took hold of the empty beer bottle in front of him and turned it in his hand. *I'm burying myself. Better get the truth over with.*

"Jacqueline suggested I hire a private investigator to find out where you were and what you were doing. Then I could decide what to do." He heard Stacey suck in her breath and tried to ignore it. "That's how I found out about BJ. And that's when I began to wonder if he was my son."

"But surely if you saw a picture—"

"I requested no pictures." Surprise and confusion at what he revealed registered clearly on her face. "I basically know everything that's happened to you since you left California sixteen years ago."

Stacey stood and moved to the kitchen sink. She turned on the cold water tap and filled a glass, drinking part of it. She turned slowly, the glass still in her hand, and leaned against the sink.

"Then you know about my second marriage and divorce?"

"Yes."

"Everything?"

He shrugged. "Most of it, I suppose." He watched her as she absorbed what he said. "I'm sorry you had to go through that. Divorce isn't easy, even when it's the right thing to do."

She bit her lip. "It's a little disconcerting to think a stranger can find out all there is to know about your life. Why didn't you just call?" Her voice had an edge to it.

JD leaned forward, rested his arms on his legs, his head down toward the floor. "I wasn't sure where you were, what you were doing, or if you were married." He glanced at her. "Jacqueline and I are the only ones besides the investigator who have seen the report. And he didn't know it was for me. Most of what he reported can be found in public records. The report has been destroyed, if that's any comfort."

He waited a few long moments, and when Stacey didn't say anything, he stood and walked toward her. "I'm sorry, Sam." He shrugged his shoulders. "I couldn't just show up and completely disrupt your life if you were married. If you had been, I would have stayed away. As it is...knowing you don't blame me...I hope there's still a chance for us." He stopped short of where she stood and shoved his hands in his hip pockets. "I've never stopped loving you, Sam."

Stacey shook her head and set her glass on the counter. "Oh, Mac...the report...it would've...." She looked into his eyes. "You must know I'm engaged."

Stacey's revelation slowly registered. "Engaged? No." He shook his head. "Nothing in the report indicated that. It only said you were dating some guy named Ken Larsen." He rubbed his hand across the top of his head. "I don't understand." He felt Stacey slipping away from him.

"I accepted Ken's proposal a week ago."

He took hold of Stacey's left hand. "You're not wearing a ring. Is he too cheap to buy you one?" He regretted the question the moment he asked it.

Stacey pulled her hand away from JD and glared at him. "That's not fair, Mac. The ring he bought me was a little too big. It's at the jeweler's getting sized."

He lowered his head. "I'm sorry. I was out of line."

"Yes, you were."

JD shook his head. "My timing's a little off again, isn't it?" He smiled, trying to ease the tension between them. He looked away from Stacey for a moment, then pressed on. "But it's still not too late. Engaged but not married. Now that I'm back in your life, there's still a chance for us."

Stacey's eyes clouded. "How do I make you understand? It took me a long time to accept Ken's proposal. He didn't give up on me, and a week ago I finally agreed to marry him. I love him, and I won't back out of my commitment. I owe him that."

*She loves him, not me.* JD shoved the thought aside, refusing to give up. "When's the wedding?" he asked, afraid to hear the answer, his heart weighted down inside him.

"Christmas break."

Relief washed over him. December was eight months away.

"Then I intend to change your mind before Christmas break." He stepped closer to Stacey and took hold of her shoulders. "I love you, Sam. Time and distance haven't changed that. Seeing you again has only reinforced my feelings. I've finally stopped feeling guilty about loving you. We belong together."

He lowered his head and brushed her lips with his. She responded to his touch, and he kissed her lightly. When her arms slipped around his neck, he pulled her close, deepening the kiss. In that instant he knew he had come home; he belonged here with her. In the next instant Stacey pushed him away.

"Please, Mac. I can't let this happen." She slipped past him and stepped toward the living room.

"Sam."

She turned as he called her name, and he noticed tears in her eyes. "Mac, I do love you. You're very special to me. But you and I can never be. Too much time has gone by. Too many things have passed

277

between us."

He moved toward her. "No, Sam. You're not thinking straight. It's the things we share that make the two of us so right together. I've caught you off guard. Give it some time."

Stacey met him halfway and put her fingers on his lips. "Mac, please, don't fight me on this. I'm committed to Ken. I believe very strongly in that commitment. Just be happy for me. Be my friend again. I need that."

She let her hand drop to her side. "I want BJ to know you. You can tell him so much about Butch that I don't even know. He's so hungry to know about his father. Please."

Warning bells sounded in JD's head. Impatience had lost her sixteen years ago. He wouldn't make the same mistake twice. As brief as it was, Stacey had responded to his kiss, sparking a tiny flicker of hope. Time was on his side. He'd find a way to change her mind.

Cradling Stacey's face in his hands, he said, "I won't leave, Sam. Not now. Not when I've found you again. And I do want to get to know BJ." He smoothed a loose strand of hair away from her face. "I intend to be a very visible presence in your life. I hope Ken is understanding."

"He is," Stacey said. "He knows you were a friend a long time ago. I think you'll like Ken."

"I already don't like him." JD lifted an eyebrow and almost grinned. "And for now, I'll be the friend you want. But I'm putting you on notice. What happened between us the first time happened too fast. I never had the chance to court you. I'm going to do that this time. You've been given fair warning."

He kissed her lightly on the lips, then left her standing in the middle of the room as he retrieved his hat and jacket from the back of the couch. "Under the circumstances, I don't think tonight is a good time to meet BJ. May I drop by tomorrow?"

Stacey turned toward him, and he watched her fight back the tears crowding her eyes. "He has a baseball game tomorrow afternoon at the park. Why don't you come to the game, and we'll do something together afterwards."

He smiled. "I'd like that. Will Ken mind?"

"He's out of town until Monday."

JD raised an eyebrow.

"He'll understand I'm spending time with an old and very dear friend."

"Then I'll see you tomorrow. What time?"

"1:30."

"1:30 it is." He winked and closed the door behind him.

~

Stacey stared at the door long after JD closed it. Her afternoon and evening had produced a roller coaster ride of emotions. Her heart filled with undeniable joy, when she saw JD standing outside her classroom. Sixteen years ago she'd left behind her best friend, and in the leaving, emptiness had taken residence in a corner of her heart. Until this afternoon. Until JD walked back into her life.

But he wanted more than friendship. He wanted to pick up where they left off, and she couldn't do that. When his lips touched hers, she wanted more. But Brian's memory loomed before her, along with her promise to Ken, and she knew that JD must remain a friend and nothing more.

Tears trickled down Stacey's cheek. What had begun as a wonderful surprise ended in confusion. "I love you, Ken," she whispered. She sank onto the couch, buried her face in her hands, and sobbed.

~

JD shielded his eyes from the sun's glare as he searched the grandstand for Stacey. In spite of his sunglasses, the brightness hurt his eyes. He hadn't slept well the night before, even after his lengthy telephone conversation with Jacqueline. She tried to reassure him that all was not lost and that his best plan of attack was to take things slowly.

"Give Stacey time to reacquaint herself with you," Jacqueline said. "She'll come around. You have to believe that."

JD wished he felt as confident as Jacqueline. He used every bit of will power he could muster to walk away from Stacey the night before. Hope was the small thread he clung to as he spotted Stacey at the top of the stands.

He worked his way toward her, trying his best not to attract any undue attention. He wore tennis shoes, Levi's, a Dodgers' baseball cap, and an autographed Grateful Dead T-shirt, a gift from Jerry Garcia. He recognized Stacey's parents and brother sitting with her and noticed a space between Stacey and Jess.

"Afternoon," he said as he reached the top row. Stacey diverted her attention from the baseball game.

"It's me, Mac."

"I know it's you," she said and grinned. "What's with the mustache? You didn't have that yesterday."

"A necessary deception." He sat down next to her. "No sense in my causing a stir."

He hoped the mustache and sunglasses altered his appearance enough so that unless someone was actually looking for JD MacCord, he probably wouldn't be recognized. The sunglasses also covered his tired bloodshot eyes. A small part of him hoped Stacey's sunglasses served the same purpose, and that she'd had a sleepless night, too. JD wanted her to realize she loved him as much as he loved her.

He shook hands with Stacey's father and brother Jess, but received a hug from Stacey's mother, Kate. Jess introduced JD to his wife Lisa only as "JD, an old friend." It was good to be among ordinary, unassuming people for a change.

"I'm sorry I'm a little late," he apologized after greeting everyone. "What's happened?"

"Bottom of the second, two outs, no score," Jess answered.

When the next batter struck out, JD watched carefully for BJ to take the field and recognized him immediately as the first baseman. He marveled at BJ's resemblance to Brian. BJ played the entire game, hitting a double and a home run, chalking up two RBIs in the process. In her excitement over BJ's home run, Stacey hugged JD, and he savored her spontaneity as long as he could. North Fork won the game six to one.

He couldn't remember the last time he'd enjoyed himself more. Watching BJ play was like watching Brian—the same movements, same long stride when running, same stance at bat. He couldn't wait to meet BJ and no longer regretted that he wasn't his son. Brian had a son to carry on for him.

As for anyone recognizing JD, or wondering about the stranger sitting with Stacey, he needn't have worried. His disguise was effective, and putting him next to Jess made him appear to be Jess's friend, not Stacey's. When the game ended, Stacey invited him out to the ranch.

"BJ will have to shower and change. I'll wait for him and meet you there," she said. "Mom baked a couple of peach pies and her famous chocolate cake. That should keep you occupied until we get home."

## Chapter 27

*I*f I didn't know better, BJ, I'd swear I'd been transported back twenty years," JD said as he shook hands with BJ. He had shed the mustache at his motel room before driving out to the ranch. "You look just like your dad did when I first met him at college."

"Thanks, Mr. MacCord." BJ said. "I'm really honored to meet you."

"Call me Mac. That's what your dad called me, and that's what you'll call me."

"Cool." BJ flushed and shifted his stance, shoving his hands in his jeans' pockets.

"Just remember, Mac is reserved for certain people, like you and your mom. I'm JD or Mr. McCord to most everyone else."

"Sure thing." BJ took the plate of chocolate cake his grandmother handed him and sat down on the couch next to Stacey.

"That was a good game today," JD said. He sat in a forest green overstuffed chair opposite the couch and accepted a plate of peach pie from Kate. "Those curve balls were giving you a little trouble, though."

"Yeah. I always seem to misjudge them. Coach has worked with me a little on it, but I still can't connect with them. I think I have a mental block."

"Your dad had trouble with a curve ball, too. It was my best pitch, and Butch and I would spend hours on end practicing with me pitching and Butch batting." JD took a bite of pie and smiled at Kate. "Now that's a piece of heaven," he said and cut another bite.

"You always told me that, especially when you wanted seconds." Kate grinned at him.

"It always worked." He glanced at BJ. "Your dad finally figured out how to hit my curve ball, and then I had to improve it. I'm a little rusty, but maybe I could help you."

"Hey, that'd be great. When do you want to do it?"

"How about now?"

"Sweet. I'll go over to the house and get my bat and ball and a couple of gloves. Gramps can catch."

"Maybe another day, BJ. You've just played a full game, and you have chores to do," Stacey said.

"Aw, come on, Mom. It's not that late. Please?"

"Do your chores first, then if it's still light enough, you can get some practice in with Mac."

"Chores will wait a while," Phil said. "If he wants to work on his batting, let him."

"Dad, I'm trying to teach him a little responsibility." Stacey gritted her teeth.

"It's not every day a young man gets a chance to play a little baseball with his favorite movie star," Kate said and winked at JD. "The chores will get done."

"I'll be happy to help him with his chores after he hits a few pitches," JD said.

Stacey glared at the four of them. "I know when I'm outnumbered." To BJ she said, "Just remember, the chores *have* to be done. And no complaining tomorrow morning about being too tired to go to church."

"I promise, Mom," BJ called on his way out the door.

Stacey glared at JD "You're not playing fair."

He grinned. "It's not going to hurt. Not this one time."

"Just remember, it's *one time*. From now on, chores and homework are first before other plans."

JD saluted her. "Yes, Mom."

Stacey threatened to flip a piece of peach pie at JD.

"Not in my house," Kate said.

"Speaking of tomorrow," JD said, as Stacey put the bite of pie in her mouth, "I've made arrangements with Tom Clark, a local real estate agent, to look at several pieces of property tomorrow afternoon. I'd like it if you and BJ could come along. You can give me some honest advice about what I'm looking at. You've lived around here long enough to know about most of the properties."

Stacey hesitated. "BJ has a commitment tomorrow afternoon. The church youth group has a work day planned."

"Are you chaperoning it?" JD asked.

"No."

"Then you're available." His gaze held hers. "I really could use your input."

"All right. Tomorrow afternoon," Stacey said.

Stacey meditated as she sat in the church pew. The large wooden cross at the front of the church gave her some comfort. The last two days, however, had left her conflicted over the flood of emotions that accompanied JD's return to her life. In spite of the number of years since she'd last seen him, they had slipped into the old familiarity of their friendship.

She closed her eyes and prayed for insight into her jumbled feelings and for guidance in handling JD's sudden presence in North

Fork. A familiar voice at the end of the pew interrupted her meditation.

"Mind if I sit with you? I don't know anyone else."

Stacey leaned forward and looked past BJ and her parents. JD, minus the mustache, was dressed in a dark blue sport coat, slacks, and a blue shirt the color of his eyes. He smiled at her as he sat down. He was barely settled when Kate suggested she and Phil move over so JD could sit next to BJ.

As soon as JD was resettled, Stacey leaned forward and whispered past BJ. "This is a surprise. I thought you wanted to remain incognito for a while."

"Are my clothes too bright or something? I tried to dress conservatively enough so I wouldn't stick out." JD inspected his attire, mischief sparkling in his eyes. "Actually, I figured if I sat with you guys in the rear of the church, no one would notice. Besides, the exits are close in case the walls crumble."

Stacey fought back a laugh. "That long since you've been to church?"

He smiled. "In truth, no. I was referring to you."

"I'll have you know I attend regul—"

"*Hold it.*" BJ interrupted in a loud whisper. "If you guys are gonna keep this up, I'm trading places with *somebody.*" He stood and waited until JD scooted next to Stacey. "Now, go on with what you were discussing," BJ said as he sat between his grandmother and JD.

JD and Stacey looked at each other and both broke into muffled laughter.

"So, I take it you started going to church again when you came home?" JD asked in a hushed voice.

The smile faded from Stacey's face. "I came to church because of my parents, but I was so mad at God, I'm surprised the walls *didn't* cave in. I blamed Him for Brian's death. It took some time, but I finally realized God wasn't to blame. And when I realized that, the healing began."

"I know what you mean. I don't know that I blamed God, but I sure didn't communicate with Him for a long time. It dawned on me one day that I was allowing my bitterness over the loss of you and Butch to rule my life. I finally turned it over to God." JD glanced at Stacey and smiled. "Just one more thing in common, Sam. A shared faith."

"Mac, I don't think just because we share—"

JD put his fingers to his lips to quiet her. She realized the organist had begun her prelude. He reached for Stacey's hand, squeezed it, and then let it go.

Stacey tried to focus on the service, but JD's presence distracted her. When he sang on the first hymn, memories of Sunday nights at the beach flooded over Stacey. She heard Brian singing off key and smiled. Tears stung her eyes as she fought back the memories of happier days. When the service ended, Stacey realized she'd heard little of the sermon.

~

"It seems like old times having you eat with us again, JD," Kate commented as she and Stacey cleared dishes from the table. "Years ago I used to wonder if I'd run out of food before you three boys got full. I don't know where you put it all."

"I don't either," JD said. He had accepted Kate's dinner invitation after church. "If I ate like that now, I'd have to do character parts. I'd be too fat to be a leading man." He chuckled at the image. "One thing's for certain, though, you're still the best cook in this part of the country."

"Flattery will get you an extra piece of pie."

287

"Better let BJ have it. He's the growing boy."

"BJ?"

"Thanks, anyway, Grandma. Can I be excused?"

"Where are you off to in such a hurry?" Stacey asked. "Remember you have the work day at the church this afternoon."

"I *know,* Mom. You don't have to constantly remind me. I'm not a kid anymore."

"You're still my kid, and as long as you are, I'll remind you about things." Stacey set some dishes on the counter by the sink and turned to face BJ. "You didn't answer my question."

"I still have over an hour before Rick's dad picks me up, so I thought I'd do some work on Ol' Bess."

"Ol' Bess is still around?" JD asked.

"Yeah," BJ answered. "Mom said I could have her once I got my driver's license, but I have a lot of work to do to get her running right. I get my permit in September."

"You want some help?" JD asked.

"You know how to fix pickups?"

"I've fixed and patched more pickups, cars, and tractors than you are old."

"You bet I could use some help. Thanks, Mac."

Stacey couldn't help but notice the sparkle in BJ's eyes when JD offered to help him with Ol' Bess. Every boy needed a father to work on cars with, and BJ had been cheated of that bond. JD put his arm around BJ's shoulders and ushered him out the door.

"Hand me your plate, Dad," Stacey said as she watched the two disappear through the door. She bit her lip. It seemed so natural to see the two of them together.

"I think I'll go out to the barn and kibitz while those two are mechanicking," Phil said and handed his plate to Stacey. "If I stay here, I'll end up having to do the dishes."

As the door shut, Kate said, "Isn't that wonderful? BJ's needed somebody who's interested in helping him fix up that old pickup. Phil just doesn't have the time or energy to help every time BJ wants to work on it."

"I suppose so," Stacey answered.

"Stacey, what's wrong? I'd think you'd be happy JD is interested."

"Oh, I am, Mom. I just wish BJ and Ken had more things in common." Stacey picked up the platter with the remnants of the chuck roast and carried it to the sink.

She worried that JD might come between the tentative relationship Ken and BJ had. They were just beginning to feel at ease with each other. Forming a friendship had taken them a while, since they had little in common. Stacey didn't want JD's presence to undermine that. She sighed and grabbed a dishtowel, pushing the concern from her mind as she remembered the glow in BJ's eyes as the two headed for the barn.

~

Countless memories bombarded JD as he stood before Ol' Bess. He was surprised at how well the old pickup had withstood the years. The bed and sides had a few minor dents along with a scratch or two, but it still appeared to be in good condition.

He rubbed his hand along the back fender. "Looks almost the same as when I last saw her," he said, more to himself than anyone, "except it isn't crammed with all of Sam's worldly goods."

"You say somethin,' Mac?" BJ asked as he donned a pair of coveralls.

"Nothing important. Just reminiscing. So, what needs to be done?"

"I've been going through the engine little by little," BJ answered.

289

"I cleaned the carburetor, but it needs a new kit. The points are shot, and the timing's off. The valves probably need to be reground—"

"Whoa! In other words, the engine needs a complete overhaul."

"Yeah, I guess so. I can't afford to have somebody else do it, so I've been doing what I can."

"Well, let's start 'er up and see how she sounds." JD removed his sport coat and tie, dropped them across a wooden sawhorse, and rolled up his sleeves.

"Better put these on." Phil handed JD a pair of coveralls.

"Thanks."

JD popped Ol' Bess's hood, and BJ started the engine.

"You're right, she's running a little rough," JD said, "but we'll have this baby purring before you know it."

"Great!" BJ grinned from ear to ear as he poked his head under the hood next to JD's.

JD smiled. *So this is what it's like to have a son.*

They worked together for nearly an hour before stopping for a break. Phil offered to get them something cold to drink, and while they waited, JD broached the subject he'd wondered about since they began working on the pickup.

"Does Ken help you work on Ol' Bess?" he asked.

"Naw. He doesn't know much about engines. Fixin' em, anyway. He pays me to change the oil in his car. That gives me money I need to put into Ol' Bess."

"I see. Do you do other things with Ken?"

"I go golfing with him sometimes. I enjoy that, but that's about all. We don't have much in common." BJ shrugged his shoulders. "He doesn't ride horses, and he never played sports in high school. He comes to most of my games, though."

"I'm surprised. I'd think your mom would be attracted to someone more like your dad." JD regretted the comment the minute he said it. He knew he had no business making comments like that to BJ.

"I think she likes Ken because he isn't like my dad," BJ said. "She doesn't like to be reminded of Dad. It makes her sad." BJ began picking up his tools. "I get along okay with Ken. He makes Mom happy, and that's good."

"You're right, BJ. I shouldn't have pried."

"That's okay."

JD helped BJ pick up the tools and wipe them clean. They had put away the last tool when Stacey entered the barn. She wore jeans, a lightweight, thigh-length teal sweater, and western dress boots. In her hands she held a Dr. Pepper and a Coke. Whenever JD saw her, she took his breath away. She had worn her hair up for church, but had taken it down and French braided it into a single thick plait. Several loose tendrils framed her face.

"Is something wrong?" Stacey asked.

JD realized he was staring. "Nothing's wrong," he said. "You look good."

Stacey moved toward BJ. "Heads up," she said and tossed the Dr. Pepper at him.

"Thanks, Mom. I'd better go clean up. Rick and his dad will be here in a few minutes. Thanks for your help, Mac."

"My pleasure. Any time you want my help, you just holler."

"I will," BJ called as he headed for the house.

Stacey tried to hand JD the can of Coke, but he refused. "Not till I get out of these." He slipped the coveralls off his shoulders and arms, stepped out of them, and hung them on the nail Phil had taken them from earlier. As he accepted the Coke, he noticed it was already open.

"Hope you don't mind," Stacey said, "but I took a couple of sips."

"I suppose if I did mind it'd be too late."

"I can get you another one."

"No," he grinned, "it's okay. I don't mind." JD took a long drink, then shoved the can toward Stacey. "Here, hold this."

"I may drink the rest."

"Go ahead." He winked. "At your own risk, of course."

He turned and slipped on his sport coat, folded his tie, and stuffed it in his pocket. When he turned back to Stacey, she was only inches from him.

"Hold still a minute." She handed the Coke back to him. "You have grease on your face." She wiped his cheek with a rag, steadying his face with her free hand.

JD closed his eyes. Warmth surged through him at her touch. He wanted to take her in his arms and kiss her, but he knew better than to push right now. He didn't want to alienate her again. Patience was his best plan under the circumstances.

"It's a good thing you had on coveralls," she said. "No telling what you would have done to your shirt. As it is, you have dirt on your jacket where it was laying on the sawhorse."

JD opened his eyes as Stacey began brushing the arm and lapel of his suit coat. "It'll clean," he said, struggling to hide the desire coursing through him.

Stacey stopped brushing and looked at JD. "Thanks for helping BJ," she said. "It means a great deal to him. And me."

"I don't mind, Sam. I enjoyed it. You've raised a great kid. You should be proud of him."

"I am," Stacey said, pride showing through her smile as tears welled in her eyes.

At the sight of moisture glistening in her soft green eyes, JD lost the battle he'd fought since she entered the barn. He slipped his free hand around her waist and pulled her closer. Stacey didn't resist, but raised her face to him. He lowered his mouth to hers, brushing her lips with a light kiss.

"I feel like I've come home," he whispered and pressed her against him. He teased her lips with another light kiss, but when he began to demand more, he felt her push away. "Don't fight it, Sam," he said, but she managed to move back a couple of steps.

"This isn't right, JD."

"You're wrong."

He reached for her, but she turned her back and moved farther away. His arm dropped to his side, and he clenched his fist. He watched her shoulders lift slightly as she took a deep breath. When she turned around, she was smiling.

"Well, we'd better get going if we're going to be on time."

JD's jaw tightened. *Patience. You almost blew it.* "On time?" he asked.

"Don't you have an appointment with Tom Clark to look at some land?"

"Right." He took his own deep breath to clear his head. "I was enjoying myself so much, I almost forgot." He smiled. "Don't just stand there. Let's get going," he said as he ushered Stacey to his rented Blazer.

## Chapter 28

*T*om Clark turned down the lane of the Hansen place. "I'm afraid this one needs a lot of work. Mrs. Hansen lived alone, but she refused to let people help her much. She was ninety when she died three months ago. Katy Jordan would come once a month and clean, but the house hasn't had any repair or upkeep done on it for years. The kitchen needs upgrading, the plumbing is old, the entire house needs rewiring, and the roof needs structural re-enforcing and repair.

"If you're interested, you'll probably want to tear down the old house and build a new one. I'm showing it to you because it fits the acreage requirements your personal assistant gave me."

As Tom talked, JD noticed the fences and fields on either side of the lane and around the house were in good shape. They, at least, had been well taken care of. Several towering maple trees surrounded the three-story house. An expansive lawn, bordered by ornamental shrubs and the remnants of a rose garden, added to the landscaping. The outbuildings needed paint and some repairs, but appeared fairly sound.

The Hansen ranch was the last property of three that Tom had shown JD and Stacey. One of the properties for sale was open ground—50 acres of alfalfa and 45 acres of adobe clay and

sagebrush. The second one had a modern ranch house and 120 acres-
-some alfalfa, some corn, and about fifteen acres of fruit. The
Hansen ranch was just over 200 acres—hay, alfalfa, and corn—and
included a quarter section of high country pasture on Black Mesa.

They stopped in front of the stately Victorian house—three stories
of what must have been one of the most beautiful homes in the
valley, but time had been its enemy. Peeling paint and shutters
hanging loose left no doubt of its disrepair. The columned wrap-
around porch sagged on one end.

"Who's been working the place?" JD asked.

"Mike Jordan. He rented the acreage from Mrs. Hansen. He's
done a good job working the land. Keeps it in good shape. He has a
signed lease through the end of this year."

"I'd like to see the inside of the house." JD started up the front
steps.

"Okay, but don't expect much," Tom said.

Stacey followed Tom and JD into the house. "When Mrs. Hansen
was younger," she said, "she kept the house in good shape. It's sad
seeing it so run down."

They stepped inside. Across the large foyer a grand staircase
faced them, wider at the bottom than the top, with oak banisters on
either side. The stairs split into opposite directions just below the
second floor landing.

On JD's right was a large room with folding oak doors of two
panels each. The doors were partially open, and he peered inside.
The room had been used as a study. Oak bookcases covered the
walls on both sides of the door, with windows dominating two of the
other walls. A large marble and brass fireplace covered the fourth
wall.

Just opposite the study, a wide archway invited them into a
spacious living room. It, too, had windows along two walls. A

flagstone fireplace, topped with an oak mantel, covered half of one wall.

When they moved back into the foyer, Stacey explained, "The hallways on both sides of the stairs meet at the back in a large dining room, with a kitchen on the left. There's a bathroom between the living room and the kitchen and a huge walk-in closet under the stairway."

JD smiled at her. "You've been here before?"

"Many times. Mom used to stop by and visit once a week when Jess and I were kids. Mrs. Hansen let us play in the attic with her son's old toys. He was killed in Korea."

With Tom leading the way, JD and Stacey explored the old house. The second floor had a master bedroom with a black and white marble fireplace, a walk-in closet, and a tiny room off the master bedroom. Two medium-sized bedrooms, a smaller bedroom, and a bathroom as big as some modern bedrooms, with a deep, claw-footed bathtub also occupied the second floor.

The third floor was mostly attic, although the ceilings were high enough to accommodate an average man. One area was partitioned off and appeared to have been a playroom. Old toy cars, trucks and tractors, balls of varied sizes, games, books, and a baseball glove lay scattered around the room.

"I can't believe they're still here," Stacey said as she picked up an old toy tractor.

"Well, that's the grand tour," Tom declared. "Shall we go?" They followed Tom downstairs, but at the door JD hesitated.

"I'd like to stay for a few minutes," JD said. "Tom, would you mind waiting for us outside?"

"Of course not. Take all the time you need."

When Tom left, JD took Stacey's hand and led her into the living room. Furniture draped in white covers posed like ghosts guarding their domain. At the windows, JD dropped Stacey's hand and opened the heavy royal blue drapes. As the drapes swept open, the bright April sun streamed into the room, and dust particles danced in the light. Stacey sneezed.

"Bless you," said JD. He waited patiently while Stacy wandered around the room.

"Sam, tell me about the Hansens and this place," he said without turning around.

Stacey rejoined him at the window. "George Hansen's grandfather was one of the early settlers in the valley. George's father built this house, replacing a smaller but similar one that burned down. The Hansen's ranch was one of the most successful operations in the valley. After their son, John, was killed in Korea, Mr. Hansen was never the same. All of us kids thought he was the meanest man in the valley, but Mom said he wasn't always that way. She said his meanness came about because he was bitter over his son's death." Stacey sighed. "When we'd come to visit, Mrs. Hansen was always so gracious, but Mr. Hansen wouldn't even speak to us. He'd just grumble under his breath.

"After he died, Mrs. Hansen ran the ranch, doing most of the outside work, taking care of the cattle, horses, and fields, with only a hired hand and seasonal help to keep the ranch going. She was an amazing woman. She kept things fixed up. Over the last few years, she sold off smaller parcels of the land a few acres at a time. She kept this place in good shape until she had her stroke. She never recovered completely. That's when she started renting the ground to Mike Jordan."

Stacey hesitated a moment and stuffed her hands in her hip pockets. "I used to imagine myself living here when I was little. I imagined it was a castle, and I'd pretend I was a princess. I could see myself floating down that beautiful staircase in the most gorgeous gown anyone had ever seen."

JD raised his eyebrows at her, and she blushed. "Silly, isn't it?" She crossed her arms in front of her and looked down.

"Not at all," he said. "In fact, I can actually see you. You look beautiful."

"Don't tease me."

"I'm not. It's a perfect picture." He smiled at the image he conjured of Stacey in a white gown, smiling at him as she descended the stairs. "Tell me about Mike Jordan," he said and shoved the picture out of his mind.

"He graduated two years ahead of Jess and Brian. He went to college a couple of years, but when his father was killed in the mine, he came home to help take care of his seven brothers and sisters. He owns a small place just up the road from here that was originally part of the Hansen place. He and Katy have five kids." Stacey shook her head. "I don't see how he does it. He manages to support his family, but I know it's a struggle. Katy helps by cleaning other people's homes."

"It would be a hardship on him, then, if he didn't have this place to work."

"Probably. I'm sure it's a big part of his income."

JD moved away from the window and stopped at the fireplace, looking it over carefully. Before they met Tom, JD changed from his sport coat and slacks to Levi's, a long-sleeved blue plaid shirt, a leather waistcoat, and boots. He laid his Stetson on top of the mantel and bent down to look up the chimney.

~

Stacey found herself studying his ruggedly handsome face and muscular build, and a shiver scurried down her spine. He had a knee-buckling smile and a way of mesmerizing people with his sky-blue eyes. Tiny electric charges rushed through her at the memory of his lips on hers. Touching her mouth with her fingers, she smiled, then frowned and dropped her hand. *You're engaged to someone else, Stacey Murcheson. Besides, you know there's no future with Mac. Not ever.*

JD turned from his inspection of the fireplace and interrupted Stacey's thoughts. "What about water rights?" he asked. Before she could answer, he added, "I know what Tom told me, but I need to know how that compares with other ranches."

"Tom failed to mention that the quarter section on Black Mesa has three springs the Hansens filed on."

JD raised his eyebrows. "Remind me to ask Tom if the springs go with the acreage, or if they are a separate deed."

"Good idea. As for water rights on the home place, it has double the shares of irrigation water needed to run it even in drought years. The Hansens were asked many times to sell some of their excess shares, but they always refused. When Mrs. Hansen sold some of the land, she sold only enough shares of water to support what she sold." Stacey smiled. "They were always willing to share their excess water with other ranchers close by and never charged them for it. It was just their way. They saved Dad a lot of headaches over the years with their generosity."

"I know your folks' place is close, but I didn't know it was close enough to share water."

"Our land borders the east end of the Hansen place. Hansen Creek separates the two. Dad and Mr. Hansen built a flume years ago to carry excess irrigation water across the creek. It wasn't used very often, but it came in handy when it was needed. In exchange for the water, Dad helped Mr. Hansen out as much as he could, especially after John was killed in Korea."

"So you like this old place, huh?" He asked.

"Always have. Some people say it's haunted by Mr. Hansen and his son, but I don't believe it."

JD picked up his hat from the mantel and turned it in his hands as he gazed around the living room one more time. "I think this is just the kind of place I need," he said.

"You're going to buy it?"

"I'm going to make an offer. You said it's a great place."

"You're going to buy it because *I* like it? Mac, it needs all kinds of work." Stacey frowned. "Unless you're going to tear down the house."

"I'm going to buy it because I think it has great possibilities. Old houses like this have a warmth about them that can't be duplicated. No way am I going to tear it down. The structure is sound. All it needs is some TLC and some elbow grease." He grinned at her.

"And a lot of money."

He moved to where Stacey stood and put his hand under her chin. "Don't fret over it, Sam. I can afford it." He winked at her, then turned and headed for the door.

After a check of the outbuildings, they drove back to North Fork. At Tom Clark's office, JD made an offer on the Hansen ranch and the mountain acreage along with the springs. When JD had asked about the springs on the mountain property, Tom stuttered over the answer, then admitted that the springs were a separate deed. Stacey suspected Tom intended to keep that information to himself. Tom and JD reached an agreement on earnest money, and Tom said he would have an answer in a week from Mrs. Hansen's sole heir, a nephew in Vermont.

When they left the real estate office, JD asked Stacey to join him for a cup of coffee at Granny's Café. Once they were seated he said, "Isn't this the booth where I held you captive on your wedding day?"

Stacey choked on a sip of coffee. She coughed and nodded her head. "I think it is. I was so mad at you that day."

"I think if you could have gotten away with it, you would have strangled me." He smiled. "I'm glad you didn't."

"So am I."

After the waitress served their coffee, JD surprised Stacey again. "I'm going to need to talk to Jess as soon as possible. I'll want him to handle the legal end of this."

"Don't you have lawyers in California that handle all your business?" Stacey asked.

JD shrugged. "They handle a lot of my business, but they don't have an exclusive. Jess is in a much better position to handle my legal affairs here." He took a sip of coffee. "Is Mike Jordan a good manager? Does he have good business sense?"

"I suppose so." Stacey frowned, wondering what he was after. "Dad and Jess know him much better than I do. But he has a reputation for honesty and hard work."

"Good. I'm going to need a ranch manager, and I was thinking of offering him the job. I could use a housekeeper, too. From what you say, Katy Jordan sounds right for that job."

Stacey couldn't believe what she heard. "I don't think Mike would want to give up his place. He's quite independent."

"I wouldn't expect him to. He can do both. That's basically what he's doing now. He'd just get a regular salary for overseeing my place. Probably more than what he's making off both places now. I'll have Jess set up a meeting with him tomorrow or the next day. What's Jess's phone number?" He pulled a small note pad and a pen from his jacket pocket.

Stacey gave him the number, marveling at the speed he made decisions. "Do you always work this fast?" she asked.

"Only when I can see...feel things falling into place."

~

JD delivered Stacey to her front door long after dark. He parked the Blazer next to a new, white Porsche.

"Oh no," Stacey whispered.

"Something wrong?" JD frowned at her.

"No. I just didn't expect Ken home until tomorrow night."

"He lives here?" A knot formed in JD's stomach.

"No, of course not. Why would you think that?" She frowned. "By home I meant North Fork."

The knot relaxed and he asked, "Do you mind if I come in and meet Ken?"

"I-I suppose it would be all right."

He noticed her hesitancy. Was Ken the jealous type? "Look, it can wait if you're uncomfortable with this." He had barely spoken the words when the front door opened. A tall man stepped out, the porch light accenting his blond hair.

"Now's as good a time as any." Stacey opened the door of the Blazer and stepped out.

Ken met her halfway, and Stacey gave him a big hug. JD fought a pang of jealousy as Ken's arms enfolded Stacey and he bent to kiss her. JD wasn't sure he could take another man kissing Stacey. He stepped out of the Blazer and cleared his throat.

Ken looked up and Stacey turned around. "Ken, I'd like you to meet JD MacCord, an old friend." She smiled at Ken, and then at JD. "Mac, this is my fiancé, Ken Larsen."

JD stepped forward and offered his hand.

"JD. Good to meet you." Ken's firm handshake and friendly greeting belied the hostility JD saw in Ken's eyes.

"Sam's told me a lot about you," JD said. Stacey had said very little about Ken, and JD hadn't asked, but the comment seemed

303

appropriate. "I'm happy to finally meet you."

"Sam?"

Stacey blushed. "JD's nickname for me." She nodded at JD. "Why don't you join us inside for some coffee?" Stacey offered.

"No thanks, Sam. It's been a long day." He started toward the Blazer, then turned back toward Stacey and Ken. "Oh, by the way, I'm planning to take Sarah and her friends out for pizza sometime this week, but I need a favor. I was hoping you two would join us as chaperones. I know it sounds strange, but a man in my position has to be careful."

Stacey frowned at JD. "I don't understand."

"You'd be surprised what some people might make out of me taking several young girls out for pizza. Other adults going along that I know and the girls know is a safeguard. BJ's welcome, too. Do you mind?"

"Not at all," Stacey said. "Let us know when and where."

"I will." He slid behind the wheel of the Blazer. "Thanks for helping me out today, Sam."

~

Stacey dropped her jacket on the couch. "This is a surprise. You're back a day early," she said to Ken.

"And none too soon."

Stacey put her arms around Ken and tried to ignore his cold stare and the tight set of his jaw. When he didn't respond to her touch, she tried to shrug it off.

"Would you like some coffee?" she asked.

"Sure, why not?"

Stacey put on a fresh pot and took two mugs out of the cupboard. "Is BJ home yet?"

Ken joined her in the kitchen and leaned against the counter.

"He's upstairs studying. You're a little late getting home, aren't you?"

"It's only nine."

"I've been here since six." Ken glared at her. "Kate said you've been gone since about two."

"I'm sorry, Ken. If I'd known you were coming home tonight, I would have been here when you arrived."

"Did you enjoy your afternoon and evening with the infamous superstar, JD MacCord?"

"What's that supposed to mean?"

"Answer the question."

"Yes, I did. Mac wanted to look at some property to buy and asked me to go along. He wanted my opinion on what he was looking at, because he knew I'd know about water rights and other pertinent things."

"I'll just *bet* that's why he asked you to go along. Your Dad or Jess could have done the same thing."

"And what's that supposed to mean?"

"You know exactly what it means."

"No, I don't." Stacey felt heat rising in her face. "Why don't you explain it in simple terms so I can understand?"

Ken gripped Stacey's shoulders and glared at her. "I saw the way he looked at you. Don't kid yourself, Stacey. He wanted your company, *not* your advice."

"Well, it was my *advice* he got."

"And your company."

Stacey tore herself from Ken's grip and turned her back to him. "You're being impossible, Ken. If you want to discuss this in a civilized manner, then I'll be happy to do that, but if you don't, you're welcome to leave right now."

A long silence followed Stacey's challenge.

"I'd rather stay and talk about it," Ken said, his voice more controlled. "You can't blame me, though, for being upset. I come home early to surprise you and find you're out with some Hollywood hunk. It's a little disconcerting."

Stacey faced Ken. "He's not just some Hollywood hunk. He's an old and very dear friend that I haven't seen in over fifteen years. Can we talk about this calmly over a cup of coffee?" She crossed her arms and glared at him.

"Look, I'm sorry I flew off the handle like that, but you need to put yourself in my place. I arrive home and you're nowhere to be found. Your mother says you're running around the countryside with a movie star, and then BJ comes home and goes on and on about this *god* that's suddenly come into his life, who's already, in the short space of a couple of days, helped him hit a curve ball and work on his pickup." Ken shrugged his shoulders in frustration. "After all that you can't expect me to take it lying down." He returned Stacey's glare.

She bit her lip to keep back the smile threatening to creep across her face. "I don't think I've ever seen you jealous."

"Well take a good look, honey, because it's rearing its ugly head."

Stacey took Ken's hand and led him to the living room. "Forget the coffee. You're wound up enough." Pulling him down on the couch beside her, she kissed him on the cheek. "Now, let's get this settled in a civilized way."

They talked long into the night, and by the time Ken left for his apartment in town, Stacey had managed to ease his fears where JD was concerned. She had failed, however, to ease her own muddled feelings over JD's sudden return to her life.

Sixteen years of separation from JD hadn't dimmed her feelings toward him. He had kissed her twice since he'd arrived in North

Fork, and each time she wanted more. But each time, her guilt over what she believed was a betrayal of Brian forced its way into her consciousness. And because of the guilt, she shoved aside any feelings she had for JD and vowed to concentrate on her relationship with Ken. He was the man in her life now. He could provide the stability and companionship she needed.

She drifted off to sleep that night praying she could somehow convince JD how much his friendship, and *only* his friendship, meant to her. She had missed him, and now he was back in her life offering that friendship to her and BJ. She knew convincing JD and Ken that friendship was all she wanted from JD would take time and patience.

She chose to ignore JD's declaration that he loved her. After seeing her with Ken, Stacey was sure JD understood how she felt. Satisfied that she could deal with JD and keep Ken happy, Stacey fell asleep believing she could accomplish the impossible.

## Chapter 29

*O*n a sunny June day, Stacey saddled Sunshine, her palomino mare, and struck out across the fields. Not a single cloud spoiled the deep blue of the Colorado sky. Stacey took her time. She was in no hurry as she pointed Sunshine toward Hansen Creek. For the first time in many weeks she had a chance to take a leisurely ride and enjoy a little peace and quiet.

Since JD's surprise visit, her life had changed dramatically. She found herself trying to balance her friendship with JD, while making sure Ken felt secure in their relationship. After Ken's initial shock at finding JD back in Stacey's life, he agreed to let the friendship continue with certain proprieties. Stacey understood Ken's reasons for them.

JD lived up to his promise to be a "visible presence" in Stacey's life. He spent a lot of time at the ranch helping BJ work on Ol' Bess, and he hired BJ to help him renovate the Hansen place. When BJ had spare time, he usually spent it with JD. Once school was out for the summer, they worked together on the house after chores were finished at the ranch.

JD surprised Stacey by showing up at her tennis practices and volunteering to help her with coaching. She welcomed his offer, since she was the only coach for twenty team members, each needing individual attention. Practices settled into hard work with positive results once Stacey relegated JD to coaching the boys. The girls lacked concentration when coached by a handsome movie star.

JD fit well into the community. He managed to make others feel at ease around him, and before long they forgot his fame and accepted him as an ordinary member of the community. He made his biggest impact, however, at the year-end carnival held each year at the school.

With JD volunteering as the primary target at the dunking booth and pledging to match whatever monies were earned, the school collected a record amount of money in the carnival's twenty years. Proceeds benefited all extracurricular activities at the school—not only the sports programs, but the drama and music programs as well.

Stacey smiled as she thought about that night. Ken, alone, spent a fortune at the dunking booth, and JD took Ken's determination to dunk him in good humor. Other than his reputation as an excellent golfer, Ken wasn't known for his athletic ability. But the night of the carnival he somehow managed to be on target more than not, and JD suffered multiple dunkings at Ken's hand. A tentative and mutual acceptance had begun that evening between the two.

At Hansen Creek, Stacey reined in Sunshine and dismounted. The fresh scent of clover filled her lungs. She removed Sunshine's saddle and bridle, and tied a long rope around her neck, securing the other end around a small tree. The length of rope gave Sunshine enough room to graze on the abundant grass and drink from Hansen Creek.

Even though Stacey had legally transferred the property to BJ, she still considered it hers and Brian's. She came here when she needed to think. The land gave her peace. There was a time when it only reminded her of what she'd lost and of the house that would never be built, but as the years passed, it became a place of comfort.

She settled under the cottonwood tree. Pulling a piece of wheat grass from its casing, she chewed on the root end as her hand absently traced the jagged scar left by the rock she heaved at the trunk sixteen years earlier. Stacey settled her back against the trunk. She sighed and rested the back of her head on the rough bark and gazed at the grandeur of the mountains that bordered the valley.

To the northeast rose Stacey's favorite mountain. Ragged Mountain, or the Raggeds as the locals referred to it, was a massive wall of granite formed by time and elements carving character and beauty from its sheer face. Snow still lingered in the shadows between the vertical ridges of rock and along the uneven razored top.

Stacey found comfort in the West Elk Range. The mountains were the one constant, other than God, she could always depend on. Guarding and defining the valley, these sentinels made her feel safe and secure, while their winter snows fed the rivers that brought sustenance to the crops. Although it was early June in the valley, patches of snow dotted the higher peaks.

Brian's peaks, she reflected as she surveyed the beauty before her. He had climbed several of those mountains and explored the foothills and valleys by horseback with her brother Jess. Pass after pass, accessible only by foot or horseback, wove through the vast West Elk Wilderness, and Brian had traveled most of them.

Tears pricked at Stacey's eyes. Brian's soul might be in heaven, but his spirit roamed the West Elks. As she absorbed the beauty and majesty of the individual mountains, Stacey could feel Brian's presence.

She tossed the used wheat grass aside and stretched out on a blanket. Removing the clip that secured her hair at the back of her neck, she reclined against her saddle. She didn't want to think about JD, Ken, or her life at the moment. She only wanted peace and quiet. She opened Robin Lee Hatcher's newest book and settled in for a peaceful morning, hoping to lose herself in someone else's life.

~

JD couldn't believe his luck. He decided to ride to Hansen Creek that morning, hoping against all hope he might see Stacey, knowing from BJ that she sometimes rode to this part of the ranch when she wanted to get away for a while. He had ridden to this spot several times since he bought the Hansen place, hoping to catch Stacey alone, but their paths never crossed.

Lately, whenever they were together, someone else was always with them. Usually Ken. JD wanted time alone with Stacey. He needed to convince her she belonged with him.

Today JD's luck changed. As he approached Hansen Creek, he saw Stacey stretched out on a blanket. Patches of sunlight broke through the shade of the cottonwood tree highlighting her hair with streaks of light gold. He reined in his mount to a spot near the edge of the creek and watched her, imagining what it would be like to lie beside her on the blanket and take her in his arms.

Across the creek, the palomino raised its head and whinnied. Stacey put her book down and glanced up.

Pushing his hat back slightly on his head, JD gripped the saddle horn with his right hand and rested his left arm on top, leaning slightly forward as he did.

"Mind if I come across?" he asked. His mount shifted under him, and he straightened in the saddle.

"Not at all." Stacey rose and secured her hair at the back of her neck with the hair clip.

JD adjusted his hat forward on his head and urged his horse across the creek just south of the flume. He dismounted and secured the reins around the saddle horn. The brown and white pinto wandered toward the palomino.

"Beautiful mare," JD commented, "and a beautiful day."

"That's Sunshine," Stacey said. "The horse, that is, and yes, it's a gorgeous day. Would you like some iced tea and cookies?" She picked up a thermos and paper sack.

"Don't mind if I do."

They shared the cup from the thermos and munched on homemade oatmeal cookies in silence, enjoying the peace and quiet of a Colorado spring day. Bees buzzed around them, and butterflies flitted and darted over the ground. A gentle breeze ruffled the grass.

"I haven't seen you around much lately," Stacey remarked. "BJ tells me you two have been working hard on the house."

"We have. I've also been out of town for a few days. Had to fly out to California. I have a movie project I'm trying to get together and it needed some personal attention."

"That's what BJ said. He felt good that you trusted him to work on the house by himself."

"BJ knows what he's doing and learns quickly. He's got a good head on his shoulders."

"That's nice to hear, even though I think you might be a little prejudiced." Stacey took the last drink of tea out of the cup. "More tea?"

"I'm fine. And I don't give praise where it's not earned, no matter who it is."

"I'm glad you're pleased with his work. He's gone on and on about everything you're doing."

"Then I'm sure he's told you we've rewired and replumbed the whole house and added modern appliances. I'm trying to restore the rest of the house to its original look as much as I can. I've left the hardwood floor in the study, but I must admit I've given in to laying carpet in the living room and bedrooms. I do like some modern comforts." He winked at Stacey.

"It sounds nice. So how's Mike Jordan working out?"

"You and Jess were right about him. He's a hard worker and honest as a summer day is long. I couldn't have asked for a better manager. We think alike, and I don't have to tell him every little thing to do. Katy cleans the house and fixes and freezes casseroles and other dinners for me, so I don't have to do a lot of cooking."

JD got up from the blanket and stretched, looking around for the first time since he'd arrived. "This is a nice little piece of ground." He stepped toward the large cottonwood and gazed at the mountains.

"I've been here before," he said. "Every time I've ridden this way, it's had a familiarity about it, but it didn't click until now." He turned toward Stacey. "Butch and I rode out here the day before the wedding. He said this was a gift from your folks, and he planned to build your ho…" JD realized what he was saying and stopped short. "I'm sorry, Sam, I didn't mean—"

"It's okay, Mac." Stacey rose and joined him under the cottonwood tree, her hands stuffed in her hip pockets. "It is where Butch and I planned to build." Stacey smiled, a faraway look in her eyes. "In fact, just after we were married, we spent an afternoon here. Butch scraped an outline of his dream house with the heel of his boot, then took me on a grand tour, ending in the master bedroom, right over there." She looked at JD, flushed, and turned away from his gaze.

He smiled. "I can imagine Butch doing it with great flare."

Stacey chuckled. "It was definitely with flare." She scuffed the dirt with the toe of her boot.

JD noticed tears glistening in her eyes. One escaped and slid down her cheek. She wiped it away with her hand.

"I'm sorry, Sam. I didn't mean to upset you by bringing up old memories."

"You'd think after all this time I'd have gotten over him, but I haven't." Another tear escaped, and she wiped it away. "I still love him, Mac. I can't help it."

"So do I, Sam. So do I." He put his arm around Stacey and pulled her to him. She laid her head on his shoulder as more tears escaped.

"There's nothing wrong with you missing Butch, and you *should* still love him. He was your first love. You never get over your first love." He squeezed her shoulder. "Not to mention the fact that he's BJ's father. I'd say that should put him in pretty solid with you."

"Yeah, I guess it does." She grinned and lifted her head from his shoulder. "When I come out here, I feel close to him. It doesn't seem fair we never had a chance to build that house."

Stacey sniffed and stepped away from JD. She turned and smiled. "Dad offered to help me build a house here after my divorce, but I refused. It wouldn't have been the same without Butch. Instead, I deeded the land over to BJ. It's his to do with as he pleases. I hope someday he'll want to build a house and raise a family here. But it's up to him."

"He'll have the money when he's ready," JD said and leaned against the tree.

Stacey looked at him and frowned.

"I think it's time I told you that when I found out about BJ, I set up a trust fund in his name. He can use the money for school or anything else he wants to use it for. It's his when he needs it."

Stacey narrowed her eyes at him. "Have you told BJ?" she asked.

"No. I didn't figure he needed to know about it right now. When the time is right I'll tell him. Probably not before his graduation."

"I think that's wise. He needs to earn his way right now. It's sometimes a hard lesson, but a good one. I don't want things handed to him."

"I agree."

"I'm glad you understand."

"You know I haven't always been rich, and definitely haven't had things handed to me. The things I've worked hardest for I've appreciated the most—my first pickup, my college education, and what I have now. It hasn't come easy."

"But kids see what you have now, and they think they should have it now, too. They don't see the work you've done to get where you are."

JD frowned. "BJ you mean."

"Kids are very impressionable."

"Sam, BJ is a level-headed, responsible, hardworking kid. I've been amazed at the work he's done on the house. He's earned every penny I've paid him. He's not likely to think things come easy."

"I just don't want money handed to him."

"He'll appreciate it when he gets it. Have a little faith in him, okay?"

"I do. I just hope you haven't done this because you feel obligated to us. Or because you thought BJ was your son. You have a right to change your mind now that you know he's not."

Anger rose inside JD. He fought to keep it under control. "I did it because I felt responsible, not obligated. At the time, whether he was my son or not didn't matter. I made a promise a long time ago to a friend, and I'm only now beginning to fulfill that promise." His jaw tightened. "The trust fund was a start. But you have to know that if you ever need anything, anything at all, you just have to ask."

"I have everything I need, Mac, thank you. You've already been very generous. BJ is earning enough to fix up Ol' Bess, which is what he's always wanted. It's funny, Ken offered to buy him a newer used pickup, but he didn't want it."

"See, I told you he was level-headed." JD's anger drained away. "I've gotten a kick out of helping him with Ol' Bess. It seems very natural to me, like it was meant to be." His gaze locked on hers.

After a moment, Stacey glanced away. "It's been good for BJ, too."

Stacey walked back to the blanket and sat down. JD sensed he had somehow made her uncomfortable. He joined her, and together they watched Hansen Creek rushing headlong toward its rendezvous with the North Fork of the Gunnison.

"By the way," he said, hoping to dispel the awkwardness stretching between them, "Jacqueline said to tell you 'hi' and that she'd call again one of these days."

"It was good to talk to her after all these years. We had quite a reunion over the phone. The call must have cost her a fortune."

"Me, you mean."

"What?"

"I have no doubt she called from the office." He grinned at Stacey. "But if it makes the two of you happy, it's okay with me."

"I'm sorry things didn't work out between you years ago."

"It's best it didn't. Jacqueline and I would never have made it as a couple. As it is, we have a great friendship and working relationship, and I like Jack and the kids. In a way they're my family."

"What about Sabrina? I thought when you married Sabrina you'd found happiness, but it was over so soon. Why?"

He frowned, and Stacey looked away. He didn't want to discuss Sabrina, but he knew he had to answer. Stacey had a right to know about his past. He knew all about hers.

"When I first met Sabrina, she reminded me of you." He waited for a reaction and getting none, continued. "I married her much too soon, and as the months went by, I discovered how little like you she really was. She finally got tired of me trying to make her someone she wasn't."

At Stacey's frown, he cleared his throat. "More than once she accused me of living with a ghost. She was right, although I refused

317

to admit it. I didn't mean to hurt her." His eyes narrowed, and he rubbed a hand across his face.

"Are you sorry you divorced her?"

"She was never committed to the marriage." He shook his head. "The truth is, she slept with a producer to get a starring role in a film. It worked."

"Oh, JD, I'm so sorry. I know the hurt that kind of betrayal can cause."

He shrugged his shoulders. "Actually, she did us both a favor. The marriage was doomed from the start. If it had lasted much longer, it would have destroyed both of us." He readjusted his hat on his head. "I'm a one woman man, Sam," he said, "and nothing's *ever* going to change that."

"Mac," Stacey bit her lip.

His gaze held hers, and his fingers touched her cheek as he tucked several loose strands of hair behind her ear. "I won't pretend you're just a friend, because it's not true, Sam. You already know that." He rested his hand on her shoulder and stroked her earlobe with the side of his forefinger.

"Please, Mac." She turned her head away, but his hand remained on her shoulder. "After John, it took me a long time to trust again. To John, BJ and I were a tax deduction. And like Sabrina, he was unfaithful.

"But with Ken it's different. He cares about both of us. Even though he doesn't have a lot in common with BJ, he cares about him and his future. I love Ken, and I'm committed to him." She turned to look at JD and laid her hand against his cheek, the large solitaire diamond on her finger reflecting the sunlight. "You need to move on, Mac. I have."

He covered her hand with his, trying to ignore the bite of her engagement ring against his palm. "I can't do that, Sam. I know better. I've never gotten over my first love, either." Turning his head, he kissed her palm.

Stacey pulled her hand away and stood. JD watched her as she stepped away from the blanket. She shoved her hands in her hip pockets and stood unmoving, her head down. He wanted, needed to hold her, to encourage her to step from behind the wall she had carefully built between them, but he realized he had pushed far enough for the moment. Any attempt at intimacy now would only build another layer onto the wall.

He stood and walked toward the horses. "It's getting close to lunch and I'm starved," he called over his shoulder. "How about riding over to the house with me and having lunch? I can show you the progress BJ and I have made on the house. I think you'll be surprised."

She didn't answer right away. He held his breath, refusing to turn and look at her. A sigh of relief escaped him when she accepted.

"Sure," she said. "I've been dying to see what the two of you have been doing. BJ's descriptions just haven't been enough."

He turned toward her. "You don't have to wait for a formal invitation you know. You're welcome any time." Without waiting for a reply, he took hold of Sunshine's rope and coaxed her away from a clump of grass.

## Chapter 30

*T*he first thing Stacey noticed as they rode toward the house was the fresh coat of paint—tan with dark brown trim—the colors blending with the surrounding landscape. They turned the horses into the corral, then JD led her to the front of the house.

"BJ and I began with the porch," he said as they ascended the front steps. "We re-enforced the end that sagged, and rebuilt the steps. A few of the posts on the porch need replacing along with some of the latticework around the bottom. I've hired a carpenter for that. I also contracted the outside painting, since neither BJ nor I wanted to climb that tall a ladder."

JD ushered Stacey into the house and paused in the foyer. New stained glass windows on either side of the front door dispersed a rainbow of color across the floor. The stairs were stripped, sanded, and awaiting a coat of stain. The banister shone with a mirror finish of golden oak. Stacey moved to the staircase and rubbed her fingers across the smooth banister.

"It's perfect," she said. "Just like I remember it."

"BJ spent hours on the banister. You'll have to compliment him." JD took Stacey's hand and led her across the polished wood floor to the study.

"The doors still need to be done," he commented, "but the paneling and the bookshelves are finished."

Stacey wandered around the room, absorbing the welcoming warmth of the study. The white marble fireplace shone, and the brass trim sparkled from careful polishing. The floor, sanded, stained, and waxed to a glossy finish, reflected their footsteps, and the long narrow windows, relieved of the old drapery, beckoned light into the room through the open venetian blinds and sheer curtains.

An over-sized antique oak desk resided in front of the windows. Stacked wooden trays sat on one corner and a telephone on the other, with several manila folders, papers, pens, and pencils scattered over the desktop.

"I haven't decided on what kind of drapes I want in here," JD explained, "or if I want any at all. I'm also thinking of putting in a hooked rug or Persian rug under the desk. I'm not sure which."

Stacey didn't comment. She was amazed at the changes that had taken place since she had last seen the house. She could picture Mrs. Hansen smiling down from heaven at the rejuvenation of her beloved home.

Like the study, the wood paneling in the living room gleamed with new life. Although the walls still needed painting, freshly stained wood trim framed the windows. The dark blue drapes had disappeared, leaving the windows bare. A cozy arrangement of a couch, two overstuffed chairs, end tables, and lamps around the fireplace left a third of the room empty.

Stacey noticed fresh stain on the wood mantel of the fireplace, polished to a deep shine, enhancing the flagstone that made up the rest of the fireplace and hearth. JD and BJ had sanded and sealed the wood floor in the living room.

JD stood midway in the empty portion of the room. "I'm going to add a baby grand piano here." He gestured toward the open area.

Stacey frowned. "I didn't know you played the piano."

He grinned. "I don't. I play guitar. Remember?"

"I know that. So why the piano?"

He shrugged. "I think it's just the touch this room needs. No home should be without a piano."

"It's a shame to have a beautiful piano and no one to play it."

"I expect it to be played."

"And who's going to do that?"

He smiled, his gaze holding her captive. "I thought you'd play it. You still play, don't you?" JD's tone hinted at more than the simple question he asked.

The corner of Stacey's mouth twitched, and she looked toward the empty space in front of her. "How did you remember that?" Not waiting for an answer, she added, "You never cease to amaze me, Mac."

"That's good."

"So, have you decided what color you're going to paint the walls?" she asked, changing the subject.

"I think I might want wallpaper on part of it, but I'm not sure. I'm not an expert at this decorating stuff, but I know what I like." He moved to one of the end tables, picked up a book, and handed it to Stacey. "Maybe you can help me pick something out while we're eating lunch.

"I didn't have any trouble with the wallpaper in the study, but I can't make up my mind about this room. I picked up rug samples late yesterday, but I haven't had enough time to look them over. What this house really needs is a woman's touch."

He winked at Stacey, and she smiled. "I'd appreciate it if you would help me pick out wallpaper and carpeting for this room and the master bedroom." He picked up several bunches of carpet samples and ushered Stacey toward the kitchen.

"Other than upgrading the wiring and appliances," he said, "I haven't had time to do anything to either the kitchen or the dining room. I'm not in a big hurry, though. One thing at a time."

"I'm amazed at how much you've accomplished. Everything you've done so far has been perfect."

"Couldn't have done it without BJ's help."

Over a late lunch of roast beef sandwiches and iced tea, Stacey and JD pored over the books of wallpaper and carpet samples. Stacey finally picked out a sculptured carpet of varied shades of brown, with flecks of gold and rust red for the living room, agreeing that the half of the room where the piano would reside didn't need carpeting.

"If you can match the red in the carpet, that's what color the drapes should be," Stacey suggested. "You can put sheer ecru curtains behind the drapes for days when you want to filter the sun, but not shut it out."

She picked up the wallpaper samples and found one with a sand-colored background and a subtle pattern of browns, golds, greens, and reds. "I think this would look good on the walls around the windows," she said, "and you could paint the rest with light beige." She cocked her head at JD. "Of course, it's just a suggestion."

"I like it. The colors will bring out the flagstone and wood already in the room. You've got terrific taste."

After lunch, Stacey accompanied JD upstairs to the master bedroom. It, too, had received a facelift. The room was wider than the study directly below and covered the front end of the house. The east end of the bedroom opened onto a small balcony above the main porch.

Windows on three sides gave the room an open and cheery look. A king-sized bed covered with a navy blue comforter, filled one corner, and a dresser and chest of drawers the other. The fireplace, opposite the foot of the bed, shared a chimney with the fireplace in the study. Like the one in the study, it was marble, but instead of white marble, the bedroom fireplace was black and white variegated marble. Blue and white print curtains covered the windows.

"Well, what do you think?" JD asked.

"It's huge." Stacey hadn't remembered the master bedroom completely spanning one end of the house. "Wasn't this two rooms? I remember a smaller room...over there." She pointed toward the south wall. A library table, lamp, and leather chair occupied the space under the south window.

"I removed the wall separating the rooms and combined the two closets on the west wall into one large walk-in closet. Now it's all one room with a master bath."

Stacey saw the pride of accomplishment in his eyes. She pivoted in a circle, absorbing all the changes. "It's wonderful."

"So, what color carpeting should I put in here?"

Stacey gazed around the room, then consulted the carpet samples. A sculptured carpet of gray, with subtle swirls of light and dark blue, black, and a hint of white stood out. "Do you like this?"

JD took the sample from her. "It's perfect. You seem to know what I like." He set the samples on the mantel of the fireplace. "We make a good team. Thanks."

His look was more than one of agreement and gratitude. Stacey turned away, unable to meet his gaze. She wandered toward the balcony, opened the double doors, and stepped out.

Bathed in shade, the balcony offered a breathtaking view of the valley. Stacey could see east across Hansen Creek to her family's ranch. Beyond it stretched green and brown foothills, the West Elk mountains and Castle Peak towering behind them.

"It's beautiful at night," JD said from the doorway. "The stars look so close you'd swear you could reach out and grab one. I spend a lot of time out here watching the night sky."

"I can imagi—oh, my gosh!" Stacey gasped as she noticed the long shadows cast by the afternoon sun across the landscape. "I have to go." She nearly ran over JD in her haste to leave.

"What's your hurry, Sam?" He stopped her and slipped his arms around her waist. "I've got no plans for the rest of today. Or tonight." He focused his gaze on her. "Stay and have supper with me."

Stacey froze in JD's arms, unable to look away from him. Butterflies danced circles around her heart, and she feared he would hear it pounding as he drew her close. Every time he was near her heart betrayed her. His azure eyes teased and pleaded, and her determination to keep him as a friend dissolved into confusion.

"I-I can't." She tried to move from his embrace, but her legs refused to work. Placing her palms against his shoulders, she pushed. "JD, please. I have to go. I'm meeting Ken for supper, and if I don't hurry, I'll be late."

Saying the words seemed to give her added resolve, and she pushed free of his embrace. Without glancing back, she slipped through the door.

"Thanks for lunch and the tour," she called over her shoulder as she rushed out of the bedroom and down the stairs.

~

JD clenched his fists at his sides, unable to move. He wanted to go after Stacey, but knew it would do no good. His jaw tightened when he heard the front door slam and Stacey's hurried footfalls cross the porch and descend the front steps.

At the sound of Sunshine's hooves pounding the ground, JD stepped to the balcony rail and gripped it. He watched horse and rider, moving as one, race toward Hansen Creek.

"What are you so afraid of Sam? Why can't you see what I already know—that we belong together?"

~

Over dinner, Stacey told Ken about her tour of JD's house and the work he and BJ had done. Ken listened, not commenting until she finished. Leaning back in his chair, he said, "So, you enjoyed giving decorating advice."

"That old house has always been a favorite of mine. I've always wondered what it would be like to live in a grand old house like that."

"If I'd known you were so interested in it, I would have looked into buying it myself."

"And what would you have done with the land around it? You're not a rancher, Ken."

"I'd have sold it off. Or subdivided it."

"And that would have been a crime. The land and that house are inseparable. They belong together." Stacey took a sip of wine. "I'm glad Mac bought it. I love that old house, and so does Mac. You can see it in everything he's done so far. I'm sure that as long as he owns it, the house and land will remain intact."

Ken's eyes narrowed. "Is it the house you love, Stacey, or the man who bought it?"

Stacey glanced away. "I-I don't know what you mean."

"Don't you?"

She turned away from his lawyer stare and focused on her half-eaten food, refusing to answer his accusation.

Ken reached across the table and took hold of her hand. "I'm sorry, Stacey, but sometimes I think you love JD far more than you love me. You keep insisting that you don't, but sometimes I get the distinct feeling you'd rather be with him."

Stacey wiped her mouth with her napkin and looked up at Ken. "I love you, Ken. I've committed to you, so you have nothing to worry about."

"I hope you're right," he said and let go of her hand. "I realize I'm not as famous and rich as he is. I can't compete with all that fame and charm he possesses that seems to drive women wild." When Stacey started to object, Ken held up his hand to stop her. "No, Stacey, let me have my say.

"Being married to someone like JD would be difficult at best. That kind of fame puts him and any relationship or family he might have in a completely vulnerable position. The public craves any kind of news about people like him, true or not. He's at the mercy of all the gossips and sensationalist newspapers that don't care about the truth. Do you really want to subject BJ and yourself to that kind of scrutiny?"

Ken rearranged his napkin on his lap and reached for Stacey's hand again. "And what about all those women he makes love to on the screen? A leading man like JD is faced with constant temptation, something any man would find difficult to ignore. I would think it would be even more difficult for a wife to deal with. Especially one who isn't in the business."

Ken shook his head. "You're not suited to life in a glass house, always wondering if the next starlet might be the one who could take your place."

He squeezed her hand. "I know this sounds cruel, but it's reality. I love you, Stacey, and I can provide the kind of stable relationship you need. JD can't. Don't forget that."

Stacey placed her free hand over Ken's, looked him in the eyes, and in a steady voice said, "Whatever you might think of actors and their lives, JD is different. He's not the kind of man you've just described. He's honorable, caring, and stable. He isn't given to whims and doesn't take life and responsibility lightly. And I do love him in a special way."

Stacey cleared her throat and withdrew her hands from Ken's. "But there are things in our past that make it impossible for us to be anything other than friends. He is, and always will be, a friend. If you can't accept that, then we have no future together."

Stacey fingered the diamond on her left hand. "It's your choice whether or not I give back your ring. I'm committed to you and our marriage in December. What will it be Ken?"

He searched her eyes for a moment, then took her left hand in his. Fingering the diamond, he said, "I like this right where it is, but I have to know how you really feel. I can't help but wonder if someday you're going to tell me you can't marry me because you love JD."

He smiled. "I'll do my best to accept your friendship with him, but don't be surprised if I get a little jealous every now and then. I've never experienced the kind of friendship you two have, and it can be quite disconcerting."

"I'm sorry if it makes you uneasy, Ken. I don't know what else to say. I've told you how I feel. You come first."

Ken raised her hand to his lips. "December can't get here soon enough."

~

Dinner with Ken left Stacey irritated at his dogmatic approach to her relationship with JD. Ken hadn't pointed out anything new about JD and his fame that Stacey hadn't already considered. But hearing about the drawbacks of his profession made Stacey realize that her friendship with JD had Ken feeling insecure.

As she slept that night, her dreams were filled with images of Brian, JD, and Ken. She was caught in a tug-of-war between Ken and JD, each one pulling her, pleading with her, telling her they loved her. And then Brian stepped in and accused her of betraying Ken the same way she had betrayed him. Stacey awoke with a start, tears streaming down her cheeks. "I promise you, Brian," Stacey whispered between sobs, "I won't do to Ken what I did to you. I promise."

JD called the following morning. "How would you like to come over this morning and help me figure out what to do with the other rooms? We're on a roll here," he said. "You had such great advice yesterday I figure we'd better go with the flow while we're hot."

Stacey bit her lip. She hated hurting his feelings, but she had an obligation to make Ken feel secure in their relationship. JD would have to do without her.

"I can't Mac. I'm busy."

"When will you be free?"

"You'll have to figure the rest out on your own. I've got way too many projects of my own going. I just haven't got the time."

"Sam, what's wrong?"

"Nothing, I'm just very busy. Yesterday was unusual. I've got to start making some plans for the wedding in December, and I need to get a passport for our honeymoon to Mexico. I won't have as much time once school starts, and I don't want to do everything at the last minute."

"I promise I won't monopolize your time, Sam. But I'm no decorator. I really do need you and your input."

She could hear the urgency in his voice and knew she had to stand her ground. "Why don't you ask Katy Jordan or my mother for advice? I know both of them would enjoy doing it, and they're more available than I am."

"It's just not the same, Sam. You know that. You know how I feel about you...us."

"Let it go, Mac, please."

"I'll never let it go, Sam. Even if you're foolish enough to marry Ken, I'll never stop loving you." He paused. "If you change your mind about helping, give me a call."

The loud click communicated his veiled anger. She slowly placed the receiver on its cradle and tried to ignore the emptiness enveloping her. She knew she'd hurt him, but it couldn't be helped. "I've made my choice, Mac," she whispered. "Accept it."

~

In his study, JD sat at the oak desk and stared at the phone long after he hung up. Anger mixed with fear churned inside him. Every time he made a little headway with Stacey, she managed to dig in her heels and stop the momentum. When she told him the wedding was set for December, he thought he had plenty of time to change her mind. But he underestimated her stubborn pride and commitment to Ken. Reluctant as he was to admit it, he had underestimated his ability to win her over.

He leaned his elbows on the desk and rested his face in his hands. He couldn't understand what was keeping Stacey from acknowledging her feelings for him. The way she responded to him whenever they were alone convinced him she loved him.

Sitting back in his chair, he closed his eyes and leaned his head against the soft leather. "It's time I pushed things a little, Sam. Make you confront whatever it is that's forcing you to lie to yourself about us. No more kid gloves. The next time I get you alone, the fur's gonna fly. We're going to settle things, whether you like it or not."

331

## Chapter 31

The warm days of June sped by, and July arrived hot and dry. JD celebrated Independence Day with Stacey, Ken, BJ, and the rest of Stacey's family. After the parade and a picnic lunch, Stacey, JD, Jess, and BJ joined a coed slow pitch softball game in the park. Ken watched from under the shade of a tree, arms folded, a slight frown on his face.

After enjoying the fireworks display, they ended the evening at the community dance. Stacey's father, BJ, and her brother Jess each danced one dance with Stacey.

"My turn," JD said as Stacey finished her dance with Jess.

"Sorry, Mac, maybe another time," she said. "I promised the rest of the dances to Ken." She shrugged as Ken, a smile on his face, ushered her onto the dance floor. JD gritted his teeth and searched around for a dance partner. Stacey's excuse for not dancing with him was feeble, at best, but causing a scene over her refusal was out of the question.

The remainder of the evening, JD never lacked for a dance partner. Finally, unable to tolerate his popularity with the ladies any longer and unwilling to endure the sight of Stacey in Ken's arms, he gave his own feeble excuse and headed for home. His disappointment over the way the evening ended was tempered by the suspicion that Stacey refused him even one dance because she didn't trust her feelings when she was close to him.

JD spent most of his July weekdays in California. BJ explained to Stacey that JD's new movie project was taking more and more of his time. She missed him, but knew his absence was best for both of them. Since the afternoon she helped him with his decorating, Stacey avoided being alone with him, concentrating, instead, on spending as much time as she could with Ken.

BJ continued to work on the house while JD was away, and when JD returned on the weekends, they spent time working on Ol' Bess and the house. Occasionally, Stacey invited JD for supper, but she always made sure Ken was present.

The latter part of July turned wet and cool. The last Sunday of July, Stacey hosted the church's youth group meeting at her house. After the meeting, she drove several of the kids home. Her last passenger, Jenna Harris, lived at the far end of Crawford Mesa. Rain had fallen all day, a steady drizzle that turned into a downpour by evening. After dropping Jenna at her house, Stacey turned for home. The wind had picked up and rain lashed the windshield.

The wipers swished back and forth, barely keeping the windshield clear enough for Stacey to see, the steady beating hypnotizing as she strained to see the rain-slick road ahead. She slowed to negotiate a sharp curve.

As she entered the curve, a shadow and six bright glowing eyes loomed in front of her. Stacey swerved and slammed on her brakes. The car skidded sideways and she fought frantically to keep it under control.

JD stirred the glowing embers in the fireplace and added another log to the fire. He was glad to be back in North Fork for a few extra days. Settling back in one of the overstuffed chairs, he rested his feet on a footstool and picked up a script he was reading. As he read, he scribbled notes with a pencil. But his mind soon wandered to thoughts of Stacey. Since his decision to bring things to a head, he'd had no time alone with her. In fact, he'd hardly seen her at all.

He rose, laid the script on the end table, and paced the living room, trying to figure out a way to get Stacey alone. Rain pounded relentlessly at the windows, like his own futile attempts at penetrating the barrier Stacey had placed between them.

He watched absently as the storm intensified. Streaks of lightning darted across the sky. A brilliant flash and deafening crash startled him from his momentary trance. He returned to the chair and picked up the script. The lights flickered, then stabilized. JD wondered what Stacey was doing.

*It's a perfect night to share with someone you love.* He closed his eyes and pictured Stacey cuddled next to him in front of the fire. The insistent doorbell shattered his reverie. He grumbled under his breath on the way to the door and wondered what kind of an idiot would be out in weather like this. Another flash of lightning and crash of thunder greeted him when he opened the door.

"*Sam.*" Stacey stood before him, soaking wet and covered in mud. He grabbed her arm to pull her inside.

"W-wait. I need t-to take my b-boots off." She struggled to control her shivering. "They're caked with m-mud."

"Forget the boots," JD ordered as he nearly dragged her inside. He set her on a bench just inside the door. "What in *hell's* name are you doing out on a night like this?" He worked to get the muddy boots off her feet.

"I-I was taking J-Jenna Harris home and a doe and two fawns..."

She shivered again. "They w-were right in the middle of the road. I didn't see them until it was t-too late." Tears rolled down her cheeks.

After removing her boots, JD peeled off her muddy and rain-soaked denim jacket as she finished explaining. "I b-braked and swerved to miss them. It all happened so f-fast. The road was slick. The car's b-buried up to its axles in the borrow ditch. Your p-place was the closest, s-so I came here." She inhaled and shuddered. "I'm sorry to b-bother you."

JD cradled Stacey's face in his hands. "It's no bother, Sam. You know that." He searched her face. "Are you hurt?" He smoothed her dripping hair away from the right side of her face.

"I'm okay. I m-missed the doe and fawns, b-but I don't know what damage I did to the car."

"Cars can be replaced," he said through gritted teeth.

Sobs broke through Stacey's tentative control. JD grasped her arms, pulled her up, and gathered her against him, letting her cry into his shoulder.

Between sobs, she murmured, "You're going to get your clothes all w-wet and m-muddy."

"They'll wash." He felt her tremble. "You're freezing."

"I'll b-be all right. I just need a ride home."

JD noticed the tight set of her jaws as she tried to control her chattering teeth. He guided her toward the stairs. "Later. Right now you're going to take a hot shower, and I'm going to throw your clothes in the washer and dryer. When you're clean, dry, and warm, I'll take you home."

"B-BJ will be worried."

"I'll call him."

JD deposited Stacey in the upstairs bathroom, set out fresh towels and a wash cloth, and pointed to a white terry cloth robe hanging on the back of the door. "You can put that on until your clothes are dry.

As soon as you're out of your clothes, throw them into the hallway. I'll take care of them. And I'll find some dry socks for you to put on to keep your feet warm. There's a warm fire in the living room," he said. "I'll wait for you down there." He closed the door behind him.

After throwing Stacey's clothes in the washer, JD changed into a clean shirt and called B.J. He made a fresh pot of coffee and cleaned her boots, setting them near the fire to dry.

He was sitting in front of the fire reading, when Stacey came downstairs to the living room. She wore a pair of his white socks that rose to her knees and the oversized terry cloth robe tied securely around her waist. She fluffed her towel-dried hair with her hands as she entered the room.

JD couldn't take his eyes off her. *She belongs in this house with me. Why can't she see that?*

"Do you have a hair dryer?" she asked.

"No," he answered, surprised that he made any sound at all. He set the script on the end table.

"Why don't you sit here," he said, setting the footstool nearer the fireplace, "and let the warmth from the fire dry your hair. I've made fresh coffee. I'll get it."

She sat on the stool and leaned toward the fire, smoothing her fingers through her hair, separating and drying the damp strands.

JD returned with two mugs. After handing one of the mugs to Stacey, he settled himself on the rug near her.

Stacey took a sip and raised her eyebrows. "This is more than just coffee."

"I put a little Irish cream in it," he said. "It'll help settle your nerves."

A frown tugged at her brows. "I've never had that happen before. As many years as I've been driving, that's the closest call I've ever had." She shuddered. "It shook me up."

Taking another sip of coffee, she surveyed the room. "The rug looks beautiful in here. In fact, everything looks great. I love the rust-red drapes."

"I told you, you have great taste."

Stacey combed her hair away from her face with her fingers. As she did, JD noticed a small cut on the left side of her forehead. He set his mug on the hearth and rose to his knees to get a better look.

"I thought you said you weren't hurt?" He cupped her face in his hands and examined the wound.

"That must have happened when I got out of the car. I slipped in the mud and hit my head against the edge of the door." She reached up to touch the wound.

"Careful," he said. "It's a small cut. I'll put a bandage on it."

He was gone only a minute, returning with a bandage and first aid cream. Taking hold of Stacey's elbow, he pulled her up and bandaged the superficial cut. He tossed the wrapper from the bandage into the fire and looked at Stacey.

"Are you sure that's the only place you're hurt?"

"Yes. I was wearing my seat belt. I'm sure I'll discover a few bruises and some sore muscles tomorrow. Other than that I'm okay." She smiled. "Thanks for caring."

JD's heart skipped a beat. Her smile had first attracted him to her, and with it, the softness that crept into her eyes. The thought of her smiling across the breakfast table at Ken instead of him spurred JD into action.

He gathered Stacey into his arms. "Thank God you weren't hurt any worse." As much as he hated the thought of Stacey's accident, it provided the opportunity he needed. The time had come to settle matters between them.

He knew he could no longer hope she would change her mind on her own. He had to help her change it. His need for her took on new life, and he sought her lips.

To his surprise, Stacey responded. Instead of pushing him away, she pressed into him. He abandoned her lips long enough to kiss her neck, her ear, and then her temple. "I love you, Sam," he whispered, "more than life itself. Marry me, Sam."

His lips found hers again, and he felt himself drowning in her warmth. Searching for the sash at the front of her robe, he loosened it and felt it separate and fall away. Her arms tightened around his back as his hands moved to her neck and eased under the robe at her shoulders.

Stacey uttered a muffled gasp, and pushed away from him. "Don't, Mac. We can't." Turning away from him, she quickly secured the robe around her and retied the sash.

Words of regret lodged in his throat. Silence flooded the room.

"I'm sorry, Sam." The apology was a lie, at least in part. He was sorry for losing control, but not for kissing her or desiring her. He loved her, but she panicked every time he touched her intimately. "I have trouble controlling myself around you. I love you and want you too much."

She turned, and he saw tears welling in her eyes. "Don't love me, Mac. We're not meant to be."

"You can't mean that. I felt you respond to me. I know you love me." He gripped her shoulders. "*Say it.*"

Grief shadowed her face. "What? That I love you? That I've loved you for a very long time?" Tears streamed down her face. "It's true," she sobbed, "and I can't bear the guilt of it!"

"Guilt? Because you're engaged to Ken?"

"No, dammit! Because of *Butch*." She wrenched away from him and turned her back again. He watched in stunned silence as she wiped the tears from her face with her hands.

When she turned around, her eyes were filled with accusation.

"Don't you feel the least bit of guilt or remorse for what happened between us sixteen years ago?"

He closed his eyes and shook his head, then squinted at her. "If you're asking if I ever felt guilty about loving you, I have to answer yes. Every time I looked at you I felt guilty about being in love with my best friend's wife. But hard as I tried, I couldn't stop feeling that way about you. I hid it as well as I could. But when Butch died, I couldn't bury it anymore."

JD turned away from Stacey's glare. He shoved his hands in his hip pockets. "As for remorse," he said, "I feel it every time I think of that night. And every time, I remind myself that I should have been more patient." He took a deep breath. "Unfortunately, I'm not good at patience where you're concerned, Sam." He paused. "It's still not too late for us. You're not married to Ken."

"I've already committed to Ken," she said.

JD combed his fingers through his hair. The fire crackled. "Does Ken stir hunger and passion in you? I *know* you felt it for me when I kissed you." He turned to face her. "Don't make another mistake." He cradled her face in his hands. "We connect, Sam. Together we're whole. Apart, something is missing."

Stacey took hold of his wrists. Fresh tears brimmed in her eyes and spilled onto her cheeks. "You and I can never be, Mac. It's time you admitted that."

"*Never.* You're not thinking straight. We belong together."

Grasping his hands, she pulled them from her face and held them against her. "Mac, there's no future for us."

"Why, Sam?"

"There just isn't."

"Give me a good reason."

"How many reasons do you want?" She took a deep breath.

JD squinted, his mouth set in a grim line. "How many reasons have you got?"

"For starters," she said and took another deep breath, "I don't want to move to California. I like it here. It's a good place to raise BJ."

He shook his head slowly. Of all the reasons she could have given, that was the last one he expected, and a weak one, at that. He suspected she was avoiding the real reason. "You don't have to. We have a home right here. Try again."

"Your fame. You have no private life. Everyone wants to know everything about you. And if they can't find out the truth, they make something up. I can't live my life in a glass house."

"I've managed to keep my personal life private for the most part. I'll continue to do so. Have you seen me hounded by the press since I moved here, or seen anything about me in the tabloids?"

"No."

"What else?"

She dropped his hands and turned toward the fire. "All those beautiful leading ladies. You're human. They must have an effect. I'm not sure I could handle that."

"You can join me on the set anytime you want. You'll find out it's hard work, and any possible attraction I might have for my co-star is buried under hot lights and getting the lines right, while dealing with a certain amount of awkwardness and numerous retakes. Besides, whenever I do a love scene, I think of you and the night we made love."

Stacey glanced at JD.

He smiled. "What else?"

"Few marriages last in the movie industry," she countered. "I need a lasting relationship, not one that will fall apart under the pressures of Hollywood."

JD rubbed his hand over his head and down the back of his neck.

341

"You'd be surprised how many marriages *have* lasted in this business. They just don't make the news. But it doesn't really matter how many marriages have or haven't lasted, because ours would. You're important enough to me to make it work."

JD took hold of Stacey's shoulders and turned her toward him. "I love what I do, Sam. It's challenging, exciting, fun, and hard work. And I'd give it all up if that was the only thing holding you back. But it isn't, is it?"

Stacey's eyes widened. "You'd really give it all up for me?"

"In a heartbeat," he answered.

She looked away. "I couldn't ask you to do that," she said. "I would never ask you to give up something you obviously love so much."

JD gently nudged Stacey's face, forcing her to look at him again. "But you *are* asking me to give up the one thing I love the most. *You*. And I can't do that."

"I don't know what to say." She bit her lip as tears stung her eyes.

"Tell me the truth, Sam. You haven't once said you don't love me. In fact, you admitted a few minutes ago that you do. What's the real reason you won't marry me?"

"I told you."

"Those are poor excuses that can be handled, Sam." He traced her cheekbones with his thumbs and searched her eyes with his. "Tell me the real reason."

"Because Butch will always be here, between us," she blurted, "reminding me of my unfaithfulness!" She took a deep breath and shuddered, then softening her voice said, "Every time I look at you, I'm reminded of my feelings for you. Feelings that began long before Butch died. Feelings that caused my final betrayal of him."

JD started to speak, but Stacey put her fingers to his mouth. "I know what you're going to say. That I couldn't be unfaithful to someone who was dead. But what you don't understand, Mac, is that Brian wasn't dead to me." She choked back her tears. "When he died I had nothing to bury. Nothing to say goodbye to. Maybe if I had..."

JD's heart ached for her. He had thought that taping the bottle of beer to Brian's surfboard and sending it out to sea had helped Stacey say good-bye to Brian. He believed the sendoff accomplished the closure she needed. When Brian died, JD grieved for him and then said good-bye. He had emotionally buried Brian, everything but Brian's spirit. That would always be alive, along with the memories.

Stacey stepped away from JD. "I betrayed Brian, emotionally and physically, and I can never change that. Never go back. If he had known how I felt about you, that, not Vietnam, would have killed him. He would never have understood that I loved you both. I didn't understand it myself."

"He would never have known how you felt if he had lived, Sam. Can't you see that? You would have gone on loving him and never given your feelings for me another thought. The two of you would have been happy the rest of your lives. I would *never* have interfered."

"It doesn't matter, Mac. His ghost stands between us. He'll always be between us." She sighed and looked past JD "Are my clothes dry?"

"They should be."

"Then I think you'd better take me home." She moved toward the arched doorway.

"You're wrong about Butch," he said.

Stacey stopped mid-step. She turned toward him. "What do you mean?"

"He's not some ghost or wall between us. He's part of us." He moved to where Stacey stood and took hold of her arms. "Butch is alive in us. He always will be. Stop making him the barrier. His

343

spirit lives in us. Let him be a part of this love we feel for each other."

"I—"

The doorbell chimed with frantic persistence.

"Who in thunder?" JD strode to the door and flung it open. "*Ken.*"

"Is Stacey here?" Ken shoved past JD. He frowned at Stacey wearing only the terry cloth robe and a pair of socks. He spun and glanced at JD, then Stacey. "What the *hell's* going on here?"

"Not a *damn* thing." JD slammed the door.

Ken ignored JD and turned to Stacey. "I called the house and BJ said you'd had an accident. What happened?"

"I skidded off the road trying to avoid a doe and her fawns. The car's buried up to its axles in mud. Mac's house was closest, so I walked here to get a ride home. By the time I arrived I was muddy and soaked to the bone.

"Mac insisted I get a hot shower before I got sick. He washed my clothes, and I've been waiting for them to dry." Stacey took a deep breath and released it in a long sigh. "Mac has done nothing more than any good neighbor would. He's been very helpful."

"I'll just *bet* he has."

Stacey glared at Ken. "I'll get dressed, and you can take me home."

When Stacey left the room, Ken stepped toward JD, but before Ken could say anything, JD spoke. "You're welcome to wait in the car." His jaw clenched. "Sam should be out in a few minutes."

Stacey left without saying another word to JD except to thank him for his help. Standing in the doorway, he watched the receding taillights of Ken's car. He'd never felt so helpless. He'd tried everything he knew to get Sam to see things his way.

When the car was no longer visible, JD slammed the door, cursing Ken's timing and lamenting the fact that he and Stacey still hadn't settled anything. *Please, God, help me.* He had to find a way to convince her they belonged together.

## Chapter 32

$T$he trip from JD's place to Stacey's was made in silence. She stared out the side window, ignoring Ken. As soon as they arrived, she jumped from the car and rushed to the front door. Ken followed her inside, insisting they talk things out, but Stacey was in no mood for another confrontation and told him she would be happy to discuss things the next day. She ushered him out the door and went to bed.

The confrontation with JD played over and over in her mind, refusing to let her settle into a peaceful sleep. Her restless night only added to the confusion in her heart and left her no answers. An hour before dawn, she fell asleep, only to be awakened three hours later by a call from JD.

"Just checking to see how you're doing," he said.

"I'm fine. A little sore, but otherwise okay."

"I went up the road to check out your car earlier this morning. It's in pretty good shape, considering. You do have a bent fender on the right side where it hit a rock."

"I'll get Dad and BJ to take the tractor up later this morning and pull it out."

"No need. Mike and I already took care of it. All they need to do is drive it home. I didn't have your keys, so rather than hot-wiring it, we left it sitting by the side of the road. It's going to need a good washing."

Stacey smiled. "I can imagine."

"We need to talk, Sam."

"Mac, I—"

"We didn't settle anything last night."

"We did. I told you, sixteen years ago I betrayed Butch, and I almost did it again to Ken."

"This time it's different. You're not married to Ken."

"I love Ken, and I'm committed to him. *Please,* let it alone."

"I can't." He paused. "When I showed up a few months back, you told me you'd forgiven me for what happened. You said you didn't blame me."

"I didn't, Mac. I still don't."

"But you blame yourself, Sam, and that's worse. It's time you forgave yourself."

"I can't," Stacey whispered. An awkward silence passed between them.

"I have to fly to California this afternoon. I'd cancel if I could, but I can't. I'll be back late Friday night. When I get back, we'll talk. There's something you need to know."

"Mac, please, just let it drop."

"No. My...our whole future depends on this. I'll call you on Saturday. I love you, Sam."

Stacey heard a click and then silence. Tears streamed down her face. "Why can't he just leave things alone?" she whispered as she replaced the receiver.

She laid her head back on her pillow and wondered why life had to be so complicated. *I would never have been attracted to Mac in the first place if I had been able to completely commit to Brian.* Youth wasn't a valid excuse.

Determined not to let the past repeat itself, she reminded herself she had committed to Ken before JD arrived in North Fork. Betraying one man over JD was enough; she wouldn't do it again.

~

JD arrived in Carmel agitated and anxious to return to North Fork. Jacqueline tried her best to assure him that, given the circumstances, he still had a fighting chance with Stacey.

"You're getting to her," Jacqueline said. "Don't give up now."

"I don't intend to. We're going to talk again when I get back. I still have a few arguments up my sleeve. I hope and pray they'll make a difference."

During the week, JD found it hard to concentrate on business. Thoughts of Stacey crowded his mind. Thanks to Jack and Jacqueline, he managed to get through his meetings in good shape.

Thankful the last of his meetings had concluded early, he paced his office, anxious to be on his way back to North Fork. When Jacqueline entered the office, he stopped behind his desk and turned to greet her, but the look on her face made him frown.

"What's wrong?"

"I'm sorry, JD. From what you told me, I thought you were getting through to her."

"Sam?"

Jacqueline nodded. "Stacey called during your last meeting. I don't know how to tell you this." Tears formed in Jacqueline's eyes. "Stacey and Ken are getting married tomorrow afternoon. At 2:00 o'clock."

She took a deep breath and waited. When he said nothing, she continued. "She called because she didn't want you finding out after you got back. They evidently decided Wednesday. Stacey says you're welcome to attend the wedding and hopes you'll support her

349

decision. Said she needs your support, but would understand if you didn't want to be there. She wants you to be happy for her and said that it's best for everyone."

JD groped for the chair behind his desk and eased into it, his eyes staring at nothing.

After long moments of silence, Jacqueline prompted him. "JD, say something," When he didn't respond, she added, "I asked Stacey if she knew what she was doing. She insisted she was doing the right thing and to please let you know. Nothing I said made any difference. She's determined to marry Ken tomorrow."

His eyes wandered to the juniper-framed picture on his desk.

"Do you want to call her? I can dial for you."

"No." JD's voice was low and barely audible. "When's my flight?" he said slightly louder.

"10:30 tonight."

"Can you arrange for something sooner?"

"I tried, JD. Everything is booked solid."

"Did you try bribery?" he asked in a controlled voice. Too controlled.

"JD."

"I'm serious." He glared at her.

"No. It wouldn't work, and anyway, that's not your style. I tried getting a charter, but they couldn't leave any sooner than the commercial flight."

"I guess I should have taken flying lessons. Remind me to do that."

"The wedding's not until tomorrow afternoon," Jacqueline reminded him. "You can talk to her first thing in the morning. You still have a chance to change her mind."

"You're an optimist."

"You said you still had an argument or two up your sleeve."

He swiveled away from her and looked out the window behind him. "I should have kept going," he said.

"What?"

"Seventeen years ago. I helped kidnap Sam after the wedding. I should've kept going and never looked back."

"JD, you're not making sense."

"No, I suppose not, but since when did my relationship with Sam ever make sense?" JD stood and stepped to the window. "It's too late, Jacqueline. I've lost her."

"She's not married until she says 'I do.'" Jacqueline moved around the desk to where JD stood. Placing her hand on his arm, she admonished, "You're *not* going to give up. Not now. Not when there's still hope. And there is hope." Tears again stung her eyes. "We both know the two of you belong together. You have to make her see that."

"I tried...and failed."

"Keep trying."

JD shook his head. "Okay, I'll give it one more shot. Just for you." He put his arm around Jacqueline's shoulder and squeezed. "I must be crazy," he said. "Only a fool would set himself up for this much rejection and pain."

Jacqueline slipped her arm around his waist. "No pain, no gain." She forced a smile.

The corner of his mouth twitched. "Remind me to give you a raise."

"I will," she replied and wiped away an escaping tear.

~

JD pounded on Stacey's bedroom door. "I hope you're decent, Sam," he warned, "because I'm coming in." He pushed the door open and leaned against the frame. Stacey sat on a stool in front of her vanity, dressed in her robe, a hairbrush in her hand. She turned toward the open door. Her eyes narrowed at him.

"Good morning." He grinned at her.

"What do you think you're doing?"

"I came to talk," he said, the grin fading from his face. "I told you we'd talk when I got back. Now, what's this nonsense about you and Ken getting married this afternoon?"

"Mornin,' Mac."

JD turned to see a grinning BJ walk past him.

"Don't mind me," BJ said. "I'm going out to do the chores."

"Mornin, BJ," JD said and returned his attention to Stacey. "Well?"

"It's not nonsense." She laid the brush on the vanity. "Ken and I decided to move the wedding date up a few months."

"Sam, don't rush into something you'll be sorry for later."

"I'm not rushing," she said. "We just didn't see any reason to wait."

"How many reasons do you want?"

"None from you."

He winced. "You're making a big mistake, Sam. You love me, not Ken. Remember? You admitted it last Sunday."

"I also told you there was no future for us. And I do love Ken. I'm committed to him."

"So you've said. Over and over. Who are you trying to convince?"

"I think it would be best if you'd leave."

"Not until you hear me out."

"Nothing you can say will make me change my mind." Stacey stood and moved to the window, her back to JD.

He stepped into the room and stood next to the vanity. "Call Ken and tell him you can't marry him. Better to let him down now, than later."

Stacey faced JD. "Let it go, Mac. I won't hurt Ken."

"But you'll hurt *me?*" In spite of his resolve to keep things civil his temper flared.

"That's not *fair,* Mac."

He threw his arms up in frustration. "I'm fighting for my life. My future. *Anything's* fair."

"I don't want to hurt you," she said, tears brimming in her eyes.

"But you are, Sam."

She sank onto the edge of her bed, unable to look at him. "I told you before, Mac, but you didn't listen. Butch will always be in our way. He'll always be between us."

"And I told you that Butch wasn't in our way. He'd be happy for us. He's a part of both you and me, Sam. Let him live through us. Give the three of us a chance." He shoved his hands in his hip pockets and watched her.

"I've made my decision. Don't make this any harder for me than you already have."

He forced a smile. "I intend to make it very hard for you." He pulled an envelope from his pocket and with great flare laid it on the vanity. "This," he said and stabbed it with his finger, "is a plane ticket.

"I'm returning to California this afternoon. I have a few more meetings that will probably last through Tuesday—Wednesday at the latest. Then I plan to go to Aztec and visit my family. My sisters are both complaining I haven't been home in a while. They're right. Come with me. Meet my family."

JD paused for a moment. Stacey remained on the edge of her bed, staring out the window. He resisted the urge to grab her and force her to look at him.

"Come with me, Sam," he repeated. "I want you to meet my

family. You'd like them."

"I can't." She looked at him. "Stay for the wedding," she said, tears spilling over onto her cheeks.

JD gritted his teeth. "No way. I won't stay here, while you marry someone else, and watch my happiness crumble before me." He stepped to the bed, grabbed hold of her arms, and pulled her up. Cradling her face in his hands, he kissed her, leaving no doubt about his feelings.

As abruptly as he started it, he ended the kiss and set her back on the bed. On his way out of the room, he paused at the door. "The plane leaves at 3:20 from Grand Junction. I have a few things to do at home, then I'm leaving for the airport around one. If you haven't called by the time I leave, I'll meet you there. Jess can drive you.

"I won't stay around here, just in case you're foolish enough to marry Ken. I don't want to be anywhere near that disaster."

He gripped the doorknob. "By the way, there's something else besides a plane ticket in that envelope. You might want to look at it. I don't make a habit of breaking promises to friends. I've done it once in my lifetime and suffered guilt over it for sixteen years. I'm about to break a second promise.

"This time I hope it will right what went wrong. I love you, Sam. Never forget that." He closed the bedroom door behind him.

~

Stacey watched from the window as JD peeled out of the driveway. She couldn't remember ever seeing him so upset. "I'm sorry, Mac," she whispered. "So sorry."

As she watched his Blazer disappear in a cloud of dust, her anger built. The more she thought about it, the more the abrupt encounter with JD irritated her. *How* dare *he force his way into my bedroom so early in the morning. He had no right!*

She sat at her vanity and picked up her brush. With angry, deliberate strokes, she brushed her long blond hair and swept it up into a soft twist. Her hands shook as she struggled with a few stray strands. Her attempt to capture them failed. Setting her jaw, she grabbed her brush again, determined to succeed on the next try.

Her image in the mirror stopped her short. She paused in mid-stroke. Green eyes, tired, reddened, and rimmed with heavy dark circles, stared at her. She hadn't slept well all week.

"Great look for a bride on her wedding day." She thought of Ken and smiled. He had dealt with the past few months better than most men, exhibiting far more patience and understanding than JD. If JD had only stayed away…

Stacey slammed the brush on the vanity, knocking the airline ticket to the floor. She glared at it, picked it up, and flung it across the room.

"*Damn* you, JD MacCord!" Hot tears stung her eyes. "Why did you have to pick now to show up?"

She spent years trying to forget JD and the feelings and passion he stirred in her. And then without warning, he barged back into her life and into her heart, causing the desires to resurface along with the guilt.

"*Damn* the feelings and *damn* the guilt. And *damn you*, Mac, for making me want you again."

She stalked to the window. The stillness and beauty of the early morning belied the disquieting events that transpired minutes earlier. Bare spots in the gravel drive marked where JD had peeled out. She closed her eyes and tried to remember his smile. Instead, she saw anger and pain. Pain that would last far longer than the anger he had unleashed.

She swiped at a tear trickling down her cheek. "I've made my decision, Mac," she said to the empty room. "I intend to honor my

355

commitment to Ken. I won't betray another man over you again. I *won't.*"

The morning sun cast golden rays as it inched above the mountains, promising a beautiful day. A perfect day for a wedding.

Stacey sighed and forced a smile. She could be happy with Ken. There were so many things about him she loved. His sense of humor. His compassion. He provided stability and logic to her life; two things she needed. *Does Ken stir hunger and passion in you?* She shoved JD's words aside.

She turned from the window. "Marrying Ken is the right decision." Lingering tears glistened in her eyes. "Now all I have to do is put a smile on my face, a song in my heart, and say 'I do' to a wonderful man who loves me."

But her declaration failed to evoke any kind of smile. She sat at the vanity and gazed at her image. Why didn't she feel the same excitement and joy she felt the first time she married? Were only the young allowed the anticipation and wonder? If only she could turn back the clock. If only Brian was waiting for her.

Stacey sighed and looked in the mirror again. *There are no second chances.* Out of the corner of her eye she spied the envelope lying on the floor where she had flung it.

The contents were half out of the envelope, beckoning to her. She stooped to pick it up. As she did, she noticed a yellowed envelope with Brian's handwriting on the outside. The envelope was addressed to JD, and the postmark indicated it was mailed from Hawaii on the day before Stacey arrived for Brian's R and R.

She trembled as she picked up the envelope and removed its contents. Sinking to the floor, she leaned against the bed and began to read. The letter was dated February 28th, 1969. Her mouth went dry as she read Brian's words.

*Dear Mac,*

*This will probably be the last letter you ever get from me, so please read it carefully and with an open mind and an open heart. I'm not going to make it home this time.*

## Chapter 33

*J*D waited to board the plane, hoping Stacey would arrive at the last minute. He glanced at his watch, then boarded the plane alone. When he was settled, he checked his watch again, but only five minutes had passed.

Surely Stacey read the letter. What if she hadn't? A wave of panic surged through him. What if she tore it up and threw it away without reading it? The panic increased. What if she read it and still hadn't changed her mind?

He squirmed in his seat. *I should have stayed behind. Waited while she read the letter. I was crazy to think she needed to read it by herself. Idiot.* He rubbed his hand over his face. *Why do I manage to do everything wrong where you're concerned, Sam?*

JD left because he didn't want Stacey to feel he was trying to influence her interpretation of the letter. He needed her to read in Brian's own words the future his friend wanted for his widow and best friend.

*Please God,* he prayed, *the letter's my ace-in-the-hole. My last chance. She has to change her mind.*

He watch showed 3:20. Time for the flight to leave, but the door remained open. *On-time departures aren't always the norm for small airports. Sam could still make it.* The flight attendant began her preflight instructions, and his gut tightened

His heart rhythm increased as a blond woman ran for the plane. He straightened in his seat, craning to get a better look, hoping, willing her to be Stacey. As the woman neared, his hopes crashed. He slumped back into his seat and cursed under his breath as the young woman hurried up the steps and into the plane.

The flight attendant secured the door and the plane taxied toward the runway. He fastened his seat belt, leaned his head back against the seat, and closed his eyes. He had lost.

As the Boeing 737 lifted into the afternoon sky, he fought back the despair closing in on him. *How can I face her again?* But he had to. He wouldn't walk out on BJ. He loved him like a son. They needed each other.

*Why God? Why couldn't she choose me?* He opened his eyes and his heart ached as the ground receded below him. Exhaustion engulfed him. He closed his eyes again and slept through most of the flight to California.

Hoping that perhaps Stacey had missed the flight, his first question to Jacqueline when she met him at the airport was, "Did Sam call?"

"No. Why? What happened?"

"I lost her." He stared past Jacqueline, his eyes lifeless, all hope gone. "She married Ken."

"I'm so sorry."

JD looked away from the sympathy in Jacqueline's eyes. He said little on the ride home, and when she offered to stay and talk, he refused her. He needed to be alone.

He sat on his patio and picked out familiar tunes on his guitar, but when he played Gordon Lightfoot's *A Minor Ballad*, it reminded him too much of Stacey. He put the guitar away.

Losing Stacey the first time had been difficult; he had been partly to blame. But losing her now was unbearable.

He slept fitfully that night. Over and over in his mind he replayed everything he said to Stacey, wondering what he could have done or said differently. Wondering again if he made a mistake by not staying while she read Brian's letter.

At first light, he dressed and went down to his office to work. He set the agenda for the meeting on Monday. Jacqueline called in the afternoon offering to cancel the meetings, but he declined. At least his work would help him forget his loss for a few hours. His new project was based on a script he had waited a long time to make into a movie. He needed to forge ahead.

With the agenda set, he cleaned out files and drawers in his office desk. When he finished, he picked up the picture in the polished juniper frame and carried it upstairs. He couldn't bear to look at it anymore. Opening a bottom drawer in a storage closet, he removed a box of mementos he had carted with him over the years, but hadn't bothered to look at in a long time.

He lifted the lid, and countless memories flooded over him. Brian's championship belt buckle rested on top of yellowed newspaper clippings and old letters. I should give this to BJ, he thought as he fingered the buckle. He pushed it aside, disturbing the items beneath it. A white, lacy object caught his eye. He lifted it from the box and memories flooded over him.

"Sam's wedding garter." He had forgotten he had it. He smiled, remembering the calculated accuracy Brian used to aim it in JD's direction. His eyes misted as he pressed it to his lips. Carefully placing it on top of the juniper-framed picture, he closed the lid of the box and shut the drawer.

The night left him restless and unable to sleep. He couldn't stop thinking about Stacey's decision to marry Ken. He wondered for the thousandth time if she had even read Brian's letter; a letter that haunted him for sixteen years. A letter whose very words reminded him he had failed a friend.

~

The meetings at the beginning of the week kept JD's painful thoughts at bay. By early afternoon on Tuesday, he concluded the necessary business to get his new project started. With the remainder of his afternoon free, and needing to be alone, he donned a dark blue tank top, denim shorts, and deck shoes.

His holdings in Carmel included oceanfront property. Although the beach was public, access to it was private. He drove in an open jeep to the cliff above the sea and made his way down a winding rocky path to the beach.

Standing where the waves raced over the sand, he prayed that God would take away the anger, resentment, and hurt that threatened to undermine his sanity. Wanting to rid himself of all reminders that he had failed to win Stacey's love, he reached in his pocket and retrieved the diamond and emerald engagement ring he had commissioned for Stacey.

The ring symbolized lost dreams. Before leaving the house, he had stuffed the ring in his pocket with the intention of heaving it into the sea.

Sure that he could change Stacey's mind, he had requisitioned the ring a couple of months earlier, hoping, no believing, he would have a need for it. He thought it ironic that the finished ring was delivered the day Stacey married someone else.

He clutched the ring in his fist and pulled his arm back, but something kept him from following through with that final act. He no longer had a need for it, yet throwing it away would be like throwing away his love for Stacey. He gritted his teeth and stuffed the ring back in the front pocket of his cutoffs. Someday he would donate it to a celebrity charity auction. At least that way, it could do some good.

Trudging back toward the cliff, he collapsed on a grassy area that gave way to the sand and then the sea. Persistent waves crashed against rocks scattered along the coastline, relentless in their quest to chip away at the stubborn stone. As he watched the endless motion, he felt the sting of loss chipping away at his heart.

JD kicked off his deck shoes, lay back, and closed his eyes. He hadn't slept much the last several days. The steady crash and gurgle of the waves lulled him to sleep.

The cry of a gull nudged JD awake. He sat up and blinked. She stood with her back to him. A steady wind blowing in from the sea lifted and tossed her blond hair about her head and shoulders. He took in her turquoise peasant blouse, denim shorts, and bare feet.

"Sam," he said and started to rise, then closed his eyes, groaned, and fell back on the grassy carpet. *I'm in worse shape than I thought. Now I'm hallucinating. I can't go on like this.*

He lay still for a few minutes, trying to clear his mind of her image, but failing. Forcing himself to sit up, he rubbed his eyes and looked again. She was gone—an apparition his tired mind and aching heart conjured.

In her place was the most beautiful sunset he had seen in years. Orange, purple, magenta, and red swirled and mixed together in glorious textures. Golden tracings outlined a large cloud, setting it apart from the others. As he watched, a shaft of light broke through, illuminating a wisp of cloud in the shape of angel's wings. Hope, he thought, never dies, and life goes on.

"God help me, Sam," he said, "I'll never stop loving you." A feeling of peace washed over him. "I can't change what's happened, but I can get on with my life. Somehow I'll face you again. It won't be easy, but I'll do it for BJ. And Lord, I promise I won't interfere with Sam's marriage."

JD rose and moseyed toward the water. The waves rushed onto the shore and swirled around his feet and ankles. He ignored the threatening thunderstorm and watched the colors of the sunset fade. When he turned to go, his gaze brushed over the beach ahead of him, and he noticed indentations in the sand where the waves hadn't reached.

Footprints. Not his. Small, like a woman's. His heart raced as he followed the footprints. Stacey appeared from behind a cluster of large rocks.

"Sam?"

She looked up when he spoke her name. "Hi." She walked toward him. "I was about to come and wake you."

He rubbed his eyes and blinked at her. He tried to speak. Stacey touched her hand to his face. He took hold of her hand and kissed its palm. With his other hand, he smoothed her hair away from her face and hooked it behind her ear.

"You are real aren't you? I'm not hallucinating am I?"

"You're not hallucinating."

Cradling her face in his hands, he kissed her, drowning in the sweet taste and warmth of her. "You didn't marry Ken," he mumbled against her lips when he forced himself to part from her.

"No, I didn't," she said and kissed him on the cheek. "I had to give the three of us a chance. You, me, and Butch. After all, we're a team, aren't we?"

He encircled her with his arms and kissed her again, afraid if he let go she would disappear. Tears of gratitude stung his eyes, but he fought them back. *Thank you, God.*

"I thought I'd lost you again," he said as he held her close. "What changed your mind?"

She pushed away from him enough to look into his eyes. "Butch's letter," she said, "and Ken. Why didn't you tell me about the letter before? Or stay while I read it?"

He brushed away the tears glistening on her cheeks. "In the letter Butch asked me not to show it to you. I thought I could change your mind without breaking my promise to him. Showing you the letter was a last desperate attempt to convince you we belonged together. As for not staying while you read it, you needed to be able to absorb it without my influence."

"I had no idea Butch..." She slipped her arms around JD's neck and leaned her forehead against him.

"What did you mean, 'and Ken'?'" he asked a few moments later.

Stacey took his hands in hers. "After I read Brian's letter, I sat on the floor of my room and cried, and talked to God, and reread the letter several times. Somewhere, somehow during the crying and the praying and the reading, I finally let go of my guilt. And I finally let go of Brian." She sniffed and looked up at JD. "I think I was afraid to let him go. I was afraid I'd forget him. So I hung onto my guilt. It was a way of keeping him alive."

"And Ken?"

"I called Ken and told him we needed to talk. I couldn't share the letter with him, but I told him everything else. About the kind of friendship the three of us had, and what happened between us after Brian died. And about my guilt. I didn't leave anything out."

She smiled. "I've never told anyone, until now. I especially couldn't tell my mother. So I bottled it all up inside and tried to bury it. Perhaps if I'd been able to talk about it I wouldn't have hung onto the guilt.

"Ken and I talked for a long time. Finally, he told me he understood. As much as he loved me and wanted to marry me, he knew that in the long run it would never work."

She took a deep breath. "He's decided to accept an offer of a senior partnership in a Denver law firm. He was going to turn it down. But under the circumstances, he's decided to accept the offer. He'll be gone by the end of next week. He wished us every happiness, Mac."

"That's decent of him. Seems I owe him."

"Ken's a good man. Why do you think I fell in love with him?"

"Do you still love him?"

"Yes. I always will, a little. But not the way I love you and Brian. I know that now. I love you more, Mac. So much more."

She wiped away the wetness on her cheeks and wrapped her arms around his neck. "Do you know how cleansing it is to finally admit how much I do love you and to know it doesn't diminish, in any way, the love I had for Brian?"

"I think I do." He closed his eyes. "When you didn't make the flight, or call me, I..." He opened his eyes and looked into her tear-stained face. Ignoring his churning emotions he asked, "Why? Why didn't you call?"

Stacey smoothed an unruly curl off his forehead and rested her hand on his shoulder. "By the time Ken and I talked things out and broke the news to BJ, Mom and Dad, and Jess and Lisa, it was too late to make the plane. I had Jess call the airline and change the ticket to the first flight he could get. That was today.

"And even though the wedding was going to be family only, we invited a few friends to a reception afterwards. They had to be called. I couldn't walk away from everything and let everyone else handle it. It was my responsibility." She sighed.

"Since I couldn't fly out until today, I had time to do some serious soul-searching. I needed time to think things through and search my heart. Make sure that this time I was doing the right thing. I've made so many mistakes. I didn't want to make another one."

She sucked in a deep breath. "I've fought my feelings for you for so long. It helped to have a couple of days to adjust to this life-changing decision and what it means, not only to us, but to BJ. He had to be considered as well."

Stacey gave JD a light kiss, slipped her arms around his back, and leaned her head against his shoulder. "I didn't call you because I knew you'd be busy with meetings. But more than anything, I didn't want to tell you over the phone. I needed to be sure of my decision to call off the wedding without listening to any outside influence about what to do next."

"You could have called today to let me know you were coming. I'd have met you at the airport."

"I figured it would be better to wait until I arrived, but when I phoned from the airport, you didn't answer. So I called Jacqueline, and she picked me up. I changed my clothes at the house." She leaned back and looked at him. "It's beautiful, JD. You've built a beautiful home."

"Never mind that. Then what?"

"Jacqueline and I waited at the house while Jack checked the stables. When he didn't find any sign of you there, Jacqueline said there was one other place you might have gone, so she drove me here.

"When I got to the beach you were asleep. I sat down near you and took off my sandals. You seemed so peaceful, so I spoke your name quietly, and when you didn't stir, I decided to let you sleep a few minutes longer. I hated to wake you. Jacqueline said you were exhausted."

He grasped her shoulders, a frown creasing his forehead. "Do you know the *hell* you've put me through the last few days?"

"Oh, Mac, I can only imagine. I'm sorry if you suffered. Please, don't be angry." New tears glistened in her eyes.

He closed his eyes a moment. "Sam, I'm sorry. I'm not angry. It doesn't matter how or when you got here, as long as this is where you want to be."

"This is where I belong."

JD knelt on one knee and fished the diamond and emerald ring out of his pocket, thankful he still had it. Taking Stacey's left hand in his, he slipped the ring on her finger. "Stacey Anne Murcheson— Sam—please marry me."

Stacey studied the ring a moment. "It's beautiful. How—"

"I'll explain later. Right now I need an answer."

She dropped to her knees in front of him, tears of joy streaming down her cheeks. "I would be honored to marry you, Mac."

They kissed, reaffirming their love for each other. When they parted, Stacey grinned and a spark of mischief glinted in her eyes. "I suppose it would be inappropriate to say it's about time you asked me to marry you."

JD frowned and in his best Humphrey Bogart voice said, "Look shweetheart, don't presh your luck."

His lips sought hers again, and as she returned his passion and hunger, he hoped he could convince her to marry him as soon as possible. As Brian had written, Stacey was worth waiting for, but JD had waited long enough. It was time he fulfilled his promise to his friend and to himself.

# Epilogue

Stacey finished peeling the potato, rinsed and quartered it, and placed it in the saucepan. She smiled at the scene out her kitchen window. Her heart swelled at the sight of BJ giving his three-year-old half-sister a ride on his horse. Her dark curls bounced in rhythm to the horse and her sky-blue eyes sparkled as she giggled at something BJ said.

Every evening ended the same since BJ came home from college for the summer. As soon as he set foot in the house after a full day of work, Brianna would beg him to take her for a ride. He would pretend he was too tired, and Brianna would act like she was about to cry. Then BJ would say, "Okay, but just a short ride." They both enjoyed the game, and the short ride around the corral lasted forty-five minutes to an hour.

A great deal had transpired in the past four years. She and JD were married at his house in North Fork a week and a half after she surprised him in Carmel.

They invited only family, Jack and Jacqueline and their kids, and Mike and Katy Jordan. BJ and Jacqueline stood up with them. Like the girl in her childhood dreams, Stacey glided down the grand staircase in a beautiful gown to meet her prince.

They spent their wedding night in the house that would become one of two homes. The following day, they flew to Carmel where they spent another two days, then JD surprised Stacey with a honeymoon to New Zealand. Everything happened so quickly that the press was unaware the marriage had taken place until Jacqueline sent out a press release a week after their arrival in New Zealand.

Stacey's school year started the last week of August, and by the end of September the doctor confirmed she was pregnant. Stacey taught until the middle of May, when Brianna's entrance into the world ended Stacey's school year several weeks early.

With a new baby, BJ's senior year of high school approaching, and JD's demanding schedule, Stacey declined to renew her teaching contract. She was content to be a wife and mother. A year and a half later, with BJ in college and Stacey free of the demands of teaching, she and Brianna joined JD in New Zealand for the filming of his newest project.

Jacqueline helped Stacey learn to handle the press, and they soon lost interest in the mystery woman that had captured JD MacCord's heart. And although she wasn't crazy about the few Hollywood social functions JD felt obligated to attend, he always made her feel at ease and treated her as though she were the most important and beautiful woman in attendance.

The MacCord's spent most of their time at the ranch in North Fork where they were the happiest, and where they were only one of many families in a small, tight-knit community. With JD, Stacey had finally found the contentment she dreamed of the day she married Brian.

Stacey smiled at the memories while she watched BJ and Brianna. "You'd be proud of your son, Butch," she said. "He's so good to his little sister. Actually, he spoils her rotten. And as I've told you many times, it wasn't hard to name a girl after you. You just had no imagination." Tears clouded her eyes, and she set the paring knife aside to wipe them away.

"You say something?"

Stacey jumped at the sound of JD's voice. "Don't startle me like that, Mac," she said without turning around.

He slipped his arms around her waist and pulled her against him. He nuzzled her neck and nibbled her ear. Leaning her head against him, she rubbed her hands along his arms, then clasped her hands over his.

"So, if I startled you, who were you talking to?"

"Butch."

"Is he staying for supper?"

Stacey laughed. "What do you mean, 'is he staying for supper?' Of course he's staying for supper."

JD smiled and rested his cheek against Stacey's head. "So, what were you telling the old reprobate?"

"That he'd be proud of his son." Stacey turned and slipped her arms around JD. "And that it wasn't hard, after all, to name our first child after him."

JD smiled and kissed her. "What are we going to name the next one?" he asked, holding her tightly against him.

"We've got plenty of time to decide on a name. The baby's not due for another seven months."

He leaned back and gazed into her eyes. "I take it Dr. Miller confirmed our suspicions today?"

"He did."

JD lifted her and swung her in a circle. Stacey laughed and kissed his forehead. Setting her down, he asked, "Want to tell the kids tonight?"

"I'd rather keep it between us for a while longer."

He cradled her face in his hands. "I love you so much, Sam, sometimes it scares me. There was a time I thought I'd never have any children of my own. But you've allowed me to be a father to BJ,

371

given me a beautiful daughter, and another baby is on the way. Life can't get any better or richer than this."

Stacey savored a long and sensual kiss from her husband and best friend. And for a moment she could have sworn she heard Brian yell, "Yee-haw!"

*About the Author:*

K. L. (Karen Lea) McKee has had a passion for writing since she was a young girl. After raising two rambunctious boys and earning her B.A. in English from Regis University, she renewed her desire to write faith-based stories.

Karen worked in the Reference Center of her local library for twenty-nine years, recently retiring to pursue writing full time. She is a member of Rocky Mountain Fiction Writers.

She and her husband reside in Western Colorado, known for its fruit orchards, wineries, majestic mountains, spectacular canyons, and strikingly beautiful desert terrain. She enjoys knitting, music—playing and singing—tennis, pickle ball, the beautiful Western Colorado outdoors, and spending time with her family.

Because she lived during the Vietnam War era, Karen is particularly passionate about how the Vietnam soldiers were treated during the war and after they returned home. It is her hope that, as a nation, we thank these soldiers who were asked to do the impossible and received little thanks from the citizens if this great country.

Karen is also the author of two other books:
*Miracle, a novella*
*In Name Only*

CPSIA information can be obtained
at www.ICGtesting.com
Printed in the USA
LVHW111610140720
660690LV00001B/85

9 781546 518525